TALK TO ME

a novel

T. Coraghessan Boyle

ecco

An Imprint of HarperCollinsPublishers

TALK TO ME. Copyright © 2021 by T. Coraghessan Boyle. All rights reserved. Printed in the United States of America. No part of this book may be used or reproduced in any manner whatsoever without written permission except in the case of brief quotations embodied in critical articles and reviews. For information, address HarperCollins Publishers, 195 Broadway, New York, NY 10007.

HarperCollins books may be purchased for educational, business, or sales promotional use. For information, please email the Special Markets Department at SPsales@harpercollins.com.

Ecco® and HarperCollins® are trademarks of HarperCollins Publishers.

FIRST EDITION

Designed by Angela Boutin

Library of Congress Cataloging-in-Publication Data has been applied for.

ISBN 978-0-06-305285-7

21 22 23 24 25   LSC   10 9 8 7 6 5 4 3 2 1

TALK TO ME

Kathleen Elizabeth Boyle (1950–2019)

I am Sam. I am Sam. Sam I am.

—DR. SEUSS, *GREEN EGGS AND HAM*

ONE

TO TELL THE TRUTH

She wasn't studying. Studying was what she was supposed to be doing, what she intended to do, what she was going to start doing any minute now. First, though, she had to wait for the album to finish—the new Talking Heads, with its bass-heavy rendition of "Take Me to the River," which she couldn't get enough of—and click through all the channels on the TV while absorbing her daily dose of disodium guanylate, autolyzed yeast extract and rendered chicken fat in her Top Ramen, which was about the only thing she was eating lately. It was cheap and fast and that was all that mattered. Not that she was happy about it—she knew she had to start eating better, but she hadn't actually cooked anything even remotely healthy for weeks, and then it was only pasta with a red sauce out of a jar and a wedge of iceberg lettuce on the side and maybe a pickle or two. Were pickles healthy? They prevented scurvy, she'd read that somewhere.

Columbus had stocked them on the *Niña*, the *Pinta* and the *Santa Maria* for that purpose, but then she wasn't on a ship at sea but in her efficiency apartment in university housing, and the problem was time. And will. Work, school, work, school—it was as if she were on a stationary bicycle pedaling furiously, going nowhere.

The Top Ramen (Lime Shrimp) was boiling on the stove. Her books were spread out on the old steamer trunk from Goodwill she used as a coffee table. She was going to eat and study at the same time, then maybe go for a walk around the block and come back and study till it was time to go to bed, which lately had been anywhere from eleven to two, depending on how bored she was and how hopeless the quest for her degree seemed at any given moment. But first she clicked the remote, just to see what was on, and the screen came alive to a scrum of earnest figures in cleats and helmets chasing a little brown ball across an expanse of gleaming grass. She clicked again: sitcom. Again: the news. Once more: game show.

The game show was one she used to watch back at home and as soon as the logo appeared on the screen she felt a quick sharp pang of nostalgia, she and her sister stretched out on the living room rug, doing their homework, their mother in the recliner rattling the cubes in her second or third vodka and soda, one Lark at her lips and the other smoldering in the ashtray. And the show, comforting in its banality, everything preordained and usual, the panel of celebrities nobody had ever heard of apart from the de facto evidence—*Kitty Carlisle*—straining to be witty and urbane, middle America's entrée into a world of martinis and limos and lathered-on makeup. Three men materialized out of the shadows to introduce themselves, each claiming to be Guy Schermerhorn—two older and wearing glasses, one younger and not—before taking their seats, stage right, at the desk reserved for the contestants. The celebrity panel was seated across from them, stage left, and it was their task to determine which two were the imposters and which the original, the one telling the truth.

She didn't have time for this, but then she did. Because the affidavit the host read out wasn't the usual sort of thing at all—Guy Schermerhorn wasn't the pedestrian husband of a hypersexualized actress or a race car driver recognizable only with his crash helmet on or the discoverer of a new element for the periodic table, but a researcher who, he claimed, was teaching apes to talk. She'd heard about that—they were doing it here too, at UCSM, weren't they? And come to think of it, the young guy, the one in the middle, looked familiar, as if she'd seen him on campus, but whether she had or not, she was sure he was the one telling the truth. The other two might have had more gravitas, but that was only because of the glasses and the age difference, and of course the producers of the show relied upon deception by way of keeping the audience guessing along with the celebrity panel, otherwise no one would have bothered to tune in.

Bill Cullen—he wore glasses too, the lenses so thick they distorted his eyes—was up first and he put his question to Guy Schermerhorn Number 1, on the left. "So what was the first thing the ape said? I'm guessing it was either 'You got a cigarette?' or 'Can you loan me a dime so I can call my lawyer and get out of this joint?'"

The audience laughed. Guy Schermerhorn Number 1 laughed too and then he composed his face and said, "They don't actually talk—it's more like sign language."

"Oh, really?" Bill Cullen leaned into the long desk the panel shared. He was enjoying this, enjoying the opportunity to show off his wit for all those people out there in the living rooms of America and relishing the fact that he was a celebrity and they weren't. "How do you say 'Make mine a martini, straight up, two olives?'"

Again, the audience laughter. But Guy Schermerhorn Number 1 dodged the question with a quip of his own, as if he were auditioning for a seat on the panel. "We try to discourage them from drinking," he said, giving the camera a deadpan look, but the thing was, he didn't attempt any sign language, which to Aimee was a dead give-away, even if she hadn't already decided on Number 2.

It was Kitty Carlisle now, looking ageless in her midnight-black bouffant, though the flesh at her throat was pulled tight as a string bag. She gave the camera a catty look, then zeroed in on Number 3. "Could you demonstrate something in sign language for us—it is sign language you use, isn't it?"

Number 3 nodded.

"How about, oh, I don't know—'Do you take your coffee black or with cream and sugar?'"

The man raised both his hands to the level of his chest and Aimee thought for an instant that she'd been wrong, that this was the real Guy Schermerhorn, but then, lamely, he dropped them to the desk and said, "We don't serve them coffee."

"Jangles their nerves?" the host put in, and everybody laughed. He was seated center stage behind his own desk, his bald head flashing under the stage lights. Aimee didn't remember his name, not that it mattered. He was a celebrity too.

Kitty Carlisle couldn't resist the joke. "What about Sanka?" she asked of nobody in particular—just threw it out there—before turning to the contestant in the middle, Guy Schermerhorn Number 2, with a penetrating look. "What about you, Number Two—can you tell us how to say 'How do you take your coffee—black or with cream and sugar?'" And now a quick aside, eyes on the camera: "I mean, in case we have an ape over for dinner some evening . . ."

Guy Schermerhorn Number 2—he was the real Guy Schermerhorn, no doubt in Aimee's mind—was in his late twenties or early thirties and he wore his hair long, parted just to the left of center and tucked behind his ears. His eyes jumped and settled and he was instantly, unshakably, calm. He used his fingers only (it was called finger-spelling, as she was later to learn), moving them so quickly and adeptly he might have been a clarinetist running through "Flight of the Bumblebee" without benefit of an instrument.

Kitty Carlisle said, "That was either the most amazing thing we've seen on this show—or pure gibberish. That's not gibberish, is it, Number Two?"

Number 2 shook his head no, then the other two panelists got their chance to quiz the three men, though it was really no contest after that, and there were three votes for Guy Schermerhorn Number 2 against a sole vote for Number 1 (Bill Cullen) and none for Number 3. But wait, wait, it wasn't over yet—instead of having the real Guy Schermerhorn stand up and take his bow, there was a surprise . . .

The backstage curtains parted and out came a chimpanzee in diapers and a polo shirt with the sleeves cut off and he wasn't walking on his knuckles but standing on two feet and swaying side to side in the kind of gait you'd expect from a toddler, which, as it turned out, was what he was. He looked out at the crowd, which had sent up a whoop when he appeared, then at the panel and the three contestants, before letting out a low hoot and scampering across the floor—knuckles now—and launching himself over the low desk where the contestants were seated to land squarely in the lap of the man in the middle, as if there had ever been any doubt. But he didn't simply land there—he embraced Guy Schermerhorn like a lover, kissing him on the lips and then swiveling his head around to stare into the camera as if this was all in a day's work. His hands were moving now, first for the camera, then for Guy Schermerhorn, who returned the gesture, or a different gesture, as if he understood what the chimp was saying and the chimp understood him—as if they were truly communicating, in real time, while the whole nation looked on.

The host, his grin as wide as the screen, couldn't resist putting one more question to the man with the ape in his lap: "What did he just say?"

"He said he wants a cheeseburger."

The audience roared.

"Does he have a name?" the host wanted to know, riding with it now, the grin ironed to his face. The camera panned over the audience, a sea of shining eyes and open mouths, then swung back to Guy Schermerhorn.

Guy Schermerhorn spoke aloud as he signed the question to the chimp: "What is your name?"

The chimp—he was adorable, a big-eared doll come to life—made a rapid gesture with one hand before flicking the back of his ear as if shooing a fly, and Guy Schermerhorn provided the translation. "His name's Sam."

But the chimp—Sam—wasn't done yet. He interjected a further comment, either in correction or addition, the gestures so rapid you couldn't follow them till Guy Schermerhorn reprised them in a slowed-down version. "And he's asking"—running through the gestures now, index finger and thumb to the side of his cheek, a finger touched to his chest and then his hand pushed out in front of him in an undulating motion—"'When can I go home?'" A pause, then the real and authentic Guy Schermerhorn spun out one more sign, both palms sliding together in a horizontal clasp: "To bed."

Behind her, on the stove, the Top Ramen was boiling over. There was a hiss of vaporizing liquid, followed by the sharp tang of incinerated Lime Shrimp flavoring, and then she was up off the couch and lifting the pot from the burner while the TV audience clapped and whistled and Guy Schermerhorn took the chimp by the hand and led him across the stage and back through the curtains. She'd been lost there a moment, gone deep—it was as if a door that had been closed all her life had suddenly swung open. This little creature with the articulate fingers and watchful eyes had not only expressed desire—to have a cheeseburger—but he'd conceptualized the future and envisioned a place beyond his immediate surroundings, which animals weren't supposed to be able to do. She'd seen it with her own eyes. Unless, of course, it was some sort of trick. Unless he'd just been *aping* what his trainer had taught him.

But what if he wasn't? Scientists were involved, weren't they? Wasn't Guy Schermerhorn a scientist? And what if it really was possible to speak to the members of another species—to converse with them, not just give commands or coach them in the way people coached parrots to regurgitate what they'd been taught to say? Or dogs. *Good boy, roll over, doggie want a treat?* It wouldn't be like that. It would be a two-way conversation, a sharing of thoughts on the deepest level. People talked about life on other planets, but this was right here in front of us, a whole other consciousness just waiting to be unlocked. Did apes have God? Did they have souls? Did they know about death and redemption? About Jesus? About prayer? The economy, rockets, space? Did they miss the jungle? Did they even know what the jungle was? What about the collective unconscious— did it extend to apes? Did they dream? Make wishes? Hope for the future?

She didn't know, and it probably was just some trick, but when she went to bed that night—not at one but earlier, much earlier, her books left scattered across the table and the paper for her psych class barely begun, let alone finished, typed and proofread—she closed her eyes and saw herself in Guy Schermerhorn's place, strolling across the set of *To Tell the Truth* and through the pleated curtains, hand-in-hand with this little creature with the big ears and clownish gait and the eyes that said, *Here I am, come and get me.*

She didn't believe in karma or serendipity or whatever you wanted to call it and she wasn't superstitious, or not particularly. She was a practicing Catholic, though admittedly she could have gone to mass more often, and at the same time, whether it was conceptually incompatible or not, she believed in the observable truths of the sciences. Still, there *was* coincidence, there was déjà vu and synchronicity and the revolving notion that we never fully inhabit our bodies, all of which hit her smack in the face when she stepped into the psych building two days later to beg Professor Lindelof for an extension and encountered Guy Schermerhorn's face staring out at her from a newspaper article tacked to the bulletin board in the hallway. He was right there, front and center, the little ape in his lap, in what was obviously a still from the television show. The headline read, "UCSM Professor on National TV."

So she *had* seen him on campus, after all. She tried to picture the circumstances, the when and where of it—no doubt it was right here in this very building or the student union maybe, or the library—but it wasn't working. She didn't even know what color hair he had, though it seemed light, maybe even blond, on TV and in the newspaper photograph, which unfortunately was in black and white. Or how tall he was or whether he dressed in suit and tie or jeans and a flannel shirt like Dr. Lindelof. Her first impulse was to slip the article into her purse so she could go off somewhere and read it in private, but there were people all around her, voices swelling and clattering, the whole building thundering in her ears with the blunt force of what was happening to her, which went beyond coincidence, way beyond.

She stood there in the crowded hallway, feeling weightless and adrift, scanning the article and hoping no one was watching her, though what would it matter if they were? She was a student reading an item on a bulletin board, that was all, and wasn't that what bulletin boards were for? The article said that Dr. Schermerhorn was an associate professor of psychology, specializing in comparative psychology, and that he was a protégé of Dr. Donald Moncrief of Davenport University, in Iowa, who'd pioneered the cross-fostering of chimpanzees in human home environments by way of studying comparative development and language acquisition. Dr. Schermerhorn was one of only six researchers handpicked by Dr. Moncrief to participate in the program nationwide and he was quoted as saying that he'd accepted the invitation from the popular syndicated television show in order to raise awareness of the research—and funding for UCSM's own fledgling program in primate behavior.

"Whoa, look—the monkey prof. Can you believe it? He was just on TV."

Two girls had crowded in beside her. The nearest one (bad skin, dog collar, coppery hair cut close to her scalp) she recognized from her statistics class. Aimee had never said a word to her, but then she never said a word to anybody if she could help it. If somebody spoke to her, she responded, certain cues demanding certain responses—that was the way society was ordered—but nobody spoke to her apart from the women at the supermarket checkout who said "Hi" and "Have a nice day," and once in a while one of her professors, but she tended to avoid them as much as possible. Public situations made her uncomfortable—that was just the way she was. She was a private person, at least that was how her mother described her, and though she was majoring in early childhood education with the notion of being a kindergarten teacher or maybe first grade, she probably would have been better off in some solitary profession, like beekeeping. Or forestry. Or writing poetry or novels, alone in her room with just the hum of her IBM Selectric to keep her company, but then she wasn't much of a writer—the words always seemed to get garbled in her head, which was why her paper was late, and why she considered herself lucky to have gotten through Freshman Comp with a C.

"Did you ever have a class with him?" This was addressed to the dog-collar girl by her companion, who was dressed in engineer boots and a rumpled T-shirt but wore her hair long, like just about everybody else on campus.

"Me? I'm an English major."

"But, I mean, freshman year—didn't you have to take Psych 101?"

"Not with him—it was Lindelof. But he looked kind of cute on TV—did you see him on TV? Night before last?"

"Uh-uh, no."

"Well, he's got this monkey thing going and he was on *To Tell the Truth*. See, in the article here?" She pointed a finger at the bulletin board.

"Chimpanzee," Aimee corrected, though she didn't look at the girl but down at her feet instead.

The girl turned her face to her as if seeing her for the first time, when of course she'd been aware of her all along. She was the one who'd crowded in so they were standing there practically shoulder to shoulder and she must have recognized her from statistics, which at least made them fellow sufferers. "What did you say?"

Aimee shot her a glance out of the corner of her eye. "I said it's a chimp, not a monkey."

"Same difference." The girl was wearing a motorcycle jacket two sizes too small for her. Her lipstick was black, her face corpse-white. This was called punk, a style that had crept up out of L.A. and begun to reach campus just that fall. The girl turned to her friend. "The monkey can talk. With his hands. Like deaf people? It was, I don't know, *weird*."

"What do you mean, 'weird'?"

The girl in the dog collar let out a laugh. "I mean, it kissed him. On the lips."

"Really?"

"Which to me is kind of perverted, actually."

"Didn't you ever kiss your dog?"

"I never had a dog. My father's allergic."

"Well, mine used to kiss me and I kissed him back. All the time."

"On the mouth?"

"No, that's not what I'm saying—I mean on the head or maybe his snout? A little peck, everybody does it. You should see my mom, not only with the dog, but with our cat, Bernie? She lifts him up right in front of her face and plants these kisses on his nose? And he loves it. Or at least pretends to. Believe me, he knows where his kibble's coming from."

"Sorry, and I don't mean to be harsh or anything, but that's just disgusting."

That was when she stopped listening, not that she'd been paying all that much attention in the first place—she was still trying to focus on the article—but in that moment she noticed the flyer next to it as if it had just materialized there on the board. And in the moment after that she had the flyer in her hand and was moving off down the hall, her late paper and Dr. Lindelof suddenly plunging to the bottom of her list of priorities. The flyer said this: "Professor Schermerhorn is currently looking for students to assist in his cross-fostering project, 10–20+ hours a week. No experience necessary. Just patience and a good strong back."

That was it—it was as cryptic as that. The only other information was a phone number. By the time she got to the nearest phone booth—in the basement of the psych building, next to the junk food and soda machines—she had it memorized.

KEY LOCK OUT

He didn't have a word for words, or not yet, anyway, but he knew words all the same. He knew KEY. He knew LOCK. He knew OUT. He was a prisoner, though he didn't have a word for that either, and even if he did it would have been meaningless. What did a word, any word, have to do with this situation in this place in the onrushing unstoppable cataract of now, and the fear—AFRAID—that came with it? He had diarrhea, which existed as a pain in the gut, a stench, a hot wet squirt of shit that needed no terminology and no afterthought. He wanted his BLANKET, a blanket, any blanket. He was cold. He was distraught. He rocked from side to side. He stared at nothing. He plucked the hairs from his arms, his chin, the crown of his head, trichotillomania, and he didn't know that term either—how could he? And what would it matter if he did? Would that get him out of here?

Sleep was his only release and it came to him in a blaze of shuffled images, the bathroom light so bright it was like the sun in the sky, a trickle of blood-warm water in the tub and the face of the one who meant most to him, whose name he'd invented in the gesture of pinching his right nipple the way he pinched hers when she was with him in the BED and they were both warm and his SHIRT was on the FLOOR. But then he woke. He always woke. To the screams and the reek and his own diarrhea and the food he refused and the din of flesh pounding on metal.

When he was thirsty, thirst came to him as a sensation, pre-verbal, non-verbal, and he picked up his cup and drained it. He didn't think DRINK, didn't sign DRINK, he just drank. Until the cup was empty, that is, and no one came to fill it for him. Then the word was there. And the sign, the gesture, thumb to the lower lip, descriptor and request both. And when no one listened, when the cup went un-filled and the box, the CAGE, the prison he measured over and over with the length and breadth of his body, spoke despair to him, spoke rage, he screamed. He screamed. He screamed.

In the morning that was no morning at all because there were no windows in this place and the lights never dimmed or faltered, they came with food for him, food he didn't want, food he refused, and he compacted his own shit in his hands as best he could and flung it through the bars at them. They didn't like that. They backed away, cursing in their alien voices, and he held one hand under his chin and waggled his fingers, cursing back at them, DIRTY, DIRTY. That didn't help. Nothing helped. He worked at the bars with his hands and his feet too, but the bars were cold steel, the bars were immov-able, and every time he looked beyond them he saw more bars and barren walls and moving shadows till he shrank down inside himself. What had he done? Where was he? Where was his bedroom, where was his house and his BED and his TREE? Where was *she* and why had she allowed them to bring him here?

He took it as long as he could, huddled in the back of the cell, the box, the CAGE, and then leapt to his feet, clung to the bars and screamed and screamed again, until the BIG MAN came through the door and every voice in the place fell silent. It was as if there had never been a voice except his echoing down the corridors and reverberating off the bare walls, but of course he didn't know that word either, the acoustic signifier, only the phenomenon it represented, the physical effect that involved eardrums and cochlea and neural pathways. The BIG MAN was coming and he had the stinger in his hand, which was called a cow prod, though that formulation was beyond him too. HURT, he knew that. And he knew COW, the big lumbering night-black creature that solidified the shadows in the scrub out back of her house, of *his* house, the place he used to be before this. But that didn't do him any good because the BIG MAN with one eye, with the black eyepatch that was like a hole drilled in his head, rose and swelled and touched him with the stinger and suddenly he was writhing on the cold cement floor, beyond the reach of words now . . . except HURT, except AFRAID.

THE LEAP

She was a slim, shy girl, so shy he practically had to conduct both sides of the interview himself. He'd just got off the phone with a representative of the local CBS affiliate, who'd seen him on *To Tell the Truth* and wondered if he'd be interested in maybe doing a segment on his research—with the chimp, of course, if that was possible, because the chimp was just . . . well, they were all agog, just blown away, everybody at the station, and could he really talk or was that just, you know, something they'd worked up beforehand?—when she appeared in the doorway. He'd left the door open for office hours, though he was half hoping no one would show up because things were beyond chaotic at home and he needed to get back ASAP or somebody else was going to quit on him. He had quizzes to correct. He needed to stop at the grocery. And the gas station. And the bank.

She didn't knock at the doorframe or say "Excuse me?" or even clear her throat but just stood there till he lifted his eyes to her and asked, "Can I help you?"

Her face flushed. "I was just wondering if now's a good time . . ." and she trailed off. "I called?"

He was drawing a blank.

"You said three?"

"Oh, of course—the job, right?" He swiveled round in his chair and got to his feet. "Forgive me, I'm just so—things've been a bit crazy lately. But come on in, have a seat." He gestured to the straight-backed chair in front of his desk.

She hesitated a moment, shooting a glance over her shoulder as if to be sure he was talking to her, then ducked into the room and settled tentatively on the edge of the chair. She was short, no more than five-one or -two, and he couldn't help thinking of Olga Korbut, whose fluent limbs and exultant grin had transfixed him during the last Olympics, but this girl was prettier than Korbut, much prettier. She had the sort of face people reflexively called "sweet," which actually made no sense because physical features were a random expression of the genes and had nothing at all to do with personality, whether it be extroverted or neurotic, nurturing or homicidal. Still, he couldn't take his eyes off her.

"So you are?" he asked.

"Aimee?" she said in a soft interrogative breath of a voice, as if she were stating and questioning it at the same time. "Aimee Villard?"

"And you're a registered student, right? Undergrad?"

"Yes."

"Psych major?"

She shook her head.

"Biology?"

"No," she said. "Education? Early childhood?"

There was a hammering from down the hall where they were renovating the office of Vic Singer, an old-school behaviorist who'd passed on a month ago—died at his desk, actually, of a heart attack. Vic should have gotten out more, that's what he was thinking, and he had a momentary stab of regret, not just for his fallen colleague but for everybody in the building, on the campus, in the profession— and himself, himself most of all. You spend a lifetime scrambling to get grants and accumulate knowledge and maybe you publish and maybe you don't, and then one day you put your head down on your desk and never lift it back up again. Science advances. You don't. They both paused a moment, listening to the erratic rhythm of the hammer, which started and stopped and started again, like an ir- regular heartbeat.

"Ever work with primates before?"

She shook her head.

"Animals, at all? Pets?"

"A dog," she said. "A cat."

"What about babysitting? You ever do any babysitting? Because that's what this is going to be like, I'm afraid, and I'm not offering much by way of participation or advancement, if that's what you're expecting." He laughed. "That's what we've got grad students for."

She didn't have anything to say to this. She just stared down at her hands, which were folded rigidly in her lap. It came to him that here was the kind of personality he could make use of, dutiful, reti- cent, no questions, no arguments. Unlike Melanie, who'd been gone three weeks now and was never coming back. Here was a girl—a sweet-faced girl—he could ride like a bicycle. Or a Vespa, full throt- tle, *rem, rem, rem.*

"You know how to cook? Clean?"

"Uh-huh."

"What about diapers—you ever change diapers?"

She shrugged. "I guess."

"You guess? Okay, tell me one thing, Aimee—it is Aimee, right? Tell me—why do you want the job?"

"Because I saw you on TV."

"And that's it? Just because you saw me on TV?"

"I want to talk to him. I really, really want to talk to him."

One other applicant showed up just as he was getting ready to leave, a heavyset girl who couldn't seem to catch her breath after climbing the three flights of stairs to his office. Her shoulders were pinched between the straps of an overstuffed backpack that was the same color as her dress, olive drab, and why anybody would wear olive drab he couldn't imagine, unless she was in ROTC, which would be a nonstarter because he needed somebody with a flexible schedule who could put in the hours. As it turned out, she was a psych major, which was a plus, and she claimed to have taken a course from him, though he couldn't place her (and he couldn't place her because he was overworked and overstressed and they still had him teaching survey courses on top of everything else). She must have seen in his face that he didn't really want to do this now, but he fought down his irritation, pulled the door back open and had her sit in the chair Aimee had vacated fifteen minutes earlier.

"So," he said, easing back into his own chair, "tell me why you want the job."

"I don't know. It sounded interesting, that's all."

"And you saw me on TV, right?"

Her name was Barbara. She wore her hair in pigtails that bushed out on either side of her head so it looked as if she were wearing earmuffs. She had fat wrists and small delicate hands. "Yes," she said, breaking into a smile. "It was great. *You* were great."

Everyone had seen him on TV. TV was a portal into another di-

mension. The students, who'd largely ignored him to that point unless they were reflexively kissing up, stopped to call out to him as he
walked across campus, and his colleagues dropped by his office on
one pretext or another to see if he'd sprouted wings yet.

"And what about Sam?"

"Oh, yeah, he was great too." Her smile widened. "So cute."

"You're not in ROTC, are you?"

"Me? No. Why?" She looked surprised, maybe even offended.

"It's just the hours—it's pretty much an around-the-clock thing
looking after a chimp. What I'm saying is, it's a real commitment.
Are you sure you're up for it?"

"Oh, yeah," she said, nodding vigorously, "I am. A hundred percent."

He gave her directions to the house, which was six miles outside
of town, isolated on a ranch one of the alumni had bequeathed to the
university, and told her the same thing he'd told Aimee—"Come by
at five and we'll introduce you to Sam, because ultimately, he's going
to be the final judge here."

He drove too fast on the way home, pedal to the metal, rushing
through his errands—bank, gas station, supermarket—and when he
hit the last straightaway to the ranch, a cop swung out behind him.
He let out an involuntary curse and shifted down, afraid to tap the
brakes because that would telegraph his awareness of his own culpability, whereas if he gradually slowed to whatever the speed limit was
here (50? 55?) he could at least present a simulacrum of innocence.
And talk his way out of a ticket, if the cop was even going to pull him
over, which wasn't necessarily the case . . . but then it was. On went
the flashing lights and here came the thin complaint of the siren.

The cop was his age, more or less, and his face showed nothing.
He was wearing Ray-Bans, the twin lenses giving Guy back his own

image in duplicate. He leaned in the window of the car and said, "You seem to be in a hurry today."

"No," Guy said, "not really. Just going home, that's all. After work."

"License and registration," the cop said.

The mountains were right there, a dun eruption of blistered rock that rose up over the road and erased the horizon. Everything was quiet. Insects irradiated by the slanting sun hung like ornaments on the air and the odor of heat-scorched chaparral came to him in a sudden ascending wave. It took him a moment to dig the documents out of the glove box and hand them over to the cop, fuming all the while. The kicker here—the pain in the ass—was that he was less than a mile from home, the ranch cradled at the base of the mountains in a bright green clutch of live oak he could see from here. He said, in a softer voice now, "I'm just going home."

"You live up at Harlow Ranch?"

"Yeah, right up there." He pointed.

The cop didn't respond. He studied the documents a moment, then looked up. "I know you, don't I?"

Guy shrugged.

"You're that professor, right? With the monkey?"

Guy didn't bother to correct him.

"And *he* lives up there with you, right there on the ranch? Is that the deal?"

"That's right." He gestured to the groceries on the seat beside him. "In fact, I'm on my way home to fix him his dinner . . ."

"No kidding?" the cop said, and he was grinning now. "What you going to make for him"—he let out a laugh—"a cheeseburger?"

It was nearly five by the time he got home. The cop—Ted Simmons, eight years on the force, married, three kids, big fan of *To Tell the*

Truth—had kept him there on the side of the road for what must have been twenty minutes. He'd spared him the ticket and moderated the lecture about speeding and how people were taking their lives in their hands just to pull out of their driveways on a stretch like this—but he wanted to know all about Sam and what he liked to eat and did he know how to use the toilet and were they planning on mating him, and then he shared a long pointless story that began with, "I had this friend that had a monkey once?"

As soon as he inserted the key in the first of the three dead bolts on the front door, Guy could hear Sam on the other side, making his good-food sounds, which meant that nobody had fed him yet. He suppressed a flare of anger. No need to get excited, he told himself, though he'd warned both Josh and Elise he might be running late. The pantry was just about bare, granted, but one or the other of them could have gone to the store, couldn't they? Was that too much to ask? Not that it mattered now—he'd bought fruit and yogurt to take the edge off Sam's appetite and depending on how things worked out he could either whip up a quick pasta or send out for pizza. Or let Josh do it. Or Elise. And just pour himself a drink and sit in the armchair for ten minutes, if that wasn't asking too much.

The thing was, the key didn't seem to want turn in the bottom lock. It jammed halfway in, another irritation, and he had to set the groceries down at his feet so as to have both hands free to manipulate it, thinking Sam must have forced something inside the keyhole when nobody was looking. Which was one of his tricks, like trying to poke things into the electrical sockets or unscrew the hinges on the cabinet doors. His hoots were louder now, more urgent, and he was slapping his palms rhythmically on the inside of the door. The instant the key finally did turn in the lock, the door jerked open and there he was, his diaper full and strawberry jam smeared across the front of his shirt, holding out his arms for a hug. In the next moment he was in Guy's arms and in the moment after that clinging to his shoulders in the way of chimps in the wild, who rode their mothers' backs off and on for the first four years of life. But Guy wasn't Sam's mother—Melanie was, or had been, till she said, "Fuck you, Guy, really, fuck you," and walked out on them—and this wasn't the wild, this was captivity. And no matter how passionately he wanted to believe in the ideal of cross-fostering, of chimps taking the place of human children, that was the fact.

The problem—*one* of the problems, and the problems were infinite—was simply keeping Sam contained. And occupied. He was watchful, alert, deceptive, always probing the weaknesses in the facility and any lapses among the staff, looking to escape, to get out, to break free and lead them all on a merry chase because this was high humor, this was fun, this was what he'd been born to do. Though they'd taken pains to chimp-proof the house, installing a whole hardware store's worth of padlocks on every drawer and cabinet and even the refrigerator and replacing all the wooden doors with steel, as well as paneling over the drywall and redoing the windows in three-and-a-half-inch-thick laminated glass, he still managed to get out often enough to put the whole project at risk. There were cars on the highway (*speeding* cars), neighbors on either side and across the street who might or might not have been inclined to reach for their deer rifles on any pretext, and an assortment of rattlesnakes, bobcats, bears, coyotes and even mountain lions roaming the slopes. The price of a chimp was $10,000. And this one had been invested with nearly three years of exhaustive language training, his every gesture and reaction catalogued, his psyche probed and development monitored step by step. He'd mastered more than a hundred signs to date. He'd been on TV. He was famous. And, more importantly, he was Guy's ticket to bigger things, like a full professorship, a book contract and TV, more TV.

"Elise? Josh?"

No answer. Which pissed him off, as did the general wreckage of the living room, chairs upended, sofa on its back, food stains on the walls, not to mention the usual accumulation of toys, blankets, puzzles and magazines scattered across the floor like so much refuse. Worse, the TV cabinet was standing on one end in the far corner, the sound garbled and the picture rotating till it swallowed itself, over and over. He let out a curse and slammed the door behind him. "Elise!" he roared. "Josh!"

Innocent of everything but the present moment, Sam clung to his back, hooting softly—he wanted his dinner, but his dinner was not forthcoming because the groceries were on the front porch, unattended and unrefrigerated, and Guy wasn't about to take the chance of propping open the door to retrieve them, even for ten seconds, not without help. *Jesus*, and where *were* they?

That was when Josh appeared in the kitchen doorway, looking sheepish. "Sorry, Guy, but he's been throwing tantrums all afternoon— he just went apeshit, okay, and now I know where *that* term comes from. In spades. It was like there was nothing we could do. Elise locked herself in the bathroom, it was that bad."

He didn't want to open up on Josh. That wasn't his nature. He was a persuader, a team player—unlike Moncrief, who he swore to himself he would never be like, no matter what it came to. Josh was one of his best grad students and he liked him, genuinely liked him, and he liked Josh's girlfriend, Elise, too—they were all in this together—but he was feeling just a bit overwhelmed at the moment, not to mention worn thin as wire. Which put him in a black mood. He pushed his way past Josh and into the kitchen, which was also—no surprise—a mess. "You're telling me I can't leave the house anymore?"

Josh was wearing a T-shirt smeared with the same strawberry jam as Sam's, which Guy could feel now as an adhesive give-and-release at the back of his neck as Sam shifted positions, still hooting softly. For food. "No, I'm not saying that, I'm just saying today was one of his difficult days—you know, since Melanie left? One of the worst, actually. He misses her. Badly. Really badly."

"Don't we all."

"And he's acting out."

"Like any other kid, right?"

"Yeah, right, that's what I'm saying. And sometimes you just have to—"

"Let him wreck the fucking house? And shit in his diapers and don't bother to change him?"

"Change him? I could barely catch up with him—I mean, he was on a tear like I've never seen. And he bit Elise, hard—drew blood— and no joke, right on her face? Like her cheek? Her left cheek? She's in there now putting alcohol and hydrogen peroxide on it and whatever . . . I mean, I don't know if after today she's even going to want to come back anymore."

"How bad is it? She's not going to need stitches, is she?"

"I don't know. Maybe."

"Maybe? Well, that's just fucking great. Because I wouldn't want her to have to go to the emergency room or anything and have people start sticking their noses in—"

"Don't blame me." Josh pointed at the chimp riding his shoulders. "Blame him. He's the one that created this situation. No matter what we did, he just wouldn't stop."

It came to him, in a flood of bitterness, that Josh was too small for this job. Literally and figuratively. He was five-seven or -eight, with an apricot fluff of hair that was already receding and an academic's anemic build, and he couldn't handle a chimp of thirty-five pounds? What was going to happen when Sam put on another fifteen pounds? Another fifty? Another hundred? If you had any hope of controlling him you had to use psychology—operant conditioning, stimulus/response/reinforcement—and Josh knew that as well as he did because Sam was already as strong or stronger than he was. Of course, Sam knew it too, and for the moment, at least, he was having none of it. He was hungry, that was all that mattered, that was the full extent of his awareness, and he swung himself fluidly down to the floor, went to the refrigerator and started tugging at the twin door handles. Which were chained shut, for obvious reasons.

"Okay, okay, it's not the end of the world. You go get the groceries—they're out on the porch—and then feed him a couple apples and his peach yogurt, one container only. Maybe we send out for pizza tonight, that's what I'm thinking." He bent to Sam and signed, WHAT YOU WANT? and Sam, pointing first to the clock set in the stove with his elongated index finger that was like the stretched-out finger of a leather glove, signed, TIME EAT.

That was when the doorbell rang. Or buzzed, actually—an insistent buzz that froze the three of them in place. Guy slapped his forehead (and where had *that* gesture evolved from?). "Oh, *shit*, I forgot all about it—that'll be the girls . . ."

"What girls?" Josh had his head down, fingering the keys he wore trucker-style on a chain clipped to his belt, sorting through them for the one to the refrigerator. He located it, which caught Sam's attention, then glanced up, looking puzzled.

Ignoring him, Guy went straight for the front door, muttering to himself—*Jesus Christ, one fucking thing after another*—but before he could get there it swung open on Barbara, the ROTC girl. Or non-ROTC girl. The eager one. The one who'd said, "You were great." She was framed in the doorway, backlit, a bag of groceries propped on each hip. He saw that she'd combed out her hair and changed her clothes, wearing shorts now and a low-cut print blouse that showed off her breasts as if she were answering an ad for a wet nurse (which, in fact, Sam *had* needed for the first six months of his life, but that time was past). "Hi," she said, stepping into the room without preliminaries. "I'm sorry, but I think somebody forgot these?" She shifted her hips, indicating the groceries, and tried for a smile.

Behind him, Guy heard Josh call out a warning, but before he could react, here came Sam, hurtling through the room on all fours, intent on the open door—which was a crisis in the making, because if he got loose it could take hours to get him back. The last time he escaped, after he'd appropriated a key that someone—*Elise*—had been careless with, it was a nightmare, but then since Melanie walked out, everything connected with the project had begun to seem like a nightmare. Guy had been in the kitchen that time too, chopping vegetables for a salad while the burgers he'd just molded hissed in the pan and the buns browned in the oven, Sam right there beside him overseeing the preparations while alternately springing up and down off the counter, feeding slices of zucchini and cucumber into his mouth, chewing on the rim of the big Tupperware bowl to admire the impression of his own teeth and drooling milk down his chin and into the dense matted hair of his chest. A moment later, he was gone, and Guy didn't think anything of it—Sam was easily distracted and the house was his to roam—until Sam appeared on the other side of the kitchen window, grinning at him. Sam signed, PLAY ME, signed, HIDE SEEK.

As it turned out, as best they could reconstruct it, he'd slipped the key off the top of the washing machine where Elise had set it down for just an instant while she took out the trash. She discovered it missing as soon as she came back through the door, and after patting down her pockets and making a quick search of the laundry room and kitchen, went directly to Sam, where he was sunk into the couch in the living room, thumbing through a magazine, all innocence. She searched him—both pockets, inside his shirt, front and back—and then overturned the couch cushions before going down on hands and knees to search beneath the furniture. She even took the magazine from him and shook out the pages, but the key was nowhere to be found.

The Cartesian view of animals had it that they were merely biological machines, driven by instinct and incapable of thought, of planning, of foreseeing future actions and consequences, but that kind of thinking was antiquated. And demonstrably wrong. In fact, Sam had not only planned the whole episode, he'd used deception as well. As they ultimately discovered, he'd stolen the key, hidden it under his tongue and managed to hold it there all the while Elise was searching him and throughout the preparations in the kitchen, waiting till the time was right, till everybody was distracted and the key could reappear again, albeit coated in a slime of saliva and masticated zucchini and whatever else he'd been chewing. Which, as long as it performed its function, was of little consequence to him. Did it stick in the lock? Was it difficult to turn? No matter: he managed it. And, as if to rub it in, as if to underscore the joke, there he was, right in the kitchen window, laughing at them all.

Now the situation was different—no key required; the door stood open—but the intent was the same. Sam could move at speed, far more physically advanced than a human child of his age and beyond, and he could easily outmaneuver anybody in the house. There was the open door. There was the grinning girl with the groceries balanced on her hips. And there was Sam, closing fast.

This was a disaster, pure and simple. Another *recrudescence of shit*, and Guy was in no mood for it. He was angry, outraged, but still he didn't cry out "Stop!" because it wouldn't have had the slightest effect. Instead, he pitched his voice high and crooned, "Oh, Barbara, you brought the *ice cream*!"

Chimps run as if on pistons, up and down, shoulders, arms, knuckles, legs, feet, and now, suddenly, the motion was arrested, and he could see the effect of those two seductive words in combination—"ice" and "cream"—as they became concept and then calculation in the neural pathways of the chimp's brain. Sam pulled up short, skidding across the floorboards and right on past Barbara, bracing himself only long enough to snatch one of the bags out of her hands. The hesitation was enough, or almost enough, to let Guy get to the door first. But just as he got there, just as he was lurching for the upper panel to slam it shut, Sam, the bag clutched in one hand, worked his shoulders between the door and the frame and wriggled through the gap, trailing groceries behind him.

Josh shouted something unintelligible, the girl—Barbara—looked paralyzed, as if she'd expected a cuddle toy and not this id on wheels that Sam had become, that Sam *was*, and then the door slammed shut and Sam was on the other side of it. Furious, Guy jerked the door open again, expecting to see him scrambling up the side of the house or hurtling down the drive for the road and the traffic and the death that awaited him beneath the wheels of the next speeding car, but that didn't happen. Sam was right there, on the porch, crouched over the tattered remains of the grocery bag and staring up into the eyes of the other girl, the shy one, the pretty-face, Aimee. He wasn't running, wasn't even moving. He shot a glance over his shoulder at Guy, who was already reaching out to snatch at him, then signed, SORRY, SORRY, and made a leap right into her arms.

NOT HER

She was not there. She was not there in any way he could perceive, not even in the faintest trace of a scent, not even in the sweet lingering odor of the shampoo she used on her HAIR and his too. He was alone, but for the shapes in the other cages that showed their teeth and screeched at him like BUGS, big black chittering BUGS, things beneath his notice, things meant to be squashed against a wall or clapped between two hands. Except that they were BIG and ugly and had teeth, which puzzled him and hurt him too because what were they and what were they doing here? The real question, though, the persistent question that was lodged in his brain in a pinched tight compartment squeezed between AFRAID and HURT, was what was he doing here, wherever this was, which wasn't with her, wasn't home, wasn't safe. Or warm. Or habitable in any way he'd ever known.

He'd known the COUCH, the TV, the BED, his TOYS. And her. She was there, always, and now she wasn't.

Another night must have gone by, though the lights wouldn't admit it, and he must have slept because here they came with food for him again and water for his cup and he signed to them with the words that were so urgent his gut constricted and the diarrhea squirted out of him all over again—KEY LOCK OUT—but they couldn't fathom those words. They were ignorant, illiterate, and the faces they showed him, the two of them, males both, were without expression of any kind except indifference. One of them had a hose. The water shot from it to sweep his shit down the drain that made its own hole in the middle of the cement floor and then it shot at him too so that he had to turn his back to keep it out of his eyes and he wanted to tell them to stop—he was COLD, he was WET—and then he did tell them, rushing at the bars till the hose was right there in his face and he didn't flinch, he didn't care, and they were laughing at him now, laughing, and he stood there and took it because it didn't matter. Nothing mattered. Not anymore.

Later—he was shivering, wrapping himself in the sad blanket of his own wet arms—he heard the quick sharp sigh of the hinges on the door at the end of the hall and it brought him instantly to life. Footsteps were coming, female footsteps, the sway, the tap, the rhythm of the hips pumping the legs and maneuvering the shoes that hid her feet and toes, and he knew it was her. And more: he smelled her! Her shampoo! Her hair! But then the footsteps turned the corner and all at once she was not her but someone else altogether, with the wrong face and the wrong hair—and beneath the shampoo, the wrong smell. It was a woman wearing the same sort of clothes she would wear, not dress-up, but work clothes, and she was smiling at him. Leaning toward the cage and holding something out to him—

ORANGE—and saying, "Come on now, little fella, cheer up. It's not so bad, is it? Look, look what I have for you—isn't that nice? It's nice, isn't it?"

The orange was in his hand. A surge of lust came over him—he wanted it—but just as quickly he remembered where he was and who she wasn't and how she'd tricked him and he pushed his hand back through the bars and dropped it at her feet. Then he signed, YOU ME GO, but she just kept on grinning till finally she picked up the orange, slipped it back through the bars and *tap-tapped* her way down the hall and out the door that gave the briefest glimpse of—could it be?—light, real light, sunlight, and a cold sweet funk of cut weeds and tall trees and a thousand other things too.

That was when he began to look around him. Really look. He was in a cage and the cage was impregnable, but there was a lock on the door and if he didn't have a KEY he could find something else, some other small and shiny thing that could work the lock that would have had tumblers in it like any other lock, though he didn't know how tumblers were called, only the fact of them—or the sound of them, the sound that made the invisible visible. He could see them in his mind, hear them click into place. The animals in the other cages, the BLACK BUGS, woofed and chittered at him, but he ignored them. He was looking for something, anything, a strand of wire, a sliver of metal or even wood, because he had a plan now, a purpose, and he was hungry suddenly, starving. He plucked up the orange, squatted on the floor in the corner of the cage and fed it into his mouth, morsel by morsel, pausing only to sign to himself, to sign KEY LOCK OUT.

LIKE PLUGGING A WIRE
INTO A SOCKET

So he'd selected her. He'd gone right by the other girl and out the door, Professor Schermerhorn chasing frantically after him, and he could have raced down the drive, hoisted himself to the roof or scrambled up the trunk of a tree, but when he saw her there on the porch he just froze, as if she were a screen or a wall or a moat brimming with water. He froze, his eyes locked on hers, and then he made his leap and she didn't flinch because she didn't have time to think about it or wonder what was happening to her—he leapt and she caught him, and it was the most natural thing in the world to wrap her arms around him and press him to her and feel the mad pounding cyclone of his heart beating against hers. It was intense. The most intense moment of her life, electric, like plugging a wire into a socket. Here was this animal she didn't know at all, a wild animal one generation removed from the jungles of West Africa, and suddenly it—he—was hers. Or she was his.

The door stood open. She was aware of the sun on her back and the steady protestation of a jay from the trees along the drive where she'd parked her car, and if she'd wanted to say anything to Professor Schermerhorn, who was framed there in the doorway, tensing himself for a footrace, or to the other girl gaping at her and the guy with the panicky expression who'd suddenly appeared behind the professor like a pop-up doll, she couldn't have found the words. The ape was in her arms, his breath hot on her throat. The jay screeched. She was in shock—or a kind of shock, the shock of awakening to something radically different from anything she'd ever experienced or expected.

Professor Schermerhorn was saying, "Sam, Sam, calm down now, it's okay, everything's okay. Time to eat, right? Are you hungry? Eat?" And he leaned forward, shifting his weight to slip an arm around the chimp's shoulders so that the three of them were locked together there on the porch, arm to shoulder to arm.

He tried to take the chimp from her, but the chimp—Sam—wasn't cooperating. She felt him tighten his grip on her, hands and feet both. The professor—they were no more than eighteen inches apart, as if they were rehearsing some weird interspecies dance routine, the ape waltz, ape tango, cha-cha-cha—gave her a naked pleading look over the back of Sam's head. That look cemented everything. She had the job, she knew that in an instant, and it didn't matter if fifty applicants came to the door, because Sam had selected her and Sam wasn't letting go.

"You all right?" he asked her.

She nodded.

"You think we could all maybe just swing around and go back in the house now—I mean, can you hold him?"

She nodded again and he said, "Good, good," and they shuffled awkwardly through the door, which the other guy slammed shut and locked behind them with a key he kept on a chain at his belt. The other girl said, "Jesus, I had no idea he was so fast, because on TV, I mean, the way he was *walking* . . ."

"You can let him down now," Professor Schermerhorn said, and Aimee gently tried to extricate herself, but Sam wouldn't let go. Which could have been a problem—as she was soon to discover, there was another girl in the bathroom, a grad student who'd been bitten on the face and was going to need a rabies shot and maybe stitches too—but strangely she wasn't afraid. It was like the time when she was five or six and the neighbors' Doberman had got loose and come charging across the yard at her, showing its teeth, and her mother screamed and the neighbor shouted and then nothing happened—the dog pulled up short, let out a soft whine and began licking her face.

She tried again, working her hands under his armpits to hoist him out and away from her as if he were a clingy preschooler, and this time he went slack and let her lower him to the floor. For a moment he just stood there, upright, staring at her as if to assess the face and figure of this new plaything in his life, and despite all the frantic activity—and the disaster he'd made of the room, which she was just now registering—he seemed eerily calm, solemn almost. His eyes—perfectly round, the color of the cinnamon sticks she liked to use to flavor her tea in the morning—never wavered. He stared right into her as if he could see what she was thinking, as if he already knew her, then reached up a hand for her to take hold of—she laughed, she couldn't help herself, glancing at Professor Schermerhorn and the other girl, who said, "Looks like you've got a new friend"—and then let him lead her across the room and into the kitchen, where he dropped her hand, took a bib down from its hook on the wall beside the refrigerator and climbed into a highchair drawn up to the kitchen table.

Everybody crowded into the kitchen behind her. The other girl was trying to make small talk by way of ingratiating herself, saying, "He scared me there for a minute, he really did, just the way he came at me so fast, I mean, I didn't—"

"Don't worry about it." Professor Schermerhorn gave her a brittle smile. His hair—it *was* blond, honey-colored, actually—hung in his eyes and he shoved it back with an impatient gesture, as if all this activity had cost him more than his tone of voice admitted. He was on trial here too, Aimee saw that now. He needed her, and maybe this other girl as well, to take some of the pressure off him, to babysit and change diapers and bring order to things while he was teaching his classes and writing his papers and whatever else he was doing. The chimp could be difficult, she'd just seen that, no different from any other pet—but then he wasn't a pet, was he? He could talk. He could reason. Chimps shared ninety-eight point nine percent of their DNA with human beings—she'd looked it up—and that set them apart from any other animal species on the planet. And more: he knew things, secrets of existence no human could ever know, and he was going to reveal them. To her. To her alone. That was what this was all about. That was what she was doing here.

"He can have that effect on people," Professor Schermerhorn said, "till you get to know him, that is. Because he's a good boy"—addressing the chimp now—"aren't you, Sam? You didn't mean to scare Barbara, did you? That wouldn't be very nice, would it?"

Sam swung round in the chair and folded back his upper lip in a grin. He'd already fastened the bib around his neck and now he made a gesture to the professor, a sign anyone could read—the fingers of his right hand pressed together and tapping at his lips—and the professor said aloud, "Okay, time to eat," while simultaneously signing it. "Josh"—turning to the other guy now—"will you do the honors? If you can manage to put the groceries away before everything turns to shit, I mean." He paused, looked to her, then glanced at the other girl.

"Sam's going to have a little yogurt and fruit as an appetizer, but then we're going to send out for pizza and a mixed salad and we'll all sit down and have a proper meal—sound good? I mean, you're invited. Both of you."

At the mention of pizza, Sam clapped his hands and began to grunt his approval. In the next moment, Josh disappeared into the other room to retrieve the groceries and the professor went to the phone hanging on the wall beside the refrigerator. "What do you girls like on your pizza, any favorites? Any dislikes? Oh, by the way"—he made as if to slap his forehead in what she would come to see as his characteristic gesture, as if he were simultaneously criticizing himself and apologizing—"Aimee, this is Barbara; Barbara, Aimee. That was Josh you just met, if only briefly, and Elise's in the bathroom. And call me Guy, by the way—there's no need for formality here."

"Hi," Barbara said, glancing up at her. "Nice to meet you." And then, turning back to Professor Schermerhorn—Guy—she said, "Anything but anchovies."

"You hear that, Sam? Barbara doesn't like anchovies. What about you, Sam, you want anchovies—you love anchovies, don't you?" he said, signing it as he spoke.

Sam—he was the center of attention, always, in any situation, in any room, the marvel set down amongst them—signed something back and then pretended to gag, drawing it out till his was the only voice in the room and Aimee had the sense that it might have gone on all night if Josh hadn't ducked back into the kitchen at that moment, a carton of peach yogurt in one hand, an apple and a banana clutched in the other.

"Okay," Guy said, already dialing, "how does this sound—two extra-large, mushrooms on one, pepperoni on the other? Everybody cool with that?"

She just nodded. Barbara said, "Yeah, sure," and Sam, who was already occupied with the yogurt, no spoon necessary, his face smeared and the bib doing extra duty, paused to clap his hands sharply, twice, then began licking the smears of excess yogurt from the front of the bib, which, Aimee now noticed, featured a color picture of the Gerber baby, front and center, a wide toothless baby grin spread across her baby face.

There was a moment of silence, during which Sam's slurping and grunting were the only sounds in the room, before Guy spoke into the phone, his voice narrowing. "Yes, hello, this is Professor Schermerhorn speaking? I'd like to place an order?"

Aimee had backed into the kitchen counter, bracing herself against the edge of the countertop. She folded her arms across her chest, then dropped them and let her hands dangle at her sides, feeling awkward and unworthy. She wasn't in her apartment. She wasn't spooning up Top Ramen and finding ways to avoid studying. She was here in a professor's house, with new people, with *Sam*, the chain of events leading to this moment so haphazard, so unlikely, it didn't seem real. She wanted to go home. She wanted to stay.

"I don't know about you," Guy said, hanging up the phone and swinging round on them, spreading his hands wide, "but I could use a glass of wine—I mean, it's been a *day*, what with my class and a faculty meeting on top of that and then I got stopped by a cop on the way home and then Sam almost got loose, which, by the way, everybody has to be attuned to, number one priority, the door is shut and locked at all times." He swept his eyes over her and then settled on Barbara, who'd been the guilty party, after all. "Unless Sam's in his harness and on his lead. Understood?"

"Understood," Barbara said in a reduced voice.

"Aimee?"

She didn't know whether he was asking her if she wanted wine, which she was going to refuse because this was all coming at her too fast, or if he meant the situation with the doors, so she just smiled, or half smiled, and dropped her eyes.

"Okay, good. But wine. I'm afraid all we can offer you is red, but it's a pretty decent pinot noir from the Santa Ynez Valley. Right, Josh? We still got a couple bottles of that left?"

Josh was hovering over Sam, dabbing at his face with a napkin while Sam tried to snatch it away from him, all in fun, everything relaxed now, crisis averted, pizza on the way. "Yeah, I think like five or six bottles and the one I already opened—I poured Elise a glass to calm her down."

Guy shot him a look, and whether it was meant to be judgmental or not, she wasn't sure, though she was good at reading people—or told herself she was. "Why don't you go see how she's doing and ask her if she wants to join us for pizza? I'll fetch the wine myself." He gestured to her and Barbara, grinning now. "That's one of the little perks here, by the way—maybe the only perk. But the owner of LaSalle Vineyards is a friend of the project and he donates a couple cases once in a while—which we tend to go through pretty fast, don't we, Josh?"

"What's a ranch without wine? Or a chimp, for that matter? You want a glass, Sam?" Josh asked, thrusting his face into Sam's line of vision and signing as he spoke. "Wine? You want wine?"

Sam glanced up at him, nodding his head and bobbing his fist up and down at the same time—the sign for yes, an enthusiastic yes.

Barbara said, "Is that true? He drinks wine?"

"Try to stop him," Josh said.

"But I thought he was still a baby? I mean, is that good for him?"

"Not strictly," Guy said, "but is it good for us? We limit him to one glass only and we like to give it to him at dinner in the hope it'll make him sleepy, which it does, and that makes it all the easier to get him to bed—which, by the way, Josh, is going to require the changing of the diaper, remember? Which is full? And stinking?"

That was when Elise emerged from the bathroom, which was just across the hall from the kitchen. She was tall, pretty, with a milky complexion and a kinked-out dome of pale red hair, and she was pressing a damp hand towel packed with ice to the side of her face. "Can you believe it," she demanded, stalking into the room and going right up to Guy as if the rest of them didn't exist, "the little shit bit me." She made an angry gesture toward Sam, who ignored her, the broad spade of his tongue probing the recesses of the yogurt carton, his head down and his shoulders slumped in indifference.

"Is it bad?" Guy took her by the arm, gently drawing her to him. He stood there a moment, searching her eyes, and, as if unconsciously, began stroking the underside of her wrist, where the blue veins stood out against the soft pale skin. It was an intimate gesture and Aimee wondered about that, because Elise was Josh's girlfriend, wasn't she? Or had she missed something?

"I thought he was going to give me a kiss, you know?" Elise bunched her lips. Her voice trembled. "Like a hundred times before, like every day? But he—the little shit." She turned to Sam now. "You little shit. I'm talking to you, yeah, *you*!"

Sam had his back to her. He peeked over one shoulder as if to gauge the level of emotion in the room, the finest calibrations of which he was a master at decoding as Aimee would soon come to learn, then shifted his eyes and went back to the yogurt carton. Which was empty now. He played with it a moment, shuffling it back and forth across the tray table with a whispery scrape, then inverted it on the tray, flattened it with an abrupt slap of one hand, and inserted the circular white disk of it in his mouth, holding it there between his lips and teeth like a sixth grader playing for laughs. He didn't grunt. Didn't hoot. Didn't sign SORRY.

"Let me see," Guy said. "Come on."

"I can't believe it! *Jesus!*" Elise snarled, jerking away from Guy and kicking the leg of the highchair so hard it rocked away from the table and then back again so that Sam had to tense his muscles to keep from going over. He looked guilty, if that was possible, and something else too: annoyed.

Aimee just stood there, taking it all in, embarrassed and fascinated at the same time. The chimp was small still, an infant, a tot, cute as a toy come to life, yet she could see how defined his muscles were, especially in the shoulders and upper arms.

"Come on," Guy repeated, taking Elise by the wrist again, trying to comfort her.

Elise's eyes were swollen and red. She stared furiously at him a moment, then peeled back the towel to reveal the raw red gash at her jawbone, just below the bow of her mouth. "Am I going to need stitches? I am, aren't I? I'm ruined, right? Fucked, I mean. You tell me, Guy, *you tell me*."

"No, no," he said, his voice soft and melodic, as if he were crooning to her. "It's not that bad, not at all. You're going to want to get a tetanus booster—and rabies, because any mammal can carry rabies, though the chances of Sam having it are like one in a trillion . . ."

"*Thanks*," she said. "Really, thanks a lot, because that's so comforting to hear . . . But I mean, isn't anybody going to take me to a doctor, or what, the emergency room? This is my *face* we're talking about, don't you get it?"

"They use silk," Aimee heard herself say, and everybody turned to stare at her as if she'd just touched down from outer space. She hadn't meant to say anything because all this was so fraught, so new, but now she was exposed and she couldn't help herself. "I had this friend? She was in a car accident?"

For an instant she thought Elise was going to turn on her—she was an interloper, a stranger, and what right did she have even to open her mouth?—but Elise ignored her, pushing herself away from Guy with a savage snap of both wrists and wheeling round on Sam in his highchair. "You!" she shouted. "You're the one that did this, you shitty little *monkey*. If you ever, I swear—"

Sam just grinned at her, his eyes unblinking, the white disk of the crushed yogurt carton catching the light like a false set of teeth.

Josh, who'd been hovering just behind her, wrapped an arm around her now. "It's going to be okay," he said, and he was crooning too. "Come on, I'll take you right now—we'll go straight to the emergency room and have somebody look at it, okay?"

The pressure in the room seemed to dissipate. Elise had a cut on her face, that was all, a wound, a minor wound. They'd stitch it up. Treat it. Bandage it. Everything was going to be all right.

At that moment, Sam leaned forward, shucked the bib, which he laid out neatly on the tray top before him, and climbed down out of the highchair. He stood there beside it, erect, as if he'd never gone on all fours, as if he was human, and signed something to Elise as she and Josh made their way out of the kitchen. "What's he saying?" Barbara asked.

"He's saying he's sorry," Guy said. "He doesn't mean to bite, doesn't even know what he's doing, really—he just gets overexcited, that's all."

"But this happened, what, like an hour ago? How does he even remember?"

Guy shrugged. And then he winked, first at her, then at Barbara. "You tell me," he said.

"Like with a dog," Barbara went on. She brought her hands into play, shaping a dog in the air. "They say you don't discipline a dog for doing his business on the rug unless you catch him in the act because otherwise he has no idea what he's being punished for and it's just like random cruelty."

"Sam's not a dog."

"Yeah," she said, "I'm beginning to realize that."

They were all moving now, through the kitchen and into the living room, Sam right behind Josh, Elise and Guy, but he wasn't hurrying, wasn't trying to make a break for the door as he'd done earlier.

Josh applied the key to the three locks, opened the door and held it for Elise. She was hunched over, pressing the ice pack to her face, and she didn't bother to look behind her to see where Sam was. But Sam wasn't a problem. He ignored the open door, settling into a green plastic kiddie chair just to the left of it and pulling his feet up to his chest as if to warm them. "Look at him," Barbara said. "He's not even trying to get out."

Guy glanced back over his shoulder and smiled. "That's because pizza's coming. Nothing'll distract him from pizza—isn't that right, Sam? Pizza's his favorite." And then, just as he was easing the door shut, he called out to Elise. "Tell them it was a bat or a squirrel or something, okay? Don't mention Sam at all, because—well, just don't mention him, okay?"

And then the door slammed shut and there were just the three of them left in the house—her, Barbara and Guy. Or four. If you counted Sam. And you always had to count Sam.

A week later, Elise was still waiting for her stitches. Josh had taken her to the emergency room at University Hospital, where by a stroke of luck they got someone to examine her right away, and that someone— a doctor not much older than they were—said he just couldn't believe a bat had been the culprit, not with a bite radius like that. He'd given Josh a cold stare and said it looked as if somebody—a human being, *Homo sapiens*, a boyfriend, maybe—had sunk his teeth into her and in the next moment they were both confessing and the doctor wound up bringing in two of his colleagues to look at the laceration because nobody had ever seen a chimp bite before. They kept her for three days, put her on an intravenous antibiotic and bandaged the wound rather than stitching it up, for fear of infection. Stitches would come later. And after that, plastic surgery.

Aimee was still at the house that night when the phone rang and

Josh, on the other end of the line, explained the situation to Guy. She, Barbara, Guy and Sam were at the kitchen table at the time, the pizza boxes spread open in the center of the table and Sam perched in his highchair, folding a slice of pepperoni pizza into his mouth. They each had a glass of wine set before them (she'd been too uncomfortable to refuse), including Sam, who lifted his glass delicately by the stem, sniffed it like a connoisseur and took dainty sips between bites of pizza and the limp oily salad he seemed to relish. Which he ate with a fork, like anybody else.

"You mean you told them?" Guy was hunched over his plate, the phone pressed to his ear, the long yellow cord snaking across the floor behind him. "For shitsake, Josh, you know better than that. What did I tell you? I said to say it was a bat or something, right? Anything. Because the only thing that matters is that she gets her shots, and we don't—"

There was a long pause, Josh's voice an unintelligible buzz leaching out of the receiver, and then Guy said, "Oh, Christ, that's all we need," and he got up, crossed the room and slammed the phone down on its hook. He circled the table twice, as if warring with himself, then sank into his chair and shifted a slice of pizza around his plate a moment before he looked up and said, "No worries, everything's fine. It's just that, well, they'll be keeping her overnight."

Aimee looked to Barbara, but Barbara's face showed nothing. They couldn't have come at a worse time, that was what she was thinking, both of them thrust into the middle of this little domestic drama while its prime mover sat there in his highchair playing with a squashed yogurt container as if it had nothing to do with him. If he'd bitten Elise, why wouldn't he bite Barbara? Or her? The pizza went cold on her plate. She took a tentative sip of wine, though she'd never liked wine, or at least hadn't found a variety that appealed to her—it sat like medicine on her tongue, like cough syrup without the heavy freight of sugar and menthol.

She could see that Professor Schermerhorn—Guy—was upset, though he was trying to hide it. There were regulations for keeping exotic animals, weren't there? Dogs got put down if they were biters, but what about chimps, research animals raised as if they were human? They couldn't be put down, could they? No, they were too valuable for that, but they could be taken away, they could be caged in some facility where they'd never bite anyone again.

"So listen, girls, I don't want to give you the wrong impression," Guy said, as if reading her mind, "but it's not always like this— Elise, I mean. There've been a few bites before—that's chimp nature, they're aggressive, they can't help it—but never on anybody's face. My wife—Melanie?—he bit her once, only once, on the hand, and she bit him right back."

Barbara said, "Tit for tat, right? What goes around comes around?" She smiled at Guy, then Sam, and Aimee wondered if Sam was capable of following the conversation. Her niece, Sophie, was two and a half, and though her spoken vocabulary was limited, she clearly understood the conversation going on around her—and chimps, at this age, were more advanced than children. But if Sam was listening, he showed no sign of it. At that moment, he miscalculated with a forkful of salad, which dropped to the tray with a wet plop, and he leaned forward to lap it up with his tongue, the fork clutched redundantly in one hand.

"That's right," Guy said, nodding in emphasis. "And that's another thing—if he bites, and I'm not saying he will—you've got to discipline him right away or he's just going to keep on doing it. With Sam"—and here, at the mention of his name, Sam glanced up, beaming—"when he was one or so he got it in his head that the best way to get attention when he wanted something or was just feeling antsy or bored was to bite somebody. Right, Sam?"

Sam didn't respond. He leaned forward, reaching for another slice of pizza, which he neatly separated from the remainder and brought to his mouth, all without spilling his wine, though the glass shifted precariously on the tray table. He looked so innocent, so harmless, she could hardly believe what had happened, and she told herself it wasn't going to happen to her, not after that embrace on the front steps. He liked her, he'd chosen her, he'd wrapped his arms around her, and maybe Elise didn't understand him, maybe she'd mistreated him, maybe she was a bitch—there were two sides to every story, weren't there?

Guy was calling her name softly. "Aimee," he said, "Aimee, you still with us?"

She looked up. Nodded. It was as if a spell had come over her.

"Good. Because I wonder if you wouldn't mind fetching the d-e-s-s-e-r-t from the k-i-t-c-h-e-n? It's in the f-r-i-d-g-e? In a bowl? The door's unlocked. And there's a can of w-h-i-p-p-e-d c-r-e-a-m with it."

"Okay, sure," she said, pushing herself up from the table.

"And another thing—I've got a question for both of you. Since they're keeping Elise overnight, I'm going to be shorthanded here. I wonder, could either of you spend the night? In the guest room, that is—it's all laid out, bed made and all that. Because I'm going to need help getting him to bed—and in the morning, the morning too. I've got an early class."

"Tomorrow morning?" Barbara looked distraught—or at least she was simulating the emotion. And who was she, anyway? A junior psych major Aimee had never seen before—but then she'd been on campus two years now and hadn't really reached out to anybody. She'd made zero friends, or zero close friends, anyway, and she'd been on exactly three dates, two with the same guy because he was persistent, though she hadn't really liked him. Steven Handler. At the end of the second date—bar, fast food, movie—he'd asked her if she wanted to have sex and she'd said no and that was the end of that. "I'd like to," Barbara said, her voice dredged in fake compunction.

"I really would, but I just can't, I'm sorry, I've got like six thousand things—" She fluttered her hands, emitted a nervous laugh. "If only I'd had a little warning . . ."

"Sorry, I didn't mean to lay it on you, but I'm afraid it's something of an emergency. Aimee? What about you?"

She was standing now, arrested on her way to the kitchen and the mission Guy had entrusted her with as if she were already part of the team. She looked first to him, then Sam, who was studying her intently, as if he was fully conscious of everything going on here, as if he knew how to spell "dessert" and "whipped cream" as well as she did. "Sure," she said. "No problem."

BLACKLY, BLEAKLY

This CAGE, this space, this prison—it was the worst place he'd ever been in his life and his life was a long shimmering string of events and impressions and memories that took him back to a memory he couldn't summon and a place he didn't know, because that was his birth, that was his awakening from a sleep into a dream and the dream was the now. Still, though he raged against it, though he screamed till the BIG MAN came with his stinger, he knew that he was in that place now. He had no recollection of it and he had nothing but hate for it, and yet the feeling was inescapable. Was it the flickering ghost of a smell? A vestigial sound he recognized in the hoots and shrieks of these other things, these BLACK BUGS? No, he insisted to himself, signing it for emphasis, over and over: NO! NO! NO! His home was with her. His home was far from here. He could close his eyes and see it, see *her*. This wasn't his home. He'd never been here before and all he wanted was to get OUT, to escape . . . but then blackly, bleakly, it came to him that there was a time before her and that HOME was just a word.

He studied the cage. He sniffed the reek of his own shit and the reek of the BLACK BUGS that terrified him with their shrieking and their blind black stupidity. He took his time. He examined every detail, every surface, every flange and jointure and crevice. There was no key. There was nothing he could use as a key, nothing, not even a fragment of plastic or a scrap of straw from a BROOM. Was he calculating? Was he logical? Was he thinking? Well, yes, because the process led him to observe the low plastered-over ceiling of the CAGE and detect the faint tracery of the pipe buried there—which presented him with an idea. He got to his feet. He reached up his arm. He began tracing the pipe with his fingers, over and over, his nails digging at the plaster that was its own kind of rock until, after a time, there were flakes of it on the floor, flakes he swept into the drain with the broom of his hand. Then he slept.

They came with food and he retreated to the back of the cage. It was no food he recognized but he was hungry and he ate it once they went away and shut the door at the end of the hall that gave onto the world of light and movement. He rested. He slept. At some point the BLACK BUGS settled down and fell silent and he went back to the pipe and the plaster till he found the place where the pipe was joined to another pipe by means of a hard steel nut, though he didn't know that term because it was already occupied by the kind of NUT he liked to eat whenever she gave it to him. But here was the thing: his fingers were steadier and stronger than any wrench in the toolbox under the sink back at home and he had patience, time on his hands, though there were no clocks here and no night or morning by which to calculate it. Minutes passed nonetheless, breath in, breath out. Then hours. Flakes of plaster fell to the floor. The nut loosened by slow degrees. After a while it was wet and then it began to dribble

WATER. That was when he really applied his strength. Almost immediately the pipe gave way, bending back from its bed in the rock of the ceiling, and what had been a dribble exploded into a hard hissing cascade of WATER—furious, unstoppable WATER.

They came running, shouting in their high strained voices till they outdid the BLACK BUGS, who were aroused themselves now, the whole world screaming in his ears, and here they were in the cage with him, cursing him, cursing the pipe and the water and stabbing at the cascade with fluttering white rags that did no good, no good at all. Who were they? He recognized them as the same two males who'd shot the hose at him when he'd signed to them over and over to stop, and he felt something rise in him, a hate, a sudden hot roaring urge to bury his terror and despair in the soft white flesh of their faces and limbs, but he fought down that urge. Because . . . because in their hurry they'd left the door ajar. DOOR! OPEN! OUT! They were distracted and he was a shadow and the shadow slid out the door in three inches of swirling water and it went up the hall while the BLACK BUGS threw themselves at the bars and steel mesh of their cages, screaming as if they were being flayed alive, and then the shadow was at the door that led to that compact scene of the sun and the trees that had been revealed in a flash the day when the female that wasn't her threw it open and slammed it shut.

It was a DOOR. It had a knob. It was locked. But the lock was the kind that twists on and off under the pressure of your hand if you know how to manipulate it. And he knew. He *knew*.

ACCOUNTABILITY

That first night, the first night Aimee spent at the house, he was too wrought up to sleep. The pizza sat on his stomach like concrete. The wine puddled in his head. He kept itching himself—fleas, Sam's fleas, and when was the last time they'd doused him with flea powder?—and twice he got up to turn on the lights and check the sheets. When he finally did get to sleep, his dreams were tense and unforgiving, compact nightmares of canceled flights, missed deadlines, TV lights extinguished like cigarette butts in the middle of his next sentence. In the morning, as soon as he could manage it, he went to see Elise in the hospital, and far from helping out—showing a little understanding, a little sympathy—she was exclusively negative, at one point even threatening to sue, as if Sam and the project meant nothing to her. As if *he* meant nothing to her. As if all that mattered was the cut on her face and the plastic tube in her arm. No, the whole business was a disaster, an ongoing disaster, and though he'd hoped to hush it up, word got out within hours and ran through the department till he couldn't walk down the hall without somebody stopping to interrogate him about it. How was Elise doing? Was it really that bad? And Sam. Sam was so sweet—it was incredible. How could he have done something like that?

His biggest fear was that they'd take Sam away, put him in a cage somewhere, the project derailed, the funding dried up. What would animal control have to say about it? The health department? The university? And there was Moncrief, never forget Moncrief, who was looming off in the distance, utterly unmoved by pleas and explanations and adhering strictly to the bottom line, which was *positive* publicity and the sort of solid record of publication that would advance his own agenda—and if Guy wasn't capable of presenting him with it, then he'd get somebody who was. When he found out about this, which he invariably would, he'd make one of his late-night calls, long distance from Iowa. "You know what?" he'd say, his voice a low rasp insinuating itself over the line. "If this keeps up, I might just have to come out there and take my animal back."

About the only good thing to come of it was Aimee. She'd stayed the night and the next day too and the other new girl—Barbara— had promised to return in the afternoon to help fill the gap left by Elise, which gave him at least a little breathing room while Elise was laid up in the hospital and Josh sitting there at her bedside with a vacant look on his face. He hired them both on the spot. "You want hours? You can have all the hours you can handle, at least till I get things straightened out here. And I appreciate it, I really do."

Of course, Barbara wasn't a natural fit, and he saw that from the beginning. She was tentative around Sam, frightened of him, actually, and Sam knew it and capitalized on it, doing everything he could to make her uncomfortable, short of biting. He would hide behind the door and spring out at her with a shriek or take hold of her hand and refuse to let go no matter how many times she tried to draw it away, his humor wedded to the power he held over the household and everybody in it. Chimp humor. *There* was a dissertation waiting to be written, higher consciousness revealed through comedic inter-action between species, the ability to conceive jokes, no matter how crude, proof positive of advanced thought processes. In Sam's case, the humor was strictly rudimentary, ranging from the practical jokes you'd expect of a preschooler—hiding objects, refashioning a cheese-burger into a Frisbee, laying a turd in somebody's shoe—to something darker, sadistic even. It was different with Aimee. She seemed to have an instant connection with him, an empathetic transference, as if she saw him as a child, a human child, and not simply a lab animal in a psychology experiment. And Sam responded in kind, on his best behavior with her, as if he were trying to sell her on the arrangement, as if he knew what was at stake here—and maybe he did, maybe he saw Melanie in her, a new mother to replace the one he'd lost.

That first night, both girls had helped clean up the kitchen, and after Barbara left, Aimee had pitched in with the nightly ritual of putting Sam to bed—drawing water for his bath, overseeing the brush-ing of his teeth and dressing him in his pajama top and a clean dia-per, then settling into bed with him and his favorite Dr. Seuss book, reading to him in a low languorous voice till he was out for the night. In the morning, when Guy forced himself out of bed, depressed and disoriented, he found Aimee and Sam in the living room, sitting side by side on the couch in front of the resurrected TV, spooning up Lucky Charms and watching cartoons.

He stood in the doorway a moment, studying them, amazed at his luck. One of the cartoon figures—Daffy Duck, wasn't it?—kicked another in the rear and Sam laughed his breathy laugh and Aimee joined in with a soft girlish giggle. "Hey, you two," he said, and they both looked up as if he was the last person they expected to see.

"That's nice, that's good. I love it. You're really getting along, aren't you?"

Aimee nodded. Sam turned back to the TV.

"You okay with everything?"

She nodded again.

"Because I'm going to be gone most of the morning and you'll have to handle things on your own, at least until Josh makes an appearance. And Barbara. Didn't she say she'd be back?"

"Yeah, I think so."

"Okay, good. Look, if he misbehaves, and I'm not saying he will—hopefully he got that out of his system yesterday—lock him in his room till he calms down. And don't take any crap from him. You've got my number at school so—" He waved a hand as if to finish the thought, the thought being that she was taking on a mountain of responsibility, for which he was both apologetic and grateful and that if anything should go wrong he'd be there for her. "As for *Sam*"—here he raised his voice—"Sam's going to get the day off, no school for him today. Is that all right with you, Sam? Do you like that? No school today?"

Sam didn't respond. Daffy Duck—yes, that was Daffy, definitely Daffy—was being chased across a cartoon landscape by a hunter with a shotgun, who kept peppering him in the backside, which got Sam laughing again, and that was response enough.

"What about you?" he asked her. "Don't you have classes? Work?"

"I'm skipping today? And as soon as Hamburg Hamlet opens, I'm calling in to quit. I mean, if that's all right." She gave him a smile, then dropped her eyes.

She was very pretty. And her feet, her bare feet, propped up on the cushions beside Sam's, were pretty too—and her pose, as if she were in a glossy ad for home furnishings and demonstrating how charming and comfortable a sofa with a chimp on it could be.

"I like your attitude," he said. "And, you know, just play it by ear—and try not to spoil him too much. Josh'll be here in an hour or so and I'll be back as soon as I can. You've got the key to the fridge and the front door and Sam'll let you know when he's hungry."

Daffy Duck said something in an unintelligible squawk. The shotgun popped. Sam laughed.

"Okay," he said, "I guess I'm off, then. Sam, you want to give me a hug?"

Sam swiveled his head to peer up at him over one shoulder, but he didn't move from the couch. He just lifted his hand and dropped it again.

As if things weren't bad enough, when he got to the office there was a note from the chairman of the department, asking to see him at his earliest convenience. Which meant sooner rather than later. To this point, he'd pretty much been given free rein with the project. He was Moncrief's golden boy, after all, he'd been awarded grants from the National Institutes of Health and the National Science Foundation, had lined up a number of private donors and polished his image on TV, and before he'd arrived nobody at UCSM had ever even seen a chimp before, let alone worked with one. Not to mention that the field of primate language studies was the hottest thing going, with half a dozen universities starting up competing programs. But he was still a member of the psych department and still subject to the kind of accountability that Leonard Biggs, the chair, was doubtless about to remind him of. He didn't want any part of it (he needed to get home, oversee things, make sure Aimee was still in one piece, though she hadn't called and Josh had promised to be there by ten, so no news was good news, as far as it went), but nonetheless, after class he found himself mounting the stairs to

Leonard's office on the third floor, figuring he might as well get it over with.

The door was open and Leonard, dressed in a suit jacket flecked with lint or maybe cat hair and a tie in a shade of yellow that concentrated all the light in the room, looked up from his bag lunch and said, "Thanks." Just that—not "Hello" or "How you doing?" but just "Thanks."

Guy shrugged and fell into the chair at the foot of the desk—the student chair. A wave of exhaustion washed over him. "What's on your mind?" he asked, and he wanted to light up a cigarette but thought better of it.

Leonard was only three years older than Guy and chairman by default—nobody else wanted the job. He wore his hair in a Beatles' shag that had gone out of fashion a decade ago and his teeth were too big for his mouth so that it looked as if he was grinning even when he wasn't. Guy had no feelings about him one way or the other—he existed, he took up space, and as long as he supported the project and knew enough not to stick his nose in, he was harmless enough, he supposed. Leonard clutched a sandwich in one hand—bologna on white with a thin stripe of mustard the same color as his tie—and a half-pint container of milk in the other. He chewed, swallowed, patted his lips with a rumpled paper napkin, then set down the sandwich and looked directly into Guy's eyes. "I hear you had an accident out at the ranch?"

"Yeah, no big deal. Sam just got a little overanimated, that's all, and he bit Elise—Elise Ritchie? I wasn't even there. And whether she misread him or not, it's just not acceptable, no way. And he did say he was sorry . . ."

"He did? Well, that's comforting—at least there's that, right?" He lifted his eyebrows and puckered his lips to underscore the sarcasm, took a swig from the milk container and set it back down on the desk. "And you actually believe he channels emotions and understands consequences?"

"If he didn't, I wouldn't be working with him. Nor would people like Donald Moncrief."

"How bad is it?"

He shrugged again, and now he did dig his cigarettes out of his shirt pocket, shake one out and light it. "She's going to need stitches."

"And?"

"There's a risk of infection, so I'm told, and they put her on an intravenous antibiotic. Which is fine. Just a precaution really."

Leonard was silent a moment. "What about liability?"

"I don't know. We're covered, aren't we? I mean, she's got student health—"

"In terms of legal liability, I mean. We can't have dangerous animals running wild around here, or at the ranch, that is, where students and staff are going to be exposed to them—and it's only going to get worse. What happens when he's an adolescent? An adult? He could go totally out of control for all we know—"

"Apeshit, you mean. That's the formal ethological expression—go apeshit."

"Jesus, Guy, give me a break. But don't they usually retire them after they're four or five? For that very reason?"

It wasn't as if he hadn't thought ahead. Leonard was right—after a certain stage most chimps eventually got returned to breeding facilities like Moncrief's or sent on for use in biomedical trials because it was just too risky to work with them. A full-grown male chimp could stand over five feet tall and weigh a hundred fifty pounds—and a chimp of that size was at least twice as strong as any human, even an NFL lineman or the winner of the Iron Man competition. But this was different. Few researchers had ever raised a chimp entirely as a human before—without any knowledge of its own species or of a cage either—and the hope was that the experiment would go on indefinitely, well into adulthood, when Sam's mental capacities would be that much more refined and his ability to express himself far beyond any limits previously known to science.

"Sam's different," he said. "And I can't promise you that there won't be problems moving forward, but I'm going to try as best I can to prevent them."

"Behavior modification?"

"More or less."

"But it's been almost three years now, hasn't it?"

Guy felt the irritation rise in him. Leonard was a functionary, a desk-sitter. He couldn't begin to conceive of the thousands of hours he and Melanie had put in, of the endless drills, the control issues, the tantrums. He said, "You have a teenage son, don't you?"

Leonard gave him a long look, then broke into a grin. "Yeah, Casey can be a handful—but at least he's not biting people's faces. Or not that I know of. Yet."

Guy grinned back at him. "Right. And not only is Sam dealing with hormonal issues, but the confusion of staff changes too."

"Melanie?"

He nodded.

"Is it—?"

"Truthfully? I don't know. We're trying to work it out . . . but in the meanwhile I've just taken on two new girls on a salaried basis and I'm hoping to attract a couple more student volunteers to cover some of the hours and help with the record-keeping." He paused to take a deep consolatory drag of his cigarette and gather himself. "I won't lie to you—it's been tough since Melanie left, not least because she had the strongest bond with him, and as far as organizing was concerned, she was a past master . . . But we're getting back to it. It's a new day, a new regime, and I for one am looking forward to really bearing down on this project, which, I don't have to remind you, has the potential to lift the roof right off of everything we've ever known about animal consciousness—and our own, our own too. I mean, can you imagine actually talking with him, beyond the stage of immediate wants and needs? About what he's *thinking*?"

"What if he's thinking what we're thinking half the time, 'Fight, kill, die'? Or better yet, 'Fight, fuck, eat'?"

"Yeah, sure, but what about the other half of the time, when we're thinking about putting men on the moon and composing symphonies—and establishing apes in human households to see what we can learn from them?"

"I'm not saying that—we're all behind the project, behind you—and what Moncrief's doing too. You're attracting a lot of attention to the program, no doubt about it, and the whole thing's, well"—he waved a hand—"fascinating, really fascinating. All I'm saying is be careful, that's all."

It was past two by the time he got back to the ranch, and the first thing he noticed was that Josh's car wasn't in the driveway. Barbara's car wasn't there either, though he hadn't really noticed what she'd been driving the night before or even if she'd driven there at all—for all he knew she could have hitchhiked. The point was that there was only one car in the long dirt drive, Aimee's white Caprice, which meant that she was in there alone. And more: that she'd been alone with Sam for something like five and a half hours now.

He cursed himself. What had he been thinking? Was this being careful? Or even responsible? His heart was pounding as he came up the front steps, picturing chaos, the house wrecked, Aimee cowering in the bathroom with her pretty face gashed and bleeding, the final stake driven through the heart of the project and everything he'd worked for evaporated in an instant. He should have canceled class, canceled the meeting, blown off Leonard, should have stayed home, but he hadn't. He was tired of being on call twenty-four hours a day, seven days a week, tired of having a hundred percent of the responsibility thrust on him because Melanie was back in New York and didn't give a damn what happened—to him or Sam. So he'd dumped it all on the new girl. And Josh had let him down. Again.

The window showed nothing, which was unusual, because as soon as he heard a car pull into the drive, Sam would go first to the window, then the door, and by the time you got the door open, he was there, always. But not now. Now everything was still, nothing moving inside or out, not even a bird or lizard. He stood there on the mat a moment, his senses on high alert, then inserted the key in the first of the locks, which was the signal for Sam to rush the door and start slapping his palms on the panels till the whole house rocked with the rhythm of it. What he was remembering in that moment was an incident from grad school. There was a new girl in the program, Laura-something, whose voice had a nagging nasal quality and who was always trying to get Moncrief's attention, always at his elbow, pushing for preference and access, sucking up. One afternoon Moncrief took her out to what he called his Chimp Farm and led her into the main facility, where there were thirty-odd chimps of all ages caged in groups and separately, some so dangerous no one was allowed to handle them, ever, and led her into a cage occupied by an adolescent female named Polly. Polly didn't move, just fastened her eyes on the girl, looking for a reaction, for weakness, in the way Sam assessed anyone he came across, whether in the house or out in public when they took him for a walk. "You want to know chimps?" Moncrief asked. Laura nodded. Polly crouched there in the back of the cage, perfectly still. "Well, this one's Polly," Moncrief said, then slipped out the door and locked it behind him.

"You want to know chimps?" Moncrief repeated.

Laura, frozen, said, "Come on, please, this isn't funny. Let me out."

"Know them from the inside, that's the most important thing. Know what it's like to be in a cage, dependent on somebody else—on us—for everything, food, water, comfort, stimulation. Know what resentment feels like."

And then he walked away.

Inside, the house was absolutely still, the TV off, heat wafting silently from the wall registers. Everything was in order, the two easy chairs lined up parallel to the couch, the magazines stacked neatly on the end table, Sam's toys in the straw basket in the corner, his paints and crayons in the coffee cans reserved for them. If anything had gone amiss, there was no sign of it. Puzzled, he started up the stairs for Sam's room—depending on how he felt, Sam would sometimes take a nap around now, but if that was the case, where was Aimee?

The door to Sam's room was ajar. It was made of steel and the frame was steel too, because when Sam misbehaved—when he threw one of his tantrums—he had to be confined where he couldn't do any damage. The original door, which was solid pine and not some flimsy hollow-core alternative, had been reduced to splinters one afternoon when something had set him off and Melanie thought to punish him by confining him to his room. That was over a year ago. Lesson learned. Same thing for the picture window in the living room, which Sam had twice smashed through in his eagerness over the arrival of the delivery boy from the pizza parlor before they replaced it with the safety glass. Taking a deep breath, Guy eased the door open and instantly felt the burden lift from him: Sam was there, in bed, asleep, his head on the pillow and the blanket pulled up over his shoulder. And Aimee was stretched out beside him, on her back, her long black hair trailing over the side of the bed. Her eyes blinked open. "Hi," she said, her voice fogged with sleep. "How was school?"

As for Laura, the girl with the irritating voice, she'd been in that cage for three hours by the time Moncrief came to release her, and in all that time, Polly, one of the least aggressive chimps in the whole colony, the lowest-ranking female whose only desire was to submit, never emerged from the corner of the cage. Laura got it, though. The resentment part, anyway.

By the time Josh showed up, all apologies, Sam was sitting placidly on the couch beside Aimee, leafing through the latest issue of *Life* while she named the objects in the pictures aloud—car, baby, airplane, dog—and Sam conjured the signs for them, almost as if he were trying to teach them to her. Guy sat across from them in the armchair, amazed all over again. He was taking notes, minute by minute, gesture by gesture, and he would have got up to dig out the video camera but for fear of breaking the spell. Like any other child, Sam resisted school. He was hyperactive, willful, difficult to control, and yet control was what this was all about, since funding depended on his ability to build and utilize his vocabulary and show it off on demand. For anywhere from three to five hours a day, he was made to sit at a desk and go through a series of drills, exercises and tests of his vocabulary and ability to employ syntax, and some days were better than others, the whole process a towering ziggurat of advancing and sliding back and advancing again. Still, this was something new— Sam doing the teaching—and it was worth seeing where it would go.

When Josh eased into the room, Sam glanced up at him, but didn't sign HI or GIVE ME HUG, which was his usual reaction on encountering people he was close to. He was too absorbed. And he stayed that way for a full thirty minutes, long enough for Guy to signal Josh to get the camera and start filming. Which was good, as good as it got—until Sam, seized by a sudden urge, did a backflip over the couch and shot twice round the room in manic display before rooting through his toy box until he found his favorite stuffed toy—a chewed-over, eyeless, one-eared cocker spaniel—and presented it to Aimee, as if he were courting her.

"For me?" she said, taking it from him. "Well, thank you, Sam, thanks a lot."

Sam just stood there, bracing himself with one hand on her knee, gazing intently at her. As a general rule, he was almost pathologically protective of his things and he didn't like anyone touching them, not even when helping him clean up before bed.

Guy said, "Sign it to him, here, like this . . ." and he made the sign for thank you, open hand to the lips, then swept graciously downward, and Aimee tried it on Sam, who got it and repeated it and then signed, YOU'RE WELCOME, and all the while Josh kept the camera rolling.

"That's it?" Aimee said.

Guy nodded.

"Wow, you mean I just talked to him?"

"It's a start," he said.

A week later, Aimee was installed in the house, spending most nights and the better part of each day, working with Sam alongside Josh, Barbara and the two new student volunteers he'd managed to recruit. She was just what he'd hoped for, a calming presence, uncomplaining, non-opinionated, eager to do whatever was necessary to lighten his load. And that was more vital now than ever because the second TV appearance was scheduled for the following week and there was interest from NBC and *The Tonight Show*, which was the apex as far as he was concerned—that would put him above anybody, even Moncrief—and he needed time to prepare. Sam had to be on his best behavior and for that he had to feel secure—had to be fussed over and coddled the way Melanie had coddled him. Josh wasn't capable of doing it, not on his own, anyway, not without Elise, because like all juvenile males, Sam was more responsive to women than men. Barbara, though she was game, had her limitations. Not Aimee, though. Aimee was a perfect fit.

He learned that she lived in student housing, alone, sans roommate, but she didn't seem to be spending much time there. As far as he could see, she wasn't making use of the guest room either, though he'd found a backpack in the closet, which, on examination, proved to contain a change of clothes and underthings and a few school texts with her name inscribed on the inside leaves in minute block letters. In green ink. Why anybody would go out of their way to find green ink, he couldn't imagine, and yet still, the backpack was there and now he knew at least something about her beyond her introversion and her pretty face: black lace brassieres and green ink. He wasn't snooping, or not exactly. He was just curious, that was all, and the fact that her things were there came as a relief to him— they were markers of her commitment. Better yet, the bed was untouched. Right from the start, she'd slept with Sam, as Melanie had most nights and he himself had been pressed into doing ever since she'd left because Sam suffered separation anxiety and needed the comfort and warmth of a living breathing body stretched out in the bed beside him. If he didn't get it—if the arrangement wasn't to his satisfaction—he'd let everybody know, stripping the bed, tearing off his diaper and humping round the room with his hair erected in full chimp display, all the while screaming in a pitch that was like an ice pick to the heart. And if you weren't up to it, if you were tired and dragged out and in no mood and you just said "Fuck it" and locked him in, he would scream all night. And still be screaming, right in your face, when you unlocked the door in the morning.

That was no longer an issue. He hadn't had to suggest to Aimee that she sleep in Sam's bed, she just did it on her own initiative, because Sam wanted it and he communicated that to her, both in the rudimentary sign language she was just beginning to pick up and through subtler signals too. People outside the field couldn't fathom the depth of communication apes were capable of, though they were willing to admit that their dogs showed moods and desires, barking at the door or fetching the leash when they wanted to go out, for instance, or that their cats' mewing served half a dozen different purposes, but what they failed to appreciate was that apes were of a different order altogether. Dogs and cats had been bred for thousands of generations to weed out the undesirable genes, domesticated to create an all but emotionally neutered animal designed to serve human needs, but apes came straight out of the wild. They were independent. Resentful of captivity. And if you stared into their eyes you saw yourself staring right back.

To put Sam in the category of a dog or cat was demeaning—and beyond that, uniformed and unimaginative to the point of stupidity. Sam had presence. He had charisma. And Guy was going to show it off to Ed McMahon and Johnny Carson and all the rest of America—and he was going to be rested when he did it, rested for the first time in weeks, because Sam was back in his own bed now. With Aimee. And his fleas. And the dreams that jerked his limbs in the middle of the night till the bed rocked like a ship at sea.

They'd just sat down to dinner one evening—he, Aimee, Sam and one of the volunteers (Sid James, nineteen, bland, suitably ape-obsessed)—when they heard the thump of footsteps on the front porch and then the rattle of keys. Sam was the first to react, jerking round in the highchair, his eyes keen with excitement. In the next instant, Sam was springing down from the chair and racing for the door on all fours while Aimee jumped to her feet and Guy found himself slapping the edge of the table and barking "No!" and "Bad!" as if it would do any good. He was annoyed. Pissed off, actually. Dinner was sacrosanct, a time to relax and enjoy Sam's company, converse with him casually without the pressure of having to perfect his signs or expand his vocabulary—this was how language was acquired, in a home environment, through observation and imitation, which was the whole point of cross-fostering in the first place. How did human children pick up language? Not in school but in the kitchen, on the playground, in the living room—in bed, at night, with a storybook spread open before them. And at dinner, dinner especially. He let out a curse, startling Sid, the new kid, who sat there immobile over his plate of spaghetti.

It was Josh at the door. And behind him, her face blanched and her jaw set beneath a pristine gauze bandage that flashed like a distress signal in the harsh glare of the entryway, was Elise. Sam signed, GIVE ME HUG, and held out his arms to Josh, who bent to embrace him, which was an invitation for Sam to scramble up onto his shoulders. Elise didn't offer a smile. Wordlessly she shifted round to shut the door and work the key successively through the three locks, though it was clear that Sam was going nowhere—the moment was far too interesting. Elise was back. With a bandage on her face. This was a new dynamic. And Sam, from his perch atop Josh's shoulders, didn't utter a sound, just stared, openmouthed.

"You caught us just as we were sitting down to eat," Guy said.

"Don't let us bother you," Josh said, flashing both palms in apology. "We're fine. We just stopped by for a minute . . . to see how things were going?"

"There's plenty, really, if you're hungry." Guy shot a glance at Aimee, who was trying not to stare at Elise's face. "Right, Aimee? It's spaghetti and meatballs, Sam's favorite—except for p-i-z-z-a, right, Sam?"

Sam had nothing to say, one way or the other. His head, which was already nearly as big as Josh's, rode above Josh like a gaudy party balloon. He was staring fixedly at Elise, at her face, at her bandage. Did he know what it was? Did he understand the sequence of events that had put that bandage in place? Did he feel remorse—or was Elise's changed appearance a curiosity that had nothing to do with him and his refractory jaws?

Aimee—shoulders slouched, face averted—glanced up at Guy and in a whisper of a voice said, "Sure, there's plenty."

Josh shook his head. "No, don't bother—we already ate."

"A glass of wine, then?" he said. "Elise?"

They were all grouped there in the entryway, the moment extending itself awkwardly, until Elise, in a controlled voice, said, "I just came for closure, that's all."

"Closure?" he echoed. "What's that supposed to mean?"

"It means"—she locked eyes with Sam—"I want some sort of accounting because maybe Josh is going to keep working with him till the next ice age, but I'm done. Finished. And I can't believe"—addressing Sam now, her voice sharpening—"that I get treated this way. What did I ever do to you, Sam? Huh? Tell me."

Sam let out a series of soft pant-hoots that could have meant anything, but he didn't bring his hands into play.

"So look, okay, I hear you, but why don't we all go out to the kitchen and sit down a minute?" Guy said, making a move to usher them in. "Where we can talk? I want to hear how you're doing, what the prognosis is—Josh says they still didn't put the stitches in, even after the intravenous?" He didn't wait for an answer, just slipped an arm around Elise's waist and guided her toward the kitchen, where the new kid was waiting for an introduction and the aroma of the marinara sauce underscored the invitation.

He pulled up two extra chairs and poured wine all around—including a glass for Sam, who'd climbed back into his highchair and addressed himself to his Tupperware bowl of pasta, sauce and meatballs as if Elise and Josh had been there all along. Elise said what she was going to say, and it was no better than what he'd heard in the hospital, and when she was done, he topped off her glass and tried to bring a little variety into the conversation. Or at least change the subject. "I don't know if Josh told you, but it looks like Johnny Carson's interested . . ."

For the first time, she smiled, though it was only half a smile and it tugged at the corner of the bandage till the bandage seemed to float free in space. "Good for you," she said. "That's great, it really is. And good for Sam too."

"And what about you?" He paused. "We could all use you back here again, Sam especially."

"Uh-uh," she said. "I'm never going to put myself through *that* again. Besides," gesturing to Aimee, who was seated in the chair Elise used to occupy, right at Sam's elbow, "I see you've already replaced me."

He was going to demur, though that was the fact (and the truth was that Aimee was better than she'd ever been or ever could be), but he didn't have the chance. Because Sam suddenly took it into his head to spring out of the highchair and onto the table, upsetting his wineglass in the process and rocking the table so that they all had to shoot out their hands to keep their own glasses from tumbling over, and whether this was hilarious or not—life with a chimp—he hadn't yet decided. Oblivious to the overturned glass, Sam just squatted there in the center of the table, his eyes fixed on Elise. Then, slow as an awakening statue, he began creeping toward the far end of the table, where she sat between Josh and Sid. Everyone hushed. Guy was bracing himself to intervene, if that was what it was going to come to, but then Sam, a look of wonder on his face, snaked out a long arm and a single long finger to tentatively explore the bandage on Elise's jaw. No one scolded him. No one said a word. Here was the experiment in real time, the chimp, the non-human, confronting his own misdeeds, feeling remorse, showing compassion—or was it something else?

For a long moment Sam crouched there before her, the table elevating him so that their faces were on a level. He reached out to touch the bandage again, then ran his finger gently up and down the length of it, as if measuring it. He grunted softly. He signed, WHITE THING, signed WRONG. And then, before anyone could stop him, he seized the edge of the bandage and tore it from her face in a single motion, slapping it down hard on the surface of the table and pounding it with his fists till the silverware rattled and the glasses rocked all over again. Josh made a grab for him, but he shrugged him off. He looked directly at Elise, then stuffed the bandage in his mouth and began grinding it, slowly and methodically, between his teeth.

CHAINLINK

There was no word for chain link in his vocabulary, but there was a word for fence and FENCE was the first thing he saw when he slipped through the door and into the hard cold sunlight of a world transformed, no leaves on the trees, the wind like a whip in his eyes, his feet gone instantly cold and his hands too, his arms, his face, and where was he? This was no world he knew. It was dead. Frozen. Like the ICE CREAM in the freezer at home, like the ICE he demanded in his Coke and the gin-tonic she made for him when they settled into the COUCH and watched TV before dinner. He was disoriented. He was AFRAID. But he didn't have time to worry over it because they would be after him and if he was going to get away from here he had to scale that fence, which he did now as easily as if he were going up the trunk of a tree—more easily, actually, because the whole structure was made of hand- and footholds, simplest thing in the world, one jump, two, and he was atop the fence.

He felt a surge of power. He was free. He was up off the ground. Safe. Safe and free. He swayed and clung with his feet and shot out his arms for balance. But there was a problem here and he recognized it even as he heard the voices shouting behind him: another fence. It stood twenty feet from this one and there were shining loops of cutting wire threaded over the top of it. He knew cutting wire from the FENCE surrounding the big buildings she used to take him to in the CAR for his tests and measurements—and he knew how to avoid it, how not to touch it and slip past it as if it wasn't even there. He was perched high. The wind was cold. All he had to do was jump down, mount the second fence and drop to the other side before they could stop him. And then? Then he would go to her, wherever she was.

But now all of a sudden the barking started up and the two dark shapes came hurtling around the corner to throw themselves at the base of the fence, their bodies heavy enough to rock him where he clung ten feet above them, DOGS, DOGS snapping their jaws at him, killer DOGS, black-and-tan DOGS with thin pointed snouts full of white, white teeth, snouts he wanted to crush between his two hands, but he was AFRAID.

"Hey!" a voice shouted at him. "Hey, Sam, over here!" And there were the two wet men at the base of the fence, waving their arms at him while the dogs barked and leapt and foamed on the other side. That was when he saw the BIG MAN emerge cursing from the door of the high-flown red building behind him, where the BLACK BUGS were screaming death and fury . . . and suddenly all his fear dissolved into anger like a pill in water and he dropped down on the dog that was closest to him and before it could bite or even react he sank his own white, white teeth into the top of its skull.

The other dog—it didn't have a tail, only the stump of a tail—let out a short stuttering shriek and bolted away from him while the one he'd bitten cowered on the ground and he took off running for the next fence, AFRAID all over again.

THE DYNAMIC

Guy talked, she listened. That was the dynamic between them. He was one of those people who needed to hear his own voice issuing from him in a constant stream of comments, counter-comments, observations, jokes, routines and whatever else came into his head. Silence was not an option for him. He was a speech-giver, a lecturer, a talker, and she appreciated him all the more for it because they could talk and talk and she didn't have to say anything beyond "Uh-huh," "Yeah" and "Really?" She never got tired of it. Being with him was an ongoing education in primatology, ethology, psychobiology and linguistics, like her own private tutorial. Maybe they hadn't settled into a formal teacher-student relationship, but that was what it amounted to. From the first day he'd been guiding her toward what she had a sudden startling new hunger to know—and what statistics and psychology couldn't even begin to give her. Which was why she'd dropped both courses by the end of the first week—and her Spanish class too. She was deep into something else now, a new field—a new life—that absorbed her totally, which was what a liberal arts education was all about, wasn't it? She read everything he gave her—Goodall, Lorenz, Tinbergen, Hrdy, Imanishi—and she enrolled in an adult-ed class in ASL, which met twice a week, after Sam had gone to bed. And she had Sam, Sam above all.

Elise wasn't coming back, that much was clear, nor was Guy's wife—*Melanie*—and he needed all the help he could get, which only underscored how crucial to him she'd already become. Josh was still in charge—he was the expert, he was the grad student—but she was the one who had to see to all the details, the grocery shopping, the cleanup, the dishes, and she spent more time with Sam, one-on-one, than all the rest of them combined, including Josh. And Guy too. How much of it Elise had handled, she didn't know, but given the way Elise had reacted to Sam that night when she'd come for "closure," as she put it, Aimee was glad she'd never have to see her again. Sam wasn't to blame. He was only trying to say he was sorry—and when he'd peeled the bandage off her he was attempting in his own way to make things right. Maybe he didn't understand, or at least not fully, but he knew something was wrong with the picture he was seeing, with this wad of white tape and gauze that obscured Elise's face so that she didn't even look like herself, and so he got rid of it. And what did she do? She exploded.

She tried to put herself in Elise's place. Sam had bitten her, after all, and here was the evidence of it etched in a dark zigzagging scab slathered with some sepia antibiotic solution and the skin around it blanched like a frog's belly—all right, okay, she got it. But Elise had let out a shriek that could have shattered the windows if they weren't three inches thick and then she'd started attacking him—with the breadboard, of all things. She slammed it down on his head, his neck, his shoulders, totally out of control, until Josh and Guy took hold of her, and all the while Sam didn't attempt to defend himself, just squatted there in the center of the table, taking it, as if he knew what he'd done and this was his penance.

The following day, she and Guy put Sam through his drills as if nothing had happened. He wasn't as restless as usual, which was a blessing, and he sat at his desk without complaint for a good half hour while Guy projected slides of various objects on the wall—plate, cup, chair, book, lamp—and Sam spun out the signs for them with ease and fluidity. All this was elementary to him, but the more advanced exercises had to be suspended in the wake of first Melanie's and then Elise's defections, at least temporarily. That was what Guy told her, anyway. And he held out the promise that it would all begin again, soon, and that she was going to be right at the center of it. In the meantime he insisted on the drills to keep Sam fresh for his upcoming TV appearance, which the producers were no longer calling a feature but a mini-documentary, whatever that meant. It was all right with her. She followed along, practicing the signs as Sam formed them, learning, settling in.

After lunch, she and Guy took Sam for a walk out back of the house, where he had a high time bristling and woofing at the cattle that roamed through the chaparral beyond the barbed wire fence. The sense of release was electric. Clearly he was overjoyed to be out of the classroom, playing tug-of-war with the lead tethering him to Guy, clowning in a scatter of leaves and dried-up grasses, signing TICKLE and CHASE over and over again. People said animals didn't have emotions, but that was ridiculous—all you had to do was take a look at him to disprove that.

"He's having the time of his life, isn't he?" she said, glancing up at Guy.

"Oh, absolutely. How about you—you having fun?"

The sun was in her eyes and she had to put up a hand to shade them. Everything smelled of whatever it was in the leaves of the big oak that dominated the yard—tannin, wasn't that it? She nodded.

"You haven't seen him climb yet, have you? That's what he really likes. What do you think, Sam"—and he signed it simultaneously— "time for your tree?"

Sam hooted his approval and led them across the yard till they were under the canopy of the oak, then sat on his haunches and looked up expectantly. Guy signed something to him and he signed back, something that must have had to do with permissions and admonitions, because obviously Guy was going to have to unhook the lead before Sam could get up in the tree without tying himself in knots. The lead was six feet long and connected to a metal loop on the back of the harness Sam wore whenever he left the house, and though he could wriggle around and tug on it with his hands and feet both, he was still at least nominally under control as long as he was hooked up. Guy had let her walk him so she could get used to the feel of it—of him, of his weight and power and the way you could jerk back and control him, though ninety percent of the time he was the one doing the jerking. It was like having a dog on a leash, but different too because dogs didn't have hands and dogs didn't climb trees, lampposts, stop signs and power poles. When Guy bent forward to release the lead, she didn't know what to expect.

"Are you sure it's all right? I mean, won't he try to get away?"

Guy just smiled at her. Sam was already high in the tree, making his happy sounds, rattling branches for the sheer joy of it. "Look around," Guy said. "You see any other trees close enough for him to swing to—brachiate, that is? That's the official term, 'brachiate,' going from branch to branch. I just love the way it sounds."

The oak was massive, its multiple trunks like the fingers of an uplifted hand. The nearest tree to it—another oak; they were all oaks here—was fifty feet away. She shook her head.

"He isn't going anywhere. And even if he could, there's no way he's going to do it. Not with you here."

"What do you mean?"

"He's in love with you, haven't you noticed?"

She shrugged, looked away from his eyes. She might have been blushing, for all she knew—she probably was. Guy had told her that blushing was unique to humans because the other species didn't have anything to blush about, and whether he was joking or not, she couldn't tell.

"And you know what?" he said.

Above them, Sam let out one of his low chuffing laughs. She shrugged again. "What?"

"I can't say as I blame him."

The first time she slept with Guy was at the end of that week, after the film crew had finished shooting, packed up and left. There had been three of them, a reporter in his forties she thought she'd seen on the local news a couple of times, though the local news had never exactly been a priority with her so she couldn't say for sure, a camera-man and a soundperson (soundwoman, actually), who dangled a microphone overhead on a telescoping pole while the reporter posed questions and Guy and Sam answered in tandem. Josh was there, off camera, holding Sam's lead as a precautionary measure, but it wasn't necessary—Sam was as well behaved and magnetic as he'd been on *To Tell the Truth*, and when the segment was aired, the audience wouldn't know anything about it or what it implied, because the lead was hidden under his shirt. At one point, the reporter asked Sam what his favorite thing in the world was and without waiting for Guy's translation, he signed, PIZZA. But then he shook his head, signed, NO, and pointed to where she was standing behind Josh, and signed her name, finger-spelling the first letter, *A*, then pinching his right nipple in the shorthand version he'd invented for her.

"He means Aimee," Guy said, "my assistant," and the camera swung round on her for one mortifying instant, capturing her startled look for all the world to see, not to mention her unwashed hair and chimp-stressed jeans and sweatshirt.

Aside from that—maybe because of it, because it was an unscripted moment that showed how sweet and charming Sam could be—it all went off beautifully. Guy was in great spirits, riding the high of it—and she could see he was feeling relief too, because all this meant so much to him. He wanted Sam to shine. Needed him to. Sam was a prodigy—his prodigy. And now he was hers too.

After the film crew packed up and they'd said their goodbyes, she, Guy, Josh and Sam lingered a moment on the front porch, watching the KCOY van recede down the drive. It was a cool overcast day in late November, a gentle onshore breeze ruffling the leaves of the oaks lining the drive and a faint whiff of woodsmoke drifting over from the house across the street. She was conscious of Guy at her side, just inches from her, his hair shining, the makeup she'd helped apply smoothing his features till he looked like a picture of himself, flawless and idealized. "So how'd I do?" he asked, turning to her. "Pretty good, huh?"

"Yeah," she said, in a voice that drained the breath out of her. What could she say? He'd been brilliant—professorial, yes, but not at all overbearing or self-obsessed like so many of the other professors at school, and entertaining too. And he'd brought out the best in Sam, treating him with real affection, almost as an equal and not just some trained animal on a leash.

"You were incredible," Josh put in. "And so were you, Sam. Congrats all around."

Sam—Josh still had his lead—sidled up to her then, wrapped his arms around her legs and buried his face in the crotch of her jeans, something he'd taken to doing the past couple of days, though according to Guy he wasn't even close to puberty yet. "Yes, Sam," she said, "you were the star, you're always the star, you good boy, you," and she bent to lift him to her chest and then her back, where he perched, grunting softly, his weight dense and compacted.

When she straightened up, she saw that Guy was watching her closely, as if she were the marvel and not Sam. A slow grin spread across his face. "In that case, let's do some celebrating," he said, pulling open the door and bowing in invitation. "I've got a couple bottles of Champagne on ice, what do you think about that? Sound good?"

She nodded, feeling the exhilaration of the moment rising in her. Sam must have felt it too—he shifted position and let out an escalating series of pant-hoots ending with a soft drawn-out coo of pleasure.

"What do you think, Sam?" Guy said, signing it at the same time. "Champagne? Does that sound good?"

Sam might not have known what Champagne was—how would he?—but Guy's tone told him everything he needed to know. He dug his knees into her sides for balance so he could free his hands long enough to clap once, twice, and never mind that he was slipping back and snatching at her sweatshirt to steady himself, he was making a point and the point was most definitely affirmative. Champagne. Sure. Why not?

If Sam hadn't tasted Champagne before, neither had she. Not real Champagne, anyway—French Champagne, which Guy explained was the only true Champagne, the sparkling wines produced up north in places like Guerneville and Napa a poor substitute, *Don't be fooled by them*—and it wasn't till he filled her glass a second time that she began to appreciate what he was talking about. The flavor was subtle, faintly sweet, faintly acidic, and the carbonation seemed to propel the alcohol content—12.5% by volume—right to her brain. When he popped the cork on the first bottle, he let it shoot across the room so Sam could have the fun of chasing after it, which gave him a moment to fill Sam's flute not with Mumm but club soda and a splash of the cheap Chablis somebody had left in the refrigerator. He winked at her. "Why waste the good stuff?"

Josh laughed. "Why, indeed?" he said, holding out his glass.

But Sam wasn't so easily fooled. He raced back into the kitchen, the cork clenched between his teeth, and sprang into his highchair, waving impatiently for his own glass. Guy leaned over the chair and handed it to him, then made a toast—"To Sam!"—and they all clinked glasses and drank. All but Sam, who took a tentative sip, watching them closely. He made a face and lifted the glass to his nostrils, sniffing. Then he set his glass down, jumped to the floor and went directly to her where she was leaning against the kitchen counter. ME, he signed, reaching for her glass, ME. She looked to Guy, who just shrugged, then handed it to Sam. Who gave it a suspicious sniff, then stuck his tongue in it, lapping like a dog, before handing it back to her. Then he glided over to the sink and poured his own glass down the drain, his eyes locked on Guy's the whole while. GOOD STUFF, he signed, holding out the glass. YOU GIVE ME—he paused to snatch a look at her to be sure she was watching—GOOD STUFF.

Later, after Josh had gone home and Sam, woozy from the effects of the Champagne, fell asleep in the middle of the story she'd been reading him, she tiptoed out of his room, leaving the door ajar so she could hear him if he awakened. From the living room came the sound of the TV, some nature show, the narrator talking in an awed subdued voice about the majesty and intelligence of humpback whales: *They can communicate to other individuals of their species from as much as a hundred miles away and their songs rely on a complex and nuanced syntax. These giants of the deep*—there was the sound of rushing water and a few orchestral shadings to underscore it—*can hold their breath for forty-five minutes at a time and migrate as far as six thousand miles each year.* This information drifted down the hallway to her and just made her feel exhausted—one more nature show about the unique attributes of a species in decline and the various cruelties we impose upon it, the depressing numbers, extinction waiting in the wings. She'd drunk too much Champagne, and dinner—takeout pizza again—didn't seem to have absorbed much of it.

She found Guy sunk into the couch, a book in one hand, a flute of Champagne in the other. On the screen, a great dark shape rose from the glassy depths, breached and spouted. He looked up at her, breathed, "Hi," and patted the pillow beside him. She was thinking she really ought to get to bed—brush her teeth, slip into her pajamas and settle in beside Sam so he wouldn't wake without her and feel abandoned, feel scared, crying out over whatever passed for bogeymen in a chimp's dreamworld, snakes, hyenas, *researchers*—but then Guy flashed a smile and she came over and sat beside him.

"Want some more Champagne?" He leaned away from her to lift the bottle from the sweating stew pot he was using as an ice bucket.

"Uh-uh," she said, shaking her head. "I think I've had enough. I think—" She was going to say she had a hazy impression she'd drifted off while reading Sam his bedtime story, but just let it drop. Too much information.

"We can't let it go to waste, can we?" He held the bottle up in evidence. "It's not like we can force the cork back in, without shaving it down, anyway, and it always goes flat. My father used to say 'You pop the cork, you're making a pledge,'" and he filled the glass he'd been drinking from and handed it to her.

"Okay," she said, "just a taste," and then she had the glass in her hand. And that was all right. This was her celebration too. It could have been Elise's, could have been Melanie's, but it wasn't—it was hers.

The whales gave way to something else—what was it, harpy eagles, perched in the treetops and ripping monkeys apart with their great hooked beaks—and Guy put his arm around her, drew her to him, and they kissed. They kissed for a long slow inebriate time, the narrator—a new narrator now, but holding forth in the same hushed tones as the whale expert—saying, *The harpy eagle's talons are longer than a grizzly bear's claws and can penetrate a monkey's skull with ease.* Then Guy took his mouth away and whispered, "Enough with nature, already, let's go to bed." He got to his feet, and for a moment she thought he was going to lift her in his arms and carry her to the bedroom like in the movies, but instead he bent to take her hand and pull her to him for another kiss, this one standing, their bodies pressed tight so that she could feel his erection through the fabric of his jeans.

"Eagles mate on the wing, did you know that?" he said, leading her toward the bedroom now. "They're locked together in the act and if they don't let go at the last minute they both hit the ground and get smashed to pulp." He laughed. "Talk about risky sex . . ."

He was caressing the back of her hand, his touch smooth and silken. She was in the moment, absolutely. She didn't think about Sam, didn't think about the fact that she was going to break the lease on her apartment at the end of the month and move in here permanently, didn't think about Melanie or Elise or anybody else who might have been here before her—she just gave way and let herself be led.

He didn't use a condom. He pulled out of her at the last second and spurted in her pubic hair. There had been no mention of birth control. He'd just led her to the bed, lit a candle and climbed in beside her, and he didn't ask if she was on the pill, which she wasn't, because until that very moment, it hadn't seemed to make any sense—why mess with your hormones for nothing? She wasn't dating anybody and her only previous experience, with Tommy Slizek, a tall skinny boy with bad breath and a croaking voice who'd asked her to the prom at the last minute, hadn't encouraged her to try again. He'd produced a condom he kept in his wallet—"For emergencies," he'd said—and then snapped it on like one of those latex gloves the gynecologist uses for an exam. Which was what sex with Tommy Slizek was like, an exam. If she was supposed to feel something, she didn't really feel it, and that was her own fault, she knew it, but she was shy with or without her clothes on and she couldn't stop thinking about what they were doing through the whole process, his fingers on her, in her, his tongue poking at hers like a hot wet animal, biology, secretions, *the mating process*. It was different with Guy. Maybe the Champagne had something to do with it. Maybe the fact that Sam was asleep in his bed down the hall made her feel proprietary and in control whether she was or not. Maybe she was in love. With Guy. With Sam. With the whole new life she was suddenly inhabiting. Could it have been that simple?

He handed her a tissue from a blue cardboard box on the night table and she wiped herself, then he put his arm around her and pulled her to him so her head rested on his chest and she could feel the pulse of his heart and take in the odor of his sweat that was its own kind of perfume and it made her feel drowsy and contented. He began to talk in a low murmur, his chest rising and falling with the shape of his words. He didn't talk about love. Didn't talk about what they'd just done and were going to do again any minute now. He talked about himself, about how relieved he was that the filming had gone well and how he really didn't think there was anybody out there who could have pulled it off the way he had. The other five researchers under Moncrief's direction—he named them, three women, two men, all of them married and all but one, Lucas Borstein, located in the vicinity of Davenport, where Moncrief could keep an eye on them—were duds as far as he was concerned. "Science nerds, you know what I mean? Except for Borstein. He's the real deal. And our main competition at this point because his chimp, Alex, is far more advanced than Sam—but he's older by two years, so we'll see how that goes."

She nodded, but that felt strange since her head was pressed to his chest and the vertical had become horizontal.

"None of them's even remotely camera-friendly—I mean, not just in a physical way, but in the way they come across too. And I may be prejudiced—I am, of course I am—but I think I have a better rapport with Sam than any of them have with their own chimps . . ." He let his hand slide down the slope of her back and brought it up again, gently massaging. He was talking, she was listening. He was thirty-two, she was twenty-one. He was a professor, she was a student. And they were both here, in this house, in this bed, because of Sam.

"And that comes across on the screen, like on *To Tell the Truth*? That was a win all the way around. Pretty much everybody I talked to—random strangers, like that cop who stopped me?—were just stunned. And you know what? As far as I can gather, only one of the others, Gina Markowitz, has been on TV, which was just some local program in Iowa, and her chimp, Alice, is three years older than Sam and not half as proficient at signing. They'd tricked her out in some frilly little dress, and all Alice did was stick her hand up her dress and play with herself while Gina droned on about lexical frequency and lemma glossing. And she never looked into the camera, not once. And when she did get Alice to sign, the signs were so sloppy you could barely read them. What we need—are you listening?"

"Uh-huh."

"We need something really big—we need Carson. And that's going to happen, I know it is. It has to. Because this is our window of opportunity, right now—Sam's not always going to be like this, you realize that, don't you?"

She wanted to say "Uh-huh," but her tongue felt thick in her mouth. She thought of the term "post-coital" from her Human Sexuality class sophomore year. She thought of oxytocin, the "love chemical." She repeated the syllables in her head, ox-y-to-cin. That was what was running through her veins—and his too.

"We've got maybe a couple years and then he's going to be too much to handle. Or maybe not. Maybe we get lucky. But the way he bit Elise, that's asserting himself. And once he realizes he's stronger than we are—and he's going to reach that stage before long—we're going to be in new territory. Which is why it's so crucial to establish bonds with him now—"

He broke off and sat up abruptly, which made her sit up too. Sam was there, in the doorway, poised over his knuckles. He looked puzzled, as if he couldn't quite piece together what he was seeing. For a long moment he just gazed at them, then pushed himself up and rose to his full height, wading into the room with that sideways motion peculiar to monkeys and chimps, as if they were perpetually negotiating the deck of a ship at sea. Guy said, "It's okay, Sam—go back to bed."

But Sam had begun to bristle now, all his hair standing on end. He let out two short barks, then sprang onto the bed. "It's okay," she said, but it wasn't okay, not as far as Sam was concerned. He gave her a long steady look, then pulled back the sheet and touched first her right breast, then the left. Then he looked at Guy, and without shifting his gaze, touched her breasts again, first the right, then the left.

CLOUD BREATH

What he was seeking in the irreversible now of the worst moment of his life, he couldn't really say because it wasn't a word and it wasn't a picture. All he knew was that he was COLD, colder than he'd ever known or imagined he could be, the movie of the sliding black-and-white birds he'd seen with her on TV no more real than the screen allowed, a white world that was made of ICE, but the ice wasn't real, wasn't COLD, not like this. Touch the screen and it was neutral, touch the ice and it was COLD. What did it mean? Why was it like this? What had happened to the leaves, to the water, to the bugs and birds? She wasn't here to explain it to him. She wasn't anywhere near here. He knew that now and it filled him with despair.

He'd run off, panicked, plunging through briars and dead yellow brush, in what direction he didn't know, as long as it was away from the FENCE and the cutting wire and the BIG MAN with the stinger.

That was when? When the sun was still high, a bright ball caught in the treetops that didn't give off any heat whatever, as if it wasn't the sun at all but some counterfeit object propped up in the sky to mock him, to torture him and make him HURT inside. Where was he? He was in the middle of a vast yellow canebrake at the edge of a LAKE composed not of water but ICE that stung his feet and made him bury his hands in his armpits for the saving warmth. He breathed in and his lungs HURT, breathed out and saw his own breath steal away from him in puffs and streamers and clouds like when he smoked a CIGARETTE with her and Guy. He wasn't smoking a CIGARETTE now, he was smoking air. And the air chilled him until he was shivering all over.

At some point he heard the DOGS again and not long after that he heard the voices coming for him. He would have been angry, would have been enraged, but the COLD weakened him and he closed his eyes and burrowed into the nest he'd made of the brittle dead reeds that barely gave back his own warmth and waited for them. They would use the stinger on him—or the dart that would suddenly appear in the flesh of his chest or belly or arms—and he would be helpless. They would take him back to the CAGE, which he saw now in his mind, the CAGE without blankets or toys or TV—or her. It was BAD, very BAD. But it was warm, warmer than this hostile forbidding place that stung him in his every pore and turned his breath to clouds. He wanted to give up. Wanted to stand on his two legs and wave his arms over his head till they stung him and darted him and took him back. That was what he wanted, that was what he resolved, but when he heard them call his name, call SAM, he didn't stir.

J. FRED MUGGS

Carson was a tease—or at least the woman insulating him was. Renee
Flowers. She walked as if she had a lamppost strapped to her spine
and wore enough mascara to paint a mural, which didn't exactly in-
spire confidence in him. She spoke in looping run-on sentences and
used the adjective "super" as punctuation, pumping you up and putting you off at the same time so you never really knew where you
stood. And the thing was, *she'd* called him, not the other way around.
She'd seen him on *To Tell the Truth* (super) and had found the KCOY
feature super-interesting, and yes, Johnny often did animal segments
(the audience loved them), but then Sam—that *was* his name, right,
Sam?—was so much more than that. Wasn't he? And how did he
see Sam fitting in on the show, because this wasn't exactly an animal
act—or was it?

He talked to her twice on the phone over the course of a six-month period as winter gave way to spring and spring to summer, and then, when he'd just about given up hope, she invited him for an interview at the studio in Burbank. Which necessitated a three-hour drive down the coast from Santa Maria with Aimee for company—and to mind Sam, who loved nothing more than riding in the car but had never been on a trip even half as long as this. He and Sam had had to fly to New York for *To Tell the Truth*, but Sam had been sedated for that—there was no other option. This time he'd be conscious the whole way, and it was anybody's guess how he'd react. Would Aimee be able to keep him entertained with his toys and the pile of magazines she brought along? Would he doze off? Lean back in the seat and watch the countryside roll by, entranced by the flicker of his own face reflected in the window? It was an experiment—Sam was going to have to learn to travel if they were going to get the message out to the public—but he was bored and restless right from the start, except when he was baring his teeth and making threatening gestures at the other drivers, who couldn't resist pulling up alongside to wave and shout till they got his attention.

By the time they did get to Burbank he was in one of his moods, jittery and hyperactive and ready to go off on a tear the moment they pulled into the parking lot. They'd stopped twice, once at a rest stop and then at a fast-food place in Woodland Hills, where they tried to placate him with a vanilla shake, cheeseburger and fries, most of which he threw up by the time they reached Tarzana, an irony that wasn't lost on Guy since the town had been named for Edgar Rice Burroughs' signature character, the man raised by apes. And how did the ape raised by man reaffirm that ancestral, albeit fictional, bond? By puking in the man's car.

It was late June. A hundred and three degrees. The car reeked. Sam was a heartbeat away from throwing a tantrum and it didn't make it any easier that the minute they flung open the door and led him out onto the pavement every human being within two hundred yards came flocking to get a look at him. What is that—is it a monkey? A gorilla? Does it bite? One boy in a Dodgers cap came running right at them as if he were chasing a batted ball and Sam made a snatch for him—if Guy hadn't seen it coming and jerked back on the lead at the last minute they would have had a situation on their hands. Which would have meant no Carson, would have meant the police and animal control and another lawsuit, like the one the lawyer Elise had hired was threatening them with. Cars glittered by. The palms faded into smog. He coaxed Sam up the walk and into the building with the towering NBC logo out front.

Once they got inside, where the security guards made their monkey jokes and a whole new clutch of people came pressing in as if they were magnetized, Aimee took Sam to the ladies' room to clean him up while he was left to sign for their visitors' passes and try to work up a smile to present to Renee Flowers, though his shirt was sweated through and he was so tense he was on the verge of vomiting himself. He took a drink from the fountain in the hall, bent over the pressurized stream of chilled water like any other ape, no cup necessary, no straws, just lips, then settled into a chair in the anteroom of the office they'd been directed to and tried to calm himself by assaying a crossword puzzle in one of the magazines laid out crisply on a low table as if this were a dentist's waiting room. Which it might as well have been. If he'd expected glamour, movie stars—or at least TV stars—he was disappointed. Everything was quiet, orderly, comfortably uncomfortable.

He went over in his head what he was going to say to Renee Flowers, then dismissed it all. Better to be spontaneous. Besides which, he wasn't the one on trial here—Sam was. Everything depended on Sam. Any sign of recalcitrance or rebelliousness—any trouble—and you could kiss the whole deal goodbye. The thought gave him a headache, and yet would that be so tragic? Ultimately? He was an academic, after all, a psychologist, not a TV personality—and there were plenty of people, both inside the department and across the field generally, who would condemn him for what he was doing, who would accuse him of trivializing the project, of using it, of using Sam, for his own aggrandizement no matter the outcome. They were right, of course, at least partially, but it didn't matter—he wanted this. Badly.

The good news was that whatever she'd done, Aimee had managed to calm Sam down, and when the two of them came through the door fifteen minutes later, hand in hand, he could see from Sam's expression and body language that he was good to go. She'd cleaned him up and dressed him in the clothes she'd selected for him—a miniature suit with a checked shirt and glossy red tie and a pair of Converse high-tops she'd found in the kids' section at the local Foot Locker, also in red. He looked jaunty and casual and almost human—which was the point, exactly the point. If we could conceal our nakedness beneath blue jeans, skirts, blouses and Hawaiian luau shirts and go about constructing the world in our own image, then why couldn't another species do it too? Or at least participate? We could reason, we could talk, and so could chimps—as he and Sam were going to demonstrate for Renee Flowers and her boss and everybody else in America.

"Wow, he looks great," he said, dropping the magazine he'd been skimming and rising out of the grip of the hard plastic chair. "Like the reincarnation of J. Fred Muggs himself—and right here at NBC too. Which is only appropriate, right?" The other people in the room—a pair of secretaries and a couple in their forties who might have been comedians or maybe an actress and her agent—broke into smiles. It was an automatic response, like sympathetic yawning—dressed-up apes were simulacra of ourselves, and that was endearing in some way, funny even, which was why circuses and sideshows had been tricking them out and putting them through their paces since the first chimps were captured in the African jungle and brought back to Europe three hundred years earlier. He bent forward, conscious of everyone's eyes on him, and held out his hand to Sam for a high-five, which Sam gave him, grinning.

"He's so cute," one of the secretaries said. "Just like a little man."

"Precious," the other one said.

Sam folded back his upper lip in a grin that showed off his teeth, which were clean and even and didn't yet feature the weaponized canines adults developed, then walked upright across the room to take a seat in the chair nearest the door leading to Renee Flowers' inner sanctum, as if he knew what he'd come for. Aimee, who had hold of his lead, sank into the seat beside him and crossed her legs. Her bare legs. She'd changed into a skirt and heels and a clinging blouse, all in the same shade of cream, very proper, very adult, very sexy. He eased into the seat beside her and took her hand. "You look great too," he said.

She ducked her head. Blushed. "Thanks," she murmured.

"Does he have a name?" the man with the woman who might have been an actress wanted to know. He was slack bellied, with puffy eyes and a long feral jaw, and he wore a bow tie, of all things. Maybe he was a comedian, after all. He had to be. Who else would wear a bow tie?

"You hear that?" Guy asked, looking past her to where Sam sat slouched in the chair, dangling his legs and attempting, with mixed results, to retie the laces of his sneakers. "Do you want to tell this gentleman what your name is?"

If he'd been hyper before, now Sam was all business. He couldn't have known what was going on here, not in any deeper sense, but all the same he seemed to appreciate the uniqueness of the situation, of the office in the tall building and the strangers there in the room with them. He signed, HELLO, I AM SAM, and Guy spoke it aloud along with him.

"Smart monkey," the man said. "Is he going to be on the show?"

"That's the hope."

"Chimp," Aimee said. "He's a chimp, not a monkey."

He could see that the man was trying to formulate a response, wheels turning, the inevitable monkey joke on his lips, but then the door pulled open and Renee Flowers, in a business suit and with her hair pulled back in a tight bun, was ushering them into her office.

There was a desk, there were chairs, a bank of windows with shades drawn against the sun. It could have been a faculty office, except that it was three times bigger and the walls were decorated with framed photos of *The Tonight Show*, Johnny mugging for the camera or grinning at one celebrity or another, most of whom Guy didn't recognize, aside from Bob Hope and who was that—Diane Keaton?

"So," Renee Flowers said, clasping her hands in front of her, "this is him, huh?" And then added, "Super."

They'd paused just inside the door, Sam standing upright between him and Aimee and grasping their hands for balance. Sam looked Renee Flowers right in the face, aware that whatever was going on, he was the focus of it and no doubt calculating that some sort of treat would be forthcoming, the way it usually was when he was in any building other than home, whether it be at the university, the supermarket or even the gas station or hardware store.

A long moment ticked by, Renee Flowers gazing down at Sam and Sam up at her, before she said, "Oh, forgive me, I'm so carried away here—I haven't even introduced myself. I'm Renee."

In order to take her hand, he had to drop Sam's, but Sam wouldn't let go—more chimp humor?—so he wound up offering his left hand. Awkwardly. Renee didn't seem to mind or even notice. She just shook her head, gazing back down at Sam and smiling. "He's really something, isn't he? If he got any cuter you'd have to get in line and pay the cute tax, wouldn't you? Super," she said, "really super," then turned to Aimee with an expectant look. "Hi," she said, "I'm Renee."

"My assistant," he put in. "Aimee Villard." Aimee gave her a tentative smile, then dropped her eyes to Sam, who still had hold of her hand.

"A pleasure to meet you, Aimee," Renee Flowers said. "You're very pretty, do you know that?" And, then, to him: "Will she be part of the act? Or no, I'm sorry, forgive me—it's not an act, of course not. What I mean is, will she be on camera with you?"

"What do you think, Aimee—want to go on the show with me and Sam?"

She shook her head. Barbara would have jumped at the chance and so would Elise—before the accident, anyway. And Melanie, Melanie had always wanted to share the spotlight, jealous of him and resentful too since to her mind she was the one who bore the outsized burden of raising Sam while he reaped all the rewards. Not Aimee, though—Aimee would rather wear a crown of thorns and walk barefoot all the way back to Santa Maria than have somebody point a camera at her.

"But let's have a seat and get acquainted, okay?" Smiling broadly, smiling till her teeth shone under the glare of the overhead lights, Renee indicated the three plush seats arrayed in front of the desk with a sweep of one hand. She might have booked animal acts before, but the animals had never showed up in her office dressed in suit and tie. Or at least that was what he was guessing.

Sam didn't hesitate. He let go of their hands and bounded into the near seat, looking up expectantly at Renee Flowers as she edged her buttocks up on her desk and Guy and Aimee took the seats on either side of him. "And can I get you anything?" Renee asked. "Coffee, tea, soft drinks?" She leaned forward then, hovering over Sam. "And what about you, Sam—would you like something to drink?"

This was a test, of course—Renee Flowers wasn't Carson's gatekeeper for nothing. Did this chimp, this animal, understand spoken English at its most rudimentary, as even a dog or parrot would? Was Sam legitimate? Was Guy himself?

Sam looked straight at her and signed, DRINK, then poked his right index finger into his left arm, as if it were a needle, the sign for COKE. Then he grinned and signed, PLEASE.

"What did he say? Did he just say something?"

Guy gave her a smile. "He said, 'May I have a Coke, please?'"

"Really? Did you catch that, Aimee?" She waited a beat till Aimee affirmed it with a nod, then said, "Amazing, truly amazing. He really understands, doesn't he? Does he know what I'm saying now? Is it okay? Can I go on?"

Guy nodded. "Yeah, sure."

"So, Sam, do you like Coke?"

Sam bobbed his fist up and down. YES, emphatically YES.

The look on Renee Flowers' face told him everything he needed to know. It was the look that softens women's faces when they're in the presence of toddlers, puppies, kittens, an instinctive look, a mothering look. They were home-free now. He was sure of it.

"What do you like better, Sam," she said, leaning closer and clipping her words as if she were addressing a child, which, in a sense, she was, "Coke or 7UP?"

Sam, his legs drawn up in the chair and folded in the lotus position, the tie a shining jewel at his throat, never hesitated. BOTH, he signed. YOU GIVE ME BOTH. PLEASE.

They took the Coast Highway on the way back, even though it would add time to the trip. Traffic was crawling on the 101, anyway (no surprise there), and the heat was killing, especially since the car's air conditioner seemed to be operating at half efficiency, so Guy decided to get off at Topanga and wind his way down to the coast, where at least it would be cooler even if the traffic was no better. They stopped at a McDonald's in Malibu, all three of them in a celebratory mood, and Sam got the same meal he'd vomited up earlier—vanilla shake, cheeseburger, fries—and kept it down this time. He was back to T-shirt and overalls now, the suit neatly folded and packed away in Aimee's bag against the next time he'd need it, which Guy fervently hoped would be soon, very soon, but as well as it had gone, in the end, Renee Flowers had made no promises. Once Sam had got his Coke and 7UP—in separate glasses, with ice, which he drank alternately, sip by sip—the conversation had wound down, as if the test had been passed and it was time to move on to the next phase.

Problem was, there wasn't a next phase. Or not that Guy could see. After Renee had given them a long repetitive description of Johnny's responses to the various animals that had appeared on the show, from boa constrictors to a pair of least weasels, one of which had climbed up on his shoulder and pissed down the back of his shirt, Guy said, "Yeah, Johnny's hilarious, he really is. That deadpan look he gives the camera? Which is why I think he's going to have a great time with Sam—who's not going to have any accidents on camera, guaranteed. The two of them can just converse, like with any of your other guests—with me there to translate, that's all. Because that's the idea, the science behind this, the whole rationale for primate language studies—Sam can talk. And we can talk to him." He paused, glanced round the room, expecting Johnny himself to appear at any moment, and why not? He imagined him sitting behind a two-way mirror—that mirror, there, in back of Renee Flowers' desk—awaiting his cue.

"He wouldn't be here now, would he? I mean, just to meet Sam? For a minute?" He was going to add, "Since we drove all the way down here," but thought better of it because of the look Renee Flowers was giving him. Her grin, which had held steady since they'd walked in the door, faded. She said, "But Johnny never meets his guests beforehand—not even the celebrities," and left it at that. She'd call him, she promised, as she showed them out the door. As soon as she could get the fall schedule worked out. Promise. Okay?

"Okay," he'd said.

"Super," she'd said.

Sam fell asleep shortly after he'd finished his meal, balled up the bag it had come in and flung it out the window in the way of any child thrilled by the sucking power of air in violent motion, and while Guy didn't like it (anything with the potential of attracting police attention was a disaster in the making), there wasn't much he could do about it since he was driving and Sam had got the window down before Aimee could stop him. But now Sam was asleep, the air was cool and moist and once they got beyond Zuma Beach the ocean began to open up before them like a movie screen. Aimee had been in back with Sam till he closed his eyes and dropped off, and now she climbed over the console to settle into the seat beside him. She fooled with the radio a minute—"There's like this new song, 'My Sharona,' and I can't get it out of my head?"—but the reception was notoriously spotty on this stretch, and after five minutes of listening to white noise interspersed with sporadic snatches of guitar, she flicked it off. They'd been talking about how well it had gone and how much it would mean, as far as attention for the program, if this actually panned out, and he really thought it was about ninety-nine percent there, didn't she?, when she turned to him and asked, "Who's J. Fred Muggs?"

"The chimp. The famous chimp that resurrected the *Today* show back in the early days of TV? But you'd be too young to remember— I'm guessing he was gone by '57. I was just a kid myself but I definitely remember seeing him in his little suit and all that . . . Actually, I wonder if in some subliminal way the seeds were planted back then—that would be wild, wouldn't it? The whole arc of my life, from being a kid glued to our little fishbowl TV to grad school and Moncrief and now Sam. And you." He was feeling good, riding the high of the meeting and of having her there beside him in her short dress and heels while the breeze lifted her hair and she turned her pretty face to him. "But J. Fred Muggs, that was just an animal act, nothing like what we're doing."

Still, that animal act had saved the show—and made it Number 1 in its time slot. And though the fields of ethology and psychobiology were in their infancy and no one had any idea of teaching him ASL or penetrating his thought processes, J. Fred Muggs eventually acquired a vocabulary of over five hundred words, and his responses to them—and the gags the show's producers came up with—entranced the viewing public, children and adults alike. Which was no small thing, since when the *Today* show premiered in 1952, it barely made a ripple. Morning TV had been the province of children's programs to that point, and the show's producers had come up with something entirely new—a show that was geared toward adults as well, albeit in a casual way, featuring a mix of news, weather reports, comedy sketches, toy demonstrations and children's books read aloud for the benefit of the kids getting ready for school, with host Dave Garroway acting as a kind of laid-back uncle, concluding each show by holding up his palm and intoning, "Peace," long before the hippies co-opted the phrase. It would prove to be a winning formula but no one knew that at the time—all they knew was that the show needed a jolt, needed something that would strengthen its hold on the children as well as the adults, and what that something would be—puppets like Howdy Doody or a clown like Clarabell?—nobody quite knew until J. Fred Muggs appeared on the scene.

Like the majority of chimps exhibited in circuses and zoos or channeled into research, Muggs had been captured in the wild. His mother had been shot out of a tree while cradling him in her arms, the standard procedure for acquiring infants without risking attack. There was no notion of ecological impact or maintaining wild populations—chimps were just another animal species whose sole value lay in what they could bring economically, like the lions and tigers of the circus or the seals trained to balance a ball on their uplifted snouts for the thin reward of a sardine. Muggs was one of the lucky ones. Nine out of ten infant chimps died in transit, but Henry

Trefflich, the veteran animal importer who'd collected Muggs and exhibited him in his pet shop in Manhattan, saw that he was held and nursed through the entire transatlantic journey, and that made the difference. When he was ten months old, two former NBC pages bought him with the notion of training him as an animal act for TV. Unfortunately they got confused as to the time of his audition for the *Today* show and missed it altogether, but one of the show's producers spotted him in a café up the street, where Muggs was dunking a doughnut in a cup of coffee like any other morning commuter, and brought him back to the studio.

Garroway wasn't particularly happy about it—*A monkey act, for Christ's sake*—nor was the newscaster, who promptly quit. But from the moment Muggs appeared opposite Garroway, who spun out an endless array of improvisatory jokes while the chimp sat there in his lap, variously pretending to read the newspaper or listen to a children's story Garroway read aloud while the camera hung over his shoulder, the ratings steadily climbed. Which ultimately was all that mattered. Garroway could have been a monkey himself, could have squatted in a cage full of monkeys, could have gone to Africa and paraded through the jungle with Muggs on his back, and the ratings would only have risen—and the ad revenues along with them. The show soared and Garroway became a certifiable star, but his celebrity hung heavily on him—he suffered from depression, and the fact that Muggs' fame quickly eclipsed his own didn't make things any better.

Within a year there were Muggs comics, books, games and dolls and Muggs was called on to christen ships and make appearances at supermarket openings while Garroway had to sit there before the camera day after day with an unpredictable animal in his lap, pretending to be genially amused when Muggs rearranged his hair or snatched off his glasses and flung them across the set. Muggs grew. His arms hardened. His grip, hands and feet both, was all but unbreakable. By the second year he'd begun to act out on the set, smart enough to know that once the camera's red light flashed on he could get away with anything without fear of being disciplined, though his handler crouched off-camera with the lead in his hand, ready to jerk him back if he threatened to bite or throw a tantrum.

Eventually the producers brought in a second chimp, an infant female they named Phoebe B. Beebe, introduced as Muggs' girlfriend, in the hope of calming him down. But he wouldn't be calmed. He began to bite, both as a way of getting attention and settling scores (like any star, he demanded immediate gratification of his every whim and he had a long memory for those who failed to provide it). He bit Garroway. He bit the comedian Martha Raye during a rehearsal. He began to run amok on the set, swatting at the microphones, the cameras, overturning furniture and throwing shrieking tantrums if anyone tried to stop him. By the time he turned five, in 1957, NBC retired him and brought on a younger, more placid chimp to replace him. It didn't help. Or at least not with Garroway, who became increasingly more erratic as the years went on, wandering off the set in the middle of broadcasts, feuding with members of the crew, brooding endlessly over his career, which, when all was said and done, had been defined by a monkey act. By 1961 he'd left the show. Not long after, Muggs went into retirement in Florida in the company of Phoebe and his trainers, where he lived a placid unhurried life under the sun while Garroway, his celebrity deserting him, cycled into depression and despair.

"I don't really remember him," Aimee said. "Or the chimp either."

He was driving. The sun burnished the water. Sam was asleep in the back and she was right there beside him, the two key pieces in the board game of his life, and never mind Melanie and Elise and Renee Flowers and all the rest of them. NBC, CBS. Borstein, Moncrief, Leonard Biggs. He was on a path and he was going to leave them all behind. He felt a sudden surge of happiness. "Why would you? I'm guessing you probably never even saw a chimp till Sam—and you didn't know a thing about primate studies until you walked into my office, right?" He laid a hand on her thigh. "Right?"

"I don't know," she said, turning her face to him. "I guess. But at least the Muggs story has a happy ending."

"For the chimp. But what about Dave Garroway?"

"Don't you always say you can count the people in the world by the billions and the chimps by the thousands?"

"That's pretty harsh, isn't it? But you're right—chimp stories don't usually have happy endings, but Muggs was lucky because his people actually cared about him, loved him, even, instead of just using him. That's rare."

"What about us?"

"You think I'm using Sam? You think I don't care about him?" This was a sore point with him. Melanie had accused him—repeatedly, daily—of putting his career before Sam's welfare. Or hers, for that matter. *Bottom line is you don't really give a shit about Sam or me or anybody else but yourself,* she said, and slammed the door in his face. "No, really, Aimee—first rule of the behavioral sciences is do not fall in love with your subject, but that went out the window a long time ago, like the first month Melanie and I had him? You know me. You've seen me in action—you really think I'm not devoted to him? Totally?"

"I *love* him," she said, giving him a fierce look. He'd never seen her angry—she was the most placid person he'd ever met, which was part of the attraction, because he definitely didn't need another Melanie—but she was angry now. "Love," she said. "L-o-v-e. But you know what I worry about?"

"What?"

"Is it really going to matter? Because the truth is we have nothing to say about it—we don't even own him, your professor does. You told me over and over how domineering he is, how manipulative, how he bullies you and everybody else—what if he decides to take

Sam back? What if he doesn't like the progress we're making or *The Tonight Show* or whatever? What if he decides to give him to somebody else?"

"I'm not going to let that happen."

"No," she said. "I'm not either."

A STILLNESS

The DOG, not the one he'd bitten, but the other one, was right there all of a sudden and it was snarling and snapping its jaws at him, and here was the bitten one edging in behind it, brave all over again, though it bore the crusting red marks of his teeth in its narrow dog skull. He saw that and registered it but he didn't move. A stillness had come over him. It was like a BLANKET, this stillness, and it took the COLD away so that he wasn't shivering anymore, wasn't doing anything except dreaming in a way that closed the world out as if he'd never been part of it. His dream, which the DOGS had interrupted, was the one of her and the bath and her eyes and lips and smooth white skin. He had no concept of death as a generality, though he had killed things—a squirrel in the yard, a rat on the floor of his CAGE—and watched them transition from the animate to the inanimate, from things that moved and had a will of their own to another state altogether, the state of meat, rapidly cooling meat. Which he'd eaten because that was what meat was for, eating.

But what was going on here? Was he close to death himself? Death from an overdose of COLD, vasoconstriction, hypothermia, at the mercy of the elements? He didn't know about any of that or the terminology of stages and conditions and he didn't care. He looked up and saw the sky with its faint fading trace of counterfeit sun and the clouds that were like drawn curtains and heard the fury of the DOGS turn to bafflement because he was giving them nothing back. They wanted to snarl. Their purpose was to snarl. But he wasn't giving them the opportunity. The moment held. He felt nothing. Then the BIG MAN was there, flanked by the other two.

One of them said, "Is he dead?"

The other said, "His eyes are open."

The BIG MAN—the stinger was dangling on a cord from his belt, but he didn't need it, not at this point—cursed and said, "Get those goddamned dogs out of here, will you? Jesus fucking Christ."

He wasn't really paying attention and most of what they were saying he didn't comprehend, but he felt a jolt of fear when the BIG MAN peeled the glove off his right hand and lifted his GUN from its holster. The GUN was an object of terror, worse than the stinger, but not even the sudden appearance of it motivated him now. Hate didn't motivate him either, though he hated the GUN and he hated the BIG MAN and the other two and the DOGS into the bargain. He lay there as if the dart was already in him—and then it was and he didn't feel a thing. No, he was doubly cold, doubly powerless, and it took all three of them to lift him from the cold crushed cane and carry him past the dead trees and the dead bushes and out to the road, where they flung open the door of the car waiting there and heaved him across the backseat like so much uninhabited meat.

ALL THE TRIMMINGS

Summer drew down, then fall, the days warm and dry and suspended on the winds that raked the canyons and flung grit at the windows every afternoon at cocktail hour, as if grit was just what you wanted in your gin and tonic. It was hard to believe she'd been on the project for nearly a year now, been here with Sam and Guy as if she'd never been anywhere else, never worried about late papers or Dr. Lindelof or what she was going to tell her mother about her progress, her grades, the corrosive drip of the days that never varied and the apartment that had begun to feel like a cage. That was all behind her. She was here now and there was no other world but this one, the one confined to the low-slung ranch house with the oak trees all around it and the steers drifting through the chaparral out back and the hawks that rode the currents overhead while Sam climbed his tree and turned his face to the sky as if contemplating the mystery of his own existence.

The day after Halloween she called her mother to say she wouldn't be home for Thanksgiving and probably not for Christmas either.

"What are you telling me?" her mother demanded, her voice a thin steady complaint like the buzzing of an insect trapped in the receiver. "Is it Guy? Your professor?"

She pictured her mother at the kitchen counter, the phone pressed to her ear, sun leaching through the pepper trees out front to illuminate the pans on the stove and decorate the wall behind her with long finger-like shadows that plunged and shifted with the wind. She could hear the refrigerator clicking on in the background—or was that the dishwasher? And the radio, the low hum of the radio tuned to the classical station. She felt a pang of longing. Her mother might as well have been a thousand miles away, though she was just two hours south, in the pink stucco house where Aimee had grown up in Calabasas, within earshot of the freeway. But that was in another lifetime.

"Yes," she said, "it's Guy. And he's not just my professor, he's my boyfriend, okay? But it's more than that too. You remember you would always tell me how bad you used to feel for the farmers' kids when you were growing up in Springville? How they could never go on vacation because of the livestock? Well, that's how it is with Sam. We can't go away, not even for a couple of days."

"I find that hard to believe. He's just the one animal, right? And it's not as if you have to milk him twice a day—and you have other students there too, didn't you tell me? And volunteers on top of that?"

"Yes. But I'm the one, Mom, the one he needs like twenty-four/seven, the one he *talks* to the most—"

Her mother made a dismissive noise. "But he doesn't really talk, does he?"

"He does. It's just that his language is gestural, like with the deaf?"

"What can he say? Can he say, I don't know, 'My tooth hurts, take me to the dentist?'"

"More or less. But we're careful about his teeth—he brushes three times a day, did I tell you that? More than most people."

"Okay, fine. Bring him here, then. Does he eat turkey? Turnips? Sweet potato pie?"

"He does. He'd love it. But it upsets him to break his routine and to have to sleep anyplace but here, where everything's familiar—in his own house, in his own bed. I mean, you can understand that, right?"

There was a pause. "Ultimately? No. I want to meet this prodigy—both prodigies, the ape and the professor both. If they can't come here, why don't I go there, then? And bring your sister along too? Claire would love to see you—and Sophie too. She's almost four now, and really, when was the last time you saw her?"

"I don't know, like last year? But sure, I guess you could come, if that's what you want. But it wouldn't be much of a Thanksgiving—I mean, there's no place for you to stay here, really . . ."

The truth was she didn't want her mother interfering—or criticizing her, which was what it would amount to the minute she walked in the door and saw the way things were between her and Sam, who might or might not take to her, and between her and Guy too. Plus, there'd be the complication of her sister and niece, of whom Sam would be instantly jealous, and Claire's husband, Bob, a thick-headed thirty-year-old bore who tried to cram as many clichés into a sentence as he could and never stopped talking long enough to hear a word anyone said in return. Which would embarrass her in front of Guy. And there was no telling what Sam would do with strangers sitting across the table from him, forking up turkey and mashed potatoes that could have gone to him no matter how full he might have been or how often she heaped up his plate.

The previous year, when she was still new to all this, she'd gone home for Christmas, so it wasn't a problem, but Sam had been inconsolable and acted out the whole time she was away, at least that was what Guy and Josh told her, and when she did return, for the first two days he pretended he didn't know who she was. She'd felt terrible about that. As if she'd betrayed him. Even worse was the way she'd left, waiting till he fell asleep, then slipping out of bed and going straight to her car without saying goodbye or offering any explanation. And, of course, he woke the minute the engine turned over, his distant shattering screams the last thing she heard as she eased down the drive.

"We can always get a motel room and have the elegant brunch at the Rodeway Inn or whatever, carrot sticks and celery with ranch dressing and turkey so dried out it might as well be jerky—if you want us at all, that is."

She was going to say "It's not that," and offer maybe to bring Sam down to Calabasas on a road trip, maybe after the holidays, if it was all right with Guy, that is, but she didn't have the chance because just then she heard Sam beginning to stir upstairs in his room. He'd gone down for his half-hour nap after lunch and he was always cranky when he woke—he'd want his snack, Oreos and an apple, right away, because he had low blood sugar, or at least that was how she'd diagnosed it. "All right, Mom," she said, "I do want you to come, I do, or maybe I'll come there, but I have to go—I hear Sam waking up from his nap and he's going to want his snack. You know how he is when he doesn't get his snack, like right away—"

"No, in fact, I don't."

"He's like any other kid."

"Yeah, well, from what I've read—and yes, I've been reading as much as I can about your new field, primatology?—he's not really a kid anymore, is he?"

"But he is, emotionally, anyway. And I'm sorry, got to run. Call you soon."

Sam was okay with sleeping alone in the afternoon, but it was always a trick to get him to settle down and she'd have to climb into bed beside him, under the covers, even if it was a stifling day in July or August, and cuddle with him till he drifted off. Then she could slip away and try to deal with the ten thousand details of life exclusive of what was going on inside his head, which she couldn't do at night because night was his time of dislocation and terror, even with the night-light aglow. Leave the bed, even for a minute, even to go to the bathroom, and he'd wake screaming until she came back to him. That wasn't healthy, she knew it, and he *was* manipulating her, she knew that too, but then she'd never raised a chimp before, hardly anybody had, and nobody knew the rules. She spoiled him. They all did. But, really, what choice did they have?

She heard him bouncing down the stairs, feet and hands both, heard the soft inquisitive hoots he emitted when he was talking to himself, and a moment later he was there, standing in the kitchen doorway. He'd shucked his diaper—he was old enough now, at four, to use the toilet, though he was indifferent to the concept and every other day or so left a mess somewhere around the house. His ancestors, through all the eons, had just let fly wherever they were and whenever the urge took them, and so why expect anything different of him? Except that this was a cross-fostering experiment as well as a linguistic one, except that he didn't know he was any different from anybody else in his life—and they all wore clothes and used the toilet and encouraged him to do the same, even if he couldn't quite manage to graduate from the anal stage. The fact was, he'd never laid eyes on another member of his own species, at least not since he was two weeks old and Moncrief darted his mother and took him from her.

Sam had no idea he was anything but human, which was the whole point. His favorite game was Categories, in which she or Guy or one of the others would lay out a series of cards imprinted with pictures of various people, animals and objects and he was to sort them into piles by category, the buildings in one pile, trees in another, lions with lions, dogs with dogs, people with people. When he came to pictures of chimps, he placed them with the pictures of gorillas, orangs and monkeys, as if he were a primatologist himself—until he came to his own photo, that is. He would pick it up, extend his lips to kiss it, then grin at her as if the joke was on him, and place it, invariably, among the photos of people—and not just the category of people he knew personally, but strangers, men, women and children alike, generalizing, selecting, making a statement.

Are animals self-aware? That was one of the big questions in the field of animal consciousness and the evidentiary standard was the mirror test, in which a sleeping animal—elephant, dog, crow, human child, ape—was tagged on the face with a bright-colored sticker and then, on awakening, presented with a mirror. If the animal noticed the sticker and reached up to examine it, to remove it, this was proof that it recognized itself as a discrete individual, which in turn meant it exhibited a higher level of consciousness. Dogs failed, cats failed, but elephants, porpoises, crows, apes and human children passed easily, and Sam was so smart he could have conducted the tests himself. Sometimes, when she was putting on her makeup, he'd perch on the sink and apply her lipstick to his own lips, mugging for her and the mirror both, though admittedly she'd have to watch him like a hawk or he'd extrude the whole tube and swallow it before she could stop him.

Now, standing there in the doorway, blinking away the effects of his nap, he signed, GOOD FOOD NOW, YOU ME, and ambled into the room, pointing at the clock set in the face of the stove.

"You want Oreos? Or what about Fig Newtons for a change? They're better for you. I think."

FIG. YOU WANT SOME TOO?

She shook her head. "I'm trying to watch my weight."

He gave her a dubious look, then sprang into his chair, pointing one finger at his ear and rotating it twice: YOU'RE CRAZY. And then he made the sign for breasts and held out his arms for a hug.

"You flatterer," she said, and she crossed the room, bent over and embraced him, his hands going to her breasts and his lips brushing the side of her face in the very place where he'd sunk his teeth into Elise. But he wasn't the same chimp he'd been a year ago. And she wasn't Elise.

As it turned out, they had their own Thanksgiving at the ranch, as planned, while her mother stayed home in Calabasas, cooking for Claire and Bob and Sophie. Which was a relief—not that she didn't love them and miss them, but given the new conditions of her life, she was afraid it just wouldn't work out, not this time, anyway. And she didn't need the added pressure. As it was, Guy had invited the chair of his department and his wife, which would be a trial in itself, but Guy insisted that Sam had to get used to strangers, had to be socialized like any other child so he'd know how to respond when he was presented with new situations and new people. Barbara and Sid would be there, as well as Janie, one of the student volunteers who Sam especially liked. Josh was coming too—and at the last minute he called to say he was bringing Elise, whom nobody had seen in months, so that was going to make things interesting.

"Can you believe Elise's coming?" She was at the kitchen counter, mashing the still-hot potatoes Barbara was peeling and handing her one by one while Sam, who'd climbed atop the refrigerator for no other reason than that he felt like it, looked on in a supervisory role, hooting softly to himself.

"Tell me about it. But I hear she's all healed now and you can't really tell anything happened. Except under real intense light and if she isn't wearing any makeup, which she always is."

"Who told you that?"

"Josh."

She didn't quite know how to take this—why was Josh confiding in Barbara and not her? And why would Elise come back at all when she'd been so bitter about the whole thing? Was she having second thoughts? Did she want her old job back? "More closure," she said, "right? But isn't closure supposed to be final? I mean, what does she *want*?"

Barbara gave her a sly look. Her hair, kinky, dark, hair that was like a black cloud rising up off her head, had broken free of the band she'd tied it up with and bobbed in front of her eyes. "Your job, my job, I don't know—she has dibs, right? And she's got Josh too."

"Don't even joke about it." She looked up at Sam, who was leaning over the face of the refrigerator rearranging the magnets that held her clippings in place ("Vegetarian Lasagna"; "Chimp Speech Experiment"; "Pumpkin Spice Plantain Chips"). "What do you think, Sam—you want Elise to come back? You want her instead of me?"

Sam's grasp of spoken English was exceptional, but sometimes he didn't quite catch the meaning of a given phrase, especially when it involved rapid speech or complex syntax or even, depending on his mood, simple pronoun-antecedent agreement. He straightened up at the mention of his name, his legs dangling over the edge of the freezer compartment, but he didn't respond. She tried again, this time signing it as she spoke aloud.

YOU, he signed, then gave it a beat, shook his head and signed, ELISE.

"What? What are you saying?"

He signed it again: ELISE.

It was as if she'd been slapped in the face. There was no one in this world closer to him than she was, not even Guy, and certainly not Elise. She was the one he'd turned on. He'd bitten her. Maimed her. And now he was saying he preferred *her*? She couldn't believe it.

"You ingrate," she snapped, angry all of a sudden, and though he might not have had the specific term in his vocabulary, he knew exactly what she was saying. "You really mean to tell me you don't want me anymore? Is that it? Huh? Talk to me, Sam, because you're in trouble now, you are, and you know it—"

He was grinning. He ran both hands over his head, then hid his face in the mask of his intertwined fingers as if he couldn't contain himself. Another beat and he peeked out at her, dropped his hands and signed, JOKE. And then, holding his arms out for a hug, he signed, YOU, and waved her to him impatiently, signing YOU ME, YOU ME, YOU ME.

Guy had been in his study all morning and into the early afternoon. He was writing up the results of the double-blind tests they'd conducted on Sam's ability to name objects and their photographic representations, all of which Josh had filmed for the record. The idea was for one researcher (her) to hold up an object or photo for Sam to identify while another (Guy), who was positioned so that he couldn't see her or the object, had to interpret it from Sam's sign alone. When Sam was fresh—before he got antsy or bored, which usually happened fifteen or twenty minutes in—he was accurate ninety percent of the time, and when he wasn't, it didn't necessarily mean he'd forgotten the sign but that his signing wasn't crisp enough and Guy misread it.

She was setting the table in the dining room when Guy poked his head in the door. "Looks great," he said. "And the turkey—wow, smells ambrosial. What did you do to it?" He came across the room and slipped his arms around her from behind.

"A secret," she said. "My mother's famous turkey baste—you'd have to torture me to get the recipe out of me."

"Sorry, got no time for torture now," he said, drifting over to the table and idly picking up one of the plates—Tupperware, exclusively Tupperware, because Sam was hard on china—and setting it down again. He glanced at his watch. "Sam's naptime?"

She nodded.

"Good. Well, looks like everything's ready to go—and thanks, thanks for that. It's huge. Especially with Leonard coming—"

"And Elise."

"Right, *Elise*. And maybe—I don't mean to lay this on you out of nowhere, but you heard the phone ringing like two hours ago? You know who it was?"

She didn't have a clue. "That woman from *The Tonight Show*?"

"I wish. But no, it was Moncrief. He's in L.A. for some conference, without his wife, for whatever reason, and he said he'd like to stop by and reconnect."

"You don't mean today? On *Thanksgiving*?"

Guy shrugged. He looked guilty, as if he'd been holding back till the last minute—which he had. "He said he had nowhere to go for Thanksgiving dinner."

"You mean you invited him?"

"Yeah. Of course. What else could I do? I mean, he is my mentor, after all, not to mention he's the one who set all this up. For which I'm eternally grateful—aren't you?"

"But that's a three-hour drive—where's he going to stay? Not here—tell me not here."

"I don't know. There's plenty of motels, right? And if he drinks too much—and he does tend to drink too much—I can always drive him back to whatever place he winds up at, probably the cheapest, knowing him. But he might not come. It's not set in stone."

But it was. Moncrief—*Donald*—always did exactly what he wanted, when he wanted, and if he said he was coming, there was no turning him back short of wildfire or earthquake, both of which she began to pray for as she set another place and lashed herself round the kitchen, trying to get as much done as she could before Sam woke from his nap. She had a glass of wine to calm herself, and Barbara, every bit as frazzled as she was, lit up a joint, the thin weedy stink of pot creeping in around the edges of the dense aroma of homemade pumpkin pie and turkey with all the trimmings.

The first guests to arrive were Professor Biggs and his wife, whose name Aimee didn't quite catch. She was bad with names, especially on first introduction, always confused and embarrassed with new people and struggling to think of what to say. But the professor's wife didn't seem to notice—she was nice enough, not at all condescending, and with a smile that darted across her lips and fluctuated in a genuine way, as if she were actually engaged and not just putting on a show. She was in her thirties, with a beauty parlor coif and dressed in a pantsuit and simple strand of pearls, which could prove an unfortunate temptation to Sam, and the coif as well—he loved to get up close and personal, aggressive and curious at the same time. Anybody with sprayed-up hair was a target, and jewelry—earrings and necklaces especially—were irresistible.

Guy had put something on the stereo to set the atmosphere—classical, with ascending and descending voices and a groundswell of cello, something she didn't recognize, though he was educating her on that score too, her favorite pieces so far being Barber's Adagio for Strings and Borodin's String Quartet no. 2. They stood there just inside the door—the Biggses, Guy, Barbara and her, while Sam, as calm as she'd ever seen him in the presence of strangers, gazed up at them benevolently and everybody bent at the waist to jabber down at him. It might not have been evident to the Biggses, but anybody who knew Sam could see in an instant that he was stoned, which wasn't necessarily a bad thing, given the circumstances. He'd slipped silently into the kitchen after his nap and before holding out his arms for a hug or demanding his snack, he made a show of sniffing the air and immediately produced the sign for STONE, right fist tapped to the top of the left, then SMOKE, two fingers pressing an imaginary cigarette to the lips. Barbara still had the joint in her hand, so there was no denying him, and of course over the past months they'd all learned that a few tokes could have a wonderful mellowing effect on him, just like his nightly cocktail or glass of red wine.

All good. The Biggses cooed over him and he accepted the adulation magnanimously, with no thought of snatching pearls or disarranging hairdos—and he looked the perfect little gentleman in the suit and tie she'd bought for the Carson audition (though the show itself was still on hold, maybe permanently, a situation that had totally deflated Guy, who called Renee Flowers on the first of every month only to have her—or her secretary—tell him she was on board with it a hundred percent and would get back to him soon. Super soon.).

Guy was wearing a tie and jacket himself and he'd encouraged her to put on a skirt, though the way she saw it her function was more on the level of server than hostess. "It's not just about Sam, you know," he'd said. "I want to show you off too, okay? You reflect on me and Sam and the whole project—let these stiffs have something beautiful to look at, that's the way I see it. Come on, do it for me. Is it really that hard to put on a skirt and some makeup?"

"What stiffs? Your colleague and his wife?"

"Yeah, my colleague and his wife. And now Moncrief on top of it."

When Josh came in with Elise, they were all standing around the fire in the living room, except for Janie and Sid, who were helping out in the kitchen like the dutiful volunteers they were. Under normal conditions, the fireplace went unused because of Sam, but Guy had insisted on having a fire in honor of the holiday. Which meant they all had to keep an eye on Sam. Fires fascinated him. He loved basking in the heat, scooting across the floor till his backside was pressed right up against the screen, but more than that it was the process, the phenomenon of this neutral thing—wood, sticks he could chew on—turning hot, glowing, falling away to ash, that really got his wheels spinning. He could never resist experimenting with it, no matter how many times he burned himself, once even racing round the room with a flaming brand till Josh caught up to him and tackled him, leaving a scorched black scar on the floorboards as testimony and admonition both.

Elise tried to behave as if nothing had happened. She shook hands with the professor and his wife, gave Guy an abbreviated hug and chirped some inanity at her and Barbara, all the while ignoring Sam, who, in turn, ignored her. Her face was fine—you could hardly tell, really—and she'd put some effort into her hair and makeup and the teal cocktail dress she was wearing, which brought out her eyes and made them shine like little glass nuggets. Josh—he was in a sports coat too—was ready for anything, you could see that in the way he positioned himself between Sam and Elise when they came in the door, and then, even before getting a drink, he pulled Sam up on his back and paraded him round the room, to Sam's delight. Sam hooted and kicked out his legs and laughed his soft aspirated laugh.

"Wow," the professor's wife said, grinning in appreciation, "he really likes that, doesn't he?"

"Oh, yeah," Josh said, swinging in close, but not so close that Sam could make a grab for her pearls. "He's my boy, aren't you, Sam? And in a minute we're going to get down and play tickle—and chase, you want to play chase?"

Sam, perched on his back, signed, YOU CHASE ME, but Josh couldn't see his hands. "What did he say?" Josh asked, canvassing the room. He was keeping Sam occupied, both by way of distracting him and showing him off for the professor and his wife.

"He says he wants you to chase him," Aimee said, and then, since she was part of the demonstration too, she signed to Sam, simultaneously speaking aloud: "Is that right? Or do you want to chase him?"

CHASE HIM.

"Are you sure? Are you sure you don't want to go in and try some of the good food first?" She'd wanted to say "hors d'oeuvres," because she was about to bring out a tray of stuffed mushrooms and the chestnuts she'd roasted specially for Sam, who liked to eat them hot, shell and all, but he didn't have the term in his vocabulary.

Sam nodded. CHASE FIRST.

"Okay, then, my friend," Josh said, swinging round and dropping Sam into the easy chair. "If you think you can catch me," and he made a face of mock fright and bolted for the stairs, Sam springing after him with a wild hooting laugh. They all watched until they were both out of sight. Everybody, including Elise, was grinning.

"So impressive," the wife said. "He really understands, doesn't he?"

"Oh, that's nothing, Margaret," Guy said, waving his glass as if in illustration. He was drinking chardonnay, courtesy of LaSalle Vineyards. He would have preferred Champagne—so would she—but grant money only took you so far. "Wait'll we sit down to eat. You know what I'm going to do? I'm going to quiz him for your benefit—and yours too, Leonard. Categories and concepts. Like, 'Do you like mashed potatoes better than French fries?' Or meat. 'What do you like better, meat or vegetables?'"

"He likes fries," Elise put in, claiming a piece of her turf back. "You should see him at McDonald's."

"But concepts are what separate the believers from the skeptics. I can ask him what kind of animal the turkey is and he'll say it's a bird. And then I'll ask him, 'But isn't it meat?' and—but wait, you just wait, you'll see for yourself."

The professor—he wasn't a stiff, not at all, and he hadn't stopped grinning since he stepped in the door—said he'd be thrilled to see it. And his wife chimed in too. "Amazing, really amazing," she said.

They were in the middle of the meal, all of them settled in at the big table in the dining room, Josh and Elise at one end and she and Sam at the other, plates heaped, wine flowing, when Sam suddenly stood up in his chair and let out a single staccato bark. Everyone looked up, startled. *"Sam,"* she warned, taking hold of his wrist to restrain him, "Sam, no!" He broke her grip as easily as if she were a child, then sprang down and shot across the room on all fours even as Guy and Josh rose from their seats and Elise threw up her arms protectively (which didn't make any sense—Sam was no danger to her, couldn't she see that?). "Jesus," the professor said.

In the next moment, the door pushed open as if under its own power, and a stranger was standing there, an outsized man who filled the doorframe. He was in his fifties, his head shaved, his goatee gone white, and he wore a black leather eyepatch over his left eye: Moncrief. She'd forgotten all about him. And here he was, a bottle of what looked to be scotch or rum in each hand, grinning, or trying to. "Sorry I'm late," he said, stepping into the room and brandishing the bottles even as Guy called out "Donald!" and Sam shrank away from him, his hair gone limp and his eyes darting uncertainly round the room. "The traffic was a bitch—or no, that's giving it too much credit. Who doesn't love a bitch? Let's just say it was a motherfucker and leave it at that. And, shit, finding this place? You'd have to be a bloodhound."

In the next moment he and Guy were embracing and then introductions went round and Moncrief—Professor Moncrief, *Donald*—sat heavily in the chair reserved for him between Guy's and Leonard's, unscrewing the cap of one of the bottles (it *was* scotch, of a brand she'd never heard of) and pouring himself half a wineglass full. The room seemed to swell and then shrink back down to size. Everyone began talking at once and Barbara got up to offer Moncrief the platter of turkey, which Guy had carved earlier, presenting the first piece ceremonially to Sam. Who'd been perfect all afternoon. Earlier, during the salad course, Guy had put him through his paces and he'd really shone, despite the pot and the fact that he'd had a glass and a half of wine (that she knew of—he often snuck sips from unattended glasses, so she could never be sure), fielding direct questions from the professor and his wife and answering fluently in sign. But all that had changed the minute Moncrief stepped into the room and she couldn't imagine why—normally he'd be right in people's faces, especially here, at home, where he could assert himself, but instead he'd crept under the table and pulled himself up into her lap, where she wrapped her arms around him and held him like the big baby he was.

She was thinking about dessert—pie, coffee and Baileys, the peach ice cream that was Sam's favorite—but couldn't very well get up and start clearing away the dinner plates while Moncrief was still eating. He dug right in, without ceremony. He ate enormously, obliviously, talking all the while, his subjects ranging from the obvious—chimps—to deer hunting, Cessna aircraft and folk music (at one point, he'd turned to her and asked if young people had ever heard of Phil Ochs and she had to admit that she hadn't). When finally he pushed his plate away, he pulled a half-smoked cigar from his shirt pocket, asked, "Anybody mind?" and lit it without waiting for a response.

One puff, two—he threw his head back and blew the smoke out over the room and the conversation fell off so that she became aware of the record again, a string quartet Guy had introduced her to, Debussy or Ravel, she couldn't remember which. She was just about to ask if anyone would like dessert, when he looked directly at her—at Sam, in her lap—and said, "So this is him, is it? The famous talking chimp. The TV personality." He turned to Guy. "*The Tonight Show*—anything ever come of that?"

"Not yet." Guy looked flushed, as if he'd had too much to drink, which, she realized in that moment, he had. "But we're close—it could happen anytime. I'm just waiting for a call."

"I don't know," Moncrief said, "I'm of two minds about it. Cheapens what we're doing, actually, as if we're not psychologists but hucksters—let's see the ape jump through the flaming hoop and parse sentences at the same time. But it draws attention. Nothing like the tube for drawing attention." He waved his hand in dismissal, took another puff of the cigar. "Not that it matters. Not anymore."

"What do you mean?" Guy leaned heavily into the table, propped up on both elbows. His wineglass was empty. His plate shone viscidly with the remnants of the meal, butter, grease, gravy. "You're not saying everybody's not a hundred percent behind this, are you? Because we are on this end, I can assure you of that. And Sam. Sam's making progress like you wouldn't believe—"

"I'm not saying shit. But if you want to know, this whole thing—language studies—is dead in the water, or about to be. You hear what Borstein, that fuck, is up to? He's saying it's all a fraud, that Chomsky was right all along—only humans are programmed for language and the apes don't have a thought in their heads except to suck up to us. For treats. Like trained seals. Or lapdogs. Or anything else with a brain bigger than a snake's. And he's going to publish in *Science*. It's a fait accompli. Nail in the coffin."

Everybody began to talk at once. Sam fidgeted in her lap. Her heart was pounding. "That's not true," she said, and somehow her voice was the one Moncrief picked out of the mix.

"You don't think so?" he said, fixing a hard look on her. Rumor had it that his left eye had been gouged out by an enraged chimp when he'd gotten careless and drifted too close to its cage one day, but Guy insisted it wasn't true—he'd been in an auto wreck when he was a teenager. She saw now that there were faint pink striations running across the bridge of his nose, under the patch and out the other side of it. "Sam," he said, his voice harsh and insistent, "are you a fraud? Do you know about death? History? DNA and heredity? Do you know why you're the prisoner and we're not?"

Guy said, "*Donald*, you know that's not fair—"

Moncrief ignored him. He just stared at Sam, and Sam, his eyes round and unblinking, stared back. "Talk to me, Sam," he said. "Come on, Sam, talk to me."

BLACK BUG

When he woke he was back in the CAGE and nothing had changed except the floor was damp, which made it even colder. There was heat, though, blowing through a vent in the hallway, and that was better than the ICE outside, better than what had happened to his fingers and toes that were numb all the same and whether he'd gotten frostbite or not he didn't know because he didn't know what frostbite was. PAIN, that was what he knew. Anguish, he knew anguish too, though he had no word for it. He was lying on his back, staring at the place in the ceiling where the pipe had been, and he didn't want to move, didn't want to push himself up, didn't want to exist. He saw faces in his mind, hers first, then Guy's, then Barbara's and Josh's, then the others, and then they all blurred and condensed as if whirling on a wheel that spun faster and faster.

Finally, he pushed himself up. He ached in his joints, in his back.

His elbows were frayed. There was a lingering PAIN where the dart had gone in, the prick of a pin, a sore spot. The floor was hard. Everything stank. But something was different—he felt it before he saw it—and then he turned his head and his heart froze: there, not three feet from him, was one of the BLACK BUGS, not in its own CAGE but in his. A silent shriek of panic jolted through him. What was this? How had it happened? What did it mean?

It meant punishment, that was what. It meant terror, it meant payback, he saw that instantly. He wanted to scream but he didn't scream because the thing was asleep, its ribs heaving and a low growling snore chuffing from its lips. It had black HAIR all over it and its feet were naked. He saw its ugly outsized ears and the two bony white ridges over its shuttered eyes that were like paint, dirty smudges of creamy paint like when he was making a PICTURE and the paint stained his hands and without realizing it he touched his face, his brow, his own nose, and she chided him and dabbed it away. But its feet. Its feet puzzled him because they weren't at all like her feet or Guy's feet or anybody else's, except—he looked down now, took first one of his numbed feet in his hand, then the other—his own.

He studied it, this BLACK BUG, this thing, for the longest time and all he felt was revulsion, all he felt was AFRAID, and then the worst thing happened, or the next to worst thing: it opened its eyes. In an instant it was on him, shrieking, tearing, pounding, biting, and all he could do was lock his hands over his head and ball up to protect himself till it was done. Its breathing was fierce, ragged. Its chest heaved, its arms trembled. It backed off two feet and then came back at him to shriek in his face with all the hot ratcheting force of its inflamed breath. It stank, it reeked, it was filthy. And now, from all the adjoining cages and the cages he couldn't see, came the shrieks of the others, a long, sustained catastrophic din that went on and on till suddenly the door flung open and every voice choked off. The BIG MAN stood there in the doorway, scowling till the gouges between his eye and the black hole were angry scars and the stinger flicked in his hand and thumped like a baton against his leg. He came down the corridor, step by step, taking his time, in no hurry, this whole horrible blistering place of suffering and confinement at his command and his alone. He glared into the cages and the BLACK BUGS shrank from him. Yes. And then he came to this CAGE where *the* BLACK BUG had been screaming seconds earlier. The stinger buzzed to life and the man's arm snaked through the bars to anoint not the screamer, not the BUG, but him, *him*, as if he were the disrupter, the guilty one, the BUG.

GOLDEN EAGLE

She wouldn't stop sobbing. When he tried to comfort her, she pushed him away, her face raw and twisted. She was sunk into the couch, a sodden Kleenex clamped over her nose and mouth, a metallic January sun dragging chains of light across the floor. The world was crippled, everything gone wrong, and he felt like sobbing himself, but he couldn't—he was the one in charge here, if only nominally, as Moncrief had just demonstrated on the other end of the phone line from someplace in Nevada, where he was spending the night before flying on to Santa Maria in the morning at the controls of his Cessna 421 Golden Eagle, the one fitted out with two cages in the back for transporting animals.

"I didn't know," he said. "I swear." He held out his palms in extenuation. He'd known it was coming, they all did, but not *today*. That was Moncrief. That was how he did things. "Jesus, summer, that's what I thought. Or at least the end of the semester."

She lifted her face, miserable, bereaved, outraged. "It's you. You're the one to blame."

"It's Moncrief, you know that. I've told you all along—and the funding, without the funding we're nothing."

It had taken two years, but the bomb Moncrief dropped on them that Thanksgiving had finally detonated, leaving everybody scared and angry and the program in tatters. It was catastrophic, nothing short. Borstein had published his paper the previous year ("Proceeding from a Faulty Premise: The Fallacy of Primate Language Acquisition Studies") and the critics of the program jumped on board, declaring it bankrupt, a fad, wishful thinking, reiterating Chomsky's assertion that only *Homo sapiens* was hardwired to acquire language as a central inescapable fact of divergent evolution. The prefrontal cortex, which was linked to the ability to process language, was twice as big in humans as it was in apes, a fact that should have provided the answer right there and saved everybody the trouble. One Chomskyite, piling on, pronounced the whole business more suited to the circus than the university. Another called it the "Dr. Dolittle Syndrome."

Moncrief was embarrassed. And because he was embarrassed he was incensed. He'd never been all that enthusiastic about language-training from the beginning—more interested in cross-fostering as a means of exploring comparative development and sexuality—but he'd gone along with it because that was where the money was. Or had been. It was astonishing how fast the grant money dried up—not only Moncrief's, but his own too, both from the NIH and NSF, which declined to re-fund the project. And why? Because no matter how unbiased they pretended to be, people were species-centric and didn't want to believe that apes could use language—or express emotions or exhibit self-referential consciousness. If they did, then what was the rationale for keeping them in cages—or worse, using them for biomedical research? Borstein's article was the tipping point, but the antipathy had been there all along. Suddenly Borstein was a hero. He was courageous. He was a truth-teller. He'd spent five years teaching Alex ASL and according to him at the end of those five years Alex was still incapable of expressing any thought deeper than YOU GIVE ME, YOU OPEN DOOR, or his big breakthrough, NIGHT IS DARK.

"No," she said, glaring at him. "No, it's you."

"What are you talking about? It's the end of my career, my research, everything—kiss it all goodbye."

"You have tenure."

"Fuck tenure. You think I want to stay here teaching survey courses till I'm brain-dead like all the rest of them? This is my *life* we're talking about."

"What about Sam's life? Why can't you stand up to your professor—he's not God, you know."

"You're the Catholic, you ought to know. But as far as Sam's concerned Moncrief *is* God and God's flying in here tomorrow in his twin-engine plane and taking him right straight to purgatory and there's nothing you or I or anybody else can do about it. God has a dart gun too, did you know that? Tipped with Sernalyn?"

She came up off the couch so fast it startled him and she was right there, right in his face, jerking her hands back and forth as if she were swatting at flies. "Get a lawyer. Sue him. Get a writ or what do you call it, a stay—"

"Of what—execution?"

"You know what I mean. A court order, whatever. He can't just take him—not without a fight."

He'd been fighting all along, but the tide was against him. Or not just the tide, it was a tsunami. He'd rewritten his grant proposals half a dozen times, harangued Moncrief in letter after letter, begged him for more time, phoned him so often Moncrief had stopped answering.

"But he *can* just take him—he owns him, or did you forget that? And sue him? Sue him for what?"

"I don't know—breach of contract? What about breach of contract?"

"There is no contract, are you kidding me? Moncrief bred him, Moncrief owns him and he loaned him out to me on his own terms, end of story. 'Take him,' he said. 'Get your grants, do your study, but when it's over he comes back here to me.'"

"That's crap. How can anybody own Sam? It's like slavery—didn't we abolish slavery?"

"He's an animal."

"He's not. He's just like a person, you know that—he can talk, he can think, he loves us. This is his home, here with us. He's never known anything else. How can you even say that?"

"Tell it to Moncrief, who's interested in him for one thing only—breeding—and the bucks he can squeeze out of the next research lab and the one after that. Tell it to Borstein, tell it to the National Science Foundation, or what, *Science* magazine, for christ's sake. You want a German shepherd, you go to the breeder and buy one and you can do anything you want with him, feed him tender little bites of filet mignon all day or tie him to a stake and starve him to death."

She hadn't moved. She was right there in his personal space, glaring up at him, accusing him, as if this was some sort of contest as to who cared the most, as if he had to prove himself to her, and it came to him then that she was no different from Melanie. Maybe she hadn't said it in so many words—*All you care about is yourself*—but that was the implication. And who was she, anyway? A student, a tiny pretty-faced long-haired child he thought he'd been in love with, and here she was in his house, in his life, his *work*, making demands, attacking him.

"You said you were never going to let this happen, you swore to me . . ."

"Look, I hate it as much as you do, but he's six now and that's already beyond the age most of them get sent back. You know that. And he's been worse than ever lately, biting everybody till it's like we're on permanent rabies watch, and how much longer do you think they're going to tolerate that down at the hospital before they call in animal control—you really want to see him put down?"

"He's barely breaking the skin, that's not really biting, not like with Elise—"

"And that woman on her bike, what was her name?"

"Jody. But that was nothing, I talked her out of it. She's like a friend now, she understands, she does."

Sam had got out a month or so back, something he was doing more frequently lately no matter how closely they monitored him, and this time he'd gone nearly a mile and wound up sitting in the middle of the sidewalk in a residential neighborhood at two in the afternoon when everybody thought he was upstairs in bed, asleep. A woman in her forties—Jody—who was on her way home from an art class, saw him sitting there in his overalls and T-shirt, looking lost and forlorn, and so she propped the bike up on its kickstand and came up to him chirping endearments as if he was a lost dog. She crouched down at his level, looked him in the face. "You look lost, little guy," she said, or some such, and when she reached out with the idea of checking his pocket for ID or a phone number to call, he took hold of her wrist. Just that. He didn't threaten her, didn't bite, just held her by the wrist. An hour later, he was still holding her, and no matter what she did he wouldn't let go—or he would, but just for a second at a time, as if it was a game, only to snatch her arm back as soon as she tried to get away. If it weren't for a pair of ten-year-olds on their way home from school who raised the alarm, Sam might have been sitting there with her all night long. Chimp humor. No damage done. But Leonard was furious and even the dean got involved after the story—"Talking Ape Keeps Local Woman Prisoner"—appeared in the newspaper.

"You know what I'm saying—as much as you love him, as much as *I* love him, we can't keep him here forever. And the cost. I can barely pay the bills as it is and, believe me, we are on the last dregs of the grant money and there's no more coming, at least not that I can see right now. Maybe things'll change, I don't know, but for now maybe this is the best way."

"What way? Putting him in a cage?"

He shrugged. He felt tired in an essential way, deeply, unconquerably tired. Nearly six years of drama, of catering to an infant who never grows up, of Leonard, the dean, Melanie, Moncrief—and now her, her too.

"I hate you," she spat, and she lurched away from him, furious, slamming her hand down on the first flat surface she came to, which happened to be the end table, piled high with Sam's books. The table rocked, and the books, which had been stacked haphazardly—by Sam—thumped to the floor, one after another, like a cannonade.

And then, all at once, Sam was there, as if he'd materialized out of nowhere. He let out a bark of alarm, rose to his full height and waded into the room, his hair standing erect. He looked first to Aimee and then to him, then back and forth again, before he went to her, and not for a hug, not for a piggyback or a kiss, but just to stand there, right in front of her, immovable, rigid, his eyes shielded in a hard glaze of light.

It was all coming down too fast and he hadn't really had time to sort things out yet, except to know that he'd exhausted his appeals— and that Moncrief was the alpha male in this particular configuration of things, which forced him into the subordinate role whether he liked it or not. And he didn't like it, even if he saw the necessity of it. *Do not fall in love with your subject.* Or your student assistant, for that matter.

Aimee was inconsolable. Fierce. Frantic. Unable to do anything but cling to Sam and pet him over and over till he got bored and went careering round the house as if he were trying to catch up to some phantom of himself. She kept saying she wouldn't let Moncrief take him and he kept reminding her they had no choice in the matter, telling her he felt just as bad as she did, though she denied it. Vehemently. "He's my world," she said. "My whole world." He'd let it go—she was wrought up and didn't know what she was saying—but if Sam was her whole world, then that didn't leave much room in it for himself or begin to address what was going to happen when the university got around to repurposing the ranch house and evicted them.

That night, still in shock, he telephoned the people who'd been closest to Sam and invited everybody over for an impromptu farewell dinner. Josh was there in fifteen minutes, looking drawn and miserable. He kept calling it the Last Supper—"And if Sam's Jesus, then who's Judas? Lucas Borstein, right?"—as if irony could make this any better. Nobody laughed. Nobody even cracked a smile. Nobody had much heart for cooking either, but Janie and Barbara took over and managed to come up with a vegetarian lasagna—and a dessert of lime Jell-O embedded with grapes and canned pineapple especially for Sam—and everybody went through the motions, trying to pretend nothing was amiss. Sam wasn't fooled. He knew something was up, though as if by agreement they all spelled out the charged and hurtful words so he wouldn't catch on. They spelled out "Moncrief," "cage," "airplane," "winter," "cold," "Iowa." Spelled out "sad," "angry," "enraged," "fucked up." Janie cried. Barbara joined her. And when Josh offered a toast to Sam and all he'd meant to them, Guy found himself choking up too. The only one who didn't have tears in her eyes was Aimee, who'd been crying all afternoon. Now she just sat there rigidly beside Sam, her eyes gone hard and distant.

Afterward, everybody wanted a final moment with Sam, vying to amuse him, hold him, read him one last story, but most of all just to talk to him, as if to convince themselves that all the hours they'd put in hadn't been wasted, no matter what Borstein and the rest of them said. Barbara kept scooping him up and pressing him tightly to her till he wriggled free and bounced round the room from one person to another, reveling in the attention and stuffing himself with forbidden treats like the Snickers bars he loved to swallow, wrappers and all. Barbara chased after him till she was winded, then came straight to where Guy was slumped in one of the kitchen chairs he'd propped up in the far corner, trying to gather himself. "I can't believe it," she said, looming over him, her hair a mess, her blouse hanging open where Sam had torn the top two buttons away. "It's like when I lost my grandmother last year? Or my dog, Lolly? Did I ever tell you about that?"

She was drunk. They all were. How could they not be?

"But this is worse, way worse. It's like if I ever had a kid and, I don't know, the Nazis or somebody came and took him away? You know what I mean?"

He was trying to be patient, trying to get through this for everybody's sake, trying to be professional about it, but all he felt was the cold drop of doom. The program was dead. His career was dead. He had a book almost completed, but where was he going to publish it? Where was he going to live even? Some shitty apartment in faculty housing? And what about Josh's dissertation? What about Barbara? What about *Aimee*?

"You think there's a chance we can get him back? Or could we at least, I don't know, go there and visit him? Where is it, again, Iowa?"

He leaned back in the chair, reached for his glass—cognac, he was finishing the cognac somebody had left behind because what was the point in keeping it around now?—and took a long slow sip so that he could taste the fire of it on his lips and tongue and all the way down his throat. He was a professor. Barbara was a student. He needed to be rational for her sake—and for his own too. She might not have been a natural fit at first but she'd stuck it out and she was as devoted to Sam as any of them. He felt for her. But of course he felt for himself too because he had so much more to lose.

"That's up to Dr. Moncrief," he said. "But Sam's too old for this now, I don't have to tell you that—who knows, maybe someday when all this dies down, we could start all over again, with a new chimp."

"I don't want a new chimp. I want Sam."

"Yeah," he said, "I hear you," and poured himself another drink.

And then, when everybody had said their farewells and headed out into the grip of a stale moonless night, Aimee stood up, put on her hooded sweatshirt, slung her purse over one shoulder and took Sam's harness down from the coat tree in the front hall. "What are you doing?" he asked.

"Sam," she called, averting her face. "Want to go for a walk?"

Sam had been in the kitchen, rattling plates around in the sink with the faucet open wide, his version of helping with the dishes. Now he came scraping into the room, glutted and looking sleepy. His bedtime was eight and it was already quarter of nine.

"A walk? At this hour?"

"Sam," she said, holding out the harness to him. "Come on."

"With your purse? What do you need your purse for if you're just taking him out in the yard?"

"I don't know," she said, and she wouldn't meet his eyes, bending now to help Sam into his harness, elbows jumping, hands in motion, all business.

She was so transparent, an innocent, a true innocent. In that moment he fell in love with her all over again. "You can't just take him, you know. What would you do with him? Where would you go? A motel?"

"I'm not. I'm just going out to his tree, that's all."

"You know what he'd do to a motel room? Jesus, I can't believe you. And Moncrief. He doesn't give a shit for your feelings or mine or anybody else's, least of all Sam's. He'd be on you in a heartbeat. You know what Sam is to him? Ten thousand dollars. Period."

She glanced up at him. Sam let out a soft grunt. There were food stains around his mouth, a dribble of red sauce on his chest. He was motionless, quiet, bent docilely to receive the harness, no different from a dog awaiting the leash. "I'm just taking him to his tree," she said.

Moncrief called from the airport first thing in the morning. "We're here," he said. "No glitches, no weather, which is a real fucking novelty for this time of year." There was a pause, noise in the background, voices, a loudspeaker. "I'm going to need you to pick us up at the airport. ASAP. And you can give him the drug now."

"Now?" He was standing in the kitchen, stirring sugar into a cup of coffee, the phone pressed to one ear. It was early yet and Aimee was still upstairs with Sam, asleep. "You mean you're not even going to spend the day?"

"I haven't got a day. What I've got is thirty-nine animals to maintain and a wife who's a pain in the ass and a bunch of grad students who might be brilliant as all hell but don't seem to understand a simple command delivered in plain declarative English."

He could feel his heart going—this was too soon, he wasn't ready. He'd pictured it for months now, dreaded it, denied it, fought it, and finally made his peace with it, but now that it was here all he could think was to stall. "Won't you be exhausted? You just flew out yesterday, right? All that way?"

"I've got Jack with me. Jack Serfis? He's one of the few grad students who actually knows his ass from a hole in the ground—he's got something like fifteen hundred hours of flight time, so I can conk out on the way back if I want to. Which I don't. You might find it hard to believe but I relish the time I get to spend in the air."

He didn't know what to say to this. His only experience was with commercial airliners, which was stressful enough—and exhausting in a way that went beyond the purely physical. He'd had window seats once or twice, but the novelty of looking down on the clouds only took you so far.

"But listen, enough already," Moncrief said, his tone shifting abruptly. "Dose him and get on down here. We're on a tight schedule."

The phone went dead but he just stood there gazing out into the yard until it began beeping and he crossed the room and put it back on the hook. There were stains on the counter, a pile of dishes in the sink where Sam had left them. The room smelled faintly of him, of his secretions that seemed to overpower any shampoo they used on him, a ghost odor, and how long would the house smell of him once he was gone? A week, a month, forever?

Aimee would want a cup of coffee to wake her up, that's what he was thinking, so he poured a cup and started up the stairs, his legs gone heavy on him as if he were asleep himself. When he eased open the door, though, he saw that she wasn't asleep. She was just lying there, curled up with Sam, her eyes open and her hair splayed across the pillow. Sam, mercifully, hadn't wakened yet.

"Aimee," he whispered. "Aimee, listen, that was Moncrief on the phone—he's here. I've got to go down to the airport and get him."

She didn't say anything, but her eyes told him everything he needed to know. She hadn't slept at all. Her mind had been stuck in a loop, channeling through the stages of despair, rage and surrender, the solid black squares of the windows giving way first to gray and then the hard cold transparency of dawn. Very slowly, degree by degree, she eased herself up on her elbows and shook out her hair, Sam snoring lightly beside her, hairy, slope-headed, a changeling slipped into the bed like a cuckoo in a sparrow's nest.

"I brought you coffee," he said, crossing the room and holding out the cup to her, but when she made no move to take it from him he set it on the night table and eased himself down on the bed beside her. "Look, I know this is hard, but we're going to have to wake him up and get him dressed now. And we're going to need to dose him, sooner rather than later. Why don't I go down and mix the stuff in his orange juice—or a smoothie, you think a smoothie would be better? Unless we could just inject him now while he's asleep, which would be easier, really . . ."

"Don't you dare."

He reached for her hand, but she jerked it away.

"Moncrief's waiting."

"Let him wait."

"Look, I've got to get down there. You really want to do this your-self?"

She began to cry then. "Go," she said. "Just go."

"You going to do it?"

"Go," she said.

Moncrief and his newest protégé were waiting just inside the door. The minute he pulled up, they emerged and ducked into the car, Moncrief up front in the passenger seat, riding shotgun, the student—Jack Serfis—in back. Serfis was twenty-eight, he'd been in the military, and from the look of him—dressed in a T-shirt despite the fact that it was in the low fifties, overcast, and with a breeze blowing in from the sea—his hobby was squaring up barbells on a rack. His handshake was authoritative. He said, "Sunny California," and gave a laugh.

"Minus five in Davenport when we left," Moncrief said, "and if we're lucky it'll probably rocket all the way up to minus three by the time we get back. So enjoy it while you can, Jack."

As they pulled out of the lot, Moncrief turned to him and came as close to delivering an apology as he was capable of. "This whole thing's a bitch, and I'm sorry about it, but fads come and go—and didn't I tell you from the beginning this language studies business was just flavor of the month?"

"Actually, no, you didn't." Guy loosened his grip on the wheel—he'd been squeezing it unconsciously, his knuckles gone bloodless and white. "You gave us your blessing, all of us, me, Gina, even Borstein, and we never looked back."

"You defend him?"

"I'm not defending him. I'm just saying he's wrong. And you're wrong too. Sam *can* talk, I'm telling you, and his comprehension is off the charts. We just needed more time—"

"Time for what? For him to maim everybody in Santa Maria? Tear the house down? You know damn fucking well nobody can control a chimp when they get to be his age. He belongs in a cage. Get over it."

From the backseat, Jack said, "It'll be okay, really—he'll be better off with his own kind," as if he knew anything about it.

When they got to the house, everything was still. The only car in the drive was Aimee's Caprice and there was no sound on the other side of the door when he turned the key in the locks. He called her name as they stepped into the front hall, but there was no answer. "She must be upstairs still," he said, and called her name again, feeling the faintest tick of apprehension—she hadn't done anything crazy, had she? "I'll be right down," he said, and started up the stairs.

He found her sitting in the chair by the window, perfectly motionless, looking down on the driveway. There were two backpacks at her feet, the one she'd kept in the guest room closet when she first moved in and a smaller one Sam liked to stuff with his toys and treats when they went on outings. Sam was still in bed, though his eyes were open and he was dressed now in his overalls and striped T-shirt.

"Hi," he said.

She said nothing.

"You injected him?"

She gave him a desolate look. "Did I have any choice? Do you think I wanted *him* to do it? With his dart gun?"

"All right, then," he said, "good. Thank you. But the easiest thing, I mean, at this point, is let's just get this over with, okay? I'll get Moncrief's new golden boy up here and the two of us'll carry him out to the car . . ." And then he was in motion, ducking back out into the hallway and calling down the stairs. "Jack? Can you come up here a minute and give me a hand with him? Aimee put him out already, so . . ." and he didn't finish the thought.

Sam made a heavy and awkward load, as big now as a black Lab, his weight unevenly distributed in the way of living things, and it was a trial getting him down the stairs, but then they were out the door and down the steps and laying him across the backseat of the car, his muscles lax but his eyes still open, and all Guy could think of was the primordial dream in which your phobias materialize to seize hold of you in every part of your anatomy and you can't move a muscle. He felt terrible. Like an apostate, a betrayer, the Judas Josh had been looking for. He said, "Okay, then," twice and looked round him at the little group gathered at the rear door of the car, Moncrief, Jack and Aimee, who stood there with her feet locked together, as if at attention.

"Drops," she said, "put drops in his eyes, don't forget," and she handed Moncrief a vial of Visine.

Moncrief examined it a moment in the palm of his hand, then slipped it in his pocket, before swinging open the passenger door and settling heavily into the seat. Jack slid in beside Sam, lifting his legs from the seat and laying them across his lap to make room. Aimee said, "I'm going with you," and Moncrief, glancing over his shoulder, said, "Sorry, no room."

"I'm small, I can squeeze in."

"Sorry," Moncrief repeated.

"Then take this," she said, handing him the smaller backpack.

"What's this?" he asked, glancing up in surprise.

She was trying to keep herself together, Guy could see that. Her eyes were red-rimmed, her shoulders bunched in defeat and resignation. "His clothes," she said. "His toys. Treats for the trip."

A long moment elapsed, the sun breaking through to illuminate the scene in a single burst, like a flashbulb, even as one of the ranch's proprietorial jays flashed its wings and shot by with a screech of fear or warning or simple equanimity, screeching because it could. The air smelled of rain. Sam stared at nothing. Aimee looked as if she were drowning, three feet under and all the oxygen gone from her lungs, and he wanted to intervene, wanted to say something, but he didn't. Finally, Moncrief shifted all the way around in the seat till he was facing her. He lifted the backpack in one hand, as if weighing it, then handed it back to her. "He won't be needing this," he said. "Not anymore."

TWO

TWO

HE CURLED UP

He curled up. He whimpered. Whimpering, he fell away into the core of himself. He rocked on his heels. Pulled out his hair. Refused their food all over again. The BUG, the greedy misshapen stinking BUG, ate his portion, champing its teeth and grunting with pleasure, then shitting on the floor till the two came with the hose and shot it down the drain. There was all that and he endured it, terrified, distraught, unable to sleep or think or stop the racing of his heart, but the BUG didn't make a move to attack him again, as if the terms had been settled once and for all. And yet now he wanted it to attack him, to punish him so that the physical HURT would rake through his veins and override everything else. There it was, right there, watching him, but he wouldn't look at it because looking at it, whether it was eating or sleeping or just squatting over its haunches gazing stupidly out on the hall without knowing or caring that the DOOR was there—KEY LOCK OUT—was hurtful in a way he couldn't have expressed whether he had the vocabulary or not.

What he had was the information delivered to him by his senses. He smelled the thing, heard it, and when it was asleep he even crept up and tentatively touched its shoulder with a single trembling finger, but most of all, what it was came to him through his vision—he saw its every detail, from its feet that were just like his to its eyes that had no whites to them to the big pale whorls of its ears. But what good was seeing? Seeing delivered the world to you but didn't show you your place in it, not unless you had a mirror, and you didn't have a mirror unless you were at HOME with her.

On the third day, he ate when they brought him his food in the morning, the BUG watching his every bite while the BUGS in the other cages hooted over their own portions and the fans blew heat and nobody opened the door to the cold dead world outside. If he could get outside again, out of this CAGE, out of that DOOR, he would do it without hesitation, whether the DOGS came for him again or the COLD ate at him till the whole world stopped like the broken clock on the inside of her car, the one that didn't move no matter how many times—or how hard—your finger tapped it. But he couldn't get out, though when they came with the food and shoved it through the slot at the bottom of the steel door he looked for any advantage he could gain even if it meant grabbing one of them by the wrist or ankle and holding on till something changed. That didn't happen. Restless, he pushed himself up and climbed the bars over and over again, his fingers and toes abraded by the diamonds of steel mesh welded across the face of them, and then he got the idea of bracing himself in the upper corner for minutes at a time, a feat of strength and will. He looked down at the BUG, which hooted at him, and he scratched at the ceiling in the hope of uncovering another pipe, more water, more cold and wet and OUT. In the intervals he dropped down to crouch in the corner across from the BUG, watching it while it watched him. At some point, he fell asleep, and when he woke it was right there beside him, tranquil, silent, its fingers probing his hair and finding things it fed into its mouth and ground between its teeth. He didn't move. Didn't resist. Very gradually, so gradually he was barely moving, he turned round and worked his own fingers through its hair—*her* hair—and felt his heart slow for the first time since they'd brought him here.

The immemorial odor, the throb of the blood—she was a she. He withdrew his hands and her eyes flashed open. I AM SAM, he signed.

Nothing. She just stared.

I AM SAM, he repeated. WHO ARE YOU?

The touch of her hands—it was like *her* touch when she groomed him. She dropped her eyes. Her hands worked, smoothing, massaging, picking.

I AM SAM, he signed, though she wasn't looking. PLEASED TO MEET YOU.

THE ROAD

The road cut a hard, unwavering line across the desert, nothing but wilted scrub as far as she could see, creosote, yucca, saltbush, ocotillo, all of it bleached of color and narrowly suspended between life and death. The radio faded in and out and when it did come in strong Jesus would be right there in your face—and not the Jesus she knew, not the Jesus of Bach and Handel and the scented candles on the altar, but some dirt-scrabble country version boring right into you until you hit the button and the cowboy music came blaring up out of nowhere. She had a thirty-ounce McDonald's Diet Coke clamped between her thighs, though it was mostly dregs now, and on the seat beside her was the crumpled grease-stained bag that had contained her two Filet-o-Fish sandwiches, which she'd eaten while easing past long undulating lines of big rigs, wiping the grease on the balled-up napkin in her lap, careful to keep one hand on the wheel and her eyes on the road. She'd left the ranch minutes after they took Sam away and she hadn't said a word to Guy about her intentions, not that she'd had a chance—they'd all just got in the car and left her there, as if she meant nothing. She didn't leave a note either.

She'd packed up her things at the ranch and went directly home, to Calabasas, dug her winter clothes out of the closet in her room—boots, sweaters, gloves, fleece-lined coat—raided the refrigerator and lifted the Fidelity folder with her name on it out of the filing cabinet in her mother's home office. Her mother wouldn't be happy about that when she discovered it—the account, which had been set up with the settlement after her father's death, was earmarked for her education and then, when the time came and she settled down and got married, to put a down payment on a house. She didn't leave a note at home either. No need. A note would only complicate things. And when her mother got back from work, distracted and exhausted and thinking only of her first vodka and soda, she might not even notice that Aimee had been in the house at all—and the Fidelity folder? It could be weeks, months, before she realized it was missing. And so what? So what if she did? It wasn't her money.

She could have stopped in Las Vegas (cheap motels, cheap buffets at the casinos, free drinks if you were gambling or at least pretending to), but she didn't. It wasn't even five hours from Calabasas and she had to make time because all she could think about was Sam locked up in a cage without his toys or his blanket or anybody who cared about him in the slightest degree. He would be terrified. Disoriented. In despair. She couldn't imagine what he was going through—it would be like being abducted as a child from your parents' house and waking up in a jail cell in some foreign country where they didn't speak your language and all you could do was cry till you gagged and then cry all over again. Somewhere along the way there was a McDonald's drive-up window and somewhere beyond that a rest stop where she could ease the pressure on her bladder and fill up an empty gallon milk jug with tap water and keep on going. She passed Ute, Moapa, Mesquite, and Bunkerville and crossed into Utah, running on adrenaline—and anger, that too. Guy had just rolled over and let them do what they wanted—and with what, a *day's notice*? He was spineless, that was what he was, a shit, a coward. He could have stood up to them, could have done something—and the look on his face when he got behind the wheel, slammed the door and put the car in gear as if he was just going down to the post office or the supermarket. *Jesus!* He was cold, that was what he was, cold and remote and self-important. He didn't love her. Or Sam either.

It was dark now, the headlights pulling her along like two ghostly arms, trucks heaving and rattling beside her, the sleek humped forms of cars sluicing out of the night, taillights flowering and receding, the radio barking and chirping and fading into static: she was exhausted. Last night had been the worst night of her life and if she'd slept at all it was in snatches only. Oblivious, Sam had conked right out and slept as if he'd already been darted, not turning over once or even twitching or kicking his legs in his sleep the way he usually did, and she'd lain there beside him, stroking him over and over till the light appeared in the windows. Then it was a two-hour drive south to Calabasas and after that the numbing rush of all the mileposts and signage and the vast draining desert emptiness that finally closed down under the lid of the night. She wanted to make it to Green River, which was something like ten and a half hours from Calabasas, but didn't know if she could. She'd begun to nod and snap awake again—and what good would it do Sam if she died in a fiery crash like her father before her? She kept looking for a turnout, anyplace where she could just stop and get out of the car, if only for a minute . . .

Finally, after drifting off and jerking herself back to consciousness twice in as many minutes, she saw the distant glow of a truck stop like a flying saucer set down in the night, spread wide and hazy with light, and willed herself to reach it. The radio scratched at her, the tires hummed along with it, and then she was there, pulling into the lot, feeling as drained and exhausted as she'd ever been in her life. She thought she might stretch out across the backseat for a few minutes—or maybe an hour, only an hour—but the parking lot was alive all around her, men in caps and wide-brimmed straw hats swinging down from big rigs, lone drivers pulling up on either side of her, headlights going on and off, and she didn't feel safe. Plus, it was cold and she didn't even have a blanket, let alone a sleeping bag. She sat there a long moment, holding her face in her hands, then crossed the lot to the coffee shop and ordered a large coffee, black, to go—and everybody was looking at her, every man, they were all men, staring—picked up a bag of Doritos and two Slim Jims for nourishment, gassed up and hit the road again. GREEN RIVER, a sign read, 150 MILES. She could make that. Couldn't she?

The next two hours were a blank, the road, the headlights, the trucks, the cars. Somewhere in the mix was the exit for Green River, and she took it. There wasn't much to the place—it was more a crossroads, really—but there was a Motel 6 just off I-70, which was going to have to fit her budget, at least till she got to Iowa and could open up a bank account and find someplace to live and get down on her knees and beg Moncrief to let her work on his chimp farm, and she'd do it without pay, do anything, clean cages, haul garbage, mop the floors, as long as she could be near Sam. That was the extent of her plan and to summon it now, to say "Sam," even silently, even to herself, made her stomach clench. It was just past eleven when she pulled into the motel lot, but when she got there and saw the brightly lit office and the woman—the night clerk—framed there in the window, she hesitated. She'd never checked into a motel in her life, not alone. What would the woman think—that she was a prostitute or a drug addict or something? And what would she say to her—*I want a room? A single? Just for tonight?* Yes, of course, *I want a room*, simplest thing in the world.

But then why was she still sitting in her car, still clutching the wheel, though she was so wiped she could barely hold her head up?

She battled herself and she might have sat in the car all night if the woman hadn't stepped outside for a smoke and seen her there. The woman was old—or *older*—and wore her hair like her mother did, feathered in the Farrah Fawcett style, and that made her seem a whole lot less threatening because all at once she was thinking of the beauty parlor, the sedative snip of scissors and the drowsy hiss of hair spray, and so when the woman said, "Can I help you, honey?" she said, "Yes."

Too tired to shower or even turn on the TV, she just threw herself down on the bed and slept straight through till the window beside the door turned gray. Then she gassed up at the Conoco, got a foam cup of coffee and a package of powdered doughnuts at the convenience store attached to it (no hassles, no penetrating looks, just *Thank you and here's your change*) and was back on the road by eight-thirty. She found a decent radio station out of Colorado Springs, the weather was clear and the mountains rising up before her and she was sailing right along, too numb to think about anything but Sam and the urgency that was driving her to get to him and worry about the details later, when all at once the car started acting up. The engine revved all on its own with a high ratcheting whine, then dropped down again whether she had her foot on the gas or not, and that scared her, terrified her, because if something was wrong with the car she was defeated before she'd even begun, and what was she going to do, hitchhike to Iowa?

She was trembling by the time she got to the next exit—Glenwood Springs, a town she'd never heard of, but then why would she?—and managed to coast into the first gas station she saw, the gears slipping so badly it felt as if she had no power at all. The mechanic was a guy with long blond hair and a Pink Floyd T-shirt who wasn't much older than she was. She could see that she made an impression on him, that he wanted to please her, to hit on her, and that shamed her the way it always did with strangers but she smiled back at him and did her best to play along, utterly at a loss. He drove the car into the bay, revved it, shifted the lever from low to drive a couple of times, then got out, lifted the hood and checked the transmission fluid. Dipstick, that was the word. The dipstick was wet with a viscous pinkish fluid that was like the blood of the car, and that was a good sign, wasn't it? He didn't say. Just shoved the stick back in place, then reached in the driver's window and killed the engine. "I see you got California plates," he said.

She was standing just inside the door. There was a tire rack, another car up on the lift next to hers, a worktable, tool chests, hoses. Everything smelled of cold grease. The phrase "lube job" came in and out of her head for no reason she could fathom other than the circumstances—she didn't even know what a lube job was, but maybe that was it, maybe the car needed a lube job. She did her best to work up a smile. "Uh-huh," she said, nodding.

He gave her a quick look, up and down, the look they all gave her. "Because I hope you're not planning on getting back there anytime soon—"

She took a deep breath. She wanted to cry. Or maybe shatter, just shatter into brittle little fragments somebody could sweep up and toss in the trash.

"The transmission's shot, that's my call. I can order you a new one, or, if you want to save on the expense we can get a rebuilt one out of Denver, which'll be just as good, really, but either way it's going to take a few days."

"A few days? But . . ." and she trailed off. She didn't have a few days—she didn't even have a few hours. She saw Sam then, huddled in a cage, terrified, depressed, refusing to eat. Chimps suffered from depression, no different from people. Some had even died from it.

"I'm guessing you don't have anybody you know around here?"

She shook her head.

"Okay," he said, "maybe we get lucky, and maybe—and I haven't looked at it yet, really—you can get by with a flush, but I'm sorry to say from the sounds of it, you're going to be here for a while."

And then another thought occurred to her. "How much?" she asked, aware that she was at his mercy—all single women were at the mercy of mechanics everywhere, no matter what, that was an axiom, that was life, but this was in a class all by itself and she was sure he could see the desperation in her eyes.

He gave her half a smile, a lifting of the lip on one side to show off a gold crown there. "There's labor involved—these things can be a bitch—and we have to see if we can find you a transmission, which shouldn't be a problem, really, but as I say, maybe we get lucky." He paused. "Anyway, you come back after lunch and I'll have an esti-mate for you. In the meantime, if it turns out the way I think it's go-ing to, I can recommend the Starlite Motel?" He turned and pointed up the street. "Three blocks straight on and then a half block up on your left. And right next to it? You've got the best Chinese food in the world." He paused and his grin widened. "Unless you want to go up to Denver, that is."

She wasn't hungry. And even if she was, she was too wrought up to eat. The mechanic—his name was Jules Wanner and he worked with his father, who owned the shop, Wanner's Auto Repair—had given her the bad news when she came back two hours later after poking aimlessly around town and nursing a coffee she didn't really want at Dunkin' Donuts, just to get out of the cold. She needed a new trans-mission. He'd located one in Denver and he could go up there, get it and install it for her by Thursday maybe, five hundred bucks out the door, delivering the news as if he were giving her a box of bonbons. It was Monday. She had maybe a hundred dollars on her, but what she could do was open an account at the local Bank of America with the Fidelity funds and then transfer the account to the local branch in Iowa when she got there. "I guess," she said.

"You guess?"

She couldn't look him in the eye. She hated this, the whole trans-action, the feeling that she was agreeing to some kind of pact of which auto repair constituted the smallest part. "All right," she said, because what choice did she have? "Yes."

"Okay, great. I'll send Luis up there first thing in the morning—he's my main man? And if you need a place to stay, there's the Starlite I mentioned, but also, if you want, I mean, I've got a fold-out couch at my place, and it wouldn't be any trouble at all—I'd even buy you some Chinese. You like Chinese?"

He wasn't bad-looking and he might have been a nice guy for all she knew, just trying to be friendly, just trying to be helpful, but the situation was right out of a slasher movie and she just shook her head no and ducked out the door. She went in the direction of the motel he'd told her about, just in case he was watching—and he was, she knew he was—but once she was out of sight, she turned up a side street and doubled back in the direction of Dunkin' Donuts and the motel she'd noticed earlier just across the street from it. And here came another ordeal, checking in while the man behind the desk who she wouldn't even look at tried to make small talk and she just nodded and murmured and paid cash and locked herself in her room. She flipped through the channels on the TV for an hour or so before she thought of the bank, which would be closing soon, wouldn't it? On a Monday?

She tore the map out of the phone book and found her way to the bank, which was open still, a small miracle, but the woman in new accounts told her it would take five business days—that is, till *next* Monday—before the funds would clear, and that was the final blow. She wouldn't be able to pay for the car, or the motel either. It was all she could do to murmur, "Thanks, anyway," and push herself up out of the chair. It was getting dark. There was a wind. Her coat—all her things except the backpack—were in the car and the car was at the garage and if she went to the garage Jules would ask her if she wanted Chinese and she didn't want Chinese or anything to do with him till she picked up the car and drove out of here—but how was she going to do that with no money?

She called her mother, collect, from the phone booth out front of the motel. She couldn't stop shivering. There was graffiti on the inside of the glass, the usual sort of thing, crude drawings of penises and testicles and women's naked torsos, and beyond it, the soft declining light of a town she'd never even imagined before, cars cruising by, traffic lights flashing their colors, stringy clouds hovering over the rooftops like tears in fabric. Her mother answered on the second ring.

"Hi, Mom," she said, after the operator had asked her mother if she'd accept charges and her mother, in a puzzled voice, had said yes.

"Collect? What's up? Where are you?"

"I don't know. It's kind of a long story? But"—and here she broke down, here it all came out of her, here she started crying, which she'd told herself she wasn't going to do—"they took *Sam*."

"What do you mean? Who took him?"

"Guy's professor?"

"*Guy's* professor? I thought *he* was the professor?"

She sniffled, wiped her nose on her sleeve. "His old professor? Dr. Moncrief? The one in Iowa?"

"Don't tell me that's where you are? Iowa? What's in Iowa?"

"Sam."

"And you're doing what, trying to get him back?"

"I don't know," she said. "I don't know what I'm doing. But I need your help"—and here she almost lost it again—"okay? Because the car broke down. In someplace called Glenwood Springs? In Colorado? And I'm going to need the money to fix it . . ."

"Is Guy there, is he with you?"

"No."

"Well, what does he have to say about all this?"

"He doesn't know—I just got in the car and left when they took Sam to the airport, because he was part of it, he didn't stop them, he didn't even try—"

"Wow, honey, Jesus, this is really coming out of nowhere. All this because of a pet chimpanzee?"

"He's not a pet. And he's the most important thing in my life—he *is* my life, and I'm his. Don't you get it?"

"Actually, no. And where are you going to live, what are you going to do for a job, because I thought you were on track for your degree and making at least decent money and Guy was a big part of it—or was I wrong? Aren't you two a couple? Didn't you tell me that?"

"I don't care about any of that. I just need to get to *Iowa*."

There was a moment's silence and when her mother's voice came back over the line, her tone had shifted. She said, "Okay, honey, okay. I'm here for you. Just tell me how much you need and where I can wire it—you know where I can wire it?"

"I don't know. I never, I mean—"

"Usually it's Western Union. They do it in places like Rite Aid—is there a Rite Aid there?"

"I don't know."

"Okay, listen, you find out and call me back—or no, why don't I call you because this is costing a fortune. Are you at a phone booth? Okay, give me the number. And what about tonight—you have a place to stay? Pick someplace safe, like Best Western or—"

"I'm okay," she said.

After she hung up, she realized she was starving, nothing on her stomach all day but the coffee and powdered doughnuts she'd got that morning in Green River when she was still suffering under the delusion that her car was going to get her to Iowa. She stepped out into the cold wind, and she couldn't tell whether it was blowing up from the plains or down from the mountains, not that it mattered—it was wind. And it was cold. She walked two or three blocks, pinching the collar of her jacket, passing up McDonald's in favor of Burger King, just to mix it up, and yes, when she got to Iowa she was going to eat salad, nothing but salad, for a week. Nobody paid any attention to her—she was just another customer at the counter of a fast-food restaurant—and she could have sat in a booth and taken her time, but after the day she'd had she just wanted to disappear and decided to take her two cheeseburgers and fries back to her room. And instead of her usual Diet Coke she thought she'd go up the street to the 7-Eleven and get a six-pack to soothe her while she worked her way through the TV channels and tried to forget where she was and put off calling Guy till she got where she was going before he could protest or berate her or try to talk her out of it.

She picked Coors because she was in Colorado and figured she'd give a nod to the local brew, though beer wasn't really her thing—she'd got used to Guy's pinot noir and the gin and tonics she drank with Sam and Guy and whoever else was around, Josh, Barbara, Sid, Janie, almost every night at cocktail hour. Was she becoming an alcoholic? Did she need alcohol every day? Did she drink alone? Well, no, no and no. It was just that today had been so awful—and yesterday, and frankly, the past few weeks leading up to it and the doom that had hung over them all and sapped everybody of any kind of joy and satisfaction they could take from their work. With Sam. Who was in Iowa. In a cage. So she bought a six-pack of Coors and some nuts and potato chips and a not-too-stale American cheese on white wrapped in cellophane for breakfast and headed back out into the wind.

She'd walked a block or so, already familiar with the streets, when the traffic seemed to slow and her sixth sense told her that someone was behind her or alongside her, watching her. She heard the sound of an engine—some sort of muscle car—rumbling in low gear, but she just stared right ahead and kept on walking, clutching the food and beer in one hand, the other pinching her collar shut. "Hey," a voice called out. "Aimee!"

It was Jules, leaning over the wheel of a Charger or Mustang or something like that, a Mexican guy in the seat beside him, the passenger-side window rolled down and the car creeping along at a walking pace. She didn't know what to do, so she stopped. And the car stopped too. Jules leaned over the Mexican guy, who must have been Luis, his main man, the one who was going to get her a rebuilt transmission in Denver, or maybe he already had. "You look cold," he said. "You need a ride?"

She shook her head.

"Well, hell, we don't bite. This is Luis, by the way, who's going to be doing you a big favor first thing tomorrow morning, right, Luis?" Luis was young too, Jules' age, and he was wearing a baseball cap with an orange brim and the figure of a horse's head on the crown. He gave her a stone face and said, "Right."

She was taken by surprise, that was all, and all she really wanted to do was lock herself in her room and eat her burgers and fries and drink her beer to the accompaniment of the TV and see how deep her despair and anger went, but she just stood there rooted to the sidewalk because they were doing her a favor, kind of, even if it was a five-hundred-dollar favor, and she didn't want to just blow them off. She said, "I'm okay." Struggled for a smile. "Really."

The exhaust rumbled. Jules' face was split wide open with his grin that would have been almost like a chimp's if he could have everted his lips. He said, "Oh, come on, lighten up. What else you got to do?" He let out a laugh. "I mean, it's not as if you've got anywhere to go, right? And Glenwood Springs might not be like what you're used to in California, no movie stars here except when they stop to gas up on their way up to Aspen, right, Luis? Didn't we see Robert Redford once? Or maybe we did—it was at least a strong maybe . . ." The smile faded, came back again. "So we can't offer you any movie stars, not tonight, but how about a drink? We've got miles of pool tables and there's this one place—Marv's?—with a jukebox you could die for . . . so what do you say?"

"I'm sorry," she said. She was freezing. Her burgers were getting cold. "I'm like really tired? From the drive? And, and—" She waved a hand to fill in the rest.

Both doors suddenly swung open wide and Luis was right there at her elbow and Jules slicing around the front of the car in a quick explosion of light and Jules was saying, "Come on, just get in the car," and then, to Luis, he said, "You get in back and let her sit up front," and then he put a hand on her elbow as if to guide her and she tried to step back, step away, but bumped up against Luis, who was right there, right on her heels . . .

"No," she said, jerking her arm away, the beer swinging its weight in the white plastic bag till she almost lost her balance, and Luis, recapitulating Jules, said, "We don't bite," and now he had a hand on her other arm and she jerked that one away too.

She would have just run, just turned around, dropped her food and her beer, and run, but it was too embarrassing and the moment froze her right there to the spot, which meant that she was going to go with them whether she wanted to or not in the same way Sam— Sam!—had gone with Moncrief and his grad student and she was already telling herself it was going to be all right, they were nice guys, just trying to be friendly . . . when the patrol car pulled up to the traffic light across the street and she sidestepped them both and walked straight for it.

For the next two days she didn't leave the room at all except to go to the Western Union for the money her mother wired her and the 7-Eleven—in broad daylight—to get cheese sandwiches and microwave burritos and beer, more beer, enough beer to float her through the interminable hours shut in that room that wasn't much more than the cage they'd thrown Sam in. The TV gave her nothing, numbness only, but numbness was what she wanted. One channel even showed reruns of old shows, including *To Tell the Truth*, which was no longer on because it had outlived its time and was as lame as TV could get. She watched it, though, hoping they'd run the episode with Guy and Sam—she'd give anything to see that—but the shows were the early ones, from the fifties, with Bud Collyer as host and Peggy Cass, Tom Poston, Orson Bean and yes, Kitty Carlisle, on the panel.

On Thursday morning, right at eight when they opened, she called the garage. An older man answered—the father?—and told her that yes, her car was ready. She stuffed her things in her backpack, which were at least clean because, thankfully, there was a laundromat next to the motel, strapped it on and walked down the street to the garage. She was in a hurry, as much of a hurry as she'd ever been in, and yet when she was half a block away she began to slow down, as if unconsciously—she did *not* want to talk to Jules or even see him, though nothing had happened, really, and she might have been misreading him all along—but she steeled herself and pushed through the door of the little square box of an office behind the plate-glass window that read WANNER'S AUTO REPAIR in black foot-high letters.

The man she'd spoken to—the older man, the father—was seated in a swivel chair pushed up to a metal desk buried in paper, magazines and car parts. He looked like Jules, only an older version, with the hair gone on top of his head. He gave her that same look they all did, then smiled. "You're the little lady with the Caprice?"

She nodded.

He sat up, clapped his hands together and fished her invoice out of a tray on the far corner of the desk. "You're all set to go. We gave it a test drive and everything's fine, better than fine—your troubles are over." He ran a hand through what was left of his hair, smiled.

"My son? Jules? He worked on it himself, and I have to say he's really got the touch, puts his old man to shame. Will that be cash or credit card?"

The keys were in the car. Jules was nowhere to be seen. Luis either. She slid into the driver's seat, turned over the engine and headed out onto the highway where it gleamed and flitted and rose up into the snowcapped mountains beyond.

SEEING HER, SMELLING HER, HEARING HER, TOUCHING HER

There was no night and no day and the stink of shit burned up his nostrils and nothing happened except when the food slid through the slot in the door and he shoved past the BUG and took it and fed it into his mouth though it wasn't like any food he knew, wasn't a CHEESEBURGER, wasn't a PIZZA, wasn't SPAGHETTI. As much as anything, it was the food that impressed on him the truth of the situation. He wasn't stupid. He knew he'd been abandoned. But why that was or where he was now remained a mystery to him, an insufferable weight pressing him down and down till he was like a speck on the stony floor. When the BUG came to comfort him, he pushed her away. When the two came with the hose, he screamed at them. When the other BUGS screamed, he screamed too. But the weight. The weight kept crushing him. He pulled his hair out. He stopped eating. And then he gave up and fell into some deep place inside him, a place that was black and hopeless, where his senses were paralyzed and nothing moved in the space of his skull, not words or images or wants or needs.

He understood punishment, the concept of it, not in the sense of right and wrong, polarities that had no meaning for him, but as an assertion of dominance, like when the BIG MAN came with his stinger or he'd bitten someone at HOME because the wires snapped in him and his teeth were doing what they were doing before he was aware of it and Guy or Josh or Aimee made him go to his room and they locked him in so he could scream and rage and shatter his toys and tear his blankets until they opened the door and he could scream some more. That was BAD. He didn't like it. It made him furious. But they always came and opened the door and there was the sun riding across the high blue cloud-flecked SKY again and she petted him and she held him until whatever it was had passed. It wasn't like that here. Here was nothing, neither reason nor redemption. Here he could fling his shit at them, he could scream and rage or just slump there in a stupor and the BIG MAN would come with his stinger, anyway, come to make him HURT.

The change came as swiftly and suddenly as if he'd been darted in reverse. He heard a faint whisper leaching down the corridor, the sound of a voice weaving in and out of the grunting howling hooting racket that made up the aural tapestry of this place: *her* voice. Wasn't it? *Wasn't it?* He sprang to his feet, pressed his ear to the bars, riveted his attention. There it was again. She was here! She was coming!

And now the door flung open in a fierce blinding flash of light and she was silhouetted there, the real her and not some imposter, her in the flesh, her hips, her feet, her face, her hair, and one of the hose men with her and she was calling to him, calling his name, "Sam, Sam, Sam," even as the BUG came rushing the bars to see what this was and he jerked back and slammed her so hard she flew like a ball of paper to the back of the CAGE and then *she* was there and he reached his hands to her, his lips, kissing her through the mesh and the hose man was shouting something and he didn't care.

"Sam," she said, crouching outside the bars and touching her hand to his through the slot at the bottom of the door, "I'm sorry, I'm so sorry," and she was crying, water on her face, and the BUG was hooting and all the rest of the BUGS were taking it up now, but it didn't matter, nothing mattered: she was here.

THE FIRST CONVERSATION HE HAD WITH HER

The first conversation he had with her, on the telephone from where she was staying in Davenport, could have defined fruitlessness. And circularity. It had been a week and he'd heard nothing from her, not a word, zero—she hadn't even left a note. She'd just disappeared. Her backpack was gone and most of Sam's things too, clothes, toys, even the two bags of Monkey Chow they'd begun working into his diet to prepare him for what lay ahead. That mystified him. And more than that, it pained him—to think that she didn't trust him enough to confide in him after all this time? She was hurting, he understood that, but so was he, so was everybody. Yet when he'd got back from the airport, feeling hopeless and impotent and wondering what he was going to say to her and how they were ever going to get through this, the first thing he noticed was that her car was missing—where it had stood for the past three years, as much a part of the landscape as the oaks and boulders and the cedar-shake roof of the house, was an empty space, a car-sized patch of bare earth. He told himself it could have meant anything—she might have gone to the airport to make some sort of final desperate plea, but he immediately ruled that out because he'd stayed there till Moncrief and his new golden boy had secured Sam in back, settled into the cockpit and lifted off into the air. Which was just as well because knowing her she probably would have darted out on the airstrip and thrown herself under the wheels.

His second thought was that she must have gone to the beach, to Pismo or Point Sal, to walk off her sorrows, which was something she did whenever things got too much for her—and on those occasions she pointedly didn't want any company, just got in her car and left. Or maybe she'd gone to a movie, another thing she liked to do. Alone. Especially when she was upset. But of course if that was the case, then why had she taken her things with her?

It wasn't until late that night, when she still hadn't made an appearance, that he began to envision other scenarios, though none of them took him as far as Iowa. She was too—what?—*self-effacing* to go off on her own like that, utterly unable to look strangers in the eye or assert herself because she'd turned away from the world and found what she wanted here, locked away as if in some fairy palace, with him and Sam and the supporting cast to sustain her. She must have been at her mother's (though he wasn't about to call and find out) or at an aunt's house or something. Hadn't she mentioned an aunt in Sacramento or Stockton or someplace? She had. He was sure she had. But then he'd never been a very good listener.

In the morning, when there was still no sign of her, he had the first intimation that she'd left him, that what she'd wanted all along was Sam, Sam and not him. It was crippling. Worse even than when Melanie had left him because when you peeled back all the layers this truly felt like a divorce, slash and burn, one parent getting sole custody of the child and the other left with nothing, not Carson or career advancement or even a book anybody would ever want to publish. He questioned Barbara and Josh and the others—nobody had heard from her—and as far as he could glean the aunt in Sacramento was nothing more than a phantasm, which left her mother. He'd have to call her mother.

He kept putting it off, hoping he'd been wrong, hoping she'd come walking through the door any minute and they could start all over again. He taught his classes, ate fast food, sat stoically at his desk and wrestled with his manuscript, reading the same paragraph over and over till it lost all meaning. It was the end of the week when he finally decided to make the call because there was no other place she could be and at this point it was no longer a matter of pride or wounded feelings but just simple necessity—he had to know. And then, just as he was steeling himself to dial the number—*Hello, Mrs. Villard? This is Guy, Guy Schermerhorn, the professor who*—the phone rang.

"Hi," she said, her voice so reduced it was barely there, but even if she hadn't said a word he would have known it was her.

"Where are you?"

Just a whisper: "Iowa."

He was standing there in the deserted kitchen of the deserted house, everybody gone now, Josh, Barbara, Janie, all cut loose to scramble for work/study and internships as best they could, which was going to be tough because the semester had already begun. He felt terrible about it and he'd already made some phone calls and talked to Leonard. But he was here now and they weren't—and Aimee was in Iowa, which he hadn't thought possible. He said, "How did you get there?"

"I drove."

"By yourself?"

"Well, you weren't about to come with me, were you?"

He ignored the question, which wasn't so much a question as a rebuke, the same old story he was sick to death of. He said, "What about Moncrief?"

"He said I could stay? I told him I'd work for free."

"And Sam, how's Sam? Is he freaking out? Is he depressed? Is he eating?"

"It's horrible. The worst thing in the world. They won't even let me in the cage with him and they threw away his clothes and they won't let me give him a blanket or his, his"—she began to cry then, a soft wheeze and rasp that sounded like static over the line—"his toy dog, the one we named Louie?"

A toy dog named Louie. Jesus. In that moment, he couldn't help asking himself what a stuffed toy had to do with science, with the project that had absorbed the last six years of his life, with language acquisition and the workings of the mind of another species—it was as if he was caught up in some dark absurdist comedy here, and who was the author, Beckett? Ionesco? The Marquis de Sade? He stood at the sink, peering out the window, envisioning that torn filthy spittle-soaked rag of a thing, and felt something constrict in him. Out there in the yard was the oak, Sam's oak, which had been standing there before any of them were born and would be there when they were gone. If it didn't burn first. And sooner or later everything out here burned, didn't it?

"When are you coming back?" he asked.

"When are you coming here? Sam misses you. I miss you."

"But I can't—the semester just started, you know that . . ."

"What about Presidents' Day? When's Presidents' Day? Next month, right?"

He should have said *I miss you too*, should have canceled his classes and caught the first flight out, but he didn't: there was a line being drawn here and he was on the wrong side of it. "But that's only three days—and I have a Tuesday class this semester, as I'm sure you're aware, so it's a day to fly there, one day trying to sort things out with who, Moncrief, and then a day to fly back? That's crazy."

There was a silence on the other end of the line.

"Aimee?" he said. "You there?"

"Yes."

Her voice was a scratch in his ear, an irritation, a reminder of what he'd lost, what he was losing, and yet, what if he did work up a new project? What if he went back and crawled to Moncrief and talked him into letting him set up video cameras in the chimp barn to see if the language-trained chimps—Sam, Alice, Alex—would sign to each other spontaneously, hold discussions among themselves, inaugurate a whole new chapter of ape evolution? He could take a leave from UC for a semester or even a year, apply for grants to support it, redeem himself. It only made sense, since the groundwork had already been laid—in fact, it would be criminal not to pursue it. But no. Moncrief had his chimps all to himself now and he was going to do his masturbation studies or take their babies away for his nature-versus-nurture experiments or subject them to something a whole lot darker because they were animals and he owned them and the first rule of the behavioral sciences—

"When are you coming back?" he asked again, and he was asking it out of frustration now, out of anger.

"I don't know," she said. "When are you coming here?"

His next call was to Moncrief, who answered on the first ring. "Donald," he said, "it's me, Guy," and before he could say anything more, Moncrief cut him off.

"Yeah, she's here," he said.

"I know."

"Well, shit, you ought to know—you sent her, didn't you? To what, spy on me? Make sure *Sam* gets his backrub each night and what, foie gras and Champagne? And doilies. Doesn't he need doilies too?"

"I didn't send her. She just took off because—and I'm sorry—it was the right thing to do, I mean, at least until he's had a chance to settle in."

"Pretty girl, a real eye-catcher." In the background, faintly, there was the sound of hooting. Moncrief lived in a farmhouse just down the hill from the barn he'd converted into an apery and even in winter, even with the windows closed and the wind raking the fields, you could always hear them, especially at mealtimes. "I have no problem with her working here on her own dime—I'm not fucking crazy. I can always use the extra pair of hands and she's good with the animals, which is a plus, considering what I've got to work with in the department here, a whole new crop of numbnuts who wouldn't know a chimp from a standard poodle. So yeah, sure, she can stay, if that's what you're worried about."

"No, that's not it—it's just, I don't know, I'm kind of at a loss here."

"You've got tenure, haven't you?"

"That's not the point."

"But it is. If you didn't have tenure you'd be out on your ass and there'd be nothing I could do to help you. Except maybe draft a letter. You want me to draft a letter?"

"I want to work with primates. It's all I know. It's all I care about."

"Oh, shit," Moncrief said, "not this again. Look, language projects are over, get used to it. You want to know the truth, the whole business, ape studies from A to Z, even what I'm doing with sexuality and maternal displacement, is on shaky ground right now. About the only thing the animals are good for at this point is biomed—they need all the chimps and monkeys they can get, what with AIDS and hepatitis and the boom in transplant surgery, but of course I'd hate to have to sell off my animals if I had any other choice . . ."

The phone in his hand was an ordinary receiver molded of yellow plastic and it weighed maybe six ounces, but it was all he could do to hang on to it—he'd known it was bad, but not this bad. Sell them off? Put them in a lab someplace in cages so small they couldn't even turn around? Inject them, bleed them, intubate them, open up their brains, their body cavities, transplant their hearts and lungs and livers?

"But not Sam," he said, hearing the edge in his voice as it batted round the plastic funnel of the receiver. "Not Alex and Alice and the rest of the home-raised chimps, right?"

"Look, Guy, I hate this as much as you do—and I'm not inhumane, don't you think that for a minute—but everything's fucked right now. Borstein's just the tip of the iceberg. There's a shitload of resentment out there and let me tell you all the pigeon peckers and rat counters have just been waiting for something like this. So as much as I appreciate how you feel about the animal I assigned you, you've got to realize in the final analysis he's just a number—I mean, truthfully, did I ever lead you to believe anything different?" Moncrief paused. There was a moist insuck, lips, liquid, a cup: he was drinking coffee. Or scotch. Was it time for scotch yet? Quarter of five there now, right on the cusp of cocktail hour.

"I keep unimpeachable records, you know that," Moncrief went on, "and in my records, he's number thirty-four, just like the tattoo says on the underside of his wrist. And I don't have to tell you this, of all people, but any other species, the rats, the rabbits, the dogs, the monkeys—all the monkeys, the thousands of rhesus macaques they used in the Salk thing—they just get euthanized when the study's over."

"But this is *Sam* we're talking about—"

"I know what we're talking about. And so does your little protégée, or she's going to find out soon enough. He's not a pet. He's not a human. He's back here now—with me. And you know what I'm going to do? I'm going to make a chimp out of him."

There was still half a bottle of cognac left, enough for a good drunk, and a good drunk was what he needed after getting off the phone with Moncrief. All the glasses were dirty—nobody had been around to wash them—so he put the bottle to his lips and settled in by the window while the afternoon closed down and the ridge out back went from amber to pink to stone cold gray. He wasn't a sentimentalist, or at least that's what he told himself, and yet he and Melanie had raised Sam since he was a newborn, raised him as if he were their own child, which created a bond that had more to do with human endocrinology—with love—than with science. He and Melanie had been there in the ape house like prospective parents at an adoption agency when Moncrief poked the barrel of his dart gun through the bars of the cage and darted Sam's mother, Elizabeth Reed, who was screaming out her rage because she knew exactly what was coming. She'd been named by one of the doctoral students after an Allman Brothers tune (no matter how acidly Moncrief disparaged anthropomorphizing them, nobody referred to any of the chimps by their numbers, even Moncrief himself), and she'd given birth five times, once to twins, and all five times the dart gun had been poked through the bars of the cage and the newborns taken from her while she lay there helpless, her eyes open wide. It had been disturbing, sickening, really, but he'd been so eager to get a chimp he'd deadened himself to it—everybody had birth trauma, chimp and human alike, and this was the very first moment of a revolutionary cross-fostering experiment, so the quicker Sam was acclimatized, the better.

Melanie, her face stony and bloodless, took the infant from Moncrief's arms and pressed him to her, Sam's tiny hands and feet already working, grasping, clutching at the world, the scent of Melanie's shampoo and bath soap in his nostrils, a scent no ape alive was able to give him. In the back corner of the cage, splayed out on the wet concrete where she'd pissed herself and wearing the padlocked collar that had never left her throat from the time she'd been captured in Gambia, his mother lay prostrate, her eyes burning and her breathing slower than slow, already forgotten.

And now Moncrief was floating the idea of biomed? It was beyond imagining. But really, what had changed in the past one hundred fifty years since Claude Bernard vivisected dogs in the operating theater in order to demonstrate their inner workings, aside from the fact that experiments were conducted behind closed doors? Bernard had prepared a specimen one afternoon—a dog, unanesthetized, so as not to interfere with the natural function of the organs—and then left it strapped down on the table overnight, only to resume his work on it in the morning. Lacking specimens one day, he appropriated the family dog ("The physiologist is no ordinary man," he wrote. "He is blind to the blood that flows. He sees nothing but his idea, and organisms which conceal from him the secrets he is resolved to discover"), which so outraged his wife and daughters they moved out of the house. Permanently. The wife not only divorced him, but founded an anti-vivisection society to boot, and still Bernard didn't get it. The sky was blue, the ocean was deep. Animals were animals and humans were humans. Period.

Chimps could live to be fifty and more, but once they'd been infected with the AIDS virus or one strain or another of hepatitis or had electrodes implanted in their brains or cancerous cells injected into their organs, they were damaged goods, useless for further experiments, and could look forward to spending the rest of their years on this earth confined to cages, without stimulus, without love or even the most rudimentary kind of interaction with people or members of their own species, too valuable in terms of breeding and supply-

and-demand to be euthanized. That wasn't going to happen to Sam, no matter what Moncrief said.

The room had gone dark. He couldn't see what was left in the bottle, so he gave it a shake and heard the enlivening slosh of liquid, which by this point was probably thirty percent saliva but worth finishing in any case, well worth finishing . . . After a while he got up and switched on the lamp, thinking he might want to dig out the phone book and jot down the number of the travel agent he'd used last time he flew anywhere, just as a point of reference. He got to his feet, feeling woozy—he'd intended to get drunk and here was the issue. He congratulated himself. "Job well done," he said, though there was no one listening.

Just then the phone in the kitchen rang and he went to it, clumsily, slamming a shoulder into the wall and barking his shin on the doorframe. He took hold of the kitchen counter to steady himself, lifted the phone to his ear and managed to utter something resembling "Hello?"

"Professor Schermerhorn?"

"Yeah."

"This is Amanda, Renee Flowers' secretary? Can you hold for Ms. Flowers?"

Everything in the room smelled of Sam, though Janie and Barbara had given the place a thorough scrubbing before they'd left. It wasn't a human smell and it wasn't easy to erase. Sam. The smell of Sam. He had tears in his eyes by the time Renee Flowers' voice came chirping through the receiver at him. "Professor Schermerhorn?" she said. "Guy, that is. How are you?"

He mumbled something in response, as disoriented as if he'd just been shoved out on the soundstage in front of a live audience while Johnny sat poised behind his desk, giving him his trademark grin.

"Super," Renee Flowers said. "So let me come right to the point— we've been following the controversy with your research and I want to say we're on board with you a hundred percent. Johnny's seen the tapes and he's super-enthused. What do you say to next week?"

"Next week?"

"Listen, I know it's been a long time, and that's our fault entirely, but we're ready to go if you are and we have a slot open next week. If Sam—it's Sam, isn't it? Yes. Right. If Sam is as good as he looks on tape or that time you brought him here to the studio, he's going to be a hit and I could see it spinning out from there."

"You mean like J. Fred Muggs?"

She let out a laugh. "Not exactly. Johnny doesn't need a mascot"— another laugh—"he's got Ed for that. But truly, it would be ideal if we could book this, just to see how things'll go, you understand . . . but my feeling? It's going to be super."

If he'd been drunk when he picked up the phone, now he was on the last lap of a downhill bicycle race to sobriety, everything laid out before him, wheels churning, darkness turned to light. The only problem was Sam. Who was in Iowa. In a cage. "Could we put it off a bit? A week or two or maybe three? Like till Presidents' Day?"

"Presidents' Day? What's that got to do with it?"

"Well, you see, we *are* on an academic schedule and the fact is Sam's not here right now—"

Another laugh, a trace more brittle than the last. "Well, I'm not exactly asking him to come to the phone . . ."

"No, no, that's not what I mean. It's just—we're going to need a bit more time on this end?"

She didn't have anything to say to this, but the silence over the line was the silence of disapproval, exasperation even: nobody said no to Johnny Carson.

"Renee," he said, and he was reeling, positively reeling. "Don't you worry, don't you worry at all. Whatever happens, I'll get him there."

YOU ME GO

The BUG was gone, back in one of the other cages with the rest of them, hooting mindlessly, hooting for nothing except the compulsion to make noise because making noise was the surest sign you were alive no matter what size box they put you in. The sliding door between the cages had suddenly pulled back and the BUG scuttled through it before it slid shut again and that was that, no wave GOODBYE, no his fingers in her hair, no her fingers in his. He would have gone with her, anything to get out of this place, even if it meant rushing headlong into the seething black shadows where the BUGS got progressively bigger and angrier, but for the fact that Aimee was there in front of his cage—Aimee!—and she had a HARNESS in her hand and she was calling his name. The excitement exploded in him and he rushed the bars, whimpering and pant-hooting his joy that rocketed all the higher because the previous day she'd gone back through that door and left him here in the CAGE and the depression rocked him all over again, driving him deeper and ever deeper with the thought that she was never coming back.

But now, here she was! There were two men with her, one of the hose men and the one he called ARMS who never wore sleeves on his shirts no matter how cold it was outside. He ignored them. He signed to her. Said, YOU ME GO.

Arms said, "It's your funeral," and she said, "Just open the door," and the hose man said, "If he gets loose—"

At first he just hugged her and then he held out his arms and climbed atop her back though he was too heavy for her, he knew that, and she had to put him down almost in the same moment, but still she was AIMEE and he was SAM. Then she put a JACKET on him and he worked his arms through the HARNESS and she attached his LEAD and the door swung open, even as Arms tapped his own stinger against his thigh as if he only needed an excuse to use it and she was leading him up the corridor and out the door into the world that was as devastated and bewildering as it had been when he'd got loose and gone through it all on his own. There was the FENCE, there the DOGS. They barked and then, seeing him, they both settled down on their haunches and the one he'd bitten began to whine. That was good, that was very good, because he'd bite him again, bite both of them, tear them, pound them, kill them, if they got near her or even made a move, a single move. He bristled and barked back at them and now they both started to whine.

"Okay, Sam," she said, signing it and speaking at the same time, "want to go for a walk, get some exercise? You must need exercise after they locked you up like that."

He did. And he was so happy to be OUT, with her, that he barely noticed the COLD and the way her breath froze and his too and how Arms shivered and rubbed himself and tried to make as if he wasn't bothered at all.

After a while, after they'd been around the fenced-in area over and over and walked out to the frozen lake and back, Arms said, "Don't you think it's time to bring him back?"

"Yes," she said, "yes, of course. This cold is inhuman." Then she laughed and added, "Insimian too," though he didn't catch that because the word wasn't in his vocabulary and if it was a joke, he didn't catch that either.

Arms was wearing a puffy vest but his arms were white and hairless and his lips were white and his cheeks too. He was as white as white got, but under that whiteness he was as red as meat—he was meat, they were all meat, even the BUGS, even the BIG MAN, even Aimee. Meat. Meat with faces. Meat. "Okay, then," Arms said. "Good. Because I'm fucking freezing—and he must be too."

They went back through the door in the FENCE and across the dead yellow lawn in the direction of the door in the building that reeked of shit and the BLACK BUGS and suddenly he had an intimation of what that meant and so he tugged back on the lead so hard she almost fell.

YOU ME GO, he said.

Very slowly she began to shake her head and he knew what that meant, knew it instantly, even before she started telling the words aloud. "I'm sorry, Sam," she said, her cloud breath hanging frozen in the air. And then she was signing, just to be sure he understood, her fist rotating over her heart, VERY VERY SORRY.

THE REGIMEN

Dr. Moncrief ran a tight ship. At least that was what he liked to think. The reality was different. The converted barn—the chimp barn, as everybody called it—was too cold in winter (and, as both Guy and Jack had told her, too hot in summer). It was noisy. It reeked. Sanitation was as primitive as it got—concrete floors sloping toward a central drain in each cage, a hose applied twice a day. She had no experience of anything like it, except maybe Zoo Camp when she was in sixth grade, of which she remembered little beyond the smell, which was so nauseating it made her stomach cramp and she wound up missing two days the first week while her sister, maddeningly, seemed to have little problem with it, getting to feed the animals and bond with the other kids, including a boy named Matthew McGuire they both had a crush on. But this was worse. Much worse. The first day, when she'd managed to beg her way in before she'd even gone to

Professor Moncrief to get his sanction and just approached whoever it was coming out the locked door, she almost gagged.

Outside it was so cold the air burned your lungs, but it was clean air, astringent, the kind of air she'd come to appreciate on ski trips to Squaw Valley and Mammoth, but when the guy opened the door for her and led her inside, it was all she could do to keep going. She was desperate to see Sam, to touch him, comfort him, but the stench was an ocean and she was drowning in it. Sam was there, though, in a cage with another chimp, and as soon as she saw him, he was all that mattered. Still, though she stayed nearly an hour squatting there in front of the cage (until the guy, one of Moncrief's techs, as he called them, told her she had to go because if anybody found out he'd let her in it could cost him his job), she couldn't get used to it. And that night, her first night in Iowa, when she checked into the nearest motel she could find, the room didn't smell of Lysol or air freshener or the stale smoke of its last occupant but the reek she brought in with her.

The next day she was up at first light, took a long shower and washed her hair, then put on the only nice outfit she had, black skirt, white sweater, boots, a knit hat and her ski jacket, and drove out to Moncrief's farmhouse to knock on the door and let him know she was there and available to do anything she could to help with the chimps—all of them, and not just Sam. What this cost her was nothing short of agony. She didn't want to knock on anybody's door. She didn't want to have to make speeches or ingratiate herself or show how desperate she was. She'd met Dr. Moncrief exactly twice. He might not even remember her. And he was as intimidating a presence as she could imagine, huge, big-bellied, big-headed, with a blaring whip-crack of a voice and the eyepatch that distorted his face until he didn't even look human. He was Guy's professor. He owned Sam. And he could do anything he wanted with Sam or any of the other chimps, or for that matter, with her—she was the one put in the beggar's position here. Probably the hardest thing she ever had to do in her life was walk up that path with its dirty crust of snow and dead brown skeletal shrubs, mount the steps to the porch and rap on the door that featured a brass knocker in the shape of a chimp and a dried-out Christmas wreath that might have been there from last month or the last century. But she did it. She had to. It was her only hope.

A woman in slippers with white hair and a red round face answered the door. She looked puzzled.

"Um, I—I'm Aimee?" she heard herself say as if she were watching the scene from afar.

"You want Donald. You're one of his students?"

"I guess," she said. "Or kind of."

"Kind of?"

There was the sound of the chimps drifting down from the barn, screams mounting upon screams as in the old Tarzan movies on TV, and she wondered if that meant it was breakfast time and what they were giving Sam and whether he was too depressed to eat it. "I just got here from California? UCSM? For the chimps?"

"Yes, the chimps, always the chimps." The woman—Mrs. Moncrief?—paused as if picturing them, the chimps, with their hands for feet, their multiplicity of needs and their stench, their sheer killing stench, and how did *she* deal with it? How did anybody? "Well, okay, then," she said, "come on in out of the cold and I'll see if he's around still or if he went up the hill already." The door swung open on a room paneled in knotty pine, with open beams, throw rugs, a couch, a pair of armchairs pulled up to a woodstove. The woman ushered her in and shut the door against the cold. "Because with him you never can tell," she said. "One minute he's here, the next he's gone, whether he's at the university teaching his classes or overseeing things on the hill or mixing up one of his batches of homemade chimp chow—you know he bakes all those loaves himself? His own recipe? The complete food, he calls it."

She turned away then and called out, "Donald! Donald, you here?"

and when she didn't get an answer, went to the stairway and shouted till his voice rose up in a kind of distant roar, "Yes, goddammit, what is it now?"

There was a door at the top of the staircase. Banister, runner, paintings on the wall. Ostrich feathers in a vase. A smell of air freshener— Spring Meadow, same as her mother used. Mrs. Moncrief gestured to the stairs and said, "Well, go ahead," and though each step was like climbing Everest, she steeled herself and managed to make her way up the stairs and deliver the lightest of interrogatory knocks—not on the door but the frame, which seemed somehow less intrusive. A voice called out, "Come in," and she turned the knob and pushed open the door and there he was.

If she expected him to bite her head off, that didn't happen. He liked women, Guy had told her that, and he liked to make up to them. Girls especially. Pretty girls. And she qualified, she knew that. She knew it from the way people had treated her all her life, guys especially, but she'd never been particularly happy about it and never used her looks to get what she wanted the way other girls did. It was too embarrassing. Demeaning, really, because what did looks have to do with who you really were? The fact was, she just wanted to be left alone, and half the time she wished she'd been born looking like anybody else, like Barbara or Janie or half the other girls on campus, and yes, she did wear lipstick and eyeliner sometimes—Guy had insisted on it—but it never felt right, let alone necessary or conducive to any kind of outcome she'd ever wanted. Still, the minute she walked into Moncrief's upstairs study—a big room with a view uphill to the chimp barn and the fields that stretched out to the horizon on either side of it—she knew what she had to do.

"Hi," she said, her voice caught in her throat. "I hope I'm not—"

He was seated at his desk, which was pushed up against the window, so that he had to swing round in his chair to see her. "Not what—bothering me?"

"Yes."

"Are you kidding? Christ, if nobody bothered me for a single second for the rest of my life, I'd still never be able to get through even a tenth of this shit, let alone what's piled up at school"—he gestured at the desk, which was cyclonic with books and papers and featured a framed photograph of a younger, two-eyed version of himself, his arm around a dark-haired incarnation of the woman downstairs. "So you may as well bother me. In fact, I welcome it. Go ahead, bother me all you want." He gave her a grin that tugged at the straps of his eyepatch till everything in his face seemed to tighten under the strain. His eye bulged like an egg boiled too long—not a chicken's egg, but a robin's egg, sky blue and candescent. "But aren't you that girl from California? Guy's—what, assistant? What was your name again?"

"Aimee."

"Right. Well, Aimee, I suppose you've come all this way because you want access to the chimp barn, isn't that right?"

She was poised in the doorway still, her feet pressed tightly together, as if she were standing at attention. Her shoulders ached. She was exhausted. She took a minute before she whispered, "Yes."

"You want to see if I'm like the villain out of some Dickens novel, what's-his-name, the beadle at the orphanage—or Simon Legree. You think I'm Simon Legree?" His voice dropped. "You are so naïve, girl. You're like a child. You *are* a child. No matter what you think you know, the thing I have to emphasize, if you want to go in there at all, is that everything you've known to this point you can throw out the window—that chimp barn is as dangerous a place as you've ever been in your life and those chimps are nothing like what you think."

The light in the room, winter light, reflecting off the crust of snow in the yard, was stark and cold, sharpening the angles of the beams, the desk, the legs of the chair he was sitting in. He was giving her the look they all gave her and all she wanted to do was turn around and walk out the door, but she didn't.

"What I mean is, if you want to go in there *again*."

She felt herself reddening.

"You really think anything goes on around here I don't know about? You think I'm that blind?" He winked his eye shut and let out a ragged laugh, then gave her a long reductive stare, as if to make sure she knew exactly what the parameters were. "Christian, my tech? He told me all about it."

"I'll work for free," she said.

"You don't know the half of it," he said.

He brought her in the back door, at the other end of the building from where Sam was, and the reek, if anything, was even worse here. It took a moment for her eyes to adjust after the glare of the snow, rafters overhead, the glint of metal, squared-off shapes looming up out of the gloom to solidify into cages—two long rows of interconnected cages equipped with sliding doors to integrate or isolate the chimps as the need arose. Chimps clung to the mesh all up and down both rows like convicts in the old prison movies, the low-wattage bulbs hanging from the ceiling making them appear even bigger and denser, all of them agitated and screaming. She and Moncrief stood there a moment just inside the doorway, the din catastrophic. She was on their turf now, the chimps' turf, and they didn't see her as anything other than an invader and a threat and she understood in that moment they would have torn her apart if they could. They didn't know language. They didn't know beds or toys or kitchen tables or even the most rudimentary gesture of kindness. They were in cages and she wasn't and all they wanted was to even the score.

"Shut up!" Moncrief shouted, startling her, and in the next moment he had a baseball bat in his hand and he was rapping it against the bars of the nearest cage till it was the only sound in the room. "That's right," he said, "and damn you all too. Now get down off those bars and behave yourselves."

One after the other, as if they'd coordinated it, they slid away from their finger- and toeholds and retreated to the backs of their cages.

"Discipline," he said. "Order. The regimen. They want to be told what to do just like anybody else."

She could feel her heart pounding. This was nothing like what she'd expected, but then what had she expected? Forty Sams holding out their arms for a hug? She'd never even seen an adult chimp before, except maybe in a zoo, but here they were, up close and personal. Their rage was terrifying. If they'd been lions or leopards or hyenas it would have been bad enough in such close quarters, but it was worse than that, far worse, because of the calculation in their eyes—they were people, just like people, furious, unhinged, calculating. How was she ever going to be able to work *here*? It was impossible. A nightmare.

Moncrief was watching her closely, a thin smile on his lips. "Well, what do you think of them now? Want to get in their cages and give them all a hug?" He gestured to the cage behind them in which an enormous male chimp crouched over the drainage hole, picking at the feces gathered there and studiously compacting them into a ball. "How about this one? You know this one? No? You didn't get the full tour yesterday? Okay, fine. Meet number six, Azazel. He's the dominant male"—a laugh—"but for me, that is. He's thirty-two years old, father of twelve and three times as wicked as the devil he's named for. He'd eat you alive." And then Moncrief shouted again, again startling her. "Put that down, you fucker! Put it down!"

The chimp dropped the ball of feces at his feet—on his feet, actually—shot Moncrief a sharp sudden glare, then focused on the floor as if it gave onto a distant vista only he could see.

"One of his tricks. He likes to fling shit at the techs. Can you imagine? How about your sweet little house chimp? How about Sam? Does he mold his shit into balls and fling it at people?"

The reek. The rustling in the cages. Moncrief. All she wanted was out. "I don't know," she whispered.

Moncrief folded his arms over his belly, rapping the bat idly against one hip. His voice suddenly barked out again. "You, Azazel, get over here. Now!"

There was a moment of hesitation, a fraction of a moment, and then, resignedly, his shoulders shifting like moving pillars, the chimp shuffled to the bars, the mesh, and stood there hanging his head. His skin was scarred from innumerable confrontations—fights, take-downs, tearings and rendings—and he'd plucked all the hair from his head, his face, his shoulders and arms.

"Fingers," Moncrief said.

The chimp extended his fingers through the mesh and when Moncrief whacked them with the baseball bat, first the right hand, then the left, he barely flinched. "What were you going to do with that ball of shit?" Moncrief demanded. "Huh? Azazel, I'm talking to you!"

Nothing. The entire room was silent. Azazel raised his eyes in acknowledgment and dropped them again.

"Good," Moncrief said. "Fine. Now your lips, I want your lips." The chimp withdrew his fingers and extended his pale puckered lips through a gap in the mesh, making a kissing noise as Moncrief held out the back of his hand to him. She saw now that Moncrief was wearing a ring, a gold signet ring with some sort of figures molded into the face of it—snakes, a pair of intertwined snakes with tiny rubies for eyes. The chimp kissed the ring and kept kissing it till

Moncrief finally withdrew his hand. "Now get to the back of the cage and stay there," he snapped. Then he turned to her and he was grinning again, as if all this—this cruelty, savagery—was a joke. She couldn't believe it. What did this have to do with science? Nothing. It wasn't science any more than a circus sideshow was—it was just an excuse to impose his will on something in a cage.

"You see what this is?" he asked her, the grin flaring and then diminishing again. "The regimen, discipline—if they can learn language they can learn not to throw shit at people, right? If you let them get away with it—get away with anything, even what you might think is the smallest little thing—then you're going to wind up with shit on your face." He took a breath, squinted down at her. "Or worse, blood."

By the time Guy got there—on Thursday ahead of the Presidents' Day weekend—she'd settled into a routine, five days a week working as an unpaid tech, hauling, mopping, scrubbing, shoving pans of food at screaming chimps, hosing out cages and doing anything else physical that needed to be done, the smell of the place almost unnoticeable to her at this point, testimony to the fact that you can get used to anything if you have to. And it wasn't half as bad as what the people in the hog-processing plants must have had to endure, which wasn't just urine and excrement but blood and viscera on top of it, the smell of death lingering in the cracks and the shrieks of the killing floor echoing off the walls. At least there was no killing done here—or not physical killing, anyway, the spirit too insubstantial to count in Dr. Moncrief's reckoning, which was all about submission and control and denial. Did animals even have a spirit? He asked her about that in a casual mocking tone when he came through the door one afternoon and found her crouching in front of Sam's cage, signing to him, and when she said yes, he said, "What about doggie heaven, you believe in that too?" Whether she did or not, she wasn't about to tell him, and whether or not he made fun of her she was there on her days off too—for Sam, to spend time with him, take him for walks, talk to him, comfort him as best she could, though it devastated her every time she had to lock him in the cage and go back to her rented room without him.

The second day, the day Moncrief had allowed her to take Sam for a walk even if it meant that Jack had to be with them to oversee things, Sam threw a tantrum when they returned to the building and then he absolutely refused to go back into the cage. She knew better than to try to force him—he was far stronger than she was and though he would never use his teeth on her, there was no telling what he might do to Jack. Who stood there, legs spread as if for action, tapping his cattle prod against one thigh. She crouched beside Sam at the open door to the cage, signing SORRY and YOU HAVE TO, but it wasn't until she stepped through the door herself that he got up and followed her in, even as Jack lunged forward to swing the door shut behind them. To calm him, she began grooming him, but every time she tried to get up and leave he took hold of her wrist and wouldn't let go, just like that time with the woman on the street, Jody, but she wasn't Jody and he'd never done anything like this before. "No, Sam," she told him, "let go," but it was as if the words had no meaning. This went on for five or ten minutes before Jack said, "Look, I can appreciate he's upset but it's not safe for you to be in there and I've got things to do, places to go, you know, people to meet? Chimps, even?"

She tried again. Sam tightened his grip. No matter what she said, he wouldn't listen. Finally, after another ten minutes of this, Jack flipped the switch on the cattle prod, which started up with an ominous hum. It was capable of delivering a four-thousand-volt shock that could persuade any animal to do anything, from a steer in the chute to a chimp throwing a tantrum to a pair of pit bulls going at each other in a pen. Or the human animal—it was the torturer's tool of choice because it got the message across in no uncertain terms and it didn't leave a mark. She'd never used one, never would, no matter what, but Dr. Moncrief made it a rule that anybody entering the chimp barn had to carry one at all times. Hers, shoved into her hand by Jack before he'd opened the door and allowed her to put the harness on Sam, dangled from her waist on a bright tricolor lanyard, braided, she later learned, by Mrs. Moncrief—to give the thing a homey touch, she supposed.

As if. She was complicit too—they all were.

Jack said, "There's just no way around it, and I'm sorry, I really am, but he's got to learn . . ."

He did learn. Of course he did. Anybody would learn, no different from the first time you laid your hand on a hot stove or touched a bare wire: pain is our first knowledge of this earth, pain of the birth canal, pain of the light, the clamor, the pain of recognition. The look he gave her was heartbreaking, as if she'd betrayed him, and she had, she *had*. He balled up on the concrete floor, whimpering, and Jack pulled her out of the cage and slammed and locked the door, and though she stayed there whispering apologies for what must have been an hour, he never once looked at her or even moved a muscle.

She'd told Guy about it, about everything, calling him daily from the efficiency apartment she'd rented in a creaking old Victorian that had been divided into apartments for students and the two old women in their fifties or maybe sixties who managed the property and had the entire downstairs of the house to themselves and their cats. He'd tried to calm her, told her he'd call Moncrief and do his best to persuade him to give Sam more stimulation and keep him isolated at least till he could get acclimated and defend himself against the bigger chimps, told her about Carson—Carson was on again, wasn't that amazing?—told her he had an idea to start a new study involving Sam and the other home-raised chimps, which meant he could be coming back to Iowa for a semester, maybe, or a year, told her (right in the middle of a sentence that stretched to ten paragraphs) that he missed her. And did she miss him?

"Yes," she murmured, and the affirmation felt sweet in her mouth, *yes*, the single syllable that put them back on track again.

He could have said then that he loved her, but he didn't. Instead he said, "I need you to pick me up at the airport."

She was half an hour early, nervous and unsure of herself, as if they hadn't slept together, lived together, washed dishes and bought groceries and raised Sam side by side. It was just that she'd been so focused on Sam she hadn't had time to think much about where she was or what she'd committed herself to or even why, but as she changed out of her work clothes and got dressed that afternoon she was as excited as if it were a first date—which, in a way, it was. He'd never asked her out. Not formally. Formally, they'd never been on a date— she'd just moved in and gone to work and then one night they had sex and that was that. Was it love? Or just getting used to another person? The magazines all said it was good to have shared interests and if that was true, they were on solid ground there. She thought about the sex, about their bed back at the ranch and the times Sam had interrupted them, which, once he'd been calmed down and put back to bed, made their lovemaking all the more intense as if he'd injected some sort of aphrodisiac into them both. She was fine. Everything was fine. She told herself she was just excited, that was all.

What she hadn't taken into account was the weather. She was half an hour early, yes, but this was Iowa, in February, and his flight out of Denver was delayed by snow so that she had to sit there in the airport for hours while Sam rotted in his cage and the Denver weather, rolling eastward, manifested itself as soft brushstrokes of sleet painted on the terminal windows. When he did finally arrive, he came slouching out of the gate as if the weight of his shoulder bag was too much to bear and he was so put-upon, so exhausted, he could barely manage a smile, let alone hold her in his arms for more than the three seconds it took him to drop his bag and hug her so formulaically he might as well have given her a handshake. In the car, on their way back to her apartment, she was the one doing the talking, and that had to be a first.

Her apartment was pinched and small, no different from the one she'd had in Santa Maria, the bed a single and a pair of cardboard boxes in the corner behind the TV serving in place of a dresser, an example of which she hadn't found time to acquire, even if she could have lugged a piece of furniture up the stairs by herself. There was a kitchen nook with a counter and two stools and a bathroom featuring an old claw-footed tub and a plastic shower curtain that could have been cleaner. She was already apologizing as she put the key in the lock but he cut her off. "I'm so wiped I don't care if I have to sleep standing up in a horse stall," he muttered, heading straight for the bathroom. His bag was on the floor. The bed was turned down. She'd bought a bottle of wine. The sounds he made—the hard hissing splash of his urine, the squeal of the taps, the thump of the towel—brought her back to the ranch and the night-light in the hall and all the times she'd crept out of Sam's bed and slipped into his, and then he was there in the room with her and he took her in his arms and they kissed and she felt the way she was supposed to feel.

They didn't make love, though she'd assumed they would, expected it, wanted to more than anything, but he was asleep on his feet and barely got his clothes off before he was facedown and unconscious on the bed. The room was cold. Wind rattled the windows in their frames. The heat—steam radiators, maybe the first ones ever cast—clanked on and off like submarines dropping down into the void of the deepest ocean while she lay there cramped against the wall listening to his breathing until she was asleep herself.

In the morning, he was more like himself, more focused and considerate, and they made love twice before she got up and fixed them cheese omelets for breakfast. If he wondered what she was doing for money, he didn't ask, though the fact was Dr. Moncrief had stopped her one day when she was walking up the hill to the chimp barn and announced he was going to start paying her minimum wage, which was what the other two techs were making. "I like your attitude," he said. "Dedication, that's what it takes, and that's what I'm seeing from you. So keep it up," and he'd reached out and chucked her under the chin as if she were a child. Or a dog. Or worse: somebody he wanted to go to bed with. And what had she done? Nothing. She'd just stood there and smiled at him. The next day he fired the more pathetic of the two techs, a gawky local in patched overalls and a dirty feed cap who seemed to spend half his time smoking weed just outside the back door of the facility.

She thought Guy would want to see Sam first thing, but instead he went straight to Moncrief's office at the university, where he was teaching class that day. She drove, he talked. Everybody in the psych building seemed to know him, from the profs to the grad students to the secretaries and even one of the janitors, which only stoked his mood all the higher, as if this were a homecoming, which it was, of sorts. He'd had two cups of coffee at breakfast and as if that wasn't enough they'd stopped at a diner so he could dash in for one more in a cardboard container, working himself up to spring his surprise on Dr. Moncrief because Carson was on board now, definitely, and this was the chance they'd all been waiting for. Renee Flowers, did she remember Renee Flowers? Renee had even said if it worked out she could see having Sam on on a regular basis, which could really turn things around in the public eye and get the program back on track again. Right? Didn't she think so?

"Yes," she said. "Yes, absolutely—nothing could be better."

They were sitting in the lounge outside the main office, waiting for Moncrief's eleven o'clock class to let out. People came and went. Machines whirred. The department secretary tapped away at her typewriter as if she were killing insects, one after another, *tink, tink tink.*

"Because we can't let Borstein have the final say on this." Guy leaned forward over the cradle of his elbows and knees so that his hair fell loose across his face, lecturing now. "He's just wrong, dead wrong, and everything that's gone down is nothing short of a crime. You know it and I know it—and Donald does too. But one thing at a time. First I've got to talk him into letting me have Sam back, if even for just a couple of days, because we can be pretty sure *The Tonight Show* isn't about to relocate to Iowa."

He flashed a smile at his own joke, pushed himself up and circled the room twice while the secretary glanced up indulgently and a student sorted mail into a phalanx of wooden slots set into the wall, then dropped his coffee in the trash and slid back into the chair beside her. "And we can't just do this blindly—we have to think of Sam, and I don't mean just how all this is going to affect him emotionally, but on the level even of where we're going to put him. I mean, I still have the ranch, at least till May, anyway, and we can keep Sam there a couple days till we do the show, but then it's going to have to be back here, right, because what else are we going to do with him? If Donald lets him go at all, that is."

She felt herself slipping, as if the seat was giving way beneath her—he was talking about taking Sam away again? "They couldn't come here?"

"Are you serious? This is *The Tonight Show* we're talking about. Filmed live before a studio audience. In Burbank. You think Johnny Carson's going to fly out to Iowa to film a segment with an animal act?"

"It's not an act. And Sam's not an animal."

"It could save us. It could set us back on course, you know that—"

"What about me?"

"You'd come, of course. What do you mean?"

"I work here now. I live here. And it's not like it's ever going to be the way it was—this is the new reality. And I hate it. But at least Sam's here with me."

He shifted in the chair, pushed his hair out of his eyes. He was wearing his black ski jacket, jeans, boots, the sweater she'd bought him for Christmas (black and white squares, alternating, very up-to-the-minute, very New Wave). "Look," he said, "don't make things any harder than they already are. You know what it cost me to set this up? You think I like the fact that Donald's got me by the balls? I need your help. He likes you, right?"

She shrugged. "I don't know."

"Just give him that pretty smile of yours." He reached over, unzipped her jacket and tugged down the front of her V-neck sweater, his fingers a hot busy fumble at her throat, like bees, like honeybees hovering over a flower. "And show him a little of this too—it can't hurt."

WHAT ICE?

He knew time, no different from any other alive thing, sunrise, sunset, the long wheeling drift of the seasons, and he knew time on the stove and the dashboard of Guy's CAR, he knew BREAKFAST TIME, GIN-TONIC TIME, STORYTIME, BEDTIME, but he didn't know time in here. Time in here was a vacant space abruptly rent by screams and violence, by the BIG MAN and his stinger, but in some dumbfounding inexplicable way suddenly it was time for her to be here too, here in this place with the BLACK BUGS whose feet were just like his—here with *him* and not them, never them. And then, suddenly, as if his whole life was starting over, so was Guy. He heard the faintest filament of a voice from outside the door, outside in the cold, Guy's voice, and he came up off the floor as if he'd been launched, hooting till the others took it up, till the whole place was a pandemonium of hooting and screaming, and here came Guy's face through the door and hers beside it and he was signing so fast he hardly knew what he was saying, COME HUG, TIME GO, YOU ME HER OUT.

There was the KEY, there the LOCK, and the door swung open and they both ducked into the cage and he was so overwhelmed he prostrated himself, face on the FLOOR, arms outstretched and fingers curled in the way of his kind, the way he knew in his deepest vestigial self and had never learned or unlearned. He didn't know why he was doing what he was doing, didn't know the rituals of his species or how nature trumps nurture or anything beyond the wet concrete and the hormones pinning him there, but when Guy reached down to touch him all restraint fell away and he came flying up like a bird and landed right in his arms and Guy let out a grunt and said, "Jesus, Sam, you're too big for this, you're killing me," and then Guy was laughing, his lips pulled back and his teeth shining white. "And who's a good boy?" he asked. "Who's my good boy?"

He felt something then that was bigger than himself, so much bigger, and he sprang down from Guy's arms and humped around the cage hooting out his exultation until he couldn't help himself and sprang back into Guy's arms to kiss him on the lips, over and over. Guy was here! Guy was in charge! Guy was the one who would get him out of here and take him back HOME to his BLANKET and his BED and the REFRIGERATOR! He could see it all, because these were no mere abstractions—these were pictures he held in his mind and he could see them as clearly as if they were right there before him.

Aimee said, "You want to go for a walk?"

He jumped back down, signed, OUT. Signed, JACKET. Signed, YOU ME GUY OUT.

And then he was wearing his jacket and harness and they were in the hallway and through the door and out into the COLD where the sun was spurious and nothing was green but he was soaring all the same because Guy was here and she was here and the prison door had just slammed shut behind him.

Aimee said something about the island and the ICE, "I'm getting him used to the island because that's the only hope here—the minute spring arrives and that ice melts, we're going to be out there all day every day. Dr. Moncrief likes the idea—for the juveniles. To give them exercise?"

Guy said something back, said, "Great. Excellent. But for now my chief concern is getting him to Burbank. All the rest can come later."

They were talking and he heard the words but he didn't try to sort them out even if he could have because he was running, tumbling, tugging at the lead and gamboling across the frozen dead arena of this new world that might have been a cruel parody of all he loved and wanted and knew, but wasn't INSIDE, wasn't bars and steel mesh and the unblinking lights that made night into day. He surged with joy. He clowned for them, springing and leaping and laughing, but there was something else here, something darker, a dark blot on his mind.

The CAGE, he thought, kept thinking, the CAGE, the BUILD-ING, the BLACK BUGS. They weren't going to bring him back in there, were they? No. Never. Not with Guy here. With Guy here they would go to the CAR and get in it and drive home and make everything green again (though, admittedly, he didn't see Guy's car anywhere he looked). But he wasn't worried. Or not yet. He was in the moment and the moment had them all out on the ICE, slipping and sliding to the place where the ice ended and the ISLAND began. When they got there and he found himself back in the yellow dried-out cane where he'd hidden the day he escaped until the dogs sniffed him out and the BIG MAN came with his dart, he settled down on his haunches just to feel the thrill of the cold on his own hairy bottom, his ASS, because that was what it was, that was what everybody called it, his ASS.

She bent over him, said, "Aren't you cold there, Sam?"

He didn't answer. Just spread one palm out on the clear cold ICE and contemplated it. Then he looked up at her, curious, puzzled, needing a word, an explanation, a key to the mystery: WHAT ICE? he asked.

She laughed. "Did you see that, Guy?" Guy was standing over him now too. They were both grinning. She said, "You know what it is. It's water"—and she signed it, WATER—"that gets frozen, like at home? In the freezer? With the ICE CUBES?"

He knew that, but it wasn't what he was asking. What he was asking was how, was why, was what it meant. He tried again, talking through his fingers that were already stiffening with the cold. WHAT ICE? he repeated. And then, because that was circular, that wasn't what he meant, he tried, WHY ICE? And then, because that wasn't it either, he asked, HOW ICE?

ALPHA, BETA

The flight was a nightmare, beginning to end. He'd booked at the last minute and wound up with a seat all the way in back, wedged up against the window beside a two-hundred-sixty-pound kid who played nose tackle for the UCSM team and wanted to know his opinion not only of all the teams in the conference but the pros as well—and what had he thought of the Super Bowl? The Raiders rock, don't they? Then there was Denver. He sat at the bar in the airport for three hours while the overhead monitors went schizophrenic, the flight now on, now off, now delayed fifty minutes, now an hour and a half, and all the while he was struggling to keep the images of Johnny Carson, Moncrief, Sam and her—her, most of all—clear in his head. What would he say to Johnny? What would he say to Moncrief (and what would Moncrief say to him when he broke the news to him)? And Aimee. He missed her more than he wanted to admit because she was the one who'd walked out on him and he didn't like that power dynamic at all—no, not one bit. And yet, by the time he did get to her, by the time she appeared there at the gate with her hopeful face and yielding eyes and her hair and lips and sweet tight jeans, he was beyond drunk and so burned out he could barely function. They hugged fleetingly, kissed like strangers. And then it was her cramped depressing apartment and the single bed pushed up against the wall.

He made up for it in the morning. The bed was barely wider than his shoulders, but they managed, the whole world gone silent and a sun pale as sliced lemon creeping in under the shades, and she needed the affirmation—the sex—as much as he did. Here she was, Aimee, sweet-faced, sweet-tempered, the ultra-capable girl who'd so thoroughly filled the vacuum left by Melanie he'd gone whole days without hearing his ex-wife's voice rattling around in the margins of his head. Aimee. He wanted her back. But she wasn't going anywhere without Sam and if the alternative was for him to come here, to her, he'd need the department to grant him a leave and the NIH or NSF or whoever to pony up and fund a new project—and Moncrief to sign on. Without Moncrief, there was nothing, no Aimee, no money, no career, no hope. All of that had him depressed almost as soon as he pulled out of her for the second time and she got up to make them omelets in her pink silk nightgown with the slit up one side and flicked on the radio to some chirpy pop song that might as well have been a dirge for all the good it did him.

Her expectation was that he'd want to see Sam first thing, but he put her off. As soon as they stepped out the door (into the bitter prairie-raking wind that made his every cell scream for California), she said, "Sam's going to be so excited to see you—and I didn't say a word to him so it's a total surprise," and he said, "First things first. If Donald's not on board, then we've got nothing—and you know how he can be. Jesus. I just want to get this over with, okay?" and she said, "I can't believe you—this is Sam we're talking about. Sam?

Remember Sam?" and maybe he snapped at her, maybe he was over-wrought, but by the time they got to campus he was flooded with nostalgia and optimism and his mood took off on the wings of the caffeine he had to keep ingesting just to get his head above water. Things were going to work out, he kept telling himself, he was sure of it. Or as sure as he could be with her at his side and Sam waiting in the wings and Donald looking to pay down the cost of housing his forty chimps, which should make Carson a no-brainer.

It was a quarter past twelve by the time Moncrief came tramping down the hall shedding students, his thermos and lunchbox in hand (his wife, Dorothy, made him lunch every day, and not just out of fru-gality, though there was that, but for health reasons too—"Donald doesn't eat processed food," she would say whenever anybody asked about it, "and he never will, not while I'm alive and breathing"). He moved with the deliberation of a big man, as if afraid of crushing things underfoot, and it took him a moment to scan the office and recognize that the two people rising to greet him were his old protégé and his newest tech. "Guy, Jesus, what are you doing here? Slum-ming, right? Or is it"—he shifted his eyes to Aimee—"something more urgent?"

"Any excuse," he heard himself say, "you know me. But if you want to know the truth, I came to see you. I've got news. Big news."

Moncrief's office hadn't changed—or not that he could see, anyway. There were the same pictures on the walls—Freud, Lorenz, Goodall, Yerkes, Harlow—and the same Steelcase desk buried in a detritus of papers, books, magazines, stained napkins and various balled-up scraps of the waxed paper Dorothy wrapped his cheese-and-onion sandwiches in. Daily. And the finger, the mysterious non-human fin-ger drifting eternally in a gallon jar of formalin, which had given rise to the rumor that Moncrief had removed it (with a pair of wire cutters) from the chimp that had gouged out his eye, a rumor Moncrief made no effort to discredit, though Guy knew better. They followed Moncrief into his office, where he waved perfunctorily to the two folding chairs at the foot of the desk, then dropped heavily into his own chair, extracted his sandwich and a packet of carrot and celery sticks from the lunchbox and began eating without another word. After a moment, chewing, he said, "Big news? What big news? Don't tell me it's Carson again—or what, Sam started speaking fluent Norwegian?"

"It's Carson. And this time it's for real. I talked to Renee Flowers—she called me—and they want us as soon as we can possibly arrange it." He wanted to go on, wanted to make his case, but he was afraid of pushing too hard. Moncrief—Dr. Moncrief, *Donald*, head of the institute, head of the department, head of everything—was as resistant to pressure as anybody alive.

"Right," Moncrief said, waving the sandwich. "And what's this going to do for us again?"

"Put us back on track. And it's not just a onetime thing—Renee says it could be, I don't know, semi-regular."

"So we'd be renting him out?"

"Not exactly. There's a nominal payment, same as all the guests get, even Joey Bishop or Joan Rivers or whoever, but that's not it—it's the exposure."

"I'm not following you—how exactly does that pay my bills?"

"Demand. We'll increase demand and get the grant money flowing again—and I've got an idea for that too I wanted to talk to you about . . ."

Moncrief set down the sandwich in its cradle of waxed paper, ran two fingers over his eyepatch, as if to assess what wasn't there. He let out a low grunt. Squared his shoulders. Fixed him with his burning one-eyed stare. "And how's he going to get there? You don't expect me to fly him out to California, do you? You have any idea what that costs? And the time—Jesus, you think I have the time to go running around the country with an animal in tow?"

"They'll pay. She already told me—Renee did."

"And what about you, Aimee?" They both turned to her; she was sitting there rigid in the straight-backed chair, a gold cross glinting at her collarbone, her face expressionless. "Tell me, truthfully—don't look at him, look at me—you really want to see your chimp put in a crate underneath some jetliner? And for what, the slim promise of a payoff down the line when everybody forgets about Borstein and rallies around the adorable little finger-spelling ape on *The Tonight Show*? You think that's going to happen? You think that'll be good for him?"

"I don't know," she said, glancing up at him and then away again. "He's starting to settle in here, I guess, because there's no other choice, really. But there's no stimulation for him and he's stuck"—her voice caught—"in a *cage*."

"Donald," he said, and he couldn't help himself, he had to cut in, "it's a chance. No guarantees, but he'd be gone a couple days, a week maybe, right? And what difference would it make—he's not old enough to breed yet. And he's just sitting there in a cage—why not make use of him? I mean, we put all that effort into him, couldn't we at least start to get something back? And if he's famous—*more* famous—doesn't that make the price go up for his offspring?"

Moncrief was regarding him steadily, a thin twitch of amusement working at the corners of his mouth. "What do you mean, like race-horses? Like Kentucky Derby winners?"

"All I'm asking is give it a chance. What have you got to lose?"

"Ten thousand dollars."

"Nothing's going to happen to him."

"Isn't it flu season? And what about TB—haven't they got a bunch of farm laborers out there from Mexico, wetbacks that have never even heard of vaccination? What if he gets infected? Worse—what if he brings it back and infects the whole colony? They have zero immunity, *zero*. It'd be like smallpox and the Indians. And then I wind up with forty dead animals on my hands. You think I want that?"

"We're not taking him to a farm. It's a TV studio. NBC. Burbank. Nothing's going to happen to him, I guarantee it."

"You do, huh? What are you going to do, make him wear a surgical mask? No, listen, the more I hear about this, the crazier it sounds—but one thing's for certain."

"What's that?"

"*I* can guarantee he's not going to contract TB or the flu or anything else—you know how?"

He did. And he cut him off because he didn't want to hear it. "Please," he said, and he was pleading now, pleading for himself, for Sam, for the whole field and the great lumpen TV audience out there sunk amidst their six-packs and corn chips, "you know this isn't right. You give up now you're just rolling over to Borstein and the rest of them, your enemies—you want your enemies to win?"

Moncrief narrowed his voice. "By keeping him here, that's how. Right here, under lock and key. And if I keep him long enough to breed him, that's my business. And if I can get a fair price for him or his offspring or any of the rest of them, that's what's called a return on investment, because right now? Right now the money's flying out of here so fast it's like the little fuckers are chewing it up and shitting it out."

The rest of the weekend was just more of the same, farce wedded to tragedy. He spoke with Moncrief twice more, both times by phone, which he could just as well have done from California, but when he got tired of wheedling and pushed back and said they really needed to iron this out face-to-face, Moncrief said he was busy and as far as he was concerned the phone was a perfectly adequate conduit of expression. He actually said that, actually used that phrase: *conduit of expression*. Jesus. It was a power play, of course it was, the alpha male setting the bounds, which was just what he'd expect from Moncrief, but that he wouldn't even go out of his way for Carson—Carson and his fifteen million viewers—was beyond belief. Moncrief shut him out. He wouldn't listen. And he ended the second conversation with a rhetorical question, delivered in a low rumbling whiskey-inflected growl: "What is it you don't understand about no?"

Aimee was distraught. She'd sat there through the whole thing, watched him demean himself, watched Moncrief piss all over him, and even when they were with Sam she barely broke a smile. On his last night in town, Sunday, he took her to dinner at a place he remembered as being at least tolerable—Pane e Vino, midwest Italian, Chianti bottles with flickering candles stuck in them, red tablecloths, classical music, waiters who had some sort of unidentifiable accent that might or might not have been Neapolitan. They shared a bottle of Valpolicella while Vivaldi's "Spring" coursed ironically through the crackling speakers hanging from macramé nets on either end of the room and the wind seethed at the windows. She didn't say a word, not even to the waiter, and so he'd ordered for her, the vegetarian lasagna, which she hardly touched. She didn't know about Moncrief's threat to sell off the chimps if things didn't improve and he didn't want to tell her. Or not yet, anyway. He said, "Looks like Carson's out. I mean, face it—it's hopeless."

"I want to cry," she said.

"Maybe you could convince him."

"Me? How?"

"I don't know—be nice to him."

There was a moment of silence during which a violin—or maybe a viola—seemed to meld with the sound of the wind hissing at the windows. Her eyes went hard. "I don't know what you're saying—and you know what, I don't want to know, okay? And for your information, I am nice to him—how do you think I got the job? And to Sam too—and to the rest of those poor chimps locked up in there like, like . . . *dogs*."

"He's going to sell them off."

"What do you mean?"

"I mean biomed."

She jolted upright in her seat and shot him a look of contempt. "You're a liar."

What could he say? She was an innocent, she would always be an innocent—until the worst happened. He shrugged. "Donald's getting older. He hasn't published in years. As long as language studies was getting us attention, he was on board, but that's over now and all that matters is dollars and cents." He picked up his napkin, dropped it on his plate. "Unless—"

"Unless what?"

"Unless Carson—"

"Screw Carson. You know what?" She was angry now, furious, her face distorted, the veins standing out in her neck. "Why don't we just take him?"

The waiter was giving him a significant look from across the room and he raised his hands and made the scribbling motion that indicated he should bring the check, sign language at its most rudimentary. Why didn't they just take him? Because that was grand theft, a felony, and because Moncrief would come after them like Javert in *Les Misérables*, and beyond that, where would they keep him? How would they pay for him? And—it came to him in that punishing instant with all the finality of a door slamming shut—he didn't really want him. Not anymore. The realization shamed him, and because it shamed him, it angered him too. He said, "That's fucking crazy."

"No," she said, "I mean it—why don't we just put him in the backseat of the car and drive away? Right now. Tonight." She leaned into the table, her face swelling in the glow of the candle till it seemed to absorb all the light of the room. There was the smell of the red sauce, of wine, of her. The violin—or viola—sawed away at the measure of spring, the waiter floated toward them, the wind hissed. "They wouldn't even know," she whispered. "Or not till tomorrow, anyway, and by then we'd be—"

"Fucked?"

"No, be serious—can't you be serious? We'd be gone," she said. "Out of here." She reached out and took hold of his hand. "Just the three of us."

SHELL GAME

The game he liked best, the game they used to play in the big room of the house with the tree and the sun that was real and actual and felt good on your back, your shoulders, your face, was the shell game. He loved the shell game. One raisin, three walnut shells, and she would put the raisin under one of the shells and shuffle them around, trying to fool him, which she never did, or almost never. He found the raisin. He ate the raisin. And then it was his turn and though he wanted to eat the next raisin too he restrained himself and hid it under one of the shells, shuffling them rapidly and feinting with his other hand to throw her off and if she found the raisin she ate it and if she didn't he ate it and it was gone and so on till the raisin BOX was empty. Did she let him win? Was she faking it? What was spatial memory? What was sleight of hand? What was deception? He didn't know, but he won the game more than he lost it and when he did lose it—when she got the raisin, or Guy, when Guy played and Guy got the raisin—he felt a sudden burning flare of anger and disappointment that shot to the tense corded muscles of his arms and the tightening wires of his hands and fingers that was so hard to control he had to groom himself right then and there, groom her, groom Guy, just to calm down.

There were raisins in the BOX, raisins you could count, separate into groups, eat individually or by the handful, but always, inevitably, at some point they were gone. Until she brought a new box. In here, in this place with the BLACK BUGS and cold concrete, there were no games and no raisins either, except when she slipped a box in under her SHIRT for a special TREAT. That was good, supremely good, but Guy was gone now too, vanished like the raisins in an empty box, and wherever he'd gone—HOME?—he hadn't taken him along. Which was devastating. Wrong. Catastrophically wrong. It made him angry, made him scream, made him lash out at the BLACK BUGS and even, once, bare his teeth at the BIG MAN, who made him pay, made him cower and writhe and know exactly and intimately who was the slave and who the master.

WHERE GUY? he asked her the first day that Guy didn't come visit with her.

HE WENT BACK.

WHERE?

He could read her face. She was thinking about that, thinking she might have to conceal the truth from him, lie to him, but after a minute she signed, HOME.

MY TREE, he signed, and then again, making it a question, MY TREE?

"Yes," she said aloud, "home to your tree."

They were in the cage, squatting on the damp concrete. She'd just taken him for a walk to the ISLAND, which was ICE, only ICE, and all the ground around it was white with the pellets that flung themselves down out of the sky like tiny white pebbles. It was a perplexing moment, a hard moment, and he was trying to make sense of it. Why wasn't Guy in the cage and not him? Why wasn't he at HOME in his bedroom instead of Guy? Or better yet, in his TREE? Why was she here with him when for so long she hadn't been? And why was the BIG MAN lurking somewhere out there in the hallway or in the house at the bottom of the hill where he lived and slept and ate and kept his dart gun and his stinger and the stick he rapped your knuckles with? Why wasn't *he* gone? Why couldn't he be the one?

But more, and worse: what was happening now would happen tomorrow and the next day and the day after that until all the days were gone and she was gone and the BLACK BUGS were gone and he was here inside these walls until the time he once knew from the face of the clock and in the long arcing trail of the sun was no more.

ROADRUNNER

The song she was thinking of, the song that came into her head out of nowhere, was "Roadrunner," one of the best driving songs of all time, along with "Radar Love" and "Born to Be Wild." She had it on her mix tape the day she left Santa Maria with her pulse racing and her stomach shrunk down to nothing, and she didn't know what it was exactly—the vocalist didn't so much sing the lyrics as speak them in a flat uninflected tone—but once it got into her head she couldn't get it out. She supposed she must have heard it on the student station at some point in the previous week, which was essentially all she listened to once she got home from work to face the bleakness of her apartment that was a kind of shadowland that didn't feature Sam or Guy or anything else she really cared about. She watched TV sometimes, in the numb way she always had, and she was back to eating Top Ramen most nights because she was too tired to cook and didn't want to waste the money going out. If she read, it was in the field—Sarah Hrdy's new book on the role females played in primate societies, journal articles, *In the Shadow of Man* (for the fifth time)—though without Guy and with Sam stuck in a cage, there was no field, not for her, anyway. She wasn't progressing or learning or advancing science in the slightest, and she wasn't getting her degree either. As depressing as it was to admit it—and she would never mention this to her mother or Guy or anybody else—she wasn't much more than a zookeeper, a jailer, a hoser of shit and scrubber of walls.

The last time she'd seen Guy—it was three months ago now—he'd been at a crisis point himself and things hadn't really improved since. He'd sent a chill through her when he told her Moncrief had raised the possibility of selling off the chimps to one of the biomed labs ("But not Sam, never Sam, don't worry"). But she was worried. More than that: she was terrified. "Let's take him," she said. "Let's just put him in the car and drive away." Yes. Sure. But that wasn't going to happen. She watched his face recompose itself around a hard little nugget of *no* and *are you crazy?* even as he scrambled for excuses and everything she felt about him went careening off a cliff like a runaway car.

In the interval, Dr. Moncrief said nothing about his plans—certainly not to her, because why would he?—and things went on as before, though she hated feeling on edge all the time. She and Guy talked a couple of times a week on the phone—he was still waiting to hear on his grant proposals to set up video cameras in the chimp barn and record any spontaneous signing the chimps might do and all the rest of it—and he promised to come visit at the end of the semester. Which was soon, very soon, but he hardly even asked about Sam because the Carson thing was dead all over again and Sam nothing more to him now than a subject in an experiment that could—maybe, might, hopefully—revive his career. Truly? She almost didn't care whether he came or not.

It was mid-May, the fields lush, the trees in leaf and the air heavy with pollen. She discovered she had allergies, itching eyes, dripping nose, and she'd never seen so many bugs in her life, bugs of every description, from the ones that bit and stung to those that seemed programmed to bat around your face every time you stuck your head out the door. There was sun, though, and it came like a small miracle after the long winnowing blast of her first winter away from the coast. As soon as the ice had melted, she'd started taking Sam and some of the other juveniles out to the island where they could go off-leash and roam free, clambering up the tree trunks, rolling in the dirt, chasing birds and squirrels and abandoning their senses to nature. Chimps didn't swim, couldn't swim, couldn't even be taught to, and so there was no worry about their escaping.

Then there came a day that seemed almost like a return to winter, overcast, temperatures in the fifties and a steady rain falling all morning while she slogged through her chores in the chimp barn. Sam, impatient as always and fiercely jealous of any attention she might give to the others—even so much as taking the hose to their cages to shoot feces down the drain—clung to the bars of his cage and chattered at her the whole time she moved up and down the aisles. She was thinking there was no way she could take him out to the island—Dr. Moncrief was afraid of the chimps getting sick, insisting that everybody who came in contact with them, techs and grad students alike, was up to date on their TB shots and strictly prohibiting any activities in the rain for fear the chimps would catch a chill. But then the sun poked through at two or so and she changed her mind.

She wound up taking Sam and two of the other juveniles out in the rowboat—Alice, who'd been cross-fostered with Dr. Markowitz until Moncrief pulled the plug on her project too, and Hobart, a young male who'd been home-reared by a pair of Peace Corps volunteers who'd brought him back from Africa and quickly realized how inadequate they were to the task—along with a hamper of snacks and the odd toy or two. The clouds fell back, the sun sparked off the water. There was the smell of the blooming biota of the pond and the manure the farmers used on their fields, mixed with a sweet heady scent of flowering things and the pollen they released in the air—which had her sniffling and rubbing her eyes, though she'd taken a Dristan tablet as a precaution. The chimps had no such problem, apparently immune to the allergies that had made her life miserable—*more* miserable, that is—over the past few weeks. They sat quietly, trying to moderate their excitement in the face of their consuming fear of the water, but then, when they were halfway there, a pair of Canada geese came sailing in for a landing and all three of them went absolutely wild, pawing at the water and hooting in chorus, and whether it was because they were affected, as she was, by the birds' beauty and grace, or simply that they wanted to throttle and devour them, she didn't know, but she pulled hard on the left oar and swung wide of them while the chimps splashed and trailed their fingers in the wake.

That had been one of the things that most surprised her the first time she read Goodall—the fact that chimps, which had previously been assumed to be vegetarians like gorillas and orangutans, not only ate meat but actively sought it out in coordinated hunts in the tree-tops. Guy had showed her a film one night of wild chimps hunting and killing their preferred prey—red colobus monkeys—and the sheer savagery of it came as a shock to her, especially since her only experience at that point was of Sam, who seemed so harmless, an innocent with his little white tail tuft and big searching eyes who only wanted to cling and cuddle. Sam was with them that night, though she wondered if it was appropriate for him to see the film, which might be too disturbing for him and confusing too (WHAT THEY? he would ask, for which she would have no explanation since everything they were doing depended on Sam identifying as human). In any case it hadn't mattered since he'd promptly fallen asleep in her lap while Guy, who'd brought the footage and projector back from school, was threading the film through the rollers.

She was sipping a glass of wine and idly stroking Sam's back and the sweet spots behind his ears, when a scrum of adult chimps appeared on the screen. They were standing erect and staring up into the treetops, gesturing excitedly. The camera jumped in a quick blur of ascending leaves and branches to reveal what they were tracking—a troop of monkeys in the treetops. The chimps immediately split up, one climbing in pursuit, the others stationing themselves below the surrounding trees to prevent escape on the ground. Within minutes they'd isolated a mother with an infant clinging to her breast. One chimp—the dominant male—chased her higher and higher till finally there was no place to go and he made a swipe at her, catching her by one leg. In the next instant he snatched the baby away and dashed out its brains, then tore the mother open and began feeding on her while she was still alive even as the others clamored for their share. "Pre-moral," Guy had said. "You have to have our consciousness to consider such niceties as pity and mercy, but not to worry, we let the guys down at the slaughterhouse take care of that for us."

When they got to the island—when they were still a boat's length away, actually—all three chimps made mighty leaps to the near bank and scrambled off hooting out their joy. For her, this was the best part of what had become an increasingly depressing job. To see them free like this, even for a couple of hours, lifted her up too. If chimps were the intellectual and emotional equals of three-and-a-half- to four-year-old children, then wasn't it beyond cruel to lock them up? She thought of her niece, of Sophie—was there anybody on this earth who would justify locking *her* in a cage? It was wrong. It was obscene. *And to stick tubes and needles in them on top of it?*

She watched the chimps awhile, then gazed out over the pond to the shore and the martialed rows of crops beyond and settled into her thoughts. Guy was coming. Guy was coming and he was going to plead and wheedle yet again and spin out schemes Moncrief was only going to reject, and that was their big hope? If he succeeded and Moncrief relented, the best-case scenario was just more of the same. And what was going to happen in five years? Ten? The chimps couldn't be placed in zoos—they were too accustomed to people, and when paying customers came to the zoo they wanted to see wild animals, not cigarette-cadging, finger-spelling demi-humans who might as well have been the winos they'd stepped over to get to the subway. They couldn't be sent back to Africa either because they wouldn't have the skills to survive in the wild—they'd be at the mercy not only of the indigenous chimps but of people too, who would try to capture them all over again, this time for sale as bush meat and trophies, since the live trade had dried up. Some cultures—the Chinese, for one—paid a premium for chimps' hands and feet, which they used in their quack medicinal concoctions or for totems or trophies. Talk about obscene.

That was when she glanced up and saw that the rowboat was missing. Hobart was sitting there at water's edge, playing with a stick, using it like an eggbeater to froth the surface, but Sam and Alice were nowhere to be seen. She rose slowly, not yet alarmed, scanning the island for them—it was small, no more than an acre and so chimp-stripped the sight lines were clear and she could take in the entire thing at a glance. She scanned the treetops—nothing—and in the next moment, trying not to panic, she ran toward the place where the boat had been. She shot a look in both directions, up and down the muddy shore, thinking Sam and Alice must have dragged it somewhere—playing house maybe, using it for a sandbox—before a movement on the other side of the bay caught her eye.

It was the boat. Sam and Alice were in it, and although the operation of oars and oarlocks eluded them (one oar trailed in the water, the other floated behind it, adrift on its own), they were using their cupped hands as paddles, Sam on the right side, Alice on the left. She called out to them, shouted their names in anger, shouted, "Bad!"

and "You come back here!" but it had little effect. She saw them pause to glance back at her, then say something to each other—hands in motion, just the sort of thing Guy would die to capture on film— then turn back to paddling. They reached the shore a minute later, Sam flashing his big toothy triumphant grin and hesitating only to sign, YOU PLAY ME, before tugging Alice by the hand and humping across the grass in the direction of the farmhouse.

It was two hundred yards to shore. The air was crisp, the water freezing. And there was the complication of Hobart, who'd have to be abandoned, at least temporarily. She never hesitated, stripping to panties and bra and plunging in, the water so cold it made her face ache, thinking with every stroke that Dr. Moncrief was going to kill her, that the chimps would be run over on the main road, that the police would chase them down and shoot them like wild beasts or Sam would grab hold of some random passerby the way he had with Jody back in Santa Maria. Or bite. He was perfectly capable of biting if the mood took him. Two hundred yards. It was nothing—four laps in an Olympic-sized pool—but it seemed to take forever. And when finally she did reach shore, she couldn't seem to get her balance, her feet fighting for purchase in the mud, reeds slapping at her face and thrashing her arms. She tripped, fell twice, and then she was on the lawn and sprinting up the path to the farmhouse.

There was no one there, a small mercy. Mrs. Moncrief had gone to see her sister in Des Moines for a few days and had taken her car and Dr. Moncrief must have been at the university because his car was gone too. ("You can call me Donald," he'd told her after the first week, "because we don't really need to be that formal, do we?" but she never had called him by his first name, nor would she: to her he was Dr. Moncrief, period, which was as familiar as she wanted to get. The truth was, he creeped her out. The way he looked at her, the way he always seemed to find an excuse for putting a hand on her shoulder or elbow or the small of her back as if guiding her to some place she'd never been before, possessive and condescending at the same time. Yes. And here she was in his yard. In her underwear.) Didn't he have class today? She couldn't remember. But where had Sam got to?

She worked her way around to the front of the house—freezing, absolutely freezing—and saw nothing amiss, no broken glass, no door left ajar or knocked off its hinges. She knew how Sam thought—he wouldn't run off randomly into the fields when the temptation of a fully stocked kitchen was right there before him. He and Alice had gone straight for the house and if they weren't outside, then there was only one place they could be. She climbed the front steps, her wet hair stinging her shoulders, and tried the front door. It was open.

The room was exactly as she'd remembered it, the knotty pine, the armchairs, the throw rugs, nothing disturbed, nothing out of place. TV. Woodstove. Antimacassars on the chairs. She caught the scent of the air freshener—Spring Meadow—that brought her back to that first day when she'd steeled herself to knock at the door, not knowing what to expect, and something else too, something darker, earthier. Shivering, she stood just inside the door, feeling like a thief, listening for the smallest sound. Chimps weren't subtle, but she could picture them hiding in the closet or behind the couch, holding their breath—hilariously, chimp humor—till she left and they could ransack the place with real dedication. Then she crossed the room to the kitchen, pushed open the door, and there they were.

Alice was up on the counter, rifling the cabinets, a box of Froot Loops in one hand, a second box—Cinnamon Grahams—tucked under one arm. Sam stood in front of the refrigerator, both doors open wide and the buttery glow of the interior light softening his features. There was a bright white smear of cream cheese on his chin and he clutched a half-eaten package of hot dogs to his breast. A carton of eggs lay smashed on the linoleum at his feet in a puddle of ketchup and milk and what looked to be raw chicken livers. He gave her a guilty look, pushed the doors closed and jammed the remainder of the hot dog package in his mouth, as if afraid she'd take it away from him, while Alice, pretending nothing was amiss, settled down on the countertop, threw her head back and began shaking Froot Loops into her mouth.

There were so many things wrong here she could barely think. She was on the verge of hypothermia and needed to get into some clothes right away, but her jeans and sweatshirt were out on the island and she'd have to row back there to get them—with one oar—which she couldn't very well do without first coaxing Sam and Alice back up the hill and into the chimp barn and then fetching and securing Hobart, after which she'd have to clean up the mess here before Dr. Moncrief got back, which could be any minute now for all she knew . . . It was all too much. "Bad," she scolded, "you bad boy, and you, Alice, you bad girl," and she felt utterly ridiculous, as if she were seeing herself from afar, in a dream or movie or some other simulacrum of real life, because this wasn't exactly the sort of interspecies communication she'd yearned for, not even close. No, this was the language of the pet owner, the circus trainer, the language one species used to subject another, and what could she expect in reply? Excuses? Apologies? A treatise on impulse control?

Sam signed, COME HUG.

Alice just sat there, working her jaws. Did she look guilty? Aimee didn't know her well enough to make that determination, but Alice must certainly have known right from wrong, if situational ethics even applied when cages and will and punishment were involved. Was it wrong to escape, to feed yourself, to be yourself? It didn't matter. All that mattered now was imposing her will on these two animals—that's what they were, *animals*—and getting them back in their cages and hiding her own culpability because she was the one who'd ultimately allowed all this to happen.

NO, she signed, NO HUG. And then raised her voice, angry

now, furious: "You get out of here, back to the barn, back to your cage—now! You hear me?"

For the longest moment he didn't react—didn't move—though she knew very well he'd understood her. It could have gone either way. He was in a state of high excitement, adrenaline surging through him, pushing the limits, and he wanted to disobey, wanted to assert himself, because who was she to presume to control him when she was so much the weaker and slower? But he did feel guilt, did feel remorse—and love, love for her—because his eyes softened and he got down on the linoleum tiles, right in the middle of the stew of shattered eggs and all the rest, and prostrated himself, face to the floor, arms outstretched, palms up.

That was when the front door slammed shut with a reverberation that sent a seismic shock through the house and Dr. Moncrief's voice called out, "Hello? Is anybody there? Dorothy, is that you?"

In the aftermath—the shock wave—both chimps vanished, panicked at the sound of Moncrief's voice. Moncrief was the authority, the bringer of pain and retribution, the last word, and if they didn't know God, they knew him. He was the one who wielded the dart gun and the cattle prod and made Azazel, to whom they all in turn submitted, submit to him. Sam and Alice were terrified, and rightly so, because she was terrified herself. There were two doorways to the kitchen, the one through which she'd come and another that gave onto a back hallway, which was where the chimps fled in a concentrated explosion of limbs and hands and feet. "Dorothy?" Moncrief called out again. "Jack?"

And then the door from the living room swung open and he was standing there staring at her, stupefied, for once at a loss for words.

"I'm . . . sorry," was all she could think to say, because how was she going to explain what she was doing there in his desecrated kitchen in her wet underwear in less than ten paragraphs?

"Jesus," he murmured. "You're what—taking a shower? Did Dorothy say you could use the shower or something?" But before she could answer he saw the truth of the matter, the smeared farrago of egg and meat and ketchup on the floor, the ransacked cabinets, smudges on the walls. "Fuck no!" he shouted. "You let them loose? Don't tell me you let them loose?"

"The rowboat. They got the rowboat."

The huge head, the glaring eye—he just stared at her.

"On the pond," she said. "I had to—to swim after them?"

He was on her in two strides, his face bloated and red, and he grabbed her by the arm and jerked her round. "Stupid," he said, "stupid, stupid." And then, tightening his grip: "You're like a rag doll, you know that? I could break you in two—or no, how about if I just throw you across my knee and give you a good spanking, would you like that?"

She tried to pull away, everything boiling up in her, hurt and disgust and shame, because he was right, she was stupid and she'd put everything at risk, but he wouldn't let go. "Answer me," he demanded. "Would you?"

Whatever was to come next, she never discovered, because Sam was suddenly there, bursting into the room and springing up onto the table with a heart-stopping screech—"Wraaaaa!"—that made Moncrief drop her arm and throw up his hands the way Elise had when Sam was so much smaller. And weaker.

"Get back!" Moncrief roared, his face working, his eye bulging, shoulders swinging into play, but she could see that he was scared. Nobody went into any of the cages with any of the chimps, unless the chimps were restrained—that was the rule, and if she was the exception and then only with Sam, there was no way Moncrief liked that either. "Too risky," he'd say to her, the grad students and techs alike, then grin and point to the black leather patch and the slick black ligature of the band digging into the flesh of his face. "Because you know what? You only get two eyes in this lifetime." It had come to her even then, the first time he went through that particular charade, that he was afraid of the chimps, even the juveniles, and here was his moment of truth. Part of her wanted Sam to go for him—Oh, how she wanted it!—but she knew it would be fatal, the end of Sam no matter how it turned out. He'd be put down. Euthanized, killed, murdered, executed, however you wanted to phrase it.

Sam let out another long withering scream, his hair erected, muscles tensed, mouth open wide to display the hard honed canines she made him brush each and every night, teeth that were weapons now, and the only thing she could think to do was take hold of him, throw her arms around him and press him to her even as Moncrief, the color gone out of his face, darted back into the living room and slammed the door.

All right. Now what? Sam's body was made of steel, every muscle tensed to the breaking point, his heart revolving like a lariat, his breath coming in short hard bursts. "It's okay," she murmured, "it's okay, Sam," and then, because she couldn't help herself, she added, "Good boy."

For a minute, two minutes, everything was still. She became aware of the intimate sounds of the house, the ticking of a clock, a drip in the sink, the soft purr of the refrigerator starting up again. She had to move, had to get Sam back in his cage—and Alice too, and Hobart—before something irreversible happened, and she was going to do that, right away, or as soon as she could calm Sam enough to lead him out the door, and she needed to find something to wear, a coat, one of Dorothy's coats, a sweater, anything, and shoes, her feet were killing her . . .

But then Sam tensed all over again, attuned to some subliminal sound she couldn't detect, a creak of the floorboards, the whisper of a breath caught and held, and suddenly the door flung back and Moncrief was there with his dart gun and before she could react— she would have taken the dart herself if she could—he was firing it point-blank at Sam's throat. The dart stuck there as if it were a bowtie and Sam screamed, flailing his arms and showing his teeth, then the second appeared in his chest, then the third, and in the next moment he went slack, all his musculature, all his being, collapsed like an empty paper bag. She heard her own voice sailing out high over the room, "You killed him!"

"Shut up!" Moncrief barked, swinging round on her. "Shut the fuck up! You don't even know what you're talking about!"

She was still holding Sam in her arms, but not to comfort him—it was too late for that. He was like a puppet, a ventriloquist's dummy without the hand and arm to animate it, gone limp now and on the verge of pitching to the floor. If she was bigger, if she was stronger, harder, fiercer, she would have gone after Moncrief with everything she had, would have killed him, she would have . . . but then Sam drew in a ragged phlegmy insuck of breath and she was back in the moment.

"Where's the other one?" Moncrief—Dr. Moncrief, the humanitarian, the educator, friend of animals and grad students alike— was loading another dart into his gun. "Down the back hall? Is that where she went?"

Her voice was very small, so small she could barely hear herself. "Yes," she said, but she was already far from this place, far from the world of cages and guns and this language she didn't speak and didn't want to speak. She would have to gas up the car, pack in a hurry, pay a visit to the bank—and then one more visit, her final visit, to the dank reeking barn on the hill.

ANOTHER BUG

Guy had left him. He was in a cage. He was bored and restless and angry and when Aimee wasn't with him—at night, especially at night—he screamed just for the sake of screaming and if it brought the BIG MAN and the PAIN, at least it was something he was in control of: scream and feel pain, stay silent and feel its absence. He wanted OUT, wanted it more than ever now that he understood what this place was and what his role was and why he was here behind bars and Guy and Aimee and all the rest of them were not—he was a BLACK BUG himself, that was it, that was everything, and he could see it in his feet and his fingers and worst of all in the little square mirror she kept in a snap case in her purse. OUT, he wanted OUT! And more, and worse: he wanted to KILL, he wanted to DIE.

But then one day there was another female, not the original one, the dumb one, but one whose fingers could construct words and make meaning. He'd known something was up from the way Aimee was acting that morning, and he couldn't guess what it was, though he was hoping for a surprise, a TREAT, a trip in the boat, raisins, candy, soda. Aimee was with him in the cage, grooming him and praising him in her soft trickle of a voice, and then when he was distracted just for a second she stepped out and locked the door behind her and he was about to protest, to scream, already working himself up, when the door at the back of the cage slid open and there she was, the new one, the female, the new female. She was older than him, bigger, and when he rushed at her in full display, his hair erect and his hands pounding at the floor and punishing the walls, she ignored him. He danced around her, hooting, beating at the air, shadowboxing (a term he didn't know and would never know, but that was what he was doing), and still she ignored him. And then all at once her eyes fastened on his and she didn't look away as the other one had—no, she stared at him till he was the one to look away. He squatted there, no more than two feet from her, feeling smaller than he had in a long time, feeling embarrassed, if he could feel embarrassed. Or ashamed. Could he feel ashamed?

When he glanced up it was into a thunderclap of amazement: she was signing to him. HELLO HOW ARE YOU?

He was so surprised he couldn't think.

I AM ALICE, she said, finger-spelling her name. WHO—she raised her eyebrows for the verb—YOU?

SAM, he signed. I AM SAM.

Just then a BUG in the next cage over, Hobart, another juvenile, hooted, because he wanted to get in on this and he couldn't. WHO HE? she asked.

Ah, but that was the question, the existential question that had been hidden from him all this time, hidden from him by Guy, by Elise and Josh and Barbara and even Aimee, but he knew the answer now, knew it in the way he knew he was a prisoner, in the way he knew hate for the BIG MAN and the dogs and the hose men and Azazel, so he told her: A BUG. LIKE ME.

She didn't understand. She said, YOU ARE SAM.

He shook his head.

WHO ARE YOU? she asked again.

He looked at his feet, looked at the wrinkled black hide of his too-long fingers, looked at her face, her ugly bristling cartoon of a face, and he snuffed the air and smelled the rank fecal stench of himself, of her, of all of them. A BUG, he signed. ANOTHER BUG.

A PERFECTLY ADEQUATE
CONDUIT OF EXPRESSION

He was just coming up the steps on his way home from class, juggling a bag of groceries, his briefcase and his dry cleaning, when he heard the phone ringing from inside the house. There was only the top lock to deal with now, and he already had his key out so he didn't have to set down the groceries or fumble through his pockets, yet by the time he got to the phone it had stopped ringing. Which was no great tragedy—the only good news he was anticipating would come via the U.S. mail bearing the logo of the NIH or NSF, and he'd already checked the mailbox, which contained nothing but flyers and bills he barely had the funds to cover after settling the project's final accounts.

Inside, everything was soft-edged and gray and the house was cold, though it must have been seventy outside. It could have been cleaner too, but that was something he'd been addressing in stages, along with packing his clothes and getting rid of the furniture. Josh and Barbara had stopped by to help him move the bigger things (couch, armchairs, kitchen set) to the apartment he'd rented on East Boone, near the campus. His bedroom was intact for now, but all Sam's things were gone, as was everything in the guest room, which depressed him. He ate standing at the counter most nights or in bed in front of the TV. Last he'd heard the school was planning on repurposing the ranch as a conference center.

There were four messages on the answering machine, all from Moncrief. The first two delivered the same injunction, "Call me," Moncrief's voice captured in a crackling burst of phlegm as if he was trying to choke down a slice of dry toast and form the words at the same time. The third, which was so clear and immediate it was as if Moncrief were standing right there next to the refrigerator, was "Jesus fucking Christ, where the fuck are you?" The fourth, delivered just fifteen minutes ago, came across in a controlled roar: "Pick up, goddammit, pick up already!"

He took his time, tearing the plastic off the shirts he'd got back from the cleaner's and hanging them in the closet before they got wrinkled, then putting the groceries away and pouring himself a glass of a local pinot noir he'd had to go out and buy himself (no more freebies from the friends of the project since there was no project, not anymore), before he picked up the phone and dialed Moncrief. He tried him at home first—it was just past seven in Iowa, so it was unlikely he'd be at school still—but Dorothy answered and said he hadn't come home yet.

"Is there anything wrong? He called four times, but I wasn't home all day and I just got his messages."

"Frankly, Guy? I don't know, but he was in one of his moods when he came down from the barn around one or so. He didn't say ten words to me—he just changed his clothes and slammed out the door—but I got the distinct impression that he had a bug under his collar, if you know what I mean, and I've learned the hard way not to ask."

"Should I try him at school?"

"Yes, Guy," she said, her voice soft and placatory, "I think that would be a good idea."

Moncrief answered on the first ring. "Where is she?" he demanded.

"Who?"

"*Who?* Your girlfriend, that's who."

He was trying to put things together, fitting the pieces in place, doing the math: Where was she? How would he know? In her apartment, the chimp barn, out on the island—or a movie, maybe she went to a movie. "I don't know, I haven't talked to her in a couple of days, if that—and I know I should call more, just to keep in touch, but it's the end of the semester and—"

Moncrief cut him off. "She stole my fucking property and I want it back."

He was at a loss. He was going to say "What property?" and then it came to him: "Sam?"

"Not a word. Nothing. Jack comes in this morning and finds an empty cage. You know how much that animal is worth?"

He did. Because every time the subject came up—Renee Flowers, *Johnny!*—he let him know. And now, since the government had imposed a ban on importing chimps because of the collapse of the wild populations, the animals the breeders had on hand were potentially worth all the more—even if they did ultimately wind up in laboratories. "There must be some explanation. Did you try her apartment?"

"What am I, a detective? A fucking bloodhound? Maybe you're not hearing me: she stole my property and I want it back. Now. Today, tonight."

"Well, okay, yeah—calm down. If I hear from her I'll tell her, of course I will."

"You'll hear from her. She's your main squeeze, isn't she? Your little fuckstress?"

"Donald, come on, you don't have to be like that—"

"Like what?"

"It's not fair to her."

"Not fair to *her*? What about me? You forgetting your priorities here or what?"

He knew exactly what his priorities were—and they involved sucking up to the man on the other end of this perfectly adequate conduit of expression and to Leonard Biggs and the granters of grant money and all the other high priests of the science foundations. He said, "I'll do everything I can."

"Everything you can? Yeah, well, that's a good start. But look. You tell her this from me—if he's not back in that cage in twenty-four hours, I'm calling Roy Stennett down at the state police division, who happens to be a personal friend of mine, and she *will* go to jail, that's a promise."

For a long while after he'd hung up the phone he sat out on the back porch with his wine and a cigarette, watching the light play off the high rock ledges behind the house. There'd been a late rain at the end of April and the chaparral was in bloom still, little white flowers like snowflakes decorating the mesquite, something else gone a vivid yellow against a low blue creep of what was it—ceanothus? Aimee would know, but then Aimee wasn't here, was she? She was out on the road somewhere, with Sam, probably with no money and no place to go. He tried to get his head around that, but all he could summon were snapshots of disaster, and was she planning on coming back here? Or to her mother's house—or maybe the aunt's, if the aunt even existed? It got worse: what if Sam glanced out the window and saw a dog or a horse or an Amish buggy he didn't like? What if he punched out the windshield or made a grab for somebody at a stoplight? At that very moment he was no doubt shitting all over the backseat or making his demands—to be groomed, to sit in her lap, play with that nice shiny revolving plastic toy called a steering wheel, twist off the key, beep the horn. Where was she going to hide him? What was she going to feed him? How was she going to pay for it?

A hummingbird shot straight up in the air, then angled down again, hovering and flitting, and two of the steers that used to so excite Sam picked their way delicately across the back lot, pausing to browse on one shrub or another, wide around as barrels. Nobody was teaching them how to talk. They were as stupid as nature made them—or actually, as smart as they had to be to survive till something crept up behind them equipped with teeth and claws or the truck to the slaughterhouse pulled into the driveway. After a while he went back in the house and began dialing numbers—Josh, Barbara, Janie, Elise, even Jack Serfis in Iowa. Nobody had heard from her. Everybody was shocked.

It wasn't till two days later—early evening, another bottle of wine, fast food out of a bag—that the phone rang again and her voice came over the line. "Don't be mad," she said.

"Are you crazy? I mean, have you gone completely out of your mind?"

Her voice tightened: "I didn't call to get yelled at."

"I'm not yelling. I just—I'm concerned, that's all. Worried about you—Moncrief called, which is how I found out, and I'll tell you, he's going ballistic."

"So?"

"So? What do you mean, 'So?' He reported you to the police, you know that, don't you? And he swears up and down he's going to press charges, which is no joke, believe me—and remind me, how many times did we discuss this? How many times did I pronounce the words 'grand theft,' 'felony,' 'jail time'? Shit, Aimee, what are you thinking? You've got California plates and a hyperactive animal just ready to explode sitting next to you in the passenger seat—how hard do you think it's going to be for the cops to find you?"

He was in the kitchen, clutching the grimy yellow receiver that still bore Sam's tooth marks, the wine buzzing in his brain like the cascabels of the snakes that routinely slithered down out of the rocks, the ones they were always so afraid would bite Sam, send him into cardiac arrest, kill him, when in fact they were killing him themselves—or at least Moncrief was. He saw Aimee's face then—and Sam's—and felt a vast sorrow open up inside him.

"Look," he said, "I'm sorry, I don't mean to lecture you. I'm glad you called—I've been worried about you."

"Really? You don't sound like it."

He should have said something with a little affection in it, something soft and intimate to remind her—remind them both—of the relationship they'd had, of love, or at least the lovemaking that was the propeller of it. He said, "I miss you. And Sam too. Where are you, anyway?"

"In a campground."

"A campground? Where?"

He could feel her presence over the line, feel her thinking, as if mental processes were transferrable, as if the words didn't need to emerge from her larynx and take shape on her palate and tongue— she wasn't going to tell him. She was going to blow him off. After all their time together, after all they'd had, it came down to this. She said, "If you're wondering about Sam, he's fine. Happy, actually. Can you believe it—he's *happy*." She paused, the moment held in equipoise. "And you know why?"

"Because he's with you?"

"Because he's not in a cage anymore."

A movement beyond the window distracted him—a squirrel making its way up the trunk of the oak, its tail beating like a pulse. He said, "But he's going to be, as soon as they catch up to you—in where, Dinksville, Iowa? They'll put him in the dog pound, you know—if you're lucky. They might just shoot him if he makes a fuss, and he will make a fuss, you know that, especially if he thinks you're under threat, which you will be. They're going to put you in a cage too—and don't expect me to bail you out."

"I don't expect anything from you, not anymore."

"Oh, come on, Aimee, please. Give me a break here. You know I don't mean that—I'm just frustrated, that's all. And worried. Deeply, fucking insanely *worried*. Okay?" He paused, shuffling across the kitchen with the phone pressed to his ear so he could pick up the half-full glass and drain it in a gulp because he suddenly had the fiercest burning thirst and a blistering headache on top of it. "But I need to know where you are—"

"I told you—a campground."

The circularity. Didn't she know how crazy she was making him? He'd thought she was malleable, easy pickings, a girl he could ride and ride, but he was wrong. "Yeah," he said. "Right. But a campground *where?*"

Now it was her turn. A long pause. The squirrel flagged its tail, a branch swayed, a stray leaf sailed to the ground. "I'm sorry," she said, her voice as shallow and toneless as the wind sifting through all the canyons of the world. "I'm really sorry."

THREE

THERE WAS NO MOON

There was no moon the night she took him and there were no stars either, the clouds low and ribbed and giving up nothing. A moon would have been nice, would have made things easier, because she certainly wasn't about to use a flashlight. She wasn't about to take the car up the drive either, so she parked out on the main road, eased the door shut and stood there in the dark a moment, letting her eyes adjust. The night was cool enough to silence the crickets and since there were no cars passing by at this hour, the only sound was the soft sporadic call of the owl that had taken up residence in the disused hayloft of the barn and regurgitated the hard little pellets of rat bone and fur she sometimes found on the doorstep in the morning. The only problem was the light burning on the second floor of the house, which meant that somebody was awake still. That light almost stopped her. She pictured Dr. Moncrief stalking around up there, unable to sleep, the leather patch dangling from a bedpost and his naked eye socket a sinkhole of puckered flesh, clocks ticking, floorboards creaking, and she felt herself losing momentum. She crouched in the weeds, fighting the urge to sneeze, and stared at the window as if she could will the light to go out.

She was dressed all in black, hooded sweatshirt, black jeans, Converse high-tops, and she planned to be quick, in and out. She'd brought along a can of Vienna sausages for the two Dobermans to keep them quiet, but the biggest problem would be getting Sam out of there before the rest of the chimps caught wind of it and started screaming. Five minutes went by. Ten. The light in the window shone steadily, mockingly, sadistically. What to do? Wait it out? But people fell asleep with the lights on, didn't they? And even if they didn't, even if Dr. Moncrief was lying there wide awake with his hearing attuned to the slightest irregularity, she was going to go up that hill, anyway, so she might as well steel herself and do it. She took a deep breath, rose silently from the bushes and followed the pale tongue of gravel up the hill to the barn, where the glow of the interior lights leached out into the darkness to orient her. Everything was still. No dogs barked, no chimps stirred, no outraged voice bellowed from the second-story window behind her.

The dogs were asleep, lying in the grass with their backs pressed up against the perimeter fence, but she called softly to them and pushed two of the sausages through the mesh and into their wet eager mouths so that they'd see it was only her and not raise the alarm when she and Sam eased out the door five minutes from now. "Good dogs," she whispered. Then she opened the door and stepped into the lighted hallway.

She expected Sam to be asleep, and he was, but the surprise—the shock—was that Alice was in the cage with him, sleeping with her head tucked into his chest and one arm thrown over his shoulder. Before she'd left work that afternoon she'd locked Alice back in her own cage, so somebody must have thought to put them together again, whether it was Jack or Christian, the other tech, and that was good, that was right—they needed company, they needed each other—and under any other circumstances she would have been pleased. But not tonight. Tonight it was just another complication, maybe even a fatal one. She was terrified, actually trembling as she inched silently across the floor, the whole plan on the verge of collapse, because how was she going to get Sam out of there without waking Alice? She could see it already: Alice would jolt awake. Alice would want out. Alice would start screaming and the whole place would erupt.

This was an eventuality she hadn't planned on, and she was so thrown off she found she already had the key in the lock before she remembered the medicine cabinet, which she had to visit first if she had any hope of getting away undetected. The medicine cabinet was located in the hallway leading to the back cages and what she wanted there were the tranquilizers they used to calm the chimps before the vet paid a call or some visiting researcher took a tour of the facilities. Sam had showed no ill effects from the Sernalyn Moncrief had darted him with yesterday afternoon (it wasn't possible to overdose on it, though no one had told her that), but it wasn't Sernalyn she was after. They kept a supply of methaqualone on hand, which was more dangerous because animals could overdose on it, but it was preferable in certain situations since it wouldn't totally immobilize them. She planned to grind up a tablet and mix it into a can of Coke—Sam's favorite, which he could never resist—by way of keeping him quiet at least until they were out of the state. After that, she didn't know. She didn't even know where she was going to take him, but what she did know, what she swore to herself, was that she was going to get him out of there. For good.

The lights held steady, though they were dimmed at night, thankfully. The chimps in the adjoining cages never stirred—they lay sprawled on the concrete like a tribe of refugees displaced by war, some on their backs, others on their sides or curled up in the fetal position cradling their heads in their arms. She thought she'd gotten used to the smell of the place, but now all of a sudden it felt like a fist punching her in the face, worse at night because there was nobody there to sluice the crap down the drains. It was so heavy she could almost taste it, ammoniac and vile—she hated it, hated this place—but after tonight she'd never have to endure it again. Nor would Sam. She'd thought of slipping the bottle of pills into her pocket when she'd gone home at the end of the day, but Moncrief kept a tight watch over the supply—students, techs, party drugs—and she hadn't wanted to take the chance of anything giving her away, so here she was, easing down the half-lit hallway and trying to breathe as much as possible through her mouth, on her way to steal drugs in the dead of night.

The key to the cabinet was taped to the top of one of the overhead pipes at the end of the corridor, just opposite Azazel's cage. She hadn't been trusted with it—Jack and Dr. Moncrief were the only ones allowed access to the cabinet—but she'd seen Jack reach up and anchor something atop the pipe one afternoon when she was hosing out the cages, and once he'd left for the day, she climbed up on a stool and found it there. At that point, she didn't have a plan beyond getting through each day without breaking down, but she filed the information away all the same, one more detail to orient her in this purgatory of a place. Now she went to the broom closet, fetched the stool and retrieved the key as noiselessly as if she were in a movie without a soundtrack.

There were two 500-count bottles in the cabinet, one half empty, the other still sealed. She took the unopened one and stuffed it in her pocket, returned the stool to the closet (no sense in alerting them to the fact that the drugs were missing too) and then went back to the cage. Neither Sam nor Alice had moved, both of them locked in a trance-like sleep, Alice's face still buried in Sam's chest, her arm still flung over his shoulder. For one wild moment, she thought of taking them both, but she fought down the impulse—this was hard enough as it was. Slowly, her movements studied and deliberate, she pulled the can of sausages from her pocket and extracted two links, then broke the seal on the bottle of pills—Sopors, as the local stoners called them—and worked a pill into each of them. She hadn't foreseen it this way, because she was going to need Sam to be able to walk on his own, hence the Coke, which she'd planned to give him once they were in the car and safely away, but then the presence of Alice changed everything. If she didn't put him out now, he'd want to play, which meant he'd make noise and noise would give them away.

The small sounds—animals shifting in their sleep, a fan switching on, the muffled hoot of the owl—and then she was in the cage and petting Sam awake, so filled with love for him she could have seized up and died right there. He always slept deeply, like any child, and she kept running her hands through his hair over and over, afraid to speak, even in a whisper. When they were together at the ranch, in the same bed, he'd always been slow to wake, content to lie there and let consciousness seep back into him filament by filament till he knew where he was and that the sun was shining and she was there beside him. She began prodding him now because he wasn't responding— they had to get out of there, each second teetering on the cusp of disaster—and she was about to take the risk and whisper "Sam, time to wake up," when suddenly his eyes flashed open and he came up fast with a hard angry grunt and a show of teeth that startled her as if this wasn't Sam at all but some wild chimp she'd never laid eyes on before. It was just an instant, but it shook her, and then he was back in the world. His eyes went soft and he stretched out his arms to her even as Alice woke and propped herself on her elbows, looking puzzled and disoriented. Sam signed, WHAT?, which covered a whole range of questions—What are you doing here? Is it morning? Time for breakfast, for a walk, for the boat and the island and treats?—and she pressed a finger to her lips and gave them both a fierce warning look.

DON'T MAKE A SOUND, she signed. I BROUGHT TREATS JUST FOR YOU—DON'T LET THE OTHERS KNOW. SHHHHH!

And then she handed each of them a sausage.

The worst part of it was sitting there in that cage with her heart pounding for a full thirty minutes before Alice's eyelids began to flicker and she slumped back against the wall. Sam was showing the effects too, his eyes grown distant and a thin silvery strand of drool clinging to his lower lip, but Sam was going to have to walk because he was almost as heavy as she was now and there was no way she could carry him or even drag him if that was what it came to. Which meant she couldn't delay a minute longer—she'd have to risk Alice spreading the alarm because Alice wasn't fully out yet and as soon as the key turned in the lock there was no telling what she'd do. She told herself to be calm. Gathering her legs beneath her, she rose slowly to her knees, Alice's eyes following her every movement. Then she was on her feet and reaching down to take Sam by the hand and Alice was trying to push herself up and at the same time reach for her other hand—if one chimp was going to GO OUT, it was only fair that they both go—but the drug wouldn't let her. Aimee was at the door, pushing it open now, and Sam, struggling for balance, was right there at her side. Slumped against the wall, her hands moving in slow motion, Alice signed, ME GO TOO, but that wasn't an option, it never had been and never would be, and Aimee signed, SORRY, which was sincere, and then TOMORROW, which was a lie.

Just as they got to the outside door, there was a violent thump, flesh on metal, and she shot a glance down the length of the hall to see Azazel clinging to the bars of his cage, staring back at her. When he was sure she was watching, he thumped the bars again, then rattled them with a quick jerk and thrust of his arms, but he didn't hoot or scream or vocalize at all. Sam didn't seem to notice. His eyelids fluttered, his limbs went slack and he clutched her hand as if he was falling out of a tree. She felt the panic rising in her. All it would take was a single scream and she'd be caught—and if she was caught she'd be fired and if she was fired she'd never see Sam again. Azazel held her eyes, then bent down and thrust his hand through the food slot at the bottom of the cage door, clutching and releasing his fingers in the GIMME gesture that didn't have to be imparted or acquired. Put a creature in a cage, any creature, and you've got a de facto beggar, but then it dawned on her that this wasn't begging—it was extortion.

"Okay," she whispered, "okay," and she dropped Sam's hand and made her way down the line of cages, holding the can of sausages out before her in offering. The sound of her own breathing roared in her ears. Her eyes teared. Her heart pounded. Even in her extremity, even though she could think of nothing but getting Sam down the hill and into the car, she knew better than to get too close, and so she stood back three feet from the cage and slid the can through the slot in the door. Azazel ignored it. He kept his hand in place, clutching and releasing his fingers in rapid succession: GIMME GIMME GIMME.

It wasn't until he rose to his feet and fingered the lock in the door that she understood: he wanted the key. He wanted OUT. But he'd never been out, not for years—if he got out he wouldn't just raid refrigerators and trash kitchens, he'd rend, crush, kill. The key was in her pocket, the can of sausages was on the floor. Sam was woozy. The night was slipping away. She pointed down at the can to distract him—he was an animal, wasn't he?—but he never even glanced at it. He tapped the lock, then gripped the bars and rattled them again. There was no way she was going to give him that key, no matter how much she hated this place and feared and despised Moncrief, and he must have seen that in her eyes because even before she turned and started running, he was screaming.

She didn't lock the door behind her or even pull it closed. In a panic, with all forty chimps instantly on their feet and shrieking, she snatched Sam's hand and tugged him out into the night even as a second light went on in the house and the dogs she'd bribed flung themselves at the chain link and barked for all they were worth. Sam was unsteady on his feet and they hadn't gone ten steps before he had to get down on all fours, which meant she had to bend double and guide him with a fierce urgent hand under one arm, pulling, jerking, twisting, anything to get him moving. "Hurry, Sam, come on," she kept repeating in a harsh whisper, the house looming ahead of her and the gravel drive like a treadmill in one of the cartoons Sam loved to watch—they were moving as fast as they could and yet they were all but standing still.

"The car, Sam," she breathed, furious, panicky, and why couldn't he *move*? The drug was a mistake, she saw that now, and should she leave him for just a second and go fetch the car no matter what was going on inside that house? Is that what it was going to take? But no, she couldn't leave him and she was never going to leave him, never again. She tugged his arm and urged him on—"Hurry, Sam, *hurry!* A ride, Sam, we're going for a ride!"

The chimps shrieked. The dogs barked. Something beat past her in the dark—the owl?—and then suddenly the outdoor light flicked on and the figure of Dr. Moncrief appeared on the porch, his face a distorted sheet of flesh bleached by the harshness of the light, and in the next instant he was shouting, "Shut the fuck up, you little shits! Shut up! You hear me?"

She froze. Sam froze beside her. They were just beyond the arc of light, shadows among shadows, and could he see them? With one eye?

At night? She brought an arm up to minimize the sheen of her face, cursing herself—why hadn't she worn a ski mask? Or blackface? Or—

"Don't make me come up there!" Moncrief boomed and let out an arpeggio of curses, his voice climbing higher and higher atop the screams till the noise planed off, then died down to a sniff and whimper and the last desolate tailing bark of one of the dogs. For a long moment he stood there glaring out into the darkness and then, satisfied, he turned and went back in the house. An instant later the porch light died and the night rushed back in, but still she didn't move. She held Sam close, petting him, shushing him, until finally—it must have been ten minutes or more—both the upstairs lights flicked off and she took Sam under the arm and led him down the drive and out to the road where she guided him into the passenger seat and wrapped him in the blanket she'd brought all the way from California and kept neatly folded on the shelf above her bed against this very moment.

She ran on adrenaline at first, then switched to the thermos of coffee she'd brought along so she wouldn't have to stop. What she was doing, though she was as scared and frazzled and jumpy as she'd ever been in her life, was reversing the route she'd taken back in January, I-80 west to I-70, pushing her limits in the hope she could get far enough away before they discovered Sam was missing. At least it was dark, when nobody would notice what species of being was slumped in the passenger seat and she could rivet her eyes on the rearview for any headlights coming up on her too fast, and maybe she was overreacting—they wouldn't even know Sam was gone till morning—but she couldn't help herself. She was wound up, burning through the night in full panic mode, her stomach acidic, her nose running, and yet the thing that mattered, the only thing that mattered, was that Sam was right there beside her.

She didn't have a destination in mind—all she knew was that she was going west, and not to her mother's house or the ranch, which would be too obvious—but as the road fled beneath the wheels and the mileposts slashed by, the image of Green River suddenly came to her. It was a good sixteen or seventeen hours from Davenport, but she remembered a campground there on the river with a grove of trees that would at least provide a little privacy—she could set up the tent she'd bought that morning at the sporting goods store and have maybe a day or two to think things through. And if she couldn't make it that far and had to pull over at a truck stop and conk out for an hour or two, it wouldn't be like before, not with Sam there—all the cowboys and truckers and garage mechanics in the world couldn't touch her. But then the main problem, the overriding problem, was Sam himself. He'd never been on a drive anywhere near this long and she couldn't keep feeding him pills, could she? Plus, he'd have to eat and relieve himself. And so would she. Could she just put him on his leash and lead him into the ladies' room at some random rest stop? Or take him out to the little circle of crapped-over grass reserved for dogs?

Why not? People traveled with dogs all the time—there were pet-friendly motels, trailer courts, backstreet apartments in towns nobody had ever heard of, not even the people who lived there themselves, PETS WELCOME, SMOKING PERMITTED, BARKING ENCOURAGED. There were pets everywhere. People loved pets, couldn't live without them. She'd seen a guy in Santa Monica once walking a bobcat on a leash and the one time she'd gone to Europe a woman in spike heels and a tight skirt walking a leopard alongside one of the canals in Amsterdam, or maybe it was an ocelot. And monkeys—a girl in her high school had a pet squirrel monkey she took with her everywhere, Baskin-Robbins, the mall, on her bike even. And once he woke up, Sam would be on his best behavior because he would be quick to assess the situation and understand that they weren't going back anymore, that they were free, both of them, and he was going to have to live in the world now like he used to when they were at the ranch and she'd take him into town to McDonald's or the post office or the park with its slides and swings and jungle gym. Her mind shuffled through the possibilities, quick cameos of the future like phantom images flickering on the roadway out ahead of her, and for whole minutes at a time she forgot just how desperate the situation was. But then, like a record on repeat, it all came back to her—who was she kidding? Sam was a magnet. The minute he showed himself, people would come flocking to him and whether he was okay with it or not depended on his mood, and even if nothing happened, they'd all remember him and if they remembered him she would be leaving a trail so obvious she might as well be sending postcards.

All those road movies, *Badlands*, *The Getaway*, *Bonnie and Clyde*. How easy it was, pretend desperadoes in their freshly applied makeup and perfect hairdos just gliding across the screen till the inevitable caught up with them—Martin Sheen, Sissy Spacek, Warren Beatty— but all they'd had to hide was themselves or the loot or whatever it was. Try hiding a chimp with the energy level of a supersonic rocket and a face nobody could ever forget. "Green River," she told herself, said it out loud under the soft pulse of her mix tape, *Roadrunner, roadrunner, going faster miles an hour*, and felt a wave of exhaustion rise up inside her till it obliterated all sense and she was reduced to a pair of prehensile hands gripping a hard black plastic steering wheel in a white tunnel of the night. She had to pee. She had to lie down. She had to keep going.

Two days later, the tent set back from the river in as protected a spot as she could find, she and Sam shared a supper of Dinty Moore beef stew with a beer each to wash it down, then drove to the nearest phone booth. The phone booth stood outside one of the gas stations that seemed to be the central attraction of Green River, and she circled the lot twice just to be sure nobody was watching before she pulled up alongside it. By now it was dark and Sam was shrunk down in the seat in any case, mellowed by the beer and her presence and the novelty of life lived in a tent instead of a steel cage, so it wasn't likely anybody would notice him. He leaned all the way back, hooting softly to himself, drunk, or at least halfway drunk. Out of habit, she admonished him to behave himself, then stepped out of the car and placed a call to Guy because she didn't know what else to do.

She thought he'd be relieved to hear from her, but he started lecturing her right from the start. She wanted help, she wanted reassurance, but all she got was a guilt trip. Finally, after three or four minutes of going back and forth and settling exactly nothing, he said, "But I need to know where you are," and she said, "I told you—a campground."

THE TENT

It was like skin, like a jacket of cool smooth blue skin that ballooned out over him and kept the sun off and the rain too, except there was no rain. He could almost see through it and then when the sun was directly overhead, all of a sudden he could—or at least make out shapes and movement and the tall straight poles of the trees. It wasn't a CAGE. Touch it and it gave beneath your fingers, touch it again and it was the same, and then again, and again. He made a game of it, tapping it both inside and out, thrusting his head and arm through the door—the FLAP, new word, finger-spell it—until she told him to stop. He signed, WHY? and she said, "Because we have to hide," and he signed, WHY? and she said, "Because they'll take you back to your cage," and he felt a hard plug of fear and hate and rage break loose and rocket through his veins, which made him breathe hard and erect all his hair until he calmed down enough to sign WHO?, though he already knew the answer, and she said, "The Big Man."

I WON'T GO.

"I won't either. That's why we have to hide and be quiet—can you be quiet for me?"

I WON'T GO, he signed, but the FLAP distracted him, the way it fell open and closed with the touch of a single finger, which led him to glance beyond it, outside where there was a view of other TENTS and CARS and the cold hard glint of the river, which was where he wanted to go and catch things that hopped and jumped and tasted like mud and slap BUGS and put his feet in the water, so he flipped open the FLAP for the hundredth time and just started running for the pure joy of it while she shouted his name and came chasing after him. It was fun—and funny too. She couldn't keep up with him, not anymore, and he ducked behind the trees, the rocks, only to pop out and sign YOU CHASE ME.

"It's not funny, Sam," she said, breathing hard. "You come over here and stop fooling around or I'll get your lead, you want me to get your lead?"

That was when a man appeared in the picture, coming up the path from the river, a man like Josh or Jack with BLUE JEANS and a T-SHIRT and a beard that was like a weed growing out of his face and he had a stick in his hand, a long thin black stick. Birds were making noise and there was the *shush-shush-shush* of tires in the distance. The trees were scrawny, with pale trunks, and the sun slapped at the water and jumped high up into the leaves. The man had a stick in his hand and he felt something he couldn't name, something beyond naming, and his hair stiffened in the same moment he snatched up a stick of his own and rose to his feet and Aimee said, "Sam, no," her voice gone high and thin in her throat. That was when he saw that what the man had in his hand was not a stick at all, but a long flexible whip-like rod that had STRING attached to it for catching FISH and it was like a thunderclap inside his head because that was exactly what he wanted to do in that moment, catch a FISH like when he and Alice and Aimee were on the island and they stabbed the hooks through the pale squirming flesh of the WORMS that tasted of the dirt they came from. He dropped the stick and went right up to the man and it didn't matter in the slightest bit that she was running toward him repeating, "No, Sam," over and over.

"Whoa," the man said, grinning now to show he was friendly, "I didn't realize what it was. He's not a dog, I can see that now. Really, I thought it was a dog at first, because you don't . . . what is he, a chimpanzee, right?"

"He's okay," she was saying, and she was right there beside him now, heaving for breath, her face as white as the paper on the roller in the TOILET out by the road. "He's harmless. He just—I think it's the fishing rod?"

He had his hand on the rod now, his fingers on the string, on the flexible bow of the rod, working the thing back and forth from the point where the man clutched it in one hand as if thinking he was going to take it away from him—which he was, which he did, and now he had it, bending and releasing it again. And again. FISH. He wanted to catch FISH.

"Really? You mean, he knows how to fish?"

She was smiling now, everything okay, everything fine, FISH! "It's his favorite thing, or one of them, anyway. Isn't that right, Sam?"

He was listening but at the same time he wasn't. He'd been in a cage. Now he wasn't in a cage. Now he was here under the trees with her and this man and a fishing rod. He nodded. Emphatically. Two times. Three.

She had her hands on her hips, gazing down at him as if she were showing him off. And she was, he understood that, and he knew his role too—to be calm, non-threatening, CUTE. That was it, that was all it took when the door of the cage or the house or the car swung open and you were out in the world where everybody strutted around on their two legs with their heads held high and shopped and ate cheeseburgers and drove down the streets in their CARS. How many times had she cooed that word to him, that designation that had no fangs in it, no nails, no grip of iron: CUTE. He was going to go fishing. He was going to take the man's rod—borrow it, use it, tangle the line and untangle it again—and the whole time he was going to make himself every bit as CUTE as he could.

DESERT HAVEN

She'd always remember the day Aimee first came to the trailer court, and not because of anything in the news, which basically just featured whatever humanitarian catastrophe was going on at the time, or the weather either, which was the same as it always was in summer, high-ceilinged and hotter than it had a right to be, but because of Sam. You couldn't forget the first time you saw him—he was a novelty, to say the least. She and Gary had never experienced anything like him before, not up close and personal, anyway, though they'd both seen the Tarzan movies on TV when they were kids living in cities a thousand miles apart, and of course, *Planet of the Apes*, but there were no apes in the desert. Which made Sam stand out all the more—Arizona didn't have a whole lot in common with the African jungle, where chimps were as ordinary as lizards out here, though from what she'd heard the Tarzan movies had been filmed in Florida.

Same difference—there was a jungle there too, wasn't there? Cheetah, that was the name of Tarzan's chimp—his sidekick, really—and if they used different chimps in different pictures, the same as with Lassie and Rin Tin Tin and all the other animal stars, they were stars just the same. Sam himself had been on TV at some point, so he was a kind of star too. Did she remember *To Tell the Truth*, which was on till just a couple years ago? She did, but in the way of distant recollection, flickering and hazy, and whether she'd seen the episode with him on it or not, she couldn't say.

The first thing Aimee asked her when she pulled into the lot, even before she inquired about price and availability, was "Do you take pets?" It was nine in the morning and she was alone in the office at the time, doing the crossword in the *Miner*, and Gary was out and about somewhere, collecting the lot rents from the people who always seemed to conveniently forget it was the first of the month. The TV in the corner was on, without sound, a jumble of images like a bright little mosaic set in the wall, and she had the fan going. It was early yet and not much more than eighty or so, but the weather said it was going to climb up into the nineties, maybe even hit a hundred, so she figured she might as well be prepared. She looked up from her crossword and saw a pretty girl standing there in the doorway, one leg in, one leg out, as if she couldn't make up her mind whether to come in or not.

"Yes," she said, "we do. As long as the owner's responsible for cleaning up after them—nobody really likes stepping in dog poo, right?" She gave her a smile but the girl didn't smile back. "But tell me—you interested in a rental or purchase? Because we've got a single-wide just came up for sale or we could do a rental—is it just you, or—?"

"Just me."

That was fine, business as usual, but Sam didn't make his appearance until things were already settled—first and last month's rent, option to buy—so any objections she might have had were moot. Aimee had parked her car just inside the entrance, a good hundred feet from the office, as if she couldn't decide if she wanted to be there or not, which as it turned out was partly from shyness and partly calculation, since she didn't know how people were going to react to the sight of her particular brand of pet. (She herself wasn't prejudiced, or not especially—she'd rented to people who kept all sorts of animals, chickens, goats, horses, even one guy, now gone, thankfully, who had six terrariums full of poisonous snakes and a Burmese python he let wander the trailer at will and twice got away through the water hookup under the sink. And was that a nightmare? First thing everybody did was get their guns out.)

When Sam did finally show himself, all head and ears and big round staring eyes, he just seemed to pop up out of nowhere when Aimee went to move her car. One minute there was nothing there, and then there was this thing, this *animal* . . . it gave her a scare, or maybe not a scare, actually, more of a surprise or jolt or whatever you want to call it. She'd thought a dog maybe, a big dog, a Rottweiler or Doberman or something, but Sam was no dog. Once you saw that, you still had to blink twice, because he looked like a buffed-up overgrown kid in his jumpsuit and polo shirt with the sleeves cut off, a sixth grader on steroids. *A chimp*, she said to herself, *how about that? A chimp like Cheetah, only bigger.*

Aimee had him in a harness with a leash clipped to it, and after she parked in front of the trailer (the last one down the second row in the spill of big boulders at the foot of the mesa), she went around the car to let him out the passenger door, though he could have opened it himself, which no dog could have done. And that was something— there he was, climbing down out of the car as nice as you please— and though she should have gone back to the office and the thousand irritating little tasks that awaited her there, she couldn't move. Or no, she could, and did, but it was in the direction of Sam. It was as if she'd been hypnotized.

Nobody else was around at that hour, which would have been unusual except that it was the first of the month and the people who conveniently forgot to pay their lot rent conveniently decided to stay out of sight and pretend they'd gone deaf when Gary knocked on the door—and that was just as well because it gave her the space to process what she was seeing without having to place it in the context of what anybody else might think. In the next moment, Sam bounced down out of the car, humped up the three steps to the door of the trailer and paused there to look back over his shoulder at Aimee, as if asking permission. Aimee said, "Yes, Sam, it's okay—this is your new house, go on in and see how you like it," and she dropped the leash and let him go free. The amazing thing was that he understood every word she was saying—he reeled in the leash, swung open the door and disappeared inside as if it was the sort of thing he did every day.

"Oh, my god," she said, coming up behind Aimee, who was pulling an overstuffed backpack and a bag of kibble (Monkey Chow, actually) out of the trunk of her car. "That is the most precious thing I've ever seen."

"Oh, hi," Aimee said, blushing as if she'd been caught out—and she had. She set the bag of kibble down on the gravel and turned round to face her. "I'm just—I mean, give me a second? Just to get settled? And I'll introduce you."

But here was the chimp, pushing the door back open and reaching up to dangle from the doorframe on the twin cables of his arms like an enormous spider, except that spiders don't have faces and spiders don't grin. He made a cooing sound and looked right at her. "This is Sam," Aimee said, glancing from her to the chimp and back. "Sam, come on down here and say hello."

He seemed to think about that a second, as if he had better things to do, but Aimee repeated his name in a low warning tone and he dropped from the doorframe and came down the steps and across the gravel in a way that managed to be both ungainly and graceful, if that made any sense, and the next thing she knew he was holding out his hand for a shake.

He was so human, but at the same time he wasn't, as if the whole point of him was to undermine the human species. All her life she'd found herself stepping back mentally at the oddest moments, seeing people in a sudden flash as just big animals tricked out in clothes, old people especially, with their elongated ears and cratered nostrils and skin rippled like a lizard's, and here was the reality come home to her. She shook Sam's hand with its long fingers and callused knuckles and it was just like shaking hands with anybody else. He held on a fraction of a moment too long, then dropped her hand, looked up to be sure she was watching and began spinning out signs with his fingers the way deaf people do. Which just made the whole thing all the stranger. She looked to Aimee. "Is he trying to say something?"

Aimee's eyes had gone soft. She had the sort of look mothers get when their children are on display, first day of school, spelling bee, gold star for deportment. "He's saying. 'Pleased to meet you, my name's Sam, what's yours?'"

That was the moment she felt her heart going out to him. It was hard to explain, and she supposed it did have to do with the human part of him, and why not? That was what gave him his personality, that was what made him so phenomenal, light-years ahead of all the dogs and cats in the world combined. And she was a dog lover herself, though she and Gary had decided not to get another one after Misty died because at their age it was just too much trouble, especially breaking in a puppy—and Gary was adamant about not wanting to adopt any shelter dogs, which to his mind were nothing but the dregs, the reflexive biters and rug chewers other people had already rejected. She bent forward, smiling so hard her face ached, and said, "My name's Brenda, pleased to meet you."

He spun his hands in reply and she turned back to Aimee and asked her what he'd said.

Aimee laughed, a soft rippling trill of a laugh that lit up her face so you could really see the beauty of her. "He said, 'The pleasure's all mine.'"

For the first month or two, Aimee kept pretty much to herself. Mornings and evenings she took Sam for long walks, not only in the wash and the flats around the property, but up on the sun-polished mesa that hovered over the place and made Desert Haven the prettiest trailer court in the greater Kingman area (of course, there wasn't much competition since the rest of them pretty much defined low-rent, lacked any kind of scenic views and didn't even have gravel in the drive, just dirt). You'd look up first thing in the morning and there they'd be, way high up—hundreds of feet above the court—just climbing and climbing. She was in great shape, Aimee (which she herself was not, sadly; she'd never been up there or even partway up because she knew full well the climb would all but kill her, not that she had any desire to scramble around a bunch of blistered rocks that were probably crawling with rattlesnakes and ready to give way under your feet every step you took), and Sam, of course, was in even better shape. It was like taking a dog for a walk, she supposed—you walk a mile, the dog runs ten. He loved to have her chase him or play hide-and-seek—you could see her way up there, climbing steadily, while he disappeared behind a rock only to pop up ten feet behind her and streak on ahead like a strip of felt whipped along at high speed. Gary said they both had to be at least fifty percent mountain goat.

During the daytime, the two of them stayed in the trailer and hardly ever went anywhere, though Aimee told her sometimes at night she'd take Sam out in the desert and let him run free where nobody could see him, though there were problems with that too (cactus spines, specifically) since he didn't wear any shoes, let alone hiking boots, and half the time he was down on his knuckles and she wasn't about to get him a pair of gloves, which she claimed would hamper him too much ("Just look at his fingers"), though that was the first thing she herself suggested. As to why she wanted to keep him from the public view, at least during those first few months, she never said—maybe she didn't want the hassle because he was sure to draw a crowd or maybe she needed a special license for him or something, who could say? One way or the other, she valued her privacy, and Brenda respected that—as did most of the other residents, who'd come here for the natural beauty and the feeling of community but at the same time liked the independence and privacy a trailer gave them, especially one that was off the beaten path. It took all kinds, and over the years they'd had their share of druggies and desert rats along with the better types, mostly retirees getting by on pensions and social security, but they *were* a community, that was the important thing, and they exhibited all the pluses and minuses of communities anywhere. Sam seemed harmless enough and if anyone objected (like Millie Vogel, who lived in the trailer next to her and Gary's and told her he scared her, *He's a wild animal, Brenda, don't you get that?*) more often than not she found herself defending him.

Besides which no animal could even come close to causing the kind of trouble she and Gary had had to put up with over the years from the members of the human race, fistfights, theft, vandalism— even a murder. Which came out of nowhere and plunged her into the worst day she'd ever lived through, SWAT team and all. It was a winter day, three or four years back, temperatures in the thirties and the sun as weak as milk and nothing, absolutely nothing, happening anywhere, boredom factor ten out of ten, when there was the sudden crack of a rifle, loud as a thunder blast, and she knew immediately it wasn't coming from any hunter up on the mesa, where you weren't allowed to hunt, anyway, for obvious reasons of safety around a populated area. Her first thought was for Gary, who'd gone over to have a little chat with Bill Terry about the fact that his rent was a week late, and call it intuition because as it turned out that shot *was* meant for him, but by the grace of God it missed. Her second thought was to dismiss it in the way we always try to minimize our fears, else how would we even get through a single day without having a nervous breakdown, telling herself it was probably just some jackass shooting at a can propped up on a rock. And it was only the one shot. She held her breath, bracing herself for the next one and the one after that, but they never came. What had happened—and Gary was white-faced when he burst through the door to dial 911 and blurt it out to the dispatcher—was that Bill Terry, drunk and depressed over losing his job, had decided to take it out on Gary because Gary was the one standing there knocking on his door and ragging him about unpaid rent. They argued. Bill told him to go fuck himself and slammed the door shut and Gary, who'd had it up to here, shouted some threat about getting the sheriff after him and stalked away and he hadn't got halfway across the lot before he ran into Stu Brazile, who stopped to chat a minute about whatever was on his mind at the time, which was plenty, because Stu was the sort of person who had theories about everything.

The single shot, fired from Bill's Marlin 336 as he stood on his porch, framed by the open aluminum door, missed Gary, but hit Stu in the back of the head, killing him instantly. He fell facedown in the gravel and Gary, who'd been in the army in Korea, went to ground right beside him. Bill could have picked him off, but once it was all over and the SWAT team had come and Bill, inside the trailer, had put the barrel of the gun in his own mouth and pulled the trigger, people theorized that he hadn't actually meant to shoot anybody, least of all Stu, and the realization of what he'd done stopped him. But there was the fact, one of their own residents, a member of the Desert Haven community, lying facedown in the gravel in a soup of his own blood and brains, and she was sorry to have to tell it that way whenever the subject came up, but she was still shocked and angry over the senselessness of it. So when Millie complained about Sam, she just reminded her of that little incident, because if you want violence you don't have to look any further than the members of your own species, especially the ones wearing beards and hand-tooled boots with a rifle in easy reach.

Then there came a day when a strange car pulled into the lot—a rental car, with a Phoenix airport sticker in the lower left-hand corner of the windshield—and a man in his thirties with blond hair hanging in his eyes thumped up the steps to the office, asking for Aimee. The weather had changed—it was fall, best season of all here, the air crisp and sweet and the sun something you sought out rather than hid from—and she'd left the door propped open to take advantage of it. The man was silhouetted there against a scene she could have painted with her eyes closed, Norv and Betty Norbert's double-wide with their candy-apple-red Chevy C/K pickup parked out front and the dun slab of the mesa rising out of view. She didn't get up from her chair. She said, "Who's asking?"

He was wearing a hooded sweatshirt and a jeans jacket and instead of the boots every man in the state of Arizona wore from birth till death, he had on a pair of soft blue running shoes with a gold flare on either side, as if he'd just come from a track meet. He gave her a megawatt smile and came right up to her desk to show her he had nothing to hide, and he wasn't an insurance salesman or repo man or Seventh-Day Adventist, she could see that at a glance. "I'm her professor?" he said, making a question of it.

That was about the last thing she expected to hear and yes, she was protective of all the residents here, but Aimee especially, who was the type that just wanted to be left in peace, cordial enough, sweet, really, but sufficient in herself. Which she respected. Because she wasn't one to pry, no matter how curious she might get. "I didn't even know she was in college," she said. "She never mentioned it to me, anyway—what college did you say you were from?"

"UC Santa Maria. I'm in the psychology department? Guy Schermerhorn? She must have mentioned me . . ."

"Not that I can recall." And then—she couldn't help herself—she said, "What, does she have a late paper due?"

He laughed then and said that if truth be told they were a little closer than professor and student—friends, really. Good friends. "She's expecting me. I mean, this *is* Desert Haven, isn't it?"

She didn't answer. "Why don't you call her and have her come get you?" She pushed the phone across the desk. "Be my guest."

He looked embarrassed. "I don't have her number. Fact is, she called me. But really, if you don't mind, can I just look around? I'd recognize her car. And Sam—Sam's with her, isn't he?"

"You know Sam?"

He looked as if he wanted to give a whole dissertation on the subject, but he just nodded.

"Number twenty-six," she said. "Last one down the second row to your left—right where those big boulders are?"

One of the mysteries about Aimee was where she got her money from. After paying rent for the first two months, she decided to buy the trailer, as is, and just sat down and wrote a check for the full amount, which was $4,495, because it was only two years old and the previous owners, Chase and Carol Abbott, had kept it in tip-top shape before Chase had his stroke and they had to move to assisted living. She did eventually get a job, four nights a week, cleaning doctors' and dentists' offices, but that was strictly minimum wage, not that it seemed to bother her—she said it was the best she could do under the circumstances, which meant that she could bring Sam along with her and nobody the wiser. He went to bed at eight—went down hard, according to her—so she bought an extra-large doggy bed at Kmart, stuck it in the backseat of the car and let him sleep while she worked. One thing she never did, as far as anybody could see, was leave him alone. Ever. And when she asked her about that one day when Aimee was coming across the lot from the laundry next to the office, Sam ambling along beside her and every eye in the whole place glued to them for the sheer entertainment value of the spectacle he provided, Aimee told her he got separation anxiety.

They were standing in the shade of one of the palo verdes Gary had planted when the two of them had first come here all those years ago, Sam settling down on his haunches in the gravel and gazing up at her benevolently. She said, "You mean he misbehaves?"

Aimee nodded.

"We had a dog like that once—Misty? First time we left her alone, she crapped all over the carpet—second time, she tore a divot out of it that must have been three feet long, and after that we took her with us everywhere we went."

Aimee nodded again. "He gets scared when he's alone. And it's not so much the carpet I'm worried about but the whole structure, the walls, the windows, the door—he doesn't know his own strength, do you, Sam?"

They both looked down at him, where he'd begun playing with the slack in his leash while Aimee balanced the laundry basket on one hip. He pulled back his lips in a grin. Whether he understood the question or not, she couldn't say—he didn't roll out any of his signs, but then the question was a rhetorical one and really didn't need an answer. And then Aimee added, "You're a good boy, aren't you, Sam?" and Sam bobbed his right fist up and down, which meant yes, yes he was a good boy who would never tear up the carpet or dent the walls or rip the door from its hinges.

There was something about him, about the way he responded,

that just made you want to hug him. "He's adorable," she said. "Cute. Cute as a button."

And Aimee, who was about as expansive that day as she'd ever been, smiled at her and said, "That's what we pay him for. All that Monkey Chow, fresh pineapple, cheeseburgers—that's it, that's the contract. Right, Sam?"

He bobbed his fist, then spun out a whole panoply of signs, his fingers a blur, until she had to ask, "What's he saying?"

Aimee shrugged, shifted the laundry basket to her other hip. "He's saying it's lunchtime, and why I ever mentioned a c-h-e-e-s-e-b-u-r-g-e-r, I don't know, but once he gets his mind fixated on something . . ." She trailed off.

"I know how it is," she said. "Gary's the same way."

The man who'd come calling—the professor (her boyfriend, actually, which was obvious the minute you saw them together)—stayed overnight. About an hour after he'd ambled across the lot in search of number twenty-six he came back into the office and asked her if it was all right to park his car next to Aimee's trailer and she told him each trailer got parking for two cars—so as long as Aimee was good with it, she was too. He'd mentioned earlier that he'd recognize her car, which would have led him right to her, but what he hadn't thought of—and she hadn't either—was that Aimee had sold her Caprice with the California plates and bought a newer model Ford van, also white, which had temporary plates on it while she waited for the permanent ones to come through in the mail. Arizona plates, that is, which told her Aimee meant to stay. What she didn't know or even suspect was that there might be other people looking for her besides her professor and that she'd got rid of the car as soon as she could so as not to give herself away. But that was the case, as would eventually come out.

Around five or so that evening she saw Aimee and the professor driving out of the lot with Sam in back, pressing his face to the window. She was in her own trailer at the time (number one, right next to the office, where she and Gary could keep an eye on the comings and goings, especially with regard to Lucy Devlin in thirty-seven, who she suspected was selling drugs; either that or she had an awful lot of boyfriends), and she just happened to glance up from the chopping board, where she was dicing carrots, onions and celery for the Crock-Pot and saw the rental car go out through the gate and turn left on Route 66, heading toward town. Dinner, was what she thought. The professor was taking her out for a nice dinner, but then she thought no, because what were they going to do with Sam? They couldn't very well bring him into a restaurant. No restaurant she knew of allowed dogs even, except for the blind, and there were health codes too, of course. For a minute there she entertained the picture of Sam perched on a chair at La Fonda, the best sit-down Mexican place in town, a napkin tucked into his overalls and his long leathery fingers plying fork and knife like anybody else, and that was hilarious, hilarious enough to call out to Gary, who was in the BarcaLounger watching football on TV. "He's taking her out to dinner, can you imagine?"

"Who?"

"The professor. Aimee's professor."

"So?"

"They've got Sam with them."

"What are you saying, how does he like his steak cooked?"

"I'll bet anything they're going to get takeout."

Gary laughed. "I'm not a betting man, you know that."

Sure enough, they were back half an hour later, Sam hanging his head out the window to catch the breeze, the car crunching across the gravel till it turned down the second row and disappeared from view, but the point was that half an hour wasn't long enough for a sit-down dinner, so they must have gone to Taco Bell or Burger King or wherever. Not that it mattered to her—people could eat whatever they wanted, whether it was healthy or not, but at least she and Gary were getting a nice homemade beef stew that positively screamed vitamins. After dinner, she watched an old movie on TV—Jimmy Stewart and Irene Dunne, or was it Jean Arthur?—while Gary snored in the recliner, and she forgot all about them.

But the next morning, there they were, the three of them, gamboling over the rocks up on the mesa, so high above the court they might have been parachuted there overnight, Sam so excited with two people to chase after he was just a blur, even with the binoculars. And how did that make her feel? Wistful, she supposed. They were young, they were in love, Sam was their surrogate baby, and whatever had happened between them in the past—late papers, bad grades, a bitter breakup, or maybe he was married already because that was the way professors were, wasn't it?—it didn't seem to affect them now. Or when they went out at lunchtime, anyway, the nuclear family, everybody all smiles, even Sam. Not that it mattered to her—she was no busybody—but it was just that she'd grown so fond of Aimee and Sam too and couldn't help feeling protective, or at the very least *interested*.

Yes. And then it was night, Saturday night, and everything went to hell. It was just after dark, the desert sky like the Hayden Planetarium when she was a kid on a school trip to New York, the coolness of the night muffling the sounds of people's TVs and stereos because they were all inside with their doors and windows shut. She and Gary were watching TV and enjoying a glass of the Dewar's Gary's brother had sent him for his birthday—neat, for the warming effect—and she was already in her nightgown. The movie they were watching, a crusty Western about a man who just wants to be left alone but gets tormented from the opening scene on by a gang of sadistic cowboys until he explodes and blows them all away, featured enough gunfire in the climactic scene to awaken the dead—until she snatched up the remote and turned the volume down, that is, which was when she first heard the sound, a high-pitched keening like a fire alarm going off. "Jesus," Gary said. "What the hell is that?"

She went to the door and stuck her head out and the noise was louder, clearer, not a mechanical sound at all but a series of cascading screams that made her throat clench against the burn of the scotch. It took her a moment before she thought of Sam. She'd heard him scream once before and it was like nothing she'd ever experienced in her life to that point. It was at night too, around this time or a little later (his bedtime, as it turned out), and it went on for a good ten minutes before she put on a sweater and her moccasins and started up the row for Aimee's trailer to see what was going on—and put a stop to it, if she could, because there were rules about excessive noise, which she'd plainly posted in the office and the laundry, along with prohibitions against untended fires and letting trash accumulate for the coons and coyotes to pick over instead of getting your ass in gear to haul it to the dump. The sound was unworldly, terrifying, nails on a blackboard, but the thing was, it stopped before she got halfway there—just cut off like a record when you jerk the needle away. She went up to the trailer in any case, just to stand there outside in the gravel drive and make sure everything was all right. She was there maybe ten minutes, enough to have a cigarette and listen to the little sounds of the night close back in, but she didn't interfere because it was none of her business—unless it started up again. (And Aimee explained it the next day—came to apologize, actually. The problem was that Sam had been feeling antsy and he just didn't want to go to bed, and yet she had to keep him on a strict schedule so he'd conk out on the nights she was working, but on this occasion he just wouldn't have it and threw a tantrum. What made it worse was that chimps, though their vocal cords don't allow them to form words, can scream two or three times louder than any human being on this earth.)

Which was what was happening now. "That's Sam," she said, lifting her sweater down from the hook by the door while Gary gave her a pained look. "Sounds like murder to me," he said, and, thinking of the professor now, because he was the odd piece in this particular puzzle, she said, "I'm going to go tell them to keep it down before somebody calls the police."

When she got closer—and people were craning their heads out of their doors up and down the row and staring numbly into the darkness—she heard the professor's voice rise up out of the mix, and Aimee's too. They were having some sort of argument, that was it, and it was clear that Sam was right at the forefront of it. The professor shouted, Aimee shouted back, and Sam just screamed till she thought her heart was going to stop. Just as she got there, just as she was about to go up the steps and rap on the door, there was a crash and then the thump of something hurtling against the inner wall of the trailer. In the next moment the door flung open and there was the professor, bleeding from a cut over one eye and hustling down the steps, shouting, "Yeah, and fuck you too," while Aimee and Sam stood there backlit in the doorway and Sam's screams went up a notch, if that was possible, and then abruptly cut off.

The professor slammed into his rental car, turned over the engine and shot out of the lot going way too fast while Aimee just stood there watching and Sam let out a single parting bark and settled down on his haunches. In the moment before she reached out to pull the door shut, Aimee caught sight of her standing there in her sweater and nightgown. Aimee's face went slack, a sliver of a face, pale as moondust and drained of emotion. She gave a little wave and tried for a smile, clearly embarrassed, but couldn't quite manage it. "Sorry," she murmured, and then she closed the door.

VARIETIES OF WRONG

The TRAILER was not a CAGE and it wasn't a TENT and the BLACK BUGS, even Alice, were just a memory now. He slept in a bed, watched TV, ate cereal out of a box whenever he wanted. Where was he? He didn't know, and if it felt foreign—the sun, the rocks, the ground that burned his feet in the middle of the day and the plants that reached out and stabbed him if he let his vigilance slip for just an instant—it didn't matter because he was with her, always, from the minute he opened his eyes till she read him his BEDTIME STORY and he fell off into a dreamless sleep. He couldn't go OUT unless she said so and that was a burden on him and it was wrong, or one variety of wrong, but he was able to consider the alternative, which was the CAGE and the BIG MAN and his stinger. They had to hide, that was what she told him, and if he understood that, if he understood the rationale behind it, it made him obedient and eager to please while at the same time it made him rocket with fury. Let the BIG MAN come. Just let him. Or ARMS or any of them. Let them come and see if they could have their way with him now.

The problem was, it all ran together, like his paints when he was making a PICTURE, and it confused him. There were times when he was as content as he'd ever been, Aimee sitting there beside him on the COUCH and grooming him with her fingers that were stiff and soft at the same time, cartoons on TV, no more lessons or drills and the words draining out of his head like water in a gutter, when all at once the thought of the BIG MAN would invade him and he'd jump under her fingers and she would say "What's wrong?" and in the instant she posed the question, the thought vanished as suddenly as it had appeared. He wanted to say "Nothing wrong," wanted to sign it, but in the duress of the moment, the wrongness of it, the sign was gone.

And then one day Guy was there, on the porch, knocking at the door. The minute she opened the door, Guy stepped in out of the light and put his arms around her and pressed her to him, which was something he didn't like at all. Guy didn't hug him, he hugged her. And though he felt a sudden wild peal of joy at the sight of him and the promise of TREATS and RIDES and all the rest he couldn't help remembering that Guy had left him in the CAGE and gone away in his CAR and hadn't come back at all. Till now. When it didn't really matter anymore.

"And how's Sam?" Guy said, letting go of her and turning to him with his arms held out for a hug. "Does he want a hug?"

He was suspicious—was this Guy, even? Guy wouldn't leave him in a CAGE, not the Guy he knew. He brought his first two fingers together and snapped them against his thumb, three times, hard, then shook his head no the way she did when she was angry with him.

Guy's face climbed up and away from him. "No?" he said. "What's the matter, Sam, don't you recognize me? Do you want to make me sad?

Do you want to make me hurt?" And then he signed, I BROUGHT TREATS FOR YOU. DON'T YOU WANT TREATS?

He did. He did want treats. CANDY especially. He held out his hand, signed GIMME TREATS and waited for Guy to dig a hand through the plastic bag in his pocket and come up with a palmful of dried apricots that were almost as good as candy and better for his teeth because he didn't want his teeth to HURT, did he?

It was a complicated transaction. He took the apricots, fed them into his mouth and held his hand out for more, and then he allowed Guy to hug him, but Guy had to bend down to him because he was too BIG now to lift and Guy knew that and so did she.

They went OUT, they climbed the rocks, played CHASE and HIDE SEEK, drove in the CAR, Guy's car, to get cheeseburgers and potato sticks and a sweet thick MILKSHAKE he sucked through a straw and when Guy was getting ready for bed the first night and standing over the toilet peeing, he couldn't stop himself from bursting through the door to taste the coiled yellow arc of his PISS as it streaked through the air, which was the final and definitive proof that this was Guy, really and actually Guy, and not some imposter who just happened to look and smell like him. He felt calm after that and ready to accept this new arrangement, her and Guy and him, just like before, as long as Guy slept on the couch and not in his BED, but then there was a moment in the night when he felt her slip out from under the covers and go to Guy and he wanted to do something about that because it was wrong but he was asleep and dreaming that he was paralyzed and couldn't move a muscle even if a snake came winding purposively through his dreams, which it did, an unraveling muscle of snakeness with its licking tongue and its hooked white fangs.

There was a whole day and then the next night, the two of them talking and talking and he too consumed with his toys and puzzles and books to pay attention except when their voices rose, which he didn't like at all. At one point, she was crying, and he tried to climb into her lap to comfort her and Guy shoved him out of the way. "You can go to hell!" Guy shouted at her. "I'm through, I mean it," and she shouted back, "Good, just go, because you're nothing to me now."

Then Guy lurched forward and flapped his hand across her face, so quickly he couldn't do anything about it, but that was wrong and it made him scream, made him snatch Guy off his feet and slam him into the wall so hard the wall roared back at him and Guy's face went bright with blood and he almost brought his teeth into play and he would have with anybody else who dared even touch her, but this was Guy, the one he used to love before her, and that saved them both. He erected his hair. He champed his teeth. He screamed. Then the door was open and Guy went through it and out into the night, gone again, gone, gone, gone.

SHE'D CALLED HIM

She'd called him, which came as a relief, but at the same time managed to stir his resentment all the more. It had been months. His life was a shambles. The fact was that her obstinacy had cost him everything, from Carson to the National Science Foundation to whatever thin threads of a relationship he still had with Moncrief. He was living in an apartment that wasn't much bigger than the bedroom at the ranch and instead of nature outside the door it was a stew of traffic and fumes and noise. He was drinking too much. His diet—fast food, Chinese takeout, beer nuts—was erasing him to the point where he barely recognized himself in the mirror. And school—school was the bare cold edge of a precipice he was just barely clinging to by his fingertips. Worse, he hadn't got laid since he'd gone to her in Iowa and he was so desperate he'd even called Melanie, who promptly hung up on him, and then he made a fool of himself trying to put the moves on an assistant professor of English in her thirties who specialized in Elizabethan poetry and wasn't even his type and then shook her head sadly at the moment of truth and informed him that she was going home to her husband, twin boys and a dachshund named Olaf.

The phone rang. He had half a glass of scotch on the counter and a cigarette jammed in the corner of his mouth and he was attempting to fold over the edge of a cheese-and-onion omelet that was already scorched on the bottom, so it took him a minute to pick up.

"Hi," her voice breathed at him. And then, superfluously: "It's me."

What did he feel in that moment? Surprise, anger and lust, in that order, but it was lust that won out. "Aimee," he said, just stating it, the fact of it, of her, as if to orient himself for what was to come.

"I just wanted to say . . . well, I miss you. And Sam does too." A pause. "Do you miss me?"

"Christ, where are you? It's been months, do you realize that? And don't tell me you're in some campground . . ."

"I'm in a house—a trailer, actually. With Sam."

"Where?"

"In Arizona?"

He wanted her. He wanted her desperately. Just the sound of her voice, a thin whisper over the phone, had given him an erection that drew all the blood to his groin instead of his brain, where it belonged. In that moment he would have done anything for her, but here was that conversation again, dodging and weaving and circling back on itself. "*Where* in Arizona?"

There was the faintest tick of hesitation, as if she'd never meant to tell him and wasn't going to tell him now. He listened to the susurrus of her breathing. Finally she said, "Kingman? Just outside of Kingman? On Route 66?"

"Kingman? How did you ever manage to wind up there?" He conjured up some bleak outpost of strip malls and used car lots hemmed in by mesquite and creosote and what, roadrunners, coyotes, jackasses. "I don't think I even know where it is—"

"In the foothills of the Hualapai range, thirty-three hundred feet high, so it's cooler than down below in the desert. It even snows here, or so they tell me."

"I would have thought you'd seen enough snow in Iowa to last you a lifetime." He threw it out there, small talk—he was making small talk when everything inside him was boiling over. "But tell me, how's Sam—is he behaving? I can only imagine him in a trailer— what are the walls made of, titanium?"

"He's been good as gold. He knows, Guy, he really knows, and people like Borstein and Moncrief can say what they will, but all Sam wants is to be with me and if that means controlling his impulses, well, he's doing it. And, of course, I never leave him alone. I mean never."

There was a pause. He was picturing that, Sam in a trailer, Sam tamping down his urges, and he wanted to ask her a thousand questions, starting with how she was paying rent, paying for groceries, paying for Sam, and more importantly what she was going to do about *him* and the project he was trying to float that wasn't going to go anywhere without Sam, access to Sam, possession of him, but then it came to him that something more essential was going on here— she'd called him. He said, "I miss you."

"I miss you too."

"You want me to come visit?"

It was a three-hour drive from the Phoenix airport, which gave him plenty of time to parse what he was doing. He loved her, he needed her, and he was speeding down some soulless highway in the middle of nowhere for the promise of expressing that in person, but there was a score to settle here too. She'd left him—again—and they were going to have to find some resolution to that little problem. One of his former students had got a job at the National Science Foundation and when he'd asked her to look into the status of his grant application she'd told him everybody was impressed and while it wasn't a sure thing it was looking very much like he was going to get funded in spite of the Borstein revolution, which meant that his number one priority was to placate Moncrief—and the only way he could do that was to get Sam back. And here was his argument: they could go back to Iowa, the three of them, and work out of the chimp barn with the signing chimps, a once-in-the-history-of-mankind opportunity, anybody could see that, and she didn't really want all that training to go to waste, did she? Video cameras, that was all they needed, just set them up to run twenty-four/seven and watch Sam talk to Alice and Alice talk to Alex and Alex talk to Sam, and what if they bred Sam and Alice and Alice used signs with the baby? What about that? What would that say to Borstein? And if Moncrief did follow through on his threat to sell off his chimps, this would at least protect Sam and Alice and some of the others too, and wasn't that worth a try? Wasn't that better than having to look over her shoulder every time she went to the grocery store or gassed up her car? Because Moncrief wasn't going to give up. That wasn't in his nature. What was in his nature was vengeance, retribution, payback.

If anything, she was prettier than he remembered, sexier, and if she'd put on a little weight it was just where it ought to be, and of course she knew that and she was wearing a low-cut top he'd never seen before and she'd let her hair grow even longer so that it was all the way down to her waist. And makeup. She didn't usually wear makeup, but she'd done her eyes and put on lipstick, just for him. He stepped in the door and the connection was instantaneous, no hesitation, no recrimination, no worries—he wrapped his arms around her and she just clung to him and they kissed, and if Sam gave him a cold hard look he couldn't help that and the minute he released her he held out his arms to Sam for a hug and when that didn't work he produced the dried apricots he'd brought along to seal the deal. Sam was bigger, he noticed that, but Sam was still Sam, and though he might have been a genius among chimps, he was still a chimp, with the emotional and intellectual range of a four-year-old child, and Guy knew how to manipulate him. Sure enough, within minutes they were hugging and grooming and it was just like before.

That night they went through the whole rigmarole of putting Sam to sleep when they were both on fire to have sex, to fuck, that is, and that was like old times too. They sat around the kitchen table drinking wine and passing a joint, making sure Sam got the lion's share, the radio tuned to the classical station, lights turned low, everything hushed and mellow. Aimee cranked the heat till the trailer was like a sauna and they kept their voices low in the hope that Sam, unable to follow along, would fall into the chasm of his own boredom and drift off to sleep. Sure enough, right at eight, right at his bedtime, he folded his arms on the table and put his head down and they both got up and helped him to bed.

He'd thought that was it, that Sam was out for the night, but five minutes later, while he was brushing his teeth and relieving himself in the cramped sweatbox of a bathroom before going to her where she was waiting for him on the sofa bed in the living room—in her negligee, her bare legs crossed and a joint glittering in her hand—Sam suddenly rocketed through the door, his mouth gaping, and sampled the stream of his piss in mid-air. Which wasn't all that unusual—it was one of Sam's little idiosyncrasies, life with a chimp—but Sam customarily reserved the honor for strangers, who might or might not have been rivals. And, of course, it had the desired effect of scaring the shit out of them. Chimps didn't have a castration complex as far as anyone knew, but when they attacked one another, when they fought to the death, one of the first things they went for was the sexual organs. So there was that to consider. But beyond that, beyond its just being unnerving, was the implication that Sam saw him as a stranger now—or worse, a rival.

In the morning, it was all good. Sam had crept out at first light and slipped into bed with them, and if he smelled the sex on them, the vaginal lubricants, the sperm drying on her skin, he didn't seem to object—he snuggled in between them and went back to sleep, snoring softly and twitching his legs in the old familiar way. Then it was breakfast, fruit, porridge and eggs over easy for Sam and Aimee, black coffee and toast for him, after which they took Sam for a jaunt up on the mesa above the trailer court and all that ape energy found its release in the kind of play that exhausted them all. By afternoon the temperature had risen to the high seventies and after lunch they sat outside in lawn chairs in back of the trailer drinking gin and tonic, Sam's favorite, and because no one was around Aimee let Sam off his lead. Which wasn't a problem—if he wandered too far she called out to him and no matter what he was doing (and he was always doing something, digging, probing, beating a stick against the side of the trailer, chucking stones at phantoms), he came back without protest.

The sun was warm on his face. The desert air washed over him, clean and astringent. He sipped his gin, watching Sam chase a lizard into the scree at the base of the mesa, and the moment felt right—*he* felt right for the first time since they'd broken up. "You know what's incredible?"

She'd been watching Sam too, but now she turned to him, her face softened with the pleasure of the moment. "What?"

"How he listens to you—it's a far cry from how it was back at the ranch when we had to guard the door every time somebody went in or out. Or when he got away and took hold of that woman and wouldn't let go. Remember that? That was a nightmare, or a potential nightmare, anyway."

"Yeah, but it wasn't, because nothing happened."

"Thank god. But really, what's your secret?"

"It's called love."

"Say that with a smile—"

"And the fact that he's growing up—and he's not in a cage. And that he knows what a cage is, which makes him want to avoid it at all costs. I explained it to him. I did. And he understands."

They both looked up at a sudden sharp percussion, a boom followed by a lithic shatter and scrape, and then the boom again. Sam was dropping a boulder the size of a suitcase on the surface of a long flat slab of rock, then picking it up and dropping it again.

"What's he doing?"

"Hunting, that's all. Watch."

In the next moment, Sam flung the boulder aside, dug his hand under the slab and came up with the limp body of the lizard he'd been chasing. He held it up by the tail, his trophy, then bit it cleanly in two, stuffing the anterior section in his mouth before scrambling across the yard to offer the remainder first to Aimee ("Oh, Sam, no") and then him ("Thanks, but I just ate—and didn't I ever tell you I'm allergic to lizard?"). Sam held the thing aloft a moment, its rear legs still twitching reflexively, then put it in his mouth, ground his teeth and swallowed.

"I wish you wouldn't do that, Sam," Aimee said. She shaded her eyes with one hand, rattled the ice in her drink. "At least not in front of me."

"Oh, come on," he said. "He's only doing what comes natural. And isn't that the beauty of him—no hang-ups, no shame, just being in the moment, and if the moment tells you to bite a lizard in two right in front of the lady you love, well, why not?"

"Still"—and she was addressing Sam now—"it's cruel. And unsanitary—DIRTY, Sam. Couldn't you just catch them and let them go?"

He was going to say something inane like "boys will be boys," making a joke of it, because that was what it was, a joke, to expect an animal to appreciate the niceties of civilization no matter the degree of cross-fostering you subjected him to, but then another lizard went scuttling across the yard and Sam shot off after it, so instead he said, "How about another drink?"

Triangulating the empty glasses between his fingertips, he mounted the three steel steps to the trailer and pushed open the door. He was thinking he'd make this second round of drinks stiffer, by way of lowering her defenses (he had a proposition to broach, after all) and at the same time mellowing out Sam so they could have a little peace for wherever the discussion of that proposition was going to take them. The gin—a half gallon of Gordon's, and was she really drinking that much, or at least drinking enough to invest in half gallons?—stood on the gouged Formica counter beside a wedge of lime and a butcher's knife. Flies decorated the air. There were crusted pans on the two-burner stove, unwashed plates in the sink, a scatter of sponges, scrubbers, balled-up plastic bags and takeout food cartons everywhere. His head grazed the ceiling, which seemed to be made of laminated cardboard—or plastic. He tapped it. Plastic, definitely plastic. The walls were plastic too, fake wood designed to simulate paneling, and everything showed the effects of Sam, the kitchen counter gnawed along the edges, the walls scuffed, panels missing to display the mustard-colored insulation beneath. This was her nest, hers and Sam's. He felt like an intruder.

She made a face when she tasted her drink. "It's too strong," she said.

"No, it's just the way you like it, or the way you used to like it." He settled back into the chair beside her.

"You're not trying to get me drunk, are you?" She looked from him to Sam, who was making use of a broomstick to probe under the slab of rock for another lizard or whatever unlucky creature might be cowering beneath it.

"I am," he said, and reached out to run a hand up her leg.

"Good," she said, closing her hand over his and leaning into him for a kiss, which was nice, which was beautiful, and he gave himself over to it, the flicker of her tongue, the pressure of her lips, but in the same moment he couldn't help feeling that this was as good a time as any to make his pitch because he only had the weekend and as delicious as this was he still had a whole life to live. And for now at least she was in control of it.

"I heard from Moncrief," he said.

He watched her face change. "Don't tell me," she said, pulling away from him. "Don't even say it."

"No, no, it's not like that—he doesn't know where you are, and it wasn't about you, anyway. Or not exactly. It was Azazel. Remember him?"

"Jesus, you gave me a scare—don't do that, Guy. *Please*. But yes, of course I remember Azazel, how could I forget him? What, did he die?"

"He hung himself."

"What are you saying?"

"He couldn't take it anymore, I guess."

"That's not possible, it must be some mistake. He must have gotten tangled up or something . . ."

Animals did not commit suicide, that was an axiom. Animals were driven by instinct to survive and reproduce, which, when you came down to it, was the sole purpose of life on this planet no matter the species. They could suffer trauma and depression, refuse food, die a solitary death, but they couldn't contemplate non-being, which was beyond the limits of their awareness. Yet Moncrief told him Azazel had planned the whole thing, secreting a length of rope one of the workers had negligently left in reach, then experimenting with knots till he fashioned a noose, looped it around his throat, tied the other end to the steel mesh at the top of the cage and lowered himself down until it tightened and tightened again.

"Not according to Moncrief. Jack Serfis found the body—and he called Donald right away because he wasn't about to go in that cage until it was a hundred percent certain Azazel wasn't just playing possum, which in itself would have been a mental feat way beyond what we would have thought he was capable of, and when Donald got there he wasn't taking any chances either and darted the body before they entered the cage. Donald felt for a pulse, but there was none. And there was the rope—and the knots."

She looked to Sam then. He'd finished probing with the broomstick and was using it now as a weapon, jabbing it over and over again into the gap under the rock. "I don't believe it," she said.

He shrugged, reached for his drink. "I'm just telling you what he told me." What he wasn't telling her, or not yet, was that the loss of his prime breeding male had made recovering Sam all the more critical to him, which was why he'd called, of course, hoping to extract information. The first thing he said, before he even mentioned Azazel, was *Have you heard anything yet?*

"I still don't believe it," she said.

He didn't answer. They sat there in silence, sipping their drinks, watching Sam as if they were watching a home movie. After a moment he said, "There was something else too . . ."

Whether they ate that night he couldn't remember. There was more drinking, but it wasn't celebratory anymore—it was defensive drinking, angry drinking. He'd barely got the words out—*Iowa, a trailer there or an apartment*—when she cut him off. "You never give up, do you?" she said.

"Well, no, of course not—I want to make this happen. For Sam, for *us*." He heard himself talking, forming the words he'd gone over in his head a dozen times already, but they sounded false somehow, as if he were not only trying to convince her, but convince himself too. "Believe me, I've thought it over till I can't think anymore—this is the best way out for everybody concerned, maybe the only way for Sam."

"Yeah, sure, and what about Dr. Moncrief? You think he's just going to forget all about it? He hates me. He'll never let me get within ten miles of that place—"

"No, no, I'll fix it up, it'll be fine, you'll see—the important thing for him is just to get Sam back. He wants to breed him when he's of age, of course he does, and if I get the funding, which is like ninety-nine percent assured at this point, and we can restore some credibility to the field, that's all to the better as far as he's concerned. And you can't go on living like this forever, can you?"

She straightened up in the chair and lifted her glass as if toasting him. "You're really too much. Don't you get it? I told you no before and I'm telling you the same thing now—there's no way Sam's going back there. That man scares me."

"He ought to. What if he comes here? What are you going to do then?"

"He won't."

"But what if, is what I'm saying?"

"He won't."

There were more drinks. Maybe there was dinner, there must have been, though he had no recollection of it. He kept pleading with her, but she was immovable, hateful, stupid, obstinate. At some point— they were in the kitchen, the windows dark, the bottle empty, both of them shouting and Sam drumming on the table in agitation—he shoved himself away from the counter and before he knew what he was doing his hand flicked out and he slapped her, hard, just to shut her up, which was wrong, inexcusable, the end of everything, finis, and he knew it in that instant. That was when Sam slammed into him because Sam had made his choice a long time ago and he'd chosen Aimee. In the aftermath, he found himself on the floor, the wind knocked out of him, bleeding from a cut over his left eye. He couldn't catch his breath. Sam was screaming. Aimee was shouting, "No, Sam, no!"

For a long moment he lay there gasping for air, then he pushed himself up, stalked into the bedroom to snatch up his bag—forget the cut, forget the blood—and pushed through the front door and out into the night, cursing over his shoulder, cursing them both. He revved the engine, spun the wheels. And then he was out on the highway, heading south.

He spent that night at a motel near the airport, and in the morning, before boarding his flight, he got a fistful of quarters from the change machine, went into the phone booth and called Moncrief.

Moncrief answered on the first ring. "Yes?" he said.

"It's me, Guy."

"Yes?"

"I found her," he said. "I know where she is."

NO LEGS

She slept late. He lay there in bed beside her, playing with her hair, but she said, "Sam, no," and so he got up and went into the kitchen to eat his CEREAL and sit on the couch and watch TV. There were figures there, in the TV, and they moved and tumbled and rose and fell till he got bored and lifted the TV and set it down on one end in the corner, which seemed to him a better arrangement. Then he got out his paints. She'd locked them in the cabinet under the sink, but the lock was nothing to him and a single jerk of his arm tore it off the door and the handle with it. Then he painted. On the TV, on the wall, on the floor, and whether she was going to like that or not didn't factor in, though she'd scolded him last time and locked him in the bedroom till he started screaming and she let him out again, which taught him that this place was different, that here he could scream and get what he wanted right away. But what he wanted in the moment was her, so he went in and played with her hair again till she woke up and hugged him and he signed, WHERE GUY, though he already knew, and she signed, GUY GONE, and then, with her mouth clamped tight, signed, FOR GOOD.

The sun came in through one window of the trailer and it went away through another and that was a day. Then there was another day and another one after that, time without a clock. He was with her all day every day and at night when she took him in the CAR and went to work and brought him home again and they went to BED. He knew the word HAPPY, a good word, not as concrete or immediate maybe as PIZZA or COKE, but good, very good, and sometimes he signed it spontaneously and she signed it back to him, I'M HAPPY TOO. Guy was gone. The sun came in one window and went out another. She was with him and he was with her.

And then one day a man was there in the trailer when he woke from his nap. He heard voices, her voice and a man's voice, and his first thought was that Guy was back because nobody else had ever been in the trailer except Brenda, and Brenda's voice was a high flutter of wings he could never mistake for anybody else's. He came through the door expecting Guy, but this wasn't Guy and that confused him and alarmed him till he felt the adrenal charge start to burn through him and Aimee said, "No, Sam, it's okay," in the voice she used to warn him off.

"So here he is," the man said. "Sam himself. How about that?"

He was tall, this man, his head as high as the ceiling, and he had no legs, or no legs anybody could see under the black screen that dropped from his shoulders to the floor, and now he bent at the waist, smiling till his teeth gleamed wet, and said, "Sam, it's a pleasure to meet you."

"Go ahead, Sam," she said. Her eyes communicated the same warning as her voice, which meant that this was an official occasion, an occasion to be responsive, to be CUTE. That was the key word here, CUTE, he recognized that, and he knew exactly what to do—hold out his hand for a shake.

The man took his hand in a soft smooth featureless grip, gave it a squeeze and dropped it.

"Sam," she said, signing simultaneously, "this is Father Curran. He's a friend. I like him very much. Can you tell him something? Can you tell him what you had for breakfast?"

PANCAKES.

"Right. Pancakes and what else?"

SAUSAGES.

She said the word aloud for the man, who wasn't literate and didn't understand the shapes he made with arms and fingers and hands.

"Do you like sausages?" the man asked, still bent at the waist, his eyebrows jumping like bugs. He was not a threat. He was tall, but he was weak, and where were his legs?

YES.

"And do you know where sausages come from?"

The question surprised him. Sausage was meat and meat was inside everything that moved. The STORE, he said.

She translated and the man laughed. She said, "He means before that, Sam, before the store?"

THEY KILL PIGS, he said.

She said the words aloud. The man laughed again. "He's amazing," he said to her. "He really is. But tell me, Sam, who kills them, who kills the pigs?"

The simplest sign, a single finger pointed right at him: YOU.

"Me? I've never killed anything in my life."

But he just shook his head, shook his head no, because that wasn't the truth.

Then it was a treat and then lunch and the man stayed with them, sat at the table and ate FRUIT SALAD and a SANDWICH, with TUNAFISH and BREAD smeared with WHITE PASTE out of a jar in the REFRIGERATOR. The man made faces at her and talked and talked and after a while he said, "Really, I don't see why not. The only question is do we perform the ceremony here or can we bring him to church? It would be more meaningful in church, don't you think?"

A CHILD OF THE LIGHT

She didn't believe, but at the same time she did. Religion was super-stition, was fear, but at least it provided answers, a cosmology, a rea-son why, which science didn't, though it had our attention, satellites creeping across the night sky and electrodes pulling images out of our brains and textbooks to explain it all. Since Sam had come into her life, she hadn't been inside a church, let alone to confession, and when Father Curran came up to the car and introduced himself in the parking lot at Dunkin' Donuts one windswept afternoon a week after the blowup with Guy, something clicked inside her. Sam was dozing in the backseat, glutted on carbs and sugar—he was mad for jelly doughnuts, amazed every time he bit into one and experienced the small miracle of jelly exploding on his palate—and she was bent over her notepad with a cup of coffee and her own doughnut, writ-ing a letter to her mother, which she tried to do at least once a week to keep in touch, since calling her on the phone just ended in a fight every time because how could she have taken that Fidelity money when it was earmarked for her wedding and a starter home and why wasn't she working on her degree and how did she expect to earn a living once the money ran out?

At some point she glanced up and there he was, a gaunt awkward young priest in a cassock that could have fit two of him, bending over to peer in the window and smiling crookedly at her. "Sorry to bother you," he said, "but I'm curious—you're the young woman with the chimpanzee, aren't you?" And then, catching sight of Sam in the backseat, "And this would be him, then, wouldn't it?"

She didn't know what to say. She was in shock—and not just because he was a priest and the sight of him flooded her with guilt and shame but because he knew who she was and who Sam was, and how could that be? If he knew—this priest, this utter stranger—then who else knew?

"I'm sorry," he said, "I didn't mean to take you by surprise." He handed her a card. "I'm Father Curran. Gary and Brenda are parishioners of mine?"

"Yes," she said, acknowledging the connection. The only thing she could think was that Brenda must have been gossiping about her, which she really didn't appreciate.

"I haven't seen you in church," he said, holding her with his eyes. "You *are* Catholic, aren't you?"

She could have denied it, but he'd caught her out, and what went through her felt almost like relief. "I don't—" she began, and broke off. "I mean, it's been hard, what with Sam—he keeps me occupied pretty much twenty-four/seven, and I know that's no excuse . . ."

"David Greybeard," he said. "Of all Goodall's chimps, he was the one who was most human, the one who bridged the gap. Tell me, is that the way it is with"—he gestured to the backseat—"your companion? What was his name?"

"Sam."

"I'm told he's able to talk."

She was a fugitive. She talked to no one but Brenda and then only when Brenda managed to catch her going to the laundry room or unloading groceries from the car. Guy was dead to her and her mother was a nagging voice over a long-distance connection. She wanted to confide in him, wanted to confess. "Yes," she said, and then she told him about it, told him at length while Sam snored in the backseat and the priest's eyes kept flicking between him and her, and when she'd told him everything, the lessons, the drills, the TV shows, the way Sam responded and how creative he was with his signing, how much he *knew*, she caught herself because this wasn't the confessional and the question of how she'd come to be here with Sam, to possess him, was something she couldn't even begin to reveal.

"That's fascinating," he said. "Amazing, really. To think that he can express himself, that he can talk—it changes everything, doesn't it? The church teaches us that animals don't have souls, or not immortal souls, in any case, but when you consider Sam or an individual like David Greybeard, allowances have to be made, don't you think?"

"Sam has a soul," she said, "I'm sure of it."

He straightened up, arched his back, then leaned forward again, his hands clasped as if in prayer even as the wind flapped the sleeves of his cassock and whipped his hair. "I wonder if I could stop by sometime, maybe next time I pay a visit to Gary and Brenda? I'd really like to talk to him." He ducked his head, tugged at his sleeves, which, she saw now, were too short by several inches, as if the cassock had been made for somebody else. He smiled. Brushed the hair out of his eyes. "And you, of course. You too."

She knew what Guy would have said about it, but she didn't really care what he thought, not anymore. In fact, Father Curran stopped by two days later and a whole new process began. Sam took to him right away, though he kept lifting the priest's cassock to inspect his legs and socks and old-fashioned garters as if they were props in a magic act, which, to Father Curran's credit, didn't seem to bother him at all—in fact he was amused by it and at one point asked Sam what he thought of the arrangement. Sam said he didn't know. The priest laughed, then asked if he'd ever seen a priest before and Sam signed no and she felt a flush of embarrassment. Then he asked Sam about Jesus—did he know Jesus? Another no, another flush of embarrassment.

"Not to worry," he said, "David Greybeard didn't know Jesus either, not as far as anybody's reported, anyway—but he could have. What do you think, Sam, do you want to know Jesus?"

Sam might not have had the proper noun in his vocabulary or understood what it signified beyond the name itself, but he was a master interpreter of body language and vocal inflection and he knew just what to do—bob his fist in an enthusiastic yes, the sort of yes that could lead to treats now and treats down the road after the priest had left, when she might be particularly disposed to show her gratitude.

She served Father Curran tea and tuna on rye and put Sam through his paces while they sat at the table eating, really drawing the priest out, because she had a motive in mind, an idea actually, that had come to her not five minutes into their conversation in the parking lot at Dunkin' Donuts. Azazel was dead. He'd lived a relentlessly cruel life, chained for eight years to a post outside the bunkhouse of a ranch in Texas after some cowboy had bought him on a whim from a circus in Mexico. He'd had no stimulus of any kind beyond what the ranch hands gave him when they remembered he was there, food tossed randomly at him, people gathering to watch him scratch his fleas or snap open a pop-top beer and see how he reacted when he was drunk, the sun eternal, a doghouse his only refuge. Then Moncrief heard about him, flew down to Texas and brought him back to a cage in Iowa, where he never again saw the sky or the sun that had scorched him through all those punishing years. He ate. He shat. He slept. He bred when Moncrief wanted him to. And then he got a rope.

What was the point of *his* life? What was the point of Sam's? What was the point of anything? She'd given herself over to something she couldn't explain, a deep connection with another soul, whether it be human or not. And she wanted guarantees. She wanted a reason. A back-up plan. Salvation.

Sam had been showing Father Curran his drawings, including the one he'd done the day before that depicted an elongated figure in a black dress—cassock?—staring straight out at you, when she said, "Please don't say this is crazy, but I was thinking I'd like to have Sam baptized. I mean, if that's possible at all—"

He was watching Sam make adjustments to the drawing with a black crayon, the cassock swelling now to take up the entire bottom half of the composition and a new figure appearing in the upper portion that was like a black ball with arms and legs radiating from it—and ears, big scalloped ears framing the smaller ball he deftly sketched atop it. "Nice, Sam," he said, "very nice. Is that me—and you?"

Sam paused to sign YES and then went back to the drawing, adding what looked to be a tree rising in the background.

"Truly?" the priest said, glancing up at her. "I don't know. I've been asked to bless just about everything you can think of, from a Harley Sportster to a hiker's shelter on the Appalachian Trail, but this is something else altogether, this is a sacrament we're talking about."

She was going to remind him of what he'd said in the parking lot about how allowances had to be made, but she didn't have to. He broke into a grin and she saw that he was wearing a retainer, which somehow made her feel better—he was the instrument of God, but

he was human too, with the same frailties and imperfections as anybody else. There was nothing to be shy about. It was okay. Everything
was okay.

"The only question," he said, "is do we perform the ceremony here
or do we bring him to church?"

She opted to have the ceremony at home, out back of the trailer, where
it was as private as it got in Desert Haven—every once in a while
a dog would careen through the yard or one of the other residents
would drift past (one skeletal old man in particular, who liked to
levitate a metal detector over the dead blasted dirt in the hope of uncovering something of value, which in itself was an act of faith), but
mostly she had the lot to herself. At first, she thought she'd like to see
Sam baptized in church, but then she wondered if she'd be expected
to contribute, which would have been awkward, not that she couldn't
spare the money, whatever it was, a token payment for services rendered, but just that she wouldn't know how to go about asking. Plus,
there would be other people there, strangers, and she had no desire
to engage in chitchat or accept congratulations or hear what they
had to say about Sam, whether it was positive or not. And there was
no telling how Sam might have reacted in a strange environment. So
she bought a redwood picnic table at Kmart, which came with two
benches, one for either side, and she put out a bowl of potato chips
and some dip and filled a cooler with ice, beer and Coke, and invited
Brenda and Gary to stand as witnesses and celebrate along with Sam
and her.

They planned the ceremony for just after Sam woke from his afternoon nap, when he tended to be at his mellowest, the sleep draining off him and his eyes still in soft focus, and that was all to the
good. Sam knew the priest and liked him and he knew Brenda and

Gary too, the only people in the court he'd had any contact with to this point, so when they gathered around the table and Father Curran began intoning the words of the sacrament, he was as patient as could be expected. And he looked the part too, all innocence in the new T-shirt and white overalls she'd bought for the occasion.

Father Curran, spindly and slope-shouldered in his vestments and with his hair combed stiffly back, leaned over Sam, where she held him in her lap. He sprinkled the holy water three times and each time chanted, "I baptize you in the name of the Father, and of the Son, and of the Holy Spirit. He now anoints you with the chrism of salvation."

Sam seemed to accept this with equanimity, though he shook his head and blinked his eyes over and over as if to say he hoped everyone present knew he was doing them an enormous favor in sitting still for whatever they might have thought this was. He was aware that potato chips were coming his way and a cake he'd helped her bake that morning, chocolate fudge with vanilla icing, and if the cost of that was to sit in her lap and endure a few sprinkles of water, a smear of oil and a speech he couldn't have fully comprehended, despite the fact that she'd gone over the details in a picture book designed for the purpose, then it was all right with him. She'd once wondered if he knew God and if he could communicate as much or at least acknowledge it, but he gave no indication. All he did was sign back to her as she read aloud to him and they both traced the figures in Michelangelo's *Creation of Adam* with their forefingers, which wound up concentrating his focus because Adam was nude with his penis exposed and God was supported by a host of naked angels.

"God the Father of our Lord Jesus Christ has freed you from sin, given you a new birth by water and the Holy Spirit, and welcomed you into His holy people," Father Curran recited as Gary lit a white candle and handed it to him. "Samuel, receive the light of Christ," the priest said, and then, raising his eyes to address her as the parent, or the nearest thing to it, he went on, "Your son, Samuel, has been enlightened by Christ and he is to walk always as a child of the light."

There was the sound of a car backfiring, which stoked Sam's attention, and then somebody in the trailer across the way turned up the volume on their radio and as if by divine intervention "Stairway to Heaven" was thumping out over the lot until it abruptly cut off and Mick Jagger was croaking, "I'm a fleabit peanut monkey/And all my friends are junkies." The irony was too much. For a moment—just that moment—everybody paused, probably thinking the same thing, and why hadn't she thought to provide her own music, one of Bach's masses or Handel or Palestrina? She was embarrassed. She felt her face flush. But then—she couldn't help herself—she burst into laughter and Brenda gave her a quizzical look even as Sam snatched the candle out of Father Curran's hand and blew out the flame, as if this were his birthday, which in a way it was. She said, "Not yet, Sam," but it was too late because the candle was out and Sam was already gnawing experimentally on the still-smoking tip of it, and if she projected, if she put herself in Sam's place, she had to admit the wax looked just like the slick vanilla icing of the cake that was waiting in the wings.

Then it was over and she was offering drinks all around, Gary and Brenda opting for beer, she and Father Curran for red wine (the same pricey California pinot noir she and Guy used to drink gratis at the ranch, the only label she really knew), while Sam expertly applied the bottle opener to his first Coke. The radio next door never let up, one tune after another, but the pedestrian sounds of the court seeped back in and nobody seemed to pay much attention to it. Brenda commented on the dip—sour cream with dill, minced onion, garlic salt and parsley folded in—and Father Curran had a second glass of wine and relaxed into the spirit of the day. Sam was perfect, once he'd spat out the candle wax, that is—he just sat there on the bench, drinking Coke, which he was allowed only on special occasions, biding his time till the cake was served. And when it was, he showed tremendous restraint while she guided his hand in cutting individual slices for the guests, though he couldn't help serving himself the first piece, all questions of decorum aside, and he did manage to decorate his baptismal outfit with a broad smear of chocolate, which by some mysterious process wound up communicating itself to the priest's robes as well. Still, whether Sam fully comprehended what all this meant and no matter what Guy and the rest of the scientific community might have had to say about it, she felt a sense of relief. The individual, the *person*, she loved best on this earth was possessed of a soul—demonstrably, in the eyes of the church—and now, no matter what came next, that soul was saved.

The days fell in place, one after the other. Nothing happened, nothing changed. She didn't hear from Guy, not that she'd expected to, and that was just fine with her. That was over. Permanently. She supposed it was like a divorce, a bad divorce, but she'd got the only asset that really mattered and now it was time to move on. Sam was her rock. He was older now, more mature—and more relaxed than she'd seen him since the days of the ranch. Every afternoon they went up on the mesa to play hide-and-seek or, if it was warm enough, spread a blanket and just lie back and watch the clouds wheel overhead. In the evenings, they sipped gin and tonic, made whatever they felt like for dinner and more often than not wound up eating in front of the TV. She wasn't getting her degree. She wasn't studying anything. She'd have to look to the future, her mother was right about that, but not now—now she was here, in her own bought-and-paid-for trailer, answerable to nobody.

Father Curran stopped by three or four times that fall to spend some time with her—or with Sam, actually. Sam learned to make the sign of the cross and Father Curran started picking up some basic signs so he could communicate directly with him on matters religious and secular both. He wanted to know what Sam knew, no different from her or Guy or any other researcher. What went on in that brain? What basic truths could it reveal? When Jane Goodall observed the chimps at Gombe dancing at the waterfall or cavorting in the rain, were they displaying a sense of awe at forces greater than themselves? And when they engaged in ritualistic behavior, like piling stones at the base of a particular tree, was this a form of worship?

If Sam knew, he wasn't forthcoming. From his point of view, the man in the black robe had once been the occasion for the production of chocolate cake and that seemed enough of a reason in itself to pay attention to him. They drank tea together at the kitchen table, ate the oatmeal cookies Father Curran never failed to bring along with him. One afternoon, after an exchange about the weather, the lizards, the rock slabs of the mesa, the cactus spines and other evidentiary features of the material world, Father Curran asked, "Who is God?" and Sam signed, GOD, which she thought was a pretty good answer since God is ineffable. Father Curran tried again. "Where is God?" he asked, and Sam, after giving her a knowing look, pointed one long determinate finger at the sky.

And then it was Halloween, a holiday Sam had loved at the ranch, when everyone would dress in costume and the treats just kept on coming, candy bars, apples, dried apricots and gum, which he seemed to like best of all, more for the concept than the taste—you chewed and chewed and didn't swallow, which he found hilarious, as if it were a charade, a delusion, food that wasn't food. She bought a pumpkin at the supermarket and let Sam help her carve a face in it, feeding him the extracted pieces, the triangles of the eyes and nose and the long jagged wedge of the mouth. Since there were no children in the court, she didn't expect any trick-or-treaters, but she bought a bag each of candy corn and Snickers bars just in case—and for Sam, who as soon as he saw the pumpkin began begging for treats.

After dinner, they settled into the couch with gin and tonics and she turned on the TV, thinking to watch one of the corny old black-and-white horror films she and Guy used to find so hilarious, especially after they'd shared a joint. She was flicking through the channels when Boris Karloff's freakishly white face appeared on the screen, his black-lipped mouth contorted in a grimace, his hair jaggedly chopped as if someone had taken a hedge trimmer to it, the telltale bolt thrust through his neck. The shadows moved, the screen flickered, the music raced. She wanted to laugh as the familiar scenes played out, the monster lurching across the colorless landscape or bursting into the blind man's shack, but then she looked at Sam. His face was set, his limbs trembling. The monster was acting like a chimp, that was what it was—and when suddenly he roared out his rage and confusion, Sam roared along with him. The villagers closed in with their torches, dogs barking, voices clamoring, and Sam sprang out of the chair to hump round the room, pounding the pillows and showing his teeth, in full hyper mode, and she kept saying, "It's okay, Sam, it's only a movie," but he wouldn't stop so she picked up the remote and shut it off right at the climax.

Sam signed, WHY?, and she didn't know if he was asking why she'd turned off the TV or why they were attacking the man with the white face. Before she could answer, he snatched the remote out of her hand and flicked the movie back on at the very moment everything collapsed in flames. She was just getting up to scold him and take it back from him, when there was a knock at the door.

Nobody ever knocked at the door, except Brenda and sometimes Father Curran—and Guy, that first night. *Guy*, she thought, and she could see his face, see the lean defined outline of him, his smile, his hair, the distressed bomber jacket he wore in cold weather, but it wasn't Guy and it was never going to be Guy, she knew that. She thought of Brenda next, even as the knock came again, this time a little firmer, a little less patient, and Sam stiffened. "Trick or treat?" a muffled voice called and she relaxed.

There were five people gathered under the yellow beam of her porch light, four of them at ground level, and one—a tall heavy big-bellied man she recognized from the next row over—on the top step, one hand clutching a beer mug, the other arrested in the act of applying his knuckles to the doorframe. All five of them—they were drunk, that was instantly clear—called out a ragged "Trick or treat?" in what was, as she would later learn, a Desert Haven tradition on Halloween, going trailer to trailer with a mug and begging to have it topped off with whatever the inhabitants had handy, all in the name of a good time and getting thoroughly sloshed. Which was fine, or would have been fine, as long as she didn't have to invite them in or be expected to make conversation beyond the usual pleasantries, and she foresaw infusing whatever they were drinking with a healthy splash of gin apiece—Halloween—but that didn't happen. Because the man on the porch, the big man, whose name was J.J. Burnside and who had his own eponymous muffler-repair shop on Stockton Hill Road, was dressed as a pirate—they were all pirates, three men and two women, her neighbors, enjoying themselves—and had made the unfortunate choice to wear an ersatz eyepatch over his left eye.

In the instant it took her to process all this, Sam let out a scream and flew at the man, and though she managed to hook an arm around his throat and tried to jerk him back, the damage was done—he hit the man like a heat-seeking missile and the man dropped his drink, threw out his arms and fell backwards down the steps. There was a shout, a curse, a gabble of voices. Sam could have flung her aside and gone after him, could have done worse, much worse, but he felt the presence of her, the grip of her arms, both her arms clutching him to her now with all her strength, and in the moment of decision he pulled back and let her hold him. One of the men shouted, "Son of a bitch!" and a woman's voice hissed, "Jesus!" in a long expiring breath. The last thing she saw before she wrestled Sam back in the house and slammed the door shut was J.J. Burnside sprawled on his back in the gravel while the shadows of the four others swelled and jerked against the reflection of the yellow light on the pale dun backdrop of the boulders behind them.

THE TASTE OF GOD

God was up in the sky. God was good. God loved everybody. And NO LEGS was God's special friend and messenger and he brought COOKIES with him when he came to visit, which was the taste of God, or at least that was the natural assumption. No Legs was harmless and weak and no threat to Aimee or him or anybody else. And No Legs was learning to make words with his hands so they could talk about what was visible and what wasn't and he sometimes understood what the man was getting at, at least partly, because if he closed his eyes he could still see things and in his dreams he could see them too. And God had a PENIS, just like him. Did God get stiff the way he did sometimes? Did God know Aimee? Did God ever come down from the sky? Was God a bird?

No Legs sat there at the kitchen table grinning at him and Aimee and it wasn't like the lessons she and Guy used to put him through, which were tedious and repetitive, but something that stirred him and invited him into a new world altogether. One time she blindfolded him and handed him objects—one of his BLOCKS with the raised letters on them, letter A, for Aimee, a TOWEL, a STICK—and asked him to identify them even though he couldn't see them. That was easy. No Legs grinned. Aimee grinned. And there was a banana in it for him.

This was his world now and it was secure in its routines, waking beside her, eating breakfast at the table with her, going OUT, going in the CAR, eating dinner and watching TV, and on the nights when she was working, sleeping in his special BED in the CAR. He didn't concern himself about the shape of his feet anymore or the BLACK BUGS or anything else but there were times when he remembered the past and then the PAIN was present with him. That was what had happened on Halloween when the man came to the door with the hole cut out of his head and the past was the now and he was AFRAID.

The next day, or maybe another day, maybe a day after that, Brenda came to the trailer and she was stiff and cold and didn't greet him or stroke his ears or offer him a treat. Aimee gave her tea, same as with No Legs, only he didn't sit at the table with them but on the couch, looking through his magazines, *Playboy* especially, his favorite, because there were no clothes in *Playboy* and they were all females and sometimes they looked like Aimee.

Brenda said, "I don't care because we just can't have another incident like this. He thought he'd broke his ankle, till they X-rayed it, but you saw him—he's still hobbling around and there's no excuse for that."

Aimee said something back to her but he wasn't listening. The pictures were boring—he'd seen them all before. He clicked the TV on and immediately the screen came to life with a line of CARS racing around in a circle and Aimee said, "Turn it down, Sam, it's too loud," and he fumbled with the button, but that only made it louder, till she got up from the table and took it from him and clicked it and clicked it again till the noise of the CARS was just a whisper. "Now you be good," she said, as if that meant anything. "I'm talking to Brenda, okay?"

They talked with their voices and he followed along till it bored him and then he got up and started banging his toy dog against the wall till she told him he was being too loud and he went into his room and banged it there. He could still hear them, their voices rising and falling, and he began to feel jealous because why was Aimee talking to her when she could be talking to him?

Brenda said, "There's plenty of other trailer courts around."

Aimee said, "You know Sam. You know he behaves himself. The man just startled him, that's all. We were minding our own business. It was Halloween. We were watching *Frankenstein*."

"Yes, but there are legal issues involved, you must know that—"

Aimee said, "Give us another chance. Please?"

ON THE ONE HAND

On the one hand, what happened to J.J. was his own fault—he was drunk, he was on Aimee's top step and Sam perceived him as a threat—but on the other hand, if there was no Sam, if she hadn't rented to Aimee in the first place, then J.J. wouldn't be hobbling around on crutches and threatening to sue not just Aimee but her too for allowing a dangerous animal to be kept on the premises. Millie Vogel had been there that night, also drunk, along with J.J. and his wife, Cindy, and Jimmy Everton, and she said she'd never been so scared in her life. "I told you somebody was going to get hurt, didn't I tell you? Didn't I?" And it wasn't just Milly and the Burnsides—half the court was up in arms. Even Gary said, "Look, I know J.J.'s full of shit, and I don't know the law or what our liability is, but maybe it's time to think about Aimee finding some other park to move her trailer to."

"What's Father Curran going to say?"

"I don't have a clue, but you think he's going to kick in for damages? Raid the poor box or the crippled orphans fund or whatever? And if Sam went after J.J., who knows who he'll go after next. I say it's time to cut our losses."

So she went to have a talk with Aimee, her mind half made up, and Sam didn't help any. He was distant, difficult, acting guilty and banging things around in the back room like an angry child, but then everything changed when all at once he glided silently into the room, laid a hand on hers and gazed up at her out of his big chocolate eyes as if he knew, as if he was apologizing. Aimee explained the whole thing, how Sam had been worked up over the movie and how no one ever came to the door so it was totally unexpected, even on Halloween, and it wasn't as if she was on the Burnsides' doorstep, right? And how all she'd ever asked since the day she moved in was for a little privacy, which was her basic right, wasn't it?

They were seated in the breakfast nook, sharing a pot of Constant Comment, and Sam climbed up beside Aimee now, making his soft hooting noises, which was his equivalent of what a cat does when it's purring. He produced a box of raisins and three plastic cups, which he inverted on the tabletop, then plucked a single raisin out of the box, hid it under one of the cups, shuffled them and pushed them toward her. "Go ahead," Aimee said. "He loves this game."

"The shell game," she said, and laughed. "I haven't played this since I was a kid, but let me see now, Sam, is it under"—and she lifted the middle cup—"this one?" But it wasn't, and Sam, giving out a laugh of triumph, overturned the right one, plucked up the raisin and popped it in his mouth. Then he pushed the box of raisins across the table to her and made signs with his hands, which meant it was her turn to hide the raisin. And what was it that made her play along—and then play again and again, though he wound up beating her almost every time? The newspaper said they were making computers you could play this very game against—or chess or checkers or solitaire—but where was the charm in that? Sam was alive. You could see him thinking. And you could see the delight in his eyes when he beat you.

Finally, she said, "Well, I came over here to give you an ultimatum, but this is—I mean, I guess it wasn't your fault. Or Sam's. But you're just going to have to keep an eagle eye on him, not that you're not doing that already, but we can't have people going around threatening to sue us. You hear me?"

"Yes," Aimee said, ducking her head, "I hear you. One more chance, okay?"

Unfortunately—*I told you so*, Gary said—that chance evaporated almost as soon as she'd granted it. At first things seemed to go back to normal and people found something else to gossip about—the DaSilvas, in number forty-six, announced they were getting divorced and they all watched Jean load up their van with everything they owned, including their two Chihuahuas and their Persian cat (whose name was either Dumbass or Lardass, she could never remember which), pull a three-point turn and wheel out of the lot for good, and one afternoon a police cruiser and a drug-sniffing dog pulled up in front of Lucy Devlin's trailer and poked around for three or four hours, but in the final analysis found nothing incriminating—but then, on a dreary socked-in weekday when everybody was focusing on the holidays and she herself was at Smith's picking up her Thanksgiving turkey and a long list of items any one of which, if overlooked, would ruin the dinner for five she was planning in honor of Gary's mother, who was flying in for the occasion, Sam got loose.

It was like this: Aimee was asleep, though it was past noon, exhausted from her night job, which didn't get her in till two or three in the morning. And Sam, who kept trying to wake her so they could go *do* something, get out of the house, climb the mesa, go to McDonald's or hike the wash or just drive around with the windows down and the breeze fanning his face, got bored. He watched cartoons for as long as he could stand it, found his paints where she'd hidden them in the secret recess under the floorboards in the kitchen closet and painted for a while, finished off a box of Lucky Charms and a bag of stale raisin muffins and then idly poked through the drawers till he came up with the Phillips-head screwdriver, which intrigued him, especially since the crank window in the living room with the smudged glass panels and shiny silver screens was held in place by screws that had just exactly the same pattern on them as the screwdriver itself. Or that fit the screwdriver, anyway. He couldn't get out the door—Aimee had seen to that, reinforcing it with a barred inner panel she'd hired a welder to put in—but the window was another story. He inserted the screwdriver experimentally and maybe he turned it the wrong way, maybe he tightened the screws rather than loosening them, but he was a quick study, Sam, and before long the screws were on the floor and the window frame and the attached screen set carefully beside them.

Once he was out, once he was free, he didn't just parade himself down the row where anybody in their yard or peering out their window could see him and raise the alarm—he was cleverer than that. As best they could reconstruct it, he must have slipped round back of the Bentons' trailer, which was right next to Aimee's, heard them talking or moving inside—they were retirees and both home at the time—and gone on to the trailer next to theirs, where Dolores Benvenidez, the only Mexican in the court (*Mexican American*, that is, as Gary was forever correcting her), lived alone with her two cats. Dolores was at work at the time—she was a nurse at the Cancer Center, a saint, actually, who specialized in children's oncology, a heartbreaking job if ever there was one. And it wasn't as if she didn't take precautions, since her trailer was one of the ones that had been broken into two years back and she had lost something like a hundred fifty dollars cash, her TV and all her financial records, which was a nightmare. In the wake of that, she'd installed double locks on the front door and always, without fail, jammed a length of two-by-four up against the frame of the sliding doors that gave onto the deck she'd built out back.

The amazing thing was that despite all that, Sam managed to get in—and without breaking anything or even making a sound that might have aroused anybody's suspicions. Gary said he must have somehow picked the locks, though no one could be sure because in the aftermath both locks had been put back and refastened so that Dolores didn't notice anything amiss till she stepped inside. It wasn't a total disaster. Nothing was broken and nothing had been stolen. But there was food scattered everywhere, the TV was on, there was a burnt Pop-Tart in the toaster oven and an unflushed turd in the toilet. It was just past four in the afternoon when Dolores got home from her shift and opened the door and was confronted with the mess. The first thing she thought of was her cats, but when she called their names there was silence, which chilled her all the more, and afraid that somebody might still be in the trailer, she slammed the door shut and came straight to the office. "There's been a break-in," she said in a voice that not only was barely under control but had an edge of accusation in it too, as if Brenda herself was being paid to keep guard over everybody's trailers and everything in them. "They trashed the place. And they might still be in there for all I know, because believe me I wasn't about to stick around and find out—"

She pushed herself up from the chair in the office, feeling more curious than anything else since the next thing Dolores told her was that the door was still locked when she'd got home and none of the windows were broken. "All right," she said, "let's have a look," and though she suspected it was all going to amount to nothing more than an overactive imagination on Dolores' part, she took the precaution of slipping the snub-nosed Colt Python Gary had given her for her last birthday into her purse, because you never knew.

The day tasted like cold metal, which was the way it sometimes was when the sky was low like this, though what that was all about, she couldn't say. She noticed a pair of vultures sliding across the sky over the bald crown of the mesa, their fringed wings dark against the clouds, and heard Gino Saks' worthless Doberman barking from the other end of the court, where he kept it chained outside when he went into town to empty his pockets at one saloon or another. When they came up the steps to the front porch at Dolores' place, Dolores said, "See, right here? I swear I locked both these locks this morning—and they were locked ten minutes ago when I got home from work too. So you tell me—"

She was no hero, and it wasn't really her job to stick her neck out—she was the manager, not the police force—but she pulled open the door and called out, "Anybody here?" two or three times and then stepped inside. Dolores' trailer was a double-wide, with a cream-and-white color scheme, which made it seem even roomier, and she was a meticulous housekeeper, nothing out of place, ever, but everything was turned upside down now, couch pillows on the floor, magazines wadded up and scattered round the room, the contents of the refrigerator and freezer dumped in a heap on the linoleum. "Jesus," she said, "whoever it was they really made a mess. You sure you didn't give anybody the key?"

"No way," she said. "Never. There's nobody I trust that much."

So they inspected the whole place, end to end, and while thankfully they did find the cats cowering under the bed, the mystery only deepened. There was nothing missing, except the bag of whole cranberries Dolores had had in the refrigerator for Thanksgiving and an unopened twelve-pack of Creamsicles that had been in the freezer. "I don't know," she heard herself say, thinking aloud, "but it looks like somebody locked a nine-year-old in here overnight," which was when the image of Sam first came into her head. And sure enough, when they went outside to test the windows and look for any signs of forced entry, they found a popsicle stick on the ground in front of the door and when they raised their eyes they saw the next one, twenty feet away and the next one beyond that, tracing a path right back to Aimee's trailer.

If anything, Aimee seemed resigned to what was coming. She didn't really protest—and it wasn't in her nature to get nasty, unlike so many of the other tenants she'd had to deliver bad news to over the years, but things just couldn't go on like this and she had no choice but to give her her thirty days' notice. At first, Aimee had no idea what she was talking about. And it wasn't play-acting, not at all—she was genuinely baffled. Brenda had felt it would be best if Dolores kept out of it, so she was the one who took it upon herself to knock on the door and confront Aimee with the evidence, including the final popsicle stick, which was located right under the trailer's front window, Sam's point of egress—and, apparently, ingress. "I can't believe it," Aimee said when she knocked at the door and told her that somebody had broken into Dolores' trailer and that that somebody was Sam. "He's been here with me all day—and we haven't gone anywhere." And then, for Sam, who was sunk into the couch with one of his Dr. Seuss books, "Right, Sam?"

"I think he got out the front window—is it broken at all?"

Aimee said, "I don't know, I don't think so, but let's have a look."

The window had been put back in, but if you examined it closely you could see that two of the screws were missing—there they were, on the rug, and the screwdriver with them. Even more damning was the bright yellow scrap of a Creamsicle carton stuck to the bottom of the curtains and two more popsicle sticks dropped casually on the kitchen floor.

"What do you know about this, Sam?" Aimee demanded, crossing the room to stand over him, hands on hips, in full interrogation mode.

And here was the thing that always amazed her, and she must have told the story a dozen times over the course of the next couple of weeks: Sam lied. Animals didn't lie. Animals just lived in the moment and if they felt guilt—a dog slinking in the corner after snatching a pork chop from the table or crapping on the floor—it wasn't so much guilt as fear of retribution, which was something, certainly a higher brain function than most people gave them credit for, but this was something else altogether. At first, Sam pretended he didn't know what she was talking about, just kept his head in his book, but you could see he knew what was coming because he wouldn't look at her. She asked again, her voice harsher now. Still nothing. Then she produced the scrap of bright yellow wrapper and waved it in his face and he looked up and signed something to her.

"Don't give me that," she said. "How could Guy do it? Guy's not even here."

Another sign, the long fingers jumping, the eyes dodging away.

"No, he wasn't. He's in California, you know that. He didn't break into that woman's trailer," she said, signing it simultaneously. "You did."

The way he smiled was to roll up his lips and expose his teeth and gums, which was what he did at that moment, and it was clownish and endearing and something else too and she saw it now for the first time and it chilled her—he was calculating. He wasn't a person and he wasn't an animal but something in between, something deformed and unnatural, even if he'd fooled Father Curran. Well, he wasn't fooling her, not anymore. Here he was, admitting to the crime and begging forgiveness at the same time because he was like a spoiled child. And who'd spoiled him? Who was ultimately responsible? Who was guilty here?

"You know we can't have this," she heard herself say. She was angry, furious really, as if she'd been taken for a fool right from the beginning. "You know this is it, don't you? The final straw?"

Stone-faced, her shoulders slumped, all the fight drained out of her, Aimee just nodded. "I know," she said.

It was just after Thanksgiving when the two men showed up. The day was cold, or cold for Kingman, anyway, in the low thirties when she got out of bed at seven, but the sun was shining and there was no wind so that made it bearable at least. She had the space heater going in the office and was doing the crossword over a microwave burrito and a cup of coffee when a strange car with two men in it swung into the lot and pulled right up to the door. The first man—he turned out to be a professor too—came in without knocking and asked for Aimee while the other one stayed in the car.

Aimee had made arrangements to have her trailer towed to Delpino's in Golden Valley at the end of the month, just ten miles away but another universe as far as views and amenities were concerned, but they weren't picky about who rented space there and pretty much anything went as far as pets were concerned. Last time she and Gary visited Joe Delpino she saw a llama tied to the tow bar of a Minnie Winnie and standing practically up to its knees in a pile of its own crap and somebody else had two of the mangiest-looking horses she'd ever seen locked up in a portable corral the size of a refrigerator box, not that it was any of her business. But it was never pleasant having to evict anybody and she'd felt sorry for Aimee and helped hook her up both with Joe and the Andrelton brothers, who'd been relocating trailers for the tenants at Desert Haven for the past twenty years. Whether Aimee was home at the moment or not, she didn't know but even after what had happened she still felt protective of her— protective of everybody in the court, for that matter—and she made it her business to find out who was asking before giving out information to just anybody.

"Yes, she lives here," she said.

Gary was a big man, six-two, two-thirty, but the man standing before her looked to be even bigger, or heavier, anyway. And Gary had gone into town in the pickup to get the brakes fixed, so he wasn't there for comparison. Or help. There was another thing about the man, aside from his manner and the way he talked, which was nothing short of condescending—he had a patch over one eye and you could see the fine lines of scar tissue wrapped over the bridge of his nose. He said, "Well, could you direct me to her?"

She thought about that for a moment, then took off her reading glasses and set them on the counter so she could see him more clearly. She couldn't help recalling how Aimee had come to her out of nowhere, without references or even a previous address, and how eager she'd been to change the plates on her car and then turn around and get rid of it altogether. What she was thinking was that this looked like trouble, and though it was no trouble of hers, she still couldn't see facilitating it in any way. "Does she know you're coming?" she asked.

"Yes," he lied.

"Well, you'll have her address, then, won't you? The lot numbers are clearly marked."

He took a minute to absorb this, studying her with the long, concentrated gaze of his working eye. "I'm afraid she didn't provide me with that information."

She was just about to do the same thing she'd done with the last visitor—push the phone across the counter to him—when she asked, almost on a lark, but to delay him too and maybe aggravate him a little, because she didn't like him one bit: "Don't tell me you're her professor too?"

The car was still running in the drive. She could see the other man sitting there in the passenger seat, younger, dressed in what looked to be a muscle shirt despite the cold. She watched him lean forward and fiddle with something—the radio dial. He was a visitor too. And maybe he was bored, but that was nothing to her either.

"In fact," the big man said, "I am a professor," and he gave his name and his title and his affiliation too—Davenport University.

"Davenport? Isn't that in Iowa?"

He nodded.

"You've come pretty far. What is it," she said, and she gave him an acid grin, "winter break?"

"All right, listen," he said, and she watched him swell out his shoulders and do a little two-step shuffle (and that was another thing that was a bit off—he was wearing a suit jacket, as if he really was a professor, but the same Timberland work boots Gary favored), "I just need to know where she is and I'll be out of your hair. The fact is, she does live here, didn't you just say so? And you are the manager of the place"—he squinted at the nameplate on the desk, which read *Brenda Sue Booth*—"aren't you? *Brenda?*"

She didn't like him. And she'd made up her mind to toy with him a little bit more just to see how he'd take it. She was going to say, in all innocence, "Oh, but I'm not Brenda, I'm Dolly. Dolly Anastasio?" but he didn't give her a chance. He was the sort who was used to getting what he wanted. He was the sort who bullied people. And never thanked anybody for anything.

He said, "This is urgent, and I think I have an obligation to tell you that. What I'm talking about is stolen property, a felony, and it would be a shame to let this, whatever it is between us here, get in the way of it or for me even to have to mention a term like harboring a fugitive." He paused to draw a handkerchief from his inner pocket and blow his nose as if to clear his head. "If you won't assist me," he said, "my best guess is that the sheriff will. You don't happen to have his number by any chance, do you?"

FIGHT KILL DIE

These were the essential words, the first words, the words that pricked rage before the fact and landed like bricks after, and he knew them in the way he knew how to breathe and swallow and move his bowels. They were the words of a story, a story already told, because when he was in the story, when it was happening to him, in real time, he didn't need words—he just acted, or reacted, like any other sentient thing. Which was how it was on the morning when she had the RECORD turned up so high it hurt his ears and she was too busy putting cans and jars and forks and spoons and knives in boxes to pay attention to him. "Not now, Sam," she kept saying, no matter what he wanted to do, whether it was to go OUT for a WALK or play CARDS or drive in the CAR. "Just watch TV, okay? Can you do that for me?"

He watched TV, though the record—thumping and thumping—fought against the TV and rendered the words of the figures inside it null and void, not that he needed to know what they were saying because he could read their body language even if she shut the sound off altogether, but he turned up the TV anyway. She came across the room, took the CLICKER from him and turned it down. He watched where she put it—atop the refrigerator—and the minute she was distracted he sidled into the kitchen, sprang up on the counter, retrieved it and clicked the sound back up. "No, Sam," she said and held her hand out for the clicker but he wouldn't give it up even when she stamped her foot and tried to grab it out of his hand, so she went back to what she was doing with the cabinets and the boxes and Daffy Duck rose up out of the cacophony and squawked, "Mine! Mine! Mine!"

Because it was so loud, he didn't hear the creaking of the three hard METAL steps up to the trailer, which was lost in the thump of her music and the crash and bang of the TV. Then there was the knock. She didn't hear it, but he did. He was trying to evaluate it, the knock, wondering if it was the knock of Brenda or No Legs or maybe—and here he felt his excitement rising—PIZZA! But it was too early for PIZZA, wasn't it? And he hadn't heard her ordering over the phone and she hadn't asked him what he wanted on it, which was EVERYTHING, piled high, GREEN PEPPERS, ONIONS, TOMATOES, SAUSAGE, MUSHROOMS, so he was confused and curious and instead of going to the DOOR he went to her and tugged on her shirt and she said, "Will you please stop pestering me, Sam?" when the second knock came and then the third, louder and louder, and she gave him a look of surprise and called out, "Okay, okay, I'm coming!"

There was a hard yellow ray of sunlight radiating through the window in a float of dust and it distracted him just a moment as she unlocked the door and pulled it back and a terrible voice insinuated itself between the noise of the record and the noise of the TV, saying, "Well, well, Miss Villard, how nice to see you again. I believe you have something that belongs to me?"

HUG ME, TEASE ME,
LOVE ME, SQUEEZE ME

That was what they were singing, the Talking Heads, doing a varia-
tion on a song by Al Green, which was also called "Take Me to the
River," or so somebody had told her—Guy?—though as far as she
knew she'd never heard the original, which couldn't have been half
as good as this. This had that magnetic bass that always seemed to
live right inside of you and it was still one of her all-time favorites,
though by now she supposed it was out of date and people on campus
were more into U2 or whoever. Who she liked when she heard them
on the radio, but she hadn't bought any albums in a while now, since
they cost money and took up space and Sam could be hard on them.
She'd put the record on the stereo and kept the volume cranked as
a means of distracting herself while giving the trailer a good scrubbing and packing her things securely in the boxes she'd got out back
of the supermarket ("Don't leave anything laying around or it'll get

beat to hell and if you read your contract we're not responsible, you are," Toby, the younger of the two Andrelton brothers, had warned her). She didn't want to pack. She didn't want to move. And she hated Delpino's, which had about as much charm as a parking lot, which was essentially what it was.

Her attachment to Sam, her love, was unconditional, but there were times—like now—when she felt the burden of it. She'd run from Iowa with him, run from the campground in Utah, and now she was running from here, the only place where she'd been able to catch her breath, really, since she left Santa Maria, but then she wasn't running exactly—she was being shoved. And what next? She could see a whole succession of *incidents* shoving her further and further away from any kind of life at all, and what would it be like in a year, five years, ten? At least at the ranch she could get out once in a while, if only to see a movie or sit by herself in one of the student hangouts and spoon up a bowl of the soup of the day without having to worry about Sam emptying the cupboards or crashing through walls or taking hold of some stranger's hand in his vise grip and holding on for three hours just for the sheer hilarity of it.

She wanted to call her mother, wanted to hear her mother's voice, wanted to go home, but none of that was possible. No cop had appeared on her doorstep, but every time she sat out in the yard and heard the slamming of a car door or a man's voice raised in conversation drifting across the yard from some hidden corner of the court— *barbecue, valve job, bring me another beer, will you, hon?*—she froze. Guy had warned her—threatened her—and though she told herself she was just being paranoid, there was always that edge of unease, no matter what she did. Moncrief was coming, that was what he'd said. Moncrief never gave up. Moncrief was a son of a bitch. And, for that matter, so was Guy, as far as she was concerned.

Sam had been antsy all morning and that was her fault. She hadn't taken him out for his walk yet because she was too busy, too stressed, and here was the burden brought home to her all over again—it wasn't as if she could just open the door and let him out to do his business and sniff at the bushes like a dog. Dogs could get in trouble, as anybody at Animal Control would testify. They could bite, run sheep, chase cars, bark for hours on end. Sam was in another category—he could devise trouble in a hundred ways and gradations. He could think. He could plan. Breaking into Dolores Benvenidez's trailer was symptomatic of a new pattern that had begun that day at Moncrief's house, an act of willfulness, delinquency even. If he was in school they would have expelled him by now.

She put the chewed-up Tupperware plates in a box, emptied the spice cabinet, set aside the cleaning supplies. She'd awakened early, before it was light out, but she hadn't got up. She'd just lain there in bed staring into nothingness until the room began to take on dimension and the black blur beside her metamorphosed into Sam. He was sleeping on his side, his legs drawn up in the fetal position, his head sunk into the pillow beside her. He tended to snore if he slept on his back, the way Guy did, and she'd sometimes have to poke him to get him to turn over, but he was fine now, his breathing easy and barely audible. She watched the light swell against the curtains and creep across the wall to infuse the pale whorls of his upturned ear, pale as a mushroom against the tight dark hairs of his neck and shoulders. The room brightened by degrees. There was no sound anywhere, not even from the birds that flitted in and out of the palo verde trees in front of the office and came to peck in the dirt behind her trailer for whatever they could find there.

Because she slept with him and because people knew that (Brenda had asked her if he slept in his doggie bed on the nights when they were home and she'd made the mistake of saying, "No, he climbs right into bed with me," and Brenda, rolling her eyes, said, "Oh, yeah, our dog Misty was like that—just try to keep *her* off the bed"), they made their dirty-minded assumptions. And she knew about it not only from what she could read between the lines with Brenda, but from a snatch of conversation she'd overhead one afternoon when she was doing her laundry, two women sitting outside in the bed of a pickup, drinking beer and listening to the radio while their clothes tumbled in the dryer, their voices clubby and confidential, *I hear she sleeps with that thing.* A laugh. *Can you blame her? Shit, I bet he's better hung than Bill.* Another laugh, both of them in chorus. *You're just disgusting, you know that?*

She'd slipped out of bed, careful not to wake him, stood under the slow dribble of the shower, ate a bagel—dry, because she was out of cream cheese and not about to restock anything till they moved—and then sat at the table for so long her left calf began to cramp. Then she pushed herself up and began putting things in boxes. The fact was that chimps and humans were basically incompatible for sex because chimps' penises are much smaller than men's and they ejaculate within ten to fifteen seconds, but Sam was like any other adolescent and he masturbated freely, which was another kind of mess to clean up and there was no bathtub here, just a stand-up shower, but that was nobody's business but hers. And Sam's.

She tried to be as quiet as she could so as not to wake him, because once he got out of bed he'd suck up all her attention, as usual, and she did have to try to get a handle on all this mess. By eight o'clock, though, there he was in the kitchen doorway, giving her his feed-me look, and she cut up some melon for him and served him a bowl of the granola he liked to sweeten with honey out of the plastic squeeze bottle till it was a mucilaginous yellow sludge, and then she put the record on the stereo, cranked the volume and went back to work. Half an hour slipped by. He kept pestering her to go out and she kept putting him off. He turned on the TV, banged things around, used a crayon on one of the walls. And when she told him to lower the sound he ignored her till she took the remote away from him and hid it atop the refrigerator, where he found it five minutes later and refused to give it back to her so that finally she just gave up and let Daffy Duck and the Talking Heads fight it out.

When the knock came she assumed it was Brenda or maybe Toby Andrelton stopping by to iron out the final details, and she wouldn't even have been aware of it what with the blare of the music and the racket of the TV but for Sam, who came up and tugged at the tail of her denim shirt for probably the tenth time that morning except that this time he pointed to the door. And there it was, a dull arrhythmic thump working in counterpoint to the music. "Okay, okay, I'm coming!" she shouted and she thought about turning down the volume on the stereo but the music was part of her now, part of the transaction of the morning, and if she was going to turn it down she'd have to fight Sam for the remote and cut the volume on the TV too, so she didn't bother. She just went to the door, unlocked it and pulled it open.

She didn't blink, she didn't breathe: Moncrief was there, right there on the top step, faintly smiling, his face a red bloat against the cincture of the eyepatch. He said, "Well, well, Miss Villard, how nice to see you again." The music was thunderous. From the TV came a stentorian voice proclaiming, "Out of the bowl or from the box!" Moncrief said, "I believe you have something that belongs to me?"

Expect the unexpected, that was what they'd taught her in driver's ed back in high school, but this wasn't unexpected, this wasn't an accident—it was consummation, the endpoint of a process that had begun four years ago with a flickering image on a black-and-white portable TV in her studio apartment at a university on the Central Coast of California. Well, here it was. His face. His voice. The inevitable moment. She lurched back, her first thought to slam the door shut, but Moncrief anticipated her, locking a hand around her wrist.

She took nothing away from the scene, not the panic or the rocketing heartbeat or the grim certainty of what was to come, because Sam took it all himself. Two leaps, the first to halve the room, the second to lash into Moncrief and fling him backwards over the rail and down the steps, just as he'd done on Halloween with Moncrief's counterfeit, as if the whole thing had been an elaborate rehearsal. Only this time he didn't stop, and in some deep part of her she didn't want him to. Moncrief went spastic, landing on his back with an impact that expelled all the air from him as if his lungs were two tires that had blown out on a racetrack, and Sam was right there on top of him, a huge black burr clinging to the man's head and chest, working his fingers and his teeth.

And then there was Jack. In his muscle shirt. Fumbling with the dart gun. Moncrief tried to roll over, to fight back, but Sam wouldn't let him. What she couldn't see yet was that Sam's incisors—fangs, Sam's fangs—had cut loose a wet red flap of Moncrief's scalp that curtained his good eye (or the place where his good eye had been before Sam's fingers got to it). There was blood all over the gravel and now she was saying it, now she was screaming, "No, Sam, stop! Stop it!" But Sam wasn't listening. Sam would have gone on in his rage till there was no point in stopping if Jack hadn't finally got the dart in the gun and fired it.

There was a hiss of air and the dart appeared for the briefest instant in Sam's shoulder before Sam reached back, snatched it out and flung it away. He gave her a look as if to say "What now?" and then he let go of Moncrief and went for Jack.

Somebody was screaming—Brenda, Brenda was screaming—and people were running toward them, legs, knees, the caverns of their open mouths, and she was down the steps and clutching at Sam's arm, trying to stop this, trying to save him, though she knew it was already too late. Moncrief lay writhing on a bed of gravel, cursing fluidly, one hand pressed to the place where his eye had been, and Jack, bleached of color, tried to raise the dart gun again but Sam wasn't having it. Sam shook her off and flew at him, snapping his jaws shut on the handle of the gun and the fingers that held it upright, that aimed it, and in the next moment Jack was waving a spurting hand in the air, the gun gone and the red curled remnant of his right thumb blossoming at his feet.

Brenda was in the picture now, screaming "Get back!," one arm thrust out stiffly in front of her and her face clamped shut, and that was when she saw that Brenda had something in her hand too, a silver flash of light that was a gun, a little snub-nosed pistol, and it wasn't a dart gun that would sting for just an instant and put you to sleep till you opened your eyes on the world again, but the real thing, the fatal thing. The gun went off then, suddenly, inadmissibly, and the noise was a punch to the heart. Her brain screamed, *Sam!*, cried it, sobbed it, but nothing came out of her mouth. She saw the gravel jump at Sam's feet and here was Brenda, right here at her elbow, taking aim again, and that was wrong beyond any level of expectation she could even begin to harbor or imagine, so she grabbed Brenda's hand, jerked it as if it were the cord of an engine that would roar to life and lift them all up and away from here, and in the same instant she shouted, "Run, Sam, run!"

Then there was the rest of it.

Brenda's face, the hand she jerked free because it belonged to her and she wanted it back, Moncrief writhing in the gravel, Jack enveloping them all with the annunciation of his pain, the severed thumb, the echoing report of the gun, the gun itself, somebody else there now with a rifle and all their voices raised in antiphony, frantic call, frantic response. And Sam? Sam was running. For the first resounding instant she was afraid he'd try to hide in the trailer or under it or atop it, but no matter how disoriented he was, how terrified, he must have known that that was where they'd look for him, where they'd trap him, kill him, and he ducked away from the still-open door and bolted across the lot, heading for the mesa. In the next moment he was a distant dark form, climbing.

People's eyes jumped at her. They didn't know Moncrief, they didn't know Jack, but they knew her. And they knew that whatever this was, this horror, this blood, she was the one who'd unleashed it and that but for the luck of the draw they could have been the ones bleeding into the gravel. Two women she vaguely recognized were down on their knees tending to Moncrief. "Somebody call an ambulance," Brenda demanded in a hard metallic voice.

When the sirens started in she slipped away without a word to anybody, let alone Brenda, mounted the three steps to the trailer and shut the door behind her. There wasn't much time. She knew what she had to do and she went about it quickly, her hands trembling. First the backpack, then the Coke—the sixteen-ounce size in the plastic bottle that molded itself to your hand—then, finally, the pills.

I AM SAM

"Run, Sam!" she said. "Run!"

Her voice was high and tight and choked in her throat, which meant she was AFRAID and that made him AFRAID too and it jolted him out of the place he'd gone to in which words had no more meaning than birdsong and the BIG MAN was down on the ground and ARMS was crying and screaming at the same time and their BLOOD was on his face and his hands and the taste of it in his mouth. "Run, Sam, run!"

He didn't want to run. There was a hard hot unbridgeable fury in him and he wanted to go back to the BIG MAN and finish what he'd started, but the GUN went off and Aimee screamed and all the faces of all the people converged on him and before his brain could tell him what to do his knuckles hit the gravel and his legs churned and he was gone. He could have darted back into the trailer and barred the door, climbed into his BED and pulled the covers over him, but the trailer was just another kind of CAGE and they would get to him there the way they always had and always would and make him feel PAIN. No, he ran till the gravel became dirt and the dirt became rock and then he was climbing to the rhythm of the blood pounding through him, climbing higher and higher till everything below him shrank away and the voices faded on the wind.

When he got to the top, when he couldn't see them anymore and they couldn't see him, he threw himself down in the shade of a great smooth uplifted slab of rock and listened to the wind breathe along with him. This was his special place, the place where he came with her to lie still with his head in her lap and watch the clouds chase the sun, the place where he knew she would come looking for him. After a while his breathing slowed. He propped himself up on his elbows and there was a LIZARD right there, not five feet away, watching him out of a half-squinted eye as if trying to make out what he was. He could have caught it—the impulse jumped to life in him but in the same instant it died. He was feeling something he couldn't have named and it had to do with what had happened, of course it did, but there was this too—he was here alone, free, without supervision, without his harness or lead, without her or anybody else. The sun warmed him, the breeze cooled him. There were BIRDS, dark small hurtling things like flung stones, and they infested the thin dry elbows of the bushes and vanished and reappeared all over again, making their way over the hard scalp of rock and pecking, always pecking. And what was this? ANTS, a whole long tapering stream of ANTS flowing right past his feet and each of them carrying a fragment of something green, flowing, ebbing, in unceasing motion. He could have prodded them with his finger, could have lifted them to his lips and tasted them, but he didn't. He just sat there, watching them. And then he was asleep.

Something woke him. A noise. And it wasn't the wind or the birds on their silent wings or the ants on their silent legs—it was a mechanical noise, a keening that was like the wind but louder, much louder, and it rose and fell and rose and fell, over and over, until he realized what it was: a SIREN. He had to sign it to remember the name because he'd learned it a long time ago, back at the ranch when there was a FIRE in the bushes that hid the black shadows of the COWS and men came with hoses to spray it with WATER and she let him climb into his TREE to watch. That was a good thing. That was enjoyable. That was fun. And more than that it was a distraction from his lessons that were a new kind of tedium repeated daily, repeated endlessly. He didn't want to sit in a chair, didn't want to be quizzed and corrected and made to conform to a model he never would have chosen for himself, but he did it. For her and for Guy and for the one before her whose name was already gone from his memory. *Good boy*, they told him, *good boy*, and that was enough. Or was it? Wasn't there something more, something he was missing? But here it was again—still—the siren keening and whooping, and it triggered something in him, made him want to whoop back at it, and he did, he did whoop, but his spirit wasn't in it and he gave up almost as soon as he'd begun.

He heard something else now: DOGS. The barking of dogs. And he was AFRAID all over again, picturing the smooth sleek heads and white, white teeth of the ones that had come after him in that place where the ICE was, where she'd deserted him, where he was alone. He felt black inside. He felt hopeless. Where was she? Where was she now?

That was when he spotted her, the concentrated white scramble of her limbs, her face, the sheen of her hair with the sun alive in it, and she was coming up the last rise as fast as she could move on her two legs and her two hands, scrambling and clutching, up, up and up. He jumped to his feet and hooted joy to her and here she came, wearing her BACKPACK like a second set of shoulders and the sight of it sent a thrill through him because there were sure to be TREATS inside it, crackers and oranges and something sweet to drink. He was thirsty, he realized that suddenly, all this sun, all that climbing—and what had come before. For an instant he saw the BIG MAN down on the ground and he felt a surge of hate and pride and triumph and then she was there, hugging him, hugging him tight.

For the longest time she wouldn't let go. There was the pressure of her, the heat, the pounding of her heart and the rasp of her lungs and the *tick, tick, tick* of her blood that told him a multiplicity of things all at once, tragic things, frightening things, things that made him sink inside himself till he was grooming her, his fingers in her hair, on her back, on her neck, on her face. Her face was wet. She said, "Sam, are you thirsty?"

He was. He was thirsty. But he was too roiled inside, too HURT, to say YES or wrap his fingers around the bottle of Coke she produced from the backpack as if she were performing a magic trick. "Coke," she said, "your favorite," holding out the bottle that still had beads of water on it from the refrigerator, but her voice wasn't right, it wasn't steady, it was wrong, and he didn't take the bottle.

The birds shot into the bushes. The lizard winked. The sirens whooped. The dogs barked.

"Sam," she said, "Sam I am," and this was the old thing she used to say with the book spread open in her lap and the sheets clean and cool and the covers pulled over their legs.

And then it was easy. He took the Coke, unscrewed the top, and if it smelled different, if it was wrong too, it didn't matter because she was Aimee and she knew who he was and this was their game. He drank.

"Drink more," she said.

He drank again.

"Sam," she said, "Sam I am."

He set the bottle down carefully so what was left wouldn't spill. Then he touched her face, rolled up his lips in the biggest smile he knew how to make and signed, I AM SAM. I AM SAM.

THE LIGHT WAS INCONVENIENT

The light was inconvenient, the sun stuck there against the drawn blinds in his office like something that had melted and the overhead fluorescents so dull and flat he was afraid he'd come out looking like an animated corpse, but this was the last interview of the afternoon and he just wanted to get it over with. He'd already done the big ones—CBS, NBC, ABC, as well as KTLA out of Los Angeles, and CNN, the new one nobody ever watched. They'd posed him in front of the psych building while a mob of students armed with skate-boards, backpacks and sports drinks formed a hushed semicircle just out of camera range, but now it was the local news—the same crew that had filmed him and Sam at the ranch in happier times—and they thought they'd do something original and portray him at his desk, surrounded by books. "The academic look, right?" the reporter had said, and he'd said, "Yeah. Right. Perfect."

The sound girl—was it the same one?—sported a nose ring, the first nose ring he'd ever seen outside the pages of *National Geographic*, and maybe it was because he was tired and overstressed, but he couldn't stop looking at it, at her. She had a body on her, that was for sure, the kind that made you drop what you were doing and just stare every time she walked across the room, the kind that made you think of anything but science, unless it was the science of reproduction. Or the practice of it.

"I like your nose ring," he said, while they were setting up.

She was down on her knees, bent over the black zippered bag that contained her equipment, and she glanced up and flashed a smile.

The ring itself wasn't much—a thin loop of gold with a tiny jewel set in it—but it made her look exotic, aboriginal almost, which meant sexy, very sexy, which was why she'd gone down to the head shop or tattoo parlor or wherever it might have been and had it put in. He said, "Does it hurt?"

The reporter—Doug Fields—was studying a notecard in his hand and he lifted his eyes and gave him an indulgent look. The cameraman—same one as last time, wasn't it?—let out with a kind of honking laugh that went on a beat too long.

She said, "Only when I sneeze," and they all laughed.

A moment later everybody was in position, the reporter seated in the student chair across the desk from him, the cameraman perched over the reporter's shoulder and the sound girl (her name was Amy, he was to discover before they were through, a joyless coincidence that came hurtling out of the black heart of the universe to pin him to the chair), stationed behind him.

The first question, a variant on the one put to him by all the others: "Did you see this coming? I mean, was there ever any indication that this animal you raised in your own home was capable of anything like this?"

He tried to smile ruefully for the camera, for her, the sound girl, whose presence he could feel like a magnetic field. Though he wanted to blink, wanted to shut his eyes in a slow dissolve and seep into some other place altogether, he restrained himself. What he was seeing was Sam, Sam in a hundred poses, in his highchair, in bed with a book, hooting out his joy from the top of his tree. "Sam was the soul of gentleness. He was as sweet and loving as anybody I've ever met."

That wasn't the answer Doug Fields was looking for. He worked a little grit into his voice: "But he did maim two people, didn't he? Permanently? You call that gentle? You call that sweet and loving? And you had him here in Santa Maria, on university property, and nobody really knew how dangerous he was, isn't that right?"

There was little to gain here. This was the news cycle, churning— "Ape Attack!" "Ape Goes Berserk!" "Lab Chimp Maims Two!"—and he was embedded in it, a thin streak of silvery consequence in a sediment of shit. He couldn't very well turn away, couldn't say "No comment," not if there was anything to salvage from all this, no matter how meager. The university expected it of him—the field, if there even was a field anymore. He turned the question back on him: "You met him, Doug. You filmed him at the ranch. What did you think? Did he seem dangerous to you?"

There was a moment of hesitation, but they could always edit that out. The problem was, Doug Fields was used to asking the questions, not answering them. "He was fine," he said finally.

"Cute, even? Charming? Charismatic?"

A shrug. "I guess so. Yes."

"Let me ask you this"—and here he stared into the camera—"do you have a dog? A cat? How about a horse, any horse aficionados out there in KCOY land?" He gave it a beat, and why was he working himself up? Really, what difference did it make now? "Well, you must know then that animals have moods, just like people. Your German shepherd? Sweetest thing in the world till some stranger comes to the door."

"But this is no German shepherd, this is a wild animal."

"Sam could talk, just like you and me. He wore clothes. He went to school."

The sun coalesced with the blinds, the fluorescents hummed, the sound girl held herself rigid. They hadn't been able to reattach Jack Serfis' thumb. Moncrief was blind.

"But he wasn't like you and me, was he? And isn't it a fact that you and the university were negligent in a host of ways and we can only be thankful this tragedy didn't unfold right here on campus? And your student, what about your student, Aimee Villard? What about her?"

What about her? What if she'd stayed out of it? What if she'd left Sam where he belonged, where he was safe, where Moncrief was determined to make a chimp out of him and breed him with the only species he was capable of breeding with and they could have mounted cameras and gone on to the next level of the research, the telling one, the one that would present definitive proof that language was trans-missible, wired into the chimp brain just as it was wired into ours, that all it took was a single Promethean spark to kick-start the next phase of their evolution?

Finally, and this was getting to be a real pain in the ass, he said, "It's pretty simple, Doug, and I'll put it in terms you or anybody else can understand—he was only trying to protect her."

Eventually, it all died down. People were shocked, riveted, but after a week or two they were shocked and riveted over something else and the TV cameras rolled on and out of his life. He taught his classes, collected his paychecks. His colleagues might have regarded him as damaged goods (worse: damaged goods with tenure), but that was nothing to him since he'd barely connected with them to begin with. As for the students, they seemed indifferent except to the fact that he'd been on TV, no matter the association, which lent him a kind of tarnished glamour as if he were an ex-rocker or politician coming out of rehab. In the evenings, he made the rounds of the bars, exploring what lack of purpose involved at its core. Twice he called Amy to ask her to dinner—the new Amy, the sound girl with the dominant body—but both times she told him she was busy.

There was rain one afternoon, the first rain of the season, which was a kind of blessed event in the thirsty foothills of coastal California, and it elevated his mood so that he found himself whistling a fragment of Borodin as he crossed the lot to his car after class. What was he thinking? Nothing too complicated—dinner and a book at a steakhouse that had a lively bar and music he could at least tolerate—then home and maybe a movie on TV just to scrape through the patina of boredom.

It wasn't till he turned down the row of rain-beaded compacts to his spot in the faculty lot that he saw her, Aimee, the original Aimee, waiting for him under an umbrella the color of a ripe peach. She had on a pair of high-heeled boots in approximately the same shade, jeans, a transparent slicker over a sweater he vaguely recognized. She was wearing makeup, which suggested something he didn't want to acknowledge—or wasn't ready to, at least not yet. When she saw him coming, when she lifted her eyes to him as he maneuvered through the rain, she smiled almost incidentally, as if it were beyond her control. "Hi," she said.

His own umbrella—black faded to a patchy gray, with one sagging strut—rattled with the rain, which was heavier now. He said, "Hi," in return, and then it was just the sound of the rain a moment till he asked, "Why didn't you come up to the office?"

"I just got here? And when I parked I saw your car and then I saw you coming . . ."

Another pause, rain drooling from the lip of his umbrella. There was a sharp working odor of renewal on the air, not that it mattered, not here in town, but up in the hills, out at the ranch, every shrub and tree and all the birds and rodents and the things that fed on them were taking it in to the degree their consciousness allowed and no doubt were feeling the same attitudinal shift that had gotten him whistling a moment earlier. He wasn't whistling now, though. Now he was standing at the door of his car, trying to make out her face under the shadow of the umbrella.

"So where are you living? Not still in—?" He was going to say "Arizona," but let that ride because of the long vista it opened up.

"I'm at my mother's? And I'm going back to school."

He felt the smallest spark of alarm. "Not here."

She shook her head, curtained by rain. "Uh-uh," she said. "Northridge? I can commute there from my mother's until I—well, until I decide. What about you?"

He was going to say "Let's get out of the rain—you want a cup of coffee?" But he didn't say it—that would normalize things and he felt too much resentment for that. Instead, he said, "So what are you doing here?"

She looked as if she were about to cry. "I wanted to see you. I wanted to talk about what happened, about *Sam*," and then she was crying.

He wasn't made of stone, he wasn't a jerk, he wasn't a user. And the fact that she'd taken his career away from him, ruined everything—*Do not fall in love with your subject*—was something he was just going to have to live with, and so what if it was every minute of every day for the rest of his life? "Okay, look," he said, "let's get a cup of coffee—you know Vesuvio's? I'll meet you there in five minutes, okay?"

Vesuvio's was packed, but he got there first and wedged himself into a two-seat booth by the window where he could see her coming. He watched her shake out her umbrella under the awning, brisk and small and barely contained, and then she saw him and waved and in the next moment she was settling in across the table from him, the ends of her hair gone dark with the wet and clinging to her shoulders. They talked. The rain held steady. Students rushed in and out the door, all carrying their own expectations, and they brought the smell of the rain in with them. There was music playing, some pop song she used to play at the ranch all the time. The coffee grinder roared to life and died. She told him about Sam and Moncrief and what had happened on top of that mesa when the dogs came and then the men after them and how she'd cradled Sam till his body lost its heat and they took him away from her. How they'd handcuffed her and how her mother had come with the bail money and got her a lawyer and the lawyer said he was going to get them to reduce the charges but now she wasn't so sure.

"What charges?" he asked.

She shrugged. "Failure to control a dangerous animal, grand theft for taking him in the first place—*as if*—and, oh, I don't know, even something about the Endangered Species Act. And Dr. Moncrief is suing for damages, if you can believe it."

She went through the details again, all of them, her voice reduced to a whisper so that he had a hard time even hearing her over the noise of the grinder and the chatter of the students. "Yeah," he said softly, every once in a while, "I understand," and, "It's not your fault," though it was ultimately, and it was his fault too for believing in something as absurd as the power of language to construct a world out of nothing.

They were there for two hours. Then he pushed his chair back and glanced at his watch, but that was just for show. "Look, I've got to go," he said, then rose to his feet, picked up his umbrella and went out the door and into the rain.

As he heard it, through the grapevine because he was out of the loop now, Moncrief closed up shop not long after the event and sold off his chimps—all of them, even Alice and Alex and the others that had been raised in human households—to a biomed lab on the East

Coast, where they were slated for use in AIDS research. There they were isolated and duly injected with the HIV virus, though none of them developed symptoms, which brought into question the underlying assumptions of the study itself, suggesting that chimps, though susceptible to so many human afflictions, both physical and psychological, are unaffected by the virus. As it happened, Alice had been pregnant at the time, though no one knew that until she gave birth in her cage in the lab, which would have been a boon in the days before Borstein, before Sam, but was just a footnote now. If they'd let her keep the baby, and there was no guarantee of that, she might have signed to it, might have taught it to say HUG and DRINK and EAT and WHAT ICE? and WHY?, but even so, even if the two of them had signed fluidly and talked through the day and into the night, every night, night after night, there would have been no one there to see it, to record it, to care.